JAMES MARSHALL

ISBN: 9798877857995

To Sarah, Daisy and Jack.
For allowing me to waste hours in my office and
inspiring me to work harder.

ACKNOWLEDGMENTS

Thanks to Pen to Print for the opportunity to write this book.

To my mentor, Catherine Coe, for her unstinting advice and support over the year.

To my writing tutors: Jenny Kane, for getting me started, and Ian Ayris for helping me improve.

To my class mates in the writing groups for listening, encouraging and sharing your excellent work.

Chapter 1

Alek Wasilewski hurdled the yellow gorse bush and sprinted towards
the cover of a low stone wall. The enemy was dug in on the edge of
a copse seventy-five metres ahead. Alek pushed his heavy helmet
back up over his sweaty forehead, his chest heaving as he tried to
regain his breath. His section commander, Swales, was signalling to
the rest of the boys to catch up.

'Get a fucking move on,' Swales said.

Alek wiped his palms on his combat trousers. His neck ached
from the rifle sling and helmet strap, his calves were burning from his
too-tight combat boots, and he needed to pee.

Swales made several hand signals to accompany his instructions
to the section. 'We'll have to go around to the left following the stone
wall.' He pointed at Murdo and Trowbridge. 'You two stay here and
lay down covering fire. The rest of you, follow me.'

Alek gripped his empty rifle and bent as low as he could to follow
Swales, keeping his head below the wall. His knees groaned after
thirty metres and screamed after sixty. He sighed when Swales held
up his fist to signal a stop.

'Hold it here.' Swales dropped to his stomach.

Alek copied Swales and wriggled forward, thankful that his legs
could rest.

'Check ammo; fix bayonets,' Swales said. 'Ski and I will take the
left trench. Evans and Williams, the middle trench, and you two –'
Swales pointed at the last members of the section – take the right-
hand trench.'

Alek pretended to check his ammo and fix his bayonet. They had
neither ammo nor bayonets but had to go through the motions.

'Ready?' Swales said.

Alek nodded.

'Go!' Swales jumped over the wall.

Alek vaulted the wall and then ran forward. 'Bang, Bang!' he
shouted, firing invisible rounds from the hip.

Swales dropped to one knee, yelling, 'Bang, bang!

Alek ran past him and knelt, aiming at the two men in the left
trench who were also shouting 'bang' as Swales ran a zig-zag
pattern to the edge of the trench. Alek leapt up to sprint and jumped
into the trench.

'Bang, bang!' He pointed his rifle at the enemy soldier still
standing.

The soldier did a theatrical spin and dive, clutching his chest and
wriggling his legs before letting out one last groan. He grinned at

4

Alek.

'Stop! End-Ex,' Corporal Sanderson, their training instructor, shouted from above them. He waved his clipboard in the air and beckoned the support soldiers up to the position. 'Well done, Swales,' he said. 'Good effort from your team.' He pointed to Murdo and Trowbridge as they walked towards the copse. 'I can see why you put those slackers in the fire support team.'

Swales turned and winked at Alek.

Alek slumped to the bottom of the cool trench and blinked as salty sweat ran into his eyes. He took a swig of the lukewarm water from his canteen, wishing it was ice-cold lemonade. He had forgotten its taste but could see the condensation on the outside of the glass and the clear bubbles floating to the top. Sugar rationing meant that lemonade was one of the many treats that were now only memories.

'Back in the trucks,' Corporal Sanderson ordered when the other two sections finished their attacks. Hulse, the red-haired and jug-eared recruit who had been appointed overall platoon leader, echoed the orders.

Alek peed into a hedge before he clambered aboard the four-tonne truck and took his helmet off, grateful that his new buzz cut meant the breeze could cool him down quickly. He shut his eyes as they rumbled back to the temporary barracks on Bodmin Moor. *Time for an essential snooze. The only good thing about this stupid army.*

Alek had been press-ganged three weeks ago while sitting in the Exeter College cafeteria, with the rest of his BTEC Exercise and Sport Science class. He had been separated from his friends and stuck in Nissen hut number four with twenty-eight strangers who formed the rest of the platoon. The last he'd seen of his best friend Callum, the person he had been with all through school, was him clambering aboard a different four-tonne truck.

Alek had kept his tears away until his first night in the bunk above Swales. When the darkness and silence had come, he'd cried as he thought about his family. He hadn't seen his parents since they'd escaped two years' ago to Looe in Cornwall to protect the family's second home from being wrecked by insurgents. He assumed they were alive, but they'd been declared traitors just for leaving. His sister, Lena, was now working in Plymouth and had come back to their family home once a month until the travel permits had been rescinded. That was four months ago, and he had no idea when he might see her again.

The next day, they were back out on exercise. The platoon were leaning against their backpacks on the lee side of a stone wall somewhere on Dartmoor. Hulse was sitting beside Corporal

Sanderson who was drinking coffee from a Thermos flask.

Alek was fatigued to the point that he could barely remember life before the army; they'd crammed so much into each day of their brief enlistment. His feet were still wet from wading through streams and sore from the marching. He had blisters upon his blisters. Swales had shown him how to pop them to drain the fluids and then wipe his urine on them to toughen up the skin, neither of which had been shown in the first morning's 'Foot hygiene' lecture.

Alek took off his boots and socks, laying them out on the wall before sitting down next to Swales. He wriggled his damp, pale toes in the sunshine. 'I'm going to get athlete's foot,' he said.

'Ha, that's what everyone thinks after a medical lecture.' Swales unzipped his combat jacket, and steam rose from his chest. He'd taken Alek under his wing a bit – shown him what was what since he'd arrived in the army a week before Alek had, after being press-ganged from his outwards bounds course at Plymouth College. Swales had told Alek he'd been in the Army Cadets when he was younger, but his dad had taken him out when they'd started to issue 'patriot badges' for reporting on misdemeanours that citizens were committing, not wanting his son to be a dobber for the Party.

Murdo was ranting in his thick Scottish accent on one of his favourite topics. 'Those nasty Continentals – they all eat frogs' legs and horses.'

'And they don't let their women shave their legs,' Trowbridge said.

Swales shook his head. 'Have either of you been to Europe?'

'No,' Murdo said, 'and I don't want to either.'

'Then how do you know what they eat?' Swales said.

'Everyone knows that. That's why we're fighting them.' Murdo looked around for approval.

'We have to make a stand,' Trowbridge said, 'otherwise they'll come over here and make us speak foreign.'

Alek kept quiet. His great-grandfather was Polish and had fought in the RAF against the German Luftwaffe. His parents had reminded him of this whenever Alek had come home from school quoting the pro-war rhetoric from assemblies.

'Right, on your feet,' Hulse said. He pointed over the wall. 'It's three kilometres to the tor over there.'

Alek put on his damp socks and tied up his boots. The recruits rocked themselves up to standing with their rucksacks on their backs. Hulse led them over a set of rocky steps that were set into the dry stone wall.

'You should be our platoon leader, not Hulse,' Alek said in a low voice to Swales as they trailed at the back of the group.

'No thanks,' Swales whispered quickly. 'Officers and NCOs are the first to get shot, unless you're in the rear. If our officer goes down

I don't want any part of being in front. Even so, since we're infantry, our life expectancy in combat will be a matter of hours.'

'Hours?' Alek blurted loudly, then lowered his voice to add. 'But we're winning all the battles.'

'Really?' Swales said. 'Then how come we've been press-ganged before we finish our college courses?'

Alek groaned as he pushed himself up a high ledge. His brain struggled to think beyond the next task, let alone the war strategy. His parents had been anti-war, he knew that. He wished he could see them but the border was closed; his parents had been unable to return. He and Lena had been left alone, and when she'd gone back to college in Plymouth, he'd had to learn to cook and clean for himself. It'd been a bad time, but that was nothing to the misery he felt now.

Hours? All this to be killed in a few hours?

'Alek, do you believe what these morons are saying?' Swales went on, his voice hushed.

'I'm too tired to think,' Alek said.

Swales tugged on Alek's sleeve. 'The army doesn't want you to think. They dehumanise the enemy so that you can kill them without remorse.'

'I thought you said that the enemy would kill us,' Alek said.

'I did. So your brain does still work!' Swales grinned. 'But the Continentals are just people like us. Sons and brothers who are being sent out to do the politicians' will.'

Alek stopped with a leg on either side of the wall. *Great-grandad was a hero and he wasn't one of the dirty Continentals. Maybe Swales is right – the Continentals are normal people too.* He climbed down the other side of the wall. *I don't want to kill or be killed by anyone.*

The following day, it was Alek's turn to be section leader, in charge of seven others. The platoon disembarked from the four-tonne trucks, each carrying a water bottle and wearing lightweight trousers, boots and their white PT shirts. Each of the three sections had been given a compass and a photocopied map. Alek was glad he had Swales alongside him as they walked to a grey boulder at the edge of the car park and Alek laid out his map. He orientated the map to the compass and looked up over the moor towards a lone tree on a rise.

His dad had insisted that Alek and Lena had learnt to read a map. 'Your spatial awareness won't develop through looking at your bloody phones all the time,' he'd said on one of their trips to Cornwall – as it had been known then.

Alek had found it annoying at first but he discovered he enjoyed studying maps. His Duke of Edinburgh Bronze Award had required Alek to walk with a group over Dartmoor. They had relied on Alek to navigate them safely.

'That tree's on a bearing of zero-seven-zero degrees,' Alek said to his section now.

'Fuck off, swot,' Trowbridge said. Three of the section laughed.

'Shut up, Trowbridge,' Swales said.

'What's it got to do with you, Swales?' Trowbridge said.

'I don't want to get lost, so let's all pay attention.' Swales stared at Trowbridge, who eventually looked away.

'That's the bearing we need,' Alek tried again. 'We should head towards that tree.'

Trowbridge pointed to their left. 'But Hulse's section has just gone that way.'

Alek looked at the ground, up at the tree and then at Trowbridge. 'I'm not worried about their section. I'm worried about ours.'

'But Hulse went that way,' Trowbridge said again.

'Hulse is an idiot; he couldn't navigate his way around Ikea,' Swales said. 'I trust Alek.'

'I'll tell him you said that,' Trowbridge said.

Alek folded the map and put it into his side pocket, thankful for Swales' support. He disliked being in charge but he was confident in his orienteering skills. 'Shall we go?'

'Yes,' Swales said. 'You look like you know what you are doing with a map. That could come in handy, soon.' He set off at a jog-trot pace along a hard track that led to a softer footpath as it entered the moorland. Alek kept pace with Swales, staying behind his right shoulder. The ground was firm with occasional tufts of longer grass: 'ankle-breakers' Alek had called them on his D-of-E expedition. Dartmoor was notorious for either tripping up the clumsy or soaking the ill-prepared when the clag came down from the tors.

The path softened and narrowed so Alek tucked behind Swales as he pushed ahead. Despite saying he wanted to avoid responsibility, Swales had a habit of taking charge.

Alek's calves were aching when they reached the solitary tree. He took a few deep breaths before looking back: the rest of the section were still fifty metres away and had slowed to a walk.

Alek took out his map and compass and scanned the undulating moorland ahead for another useful marker on their bearing.

'Listen,' Swales said in a hushed voice. 'Do you want to die with this mob?'

Alek looked over his shoulder. 'I don't want to die with anyone.' *What a stupid question.*

'Neither do I,' Swales said. 'I've got an idea about avoiding that. I could use a decent navigator.' He put a forefinger across his lips.

Murdo panted towards them like a springer spaniel on a hot June

8

day. 'What are you two girls whispering about?' he said.

'Navigation and map-reading,' Swales said. 'You'd best watch and learn.'

Murdo took a step towards Swales, his hands clenched into fists, his jaw jutting forward. 'You talk too much.'

Swales turned his body to half face Murdo, tucked his chin into his left shoulder and held his hands up and out in front of his face.

Trowbridge called out, 'Go on, Murdo, do him.'

Murdo lumbered forward. Swales moved around to his left, his heels off the floor, hands protecting his face.

'Stop it!' Alek stepped between the two belligerents and waved his map in the air like a rugby linesman signalling 'touch'. 'We're supposed to be working together, not fighting each other.'

'Get out of my way, you creep,' Murdo said, sticking his chest out and pushing against Alek.

Alek could tell that Murdo had lost heart from the push, which was more of a lean. It was easy to talk a good game when there was someone blocking the path to a dangerous-looking Swales.

'If we get behind now, we'll get beasted when we get back, and none of us want that, do we?' Alek looked towards Trowbridge and the rest of the section.

'He's right, Murdo,' Trowbridge said. 'Leave it for the barracks.'

Murdo unclenched his fists and pointed at Swales. 'I've got your number, you bum-fucking knobhead.' He shoved Alek. 'And yours.'

Alek flinched at the verbal onslaught.

Swales lowered his hands but kept his eyes focused on Murdo.

Alek swallowed. *That was close.* He pointed his compass and took his bearing. *What did Swales mean about needing a good navigator?*

Chapter 2

Lena took the England flag from Trevor, her supervisor, as he passed them out while walking down the line of women standing on the shaded pavement outside the warehouse. The local news team shivered nearby in the shade; a thin lady with a sharp nose and rigid blonde hair was standing in front of a cameraman who had a sound boom extending from the shoulder harness of his portable rig.

It was a break in their normal routine for the female artists that morning. They'd been led outside their office block and up the hill to an old industrial unit so they could witness the opening of a new factory. Lena shuffled her damp feet and rubbed her arms; they'd got caught in a shower that lasted as long as their journey. Water had leaked into her patched shoes. *Patches upon patches upon patches. But I've run out of black masking tape to do any more fixes.* She begrudged having to put her shoes through an unnecessary journey – especially in the rain.

Two electric motorcycles whined to a halt in front of the warehouse. A black car followed and out stepped a short, grey-haired man, his belly leading the way. His suit jacket was undone, a blue tie hanging above his straining belt. He had a St George's Cross England badge pinned on his lapel. Lena knew exactly who this was: John Parrish, MP.

He shook hands with the factory manager. Words were exchanged that Lena couldn't hear.

'Wave your flags,' Trevor said to the women.

Lena moved her arm fast; it would help warm her up. The paper flag fell off the stick and fluttered into a puddle.

'Pick it up,' Trevor said.

Lena did as she was told and tried to stick the flag back together, without success. She held the paper corner and waved the flag without the stick. *Cheap tat.*

'I'm glad to open...' The MP's words carried on the breeze.

The news lady collared Parrish. 'A joyous occasion, here in Plymouth, as our MP opens the new flag factory.' She shoved the microphone under his chin.

Lena stifled a yawn. There was no point in the journalist being there except for the show. There was no semblance of questions, only prompts for the scripted reply.

Parrish smiled. 'It's fantastic to be able to create new jobs and employ local people. Manufacturing is a vital component of the economic success of this great country of ours.'

Lena watched the cameraman as he scanned the line of workers, pausing at Lena. She blushed and fiddled with the flag and stick, forcing a smile and a wave.

The MP and his entourage moved inside the warehouse.

'Right, back to work, ladies,' Trevor said.

Lena led the way up the hill to the office, crossing the street to walk in the crisp sunshine that had broken through the gloom, hoping to dry her toes out. Her stomach rumbled. The walking and fresh air had exacerbated her hunger. *Two hours until lunchtime.* The dry toast she'd had for breakfast filled her stomach for a short time but left her hungry by mid-morning. She walked past a shuttered coffee shop, remembering the time she would have popped in for a coffee and muffin. *Don't do that to yourself. Those days are gone.*

Back in the office, Lena sat at her desk and scribbled as she watched the clock tick towards 13:00. The big hand whirred round to the twelve and a dozen pencils hit desks in unison, a dozen chairs scraped back. Lena filed out behind the other women to the canteen. The whole floor smelt of cabbage. Even when it wasn't on the menu.

'Cabbage soup for lunch again,' Jane said over her shoulder.

'Soup is a bit optimistic,' Lena said. 'Soup's raggedy cousin, more like.'

Jane sniggered, covering her mouth with her hand.

They sat down on the orange plastic chairs behind a Formica table that overlooked the car park. 'Car graveyard' Lena called it. Six derelict cars sat in the same places, unused since diesel had been rationed.

Sure enough, soup was the offering again today. Lena gazed at the two cabbage leaves and a piece of swede floating in the bowl of warm water. *Not swede – yellow turnip.* The term 'swede' had been banned after Sweden had joined the EU. Once pig fodder, turnips were now a staple part of the diet. So were parsnips, potatoes and carrots: vegetables that required rooting around in the dirt to harvest. Lena had to do without the cleanly packaged avocados, tomatoes and melon slices that had been her favourite student food, and the pasta and rice that had given her energy. Her body craved carbs, protein and animal fat that would have flavoured her meals and satiated her appetite.

She stirred her bowl of flavoured water that aspired to be soup. Salt and pepper were distant memories. Sugar too. She picked up a limp cabbage leaf with her spoon. 'Hmm, delicious,' she said before wolfing it down.

Jane snorted soup from her nose.

'Don't waste it,' Lena said. 'It took a lot of time and effort to prepare this gourmet delight.'

'Then stop it,' Jane said, her eyes watering. 'I can't eat if you keep making me laugh.'

Lena grinned and picked up another cabbage leaf. If they didn't have gallows humour, they wouldn't have any humour at all. *What I wouldn't give for a pork chop right now.*

Lena slumped in her desk chair after lunch, doodling on her pad; the deadline for the painting to be finished was four o'clock but she had only sketched a picture of Salcombe Sands. She chewed on the end of her pencil and looked around the office for inspiration. The twelve artists' desks were arranged in three rows, surrounded by grey, windowless walls with a solitary clock for decoration behind the supervisor's desk at the front. *What would Monet paint if he worked here; a series of watercolours about pencil sharpeners and swivel chairs?*

'Sit down and create' was how she described her job. The grey-faced supervisor and his bosses treated the artists like factory workers. *I may as well make crappy flags.* Hardly what she had been led to expect years ago when her mum had told her she could do anything she wanted if she just tried hard enough.

But that was before the war. Lena had been hired by the Ministry of Information for her creativity – one of many graduates in art or design who'd been recently recruited. Her Social-Credit score had been in the top percentile back then, indicating a loyal citizen; she had attended patriot rallies, given money to soldier charities and cheered for the workers every Tuesday lunchtime at college. Some of her friends were better artists than she but had lost Soc-Cred points by playing computer games too long, having more than one lover and even jaywalking.

Lena knew that a better Soc-Cred score led to an easier life. But when her parents were labelled as traitors, her Soc-Cred had plummeted. She was working hard to build it up again, and to get better rations. Her always-empty stomach led her actions, rather than an innate sense of patriotism.

Lena looked at the quote she had been given to include on the poster:

'*Victory at all costs, victory in spite of terror, victory however long and hard the road may be, for without victory there is no survival.*'

She was angry at the constant use of Churchill quotes; her father's grandfather had been Polish and a pilot sergeant in the RAF in 1940. He had fought to overturn the invasion of the Low Countries from the East. Now she was being asked to celebrate their invasion from the West and to demonise every foreigner. Including those from Poland.

'No time for daydreaming, Lena,' Trevor said, tapping his pen on her desk. 'You have to finish the poster. Remember how important it is for our citizens to know why we will succeed.'

Lena put the soggy pencil down, picked up her brush, dipped it into the water pot and chose a grey paint. She started to paint a face in profile over the beach. A leering Eastern European face – dark skin, a moustache and big eyebrows. That always went down well. She would add some young girls in bikinis looking scared. Titillation proved popular with the bosses too.

Sorry, Great Grandpa, but I need to eat.

Warm rain was falling as Lena left work. She put up her umbrella and walked past Drakes Circus on her way back to the apartment she shared with some of the other 'artists'. The once-mighty retail emporium was permanently shut. The war meant that cheap imports had stopped and most electrical gadgets had been made redundant as soon as the satellites had been destroyed. No more phones, no more social media, no more streaming of TV and music. Lena thought back to her old life with its myriad of connections. Her posts had always got a ton of likes because of her artist's eye for light, shape and contrast. It was satisfying to have her work appreciated by an adoring public, even thought it was only on social media. She had aspirations of having her own art exhibition in one of the local galleries. Now her audience was her supervisor grunting over her shoulder before her work was mass-produced. *Thankfully, it was anonymous.*

The boats in Sutton Harbour were sitting idle. Lena liked to take this longer route home so that she could stop and fantasise about owning one of the yachts; it was worth the extra wear on her shoes. Her favourite boats changed every week; sometimes she wanted a small and compact sailing dinghy, other times one of the large floating gin palaces. *I'm not fussy. As long as I can enjoy a cool drink in the warm sunshine after a hot meal, and feel the breeze on my cheeks.*

Today she chose a catamaran with a small cabin and tinted windows: sleek and fast. Lena leant on the white railings and imagined taking photos of the waves from the netting deck. Not that there was any chance of that; the boats hadn't left the harbour for eighteen months, the walkway now closed after the initial exodus. The boat owners with fuel and supplies and disbelief of the Party's assurances had left early. The rest had only been able to watch their boats gather rust and barnacles.

Lena pushed off the railings and walked along the cobbled streets of the Barbican towards home. Not that it felt like home, sharing with the other women – strangers thrown together a year ago. But she knew she shouldn't complain too much. She was lucky to be allowed to work and to live independently: the children of people accused of being traitors were often imprisoned in a Recreant Camp. Lena's previously high Soc-Cred had kept her free for now.

Not for the first time, Lena thought back to the evening her parents had decided to visit their second home in Looe, Cornwall. She'd been home from college for the weekend and was looking forward to getting her laundry done and one of her dad's roast dinners. But Filip and Emma Wasilewski had been alarmed by reports of 28,000 homeless and hungry Cornish residents taking over some of the 15,000 empty second homes – so much so that they'd packed their overnight bags and left. When Lena had arrived, their only communication was a hurried kiss goodbye and instructions to only use the debit card in an emergency and for the Sainsbury's shop if they weren't back by Friday. Lena had given her two cats a cuddle and cried as they squawked inside their travel boxes.

That was two years ago. The house in Cornwall had seemed important at the time, to all of them, but when her parents hadn't returned by Friday, nor the next Friday, Lena had realised that her parents had made the wrong choice. By then, the Cornish traitors had renamed their land Kernow. The Party put barriers up on the Tamar Bridge and the A30, to protect the English from foreign contamination, then a barbed wire fence along the Tamar. Filip and Emma could not return, even if they'd wanted to.

Why did you have to leave?

The power cuts had become more frequent, forcing Alek and Lena to huddle together and listen to the news on the battery-powered radio in candlelight. Lena comforted the sobbing Alek, on the night the barriers were put up, when he realised his parents weren't coming back. He cooked a stew on his D-of-E gas stove and they ate in silence. She had felt even worse when she'd told him she was going back to college.

'I'll come to see you at weekends, but Mum and Dad would want me to finish my course,' she told Alek. The truth was she didn't want to hang around looking after her annoying little brother who spent most of his time playing Call of Duty on his PlayStation. She enjoyed the independence of college and the coursework she was doing. Alek was capable of looking after himself – if he wanted to.

Lena's socks were sopping by the time she returned to the grey, pebble-dashed apartment building. The black masking tape around the split seams of her shoes had stretched and curled in the rain. She punched in the key code and turned to step backwards into the hallway, folding her umbrella outside and shaking off most of the water before placing it in the stand. Rainwater dripped onto the

14

brown linoleum. There was always a slight smell of dust and staleness in the building, like returning to a house after a holiday, no matter how often the door was opened.

She glanced at the wooden table in the hallway and spotted a brown envelope perched up against the lime green wall, a leftover from brighter days. Receiving post was unusual. Lena dashed over to the table, wiping rainwater from her nose and rubbing her hand dry on the inside of her jacket. The envelope had her name on it.

She looked around the empty atrium before ripping open the envelope. Her eyes widened as she read the official communication.

It explained that Alek had volunteered to serve in the 51st Patriot Division. He was currently in recruit training and was now part of the heroic war effort. As his named next-of-kin, Lena should be proud of her brother's contribution. As his work was secret, she should not expect any communication from him soon.

Lena trudged up the stairs to the third floor and leant against the door to their apartment. She struggled to rationalise what she had read. She thought it strange that Alek would volunteer to fight. He had been quiet and withdrawn since their parents had left. *Is it because the rest of his rugby mates did it and he followed? I should have come and seen you more often.* Her weekend visits had dropped to monthly after the transport rationing – and then down to nothing. *None of this would have happened if Mum and Dad hadn't been more worried about their stupid second home than their children. They would have kept him in college; there's no way they'd have let him join the army.*

She unlocked the apartment door and dropped her key onto the small table beneath a vanity mirror. The women she shared it with – mostly artists – were quartered two to a room. It meant very little privacy, which Lena craved; one of the reasons why she took the longer walk home. Right now, she needed time to think about Alek and how to get in touch with him. *Is it too late to get him out of the army? I don't want him getting hurt. He's too young to go to war.*

Alice was sitting on the bottom bunk of the tiny room they shared, her black hair unpinned and the curls unleashed. She worked an early shift at the naval mess as a catering assistant.

Lena sighed. There was always something with Alice. 'Hey, get off my bunk will you?'

'Sure – I was just stretching my legs.' Alice climbed onto the top bunk, leaving black hair strands on Lena's frayed pillowcase. The shower drain was continually blocked and all the women knew who was responsible.

'You're late – been shopping?' Alice made the tired joke, but it was an effort all the same.

'No, I went for a coffee,' Lena said without humour.
Alice laughed.

Lena took off her shoes, pushed the window open and hung her socks out. She took off her splattered trousers and put on her pyjama bottoms and a clean pair of thick socks. The bathroom rota was pinned on the edge of the bunk. 18:50–19:00 was Lena's evening slot, meaning only half an hour to wait. She shivered. The flat was cold. The power was cut off for most of the day in residential areas to ensure it was available for the essential services and workplaces.

'Do you know what's for dinner?' Alice leant over the bunk rail. 'It's Beth and Tamsin, so I bet it's lentils again.'

'I need something hot. It's chilly even for April.' Lena scrabbled under her duvet, unable to ignore her empty stomach. Lentils would at least fill her up.

'Shall we listen to the radio?' Alice jumped down from her bunk. There was a radio in the living room that played a crackly medium wave. One of the girls had found it in her grandmother's sideboard. The BBC still broadcast but the girls had found PIRATE MW, which played music they could dance to. They were committing an offence but none of them wanted to listen to the BBC's reports about the war after a day of making posters or serving naval officers. As long as they kept the volume down they thought the risk was worth it.

'I don't feel like it.' Lena poked her head out to speak, but put the duvet over her head again quickly. The smell of steamed cabbage was drifting into their room. Lena shuddered. *Not again – even the lentils had run out.* Alice would be farting in the night. But Lena's disgruntled stomach overruled her sensibilities. She would have to eat the cabbage, if she didn't want to be awake all night with hunger pains.

Alice whispered, 'I had a slice of pork earlier. Leftover – it was going in the bin.' 'Not many of them in today, and mostly oldies. I can dodge them easily when they try to pinch me.'

Pork. When was the last time I had pork? Lena groaned. 'Stop torturing me with your food tales, Alice.'

'Sorry,' Alice said. 'Come on – stop moping and be sociable.' She pulled the duvet off Lena's face.

'All right, all right.' Lena kicked the duvet off the rest of her body, realising all hope of privacy was lost. Her stomach rumbled as she followed Alice towards the living room, hunger pushing thoughts of Alek out of her mind.

Chapter 3

Alek led the section down a sunken lane, an old dry stone wall sheltering them on its western side. He climbed up the grass bank and looked over the wall. 'I can see the trucks. That's our final checkpoint.' He checked his watch. 'We're an hour early.'

Swales joined him. 'There's no point finishing too early; we'll only get beasted or shouted at.'

Alek checked his map once more while the section watched him in silence. He hadn't been interrupted since they had reached the first checkpoint in good time and without errors. 'We could rest for thirty minutes and still finish early.' He looked up and saw a row of grinning faces.

Half an hour of freedom. The recruits stretched out against the wall. Alek took off his boots and socks and wriggled his pale, wrinkly toes in the sunshine. He drank the last drops of his water and watched the butterflies and bumblebees flit along the wildflowers growing on the verge.

'I used to think that watching wildlife was boring,' said Alek, 'but actually it's quite relaxing.'

Trowbridge scoffed, 'What are you, queer? Talking about butterflies?'

'Shut up, Trowbridge,' Swales said. 'I bet you'll wish for this moment when you're under fire, cowering from the enemy.'

'Fuck off, Swales,' Trowbridge said. 'I'll be too busy killing Conts.'

'When do you think we'll go?' Alek said, his serenity interrupted. The war had seemed so far away for a precious few moments.

'The sooner the better,' Trowbridge said.

A buzzard screeched and the section looked upwards as the bird soared with its broad wings outstretched high above them. A crow flew up to meet it and a dogfight ensued. The crow darted in and out, pecking the less-agile buzzard and forcing the larger bird down onto the field. The crow flew up into the air, cawing its victory.

'It's not the size of the bird in the fight, it's the size of the fight in the bird,' Swales said.

Better not to be in a fight at all. Alek was happier doing orienteering than the pretend war games, shouting 'bang' at his 'enemies'. *The enemy won't be shouting bang at us.*

Alek had bought an air rifle when the rationing started and the government had encouraged citizens to shoot pigeons and squirrels to supplement their diet. He had no compunction in killing for food but killing another human being was abhorrent.

Alek spent the next thirty minutes absorbing the countryside scenery. It might be the last time he'd do this before he was sent to die. He was reluctant to leave this spot but he had no choice.

'Right, time to go,' Alek said and struggled to his feet, his back stiff and complaining. He stretched his arms backwards until his back cracked, put on his socks and boots, and then stamped his feet onto the ground to get the circulation going.

The section bimbled down the lane until they saw the open moor ahead of them and the three trucks.

'We'd best jog in to make it look like we're rushing,' Swales said. 'We don't want them thinking we had it too easy.'

'Good idea,' Alek said. 'Form up in a file.' He led them in an easy jog for 700 metres across the moor with Swales at his side. They slowed down fifty metres from the trucks. Corporal Sanderson was watching them with his clipboard under one arm. Next to him was a pale, thin man with red cheeks that looked as if they had been painted by a child.

The section marched to the finish and halted together. Alek handed his checklist and map to Corporal Sanderson.

'Well done, Wasilewski, you're the first ones back in,' the corporal said, looking down at the sheet. 'All correct and with fifteen minutes to spare.' He pointed to the furthest truck. 'Grab yourselves a brew, lads.'

'Excuse me, Corporal,' the pale man said. 'Shouldn't they be saluting me?' He pointed to the insignia on his shoulder tabs.

Alek looked at the pip on each tab and the holstered sidearm on the young man's belt before looking blankly at Corporal Sanderson.

'Sir, they are not wearing headgear so they don't salute, remember?' Corporal Sanderson said. 'And when we're in the field, you don't want them saluting you because it tells the enemy that you are an officer.'

Alek watched the officer's cheeks redden further.

'Wasilewski!' Corporal Sanderson's sharp voice made Alek jump to attention.

'Yes, Corporal.'

'This is Second-Lieutenant Winslow,' Corporal Sanderson said to the whole section. 'He's our platoon commander. You will call him "Sir" and acknowledge his presence without saluting.'

'Yes, Corporal,' Alek and the section replied in unison. He didn't know how to salute anyway – that hadn't been covered in training. He walked up to the officer and said, 'Good afternoon, Sir.'

The rest of the section followed before heading to the back of the truck where a jerry can and a stack of mugs were sitting on the tailgate that was folded out like a table. Alek turned the tap on the jerry can and filled his mug with the steaming hot dark tea. 'Cheers,' he said and raised his mug.

'It pays to be a winner,' Swales said and clinked his mug to Alek's. 'Well done on the navigating. It's not often you can beat the army at its own game.'

Alek sipped his tea and smacked his parched lips. He sat in the shade of the truck and stretched out his legs. He had time to get a snooze in.

Shouts woke Alek up. His body was stiff and his tea was cold.

One of the drivers was leaning out of the truck's cab. 'Corporal, look,' he said, pointing down the road.

Alek stood and stretched, spotting a straggle of recruits shuffling up the road. They were coming from the west, not the south as Alek's section had.

'Where the fuck have they been?' Corporal Sanderson said.

Hulse was at the front, red-faced, sweating and breathless as he staggered into the car park. The remainder of the recruits limped behind him. Hulse handed over his crumpled, damp checklist and map.

Corporal Sanderson screwed them up and threw them at Hulse's chest. 'Don't hand me this rubbish. You got lost. You're two hours late!' He pointed at the recruits, who were now sitting on the gravel or bent over with their hands on their knees. 'Fall in! Stand up straight.'

Corporal Sanderson held them at attention, watching them sway as they struggled to stay upright.

'It's not our fault,' Hulse said, 'the maps are out of date.' There had been no map updates for five years: the Ordnance Survey had relied on satellite technology for tracking and imagery for so long that it had lost most of its practical surveying skills. That, and the lack of printing ink, meant that planning and navigation were reliant on older maps. The pecking order for the best information meant that the recruits were left using twenty-year-old maps.

Corporal Sanderson shook his head and shouted, 'Wasilewski!'

'Yes, Corporal.' Alek ran forward.

'Did you make all the checkpoints?' Corporal Sanderson said.

'Yes, Corporal.' Alek glanced at the line of exhausted recruits.

'Was your map accurate?'

'Yes, Corporal.'

'Dismissed.' Corporal Sanderson turned to Hulse. 'Right, you're busted. You can't lead men if you don't know where you're going.' He took a step back. 'Fall out! Get in the trucks now.'

The recruits ran to the back of their trucks. Hulse climbed into the first one and glared at Alek. 'You tosser. You deliberately made me look bad.'

Alek swallowed. 'I'm sorry, I didn't mean to. I just did what I was told.'

Hulse pointed a finger towards Alek's face. 'Because of you, I got busted. Watch it, you Polish creep.'

Alek leant his head back against the canvas side and closed his eyes. *So much for having a good day. Hulse is an idiot – but a dangerous one. I don't need him as an enemy.*

Alek's pleasant afternoon snooze was a distant memory once they returned to the barracks. The two-hour delay meant they had to shower and clean their kit in twenty minutes before being called to the rec room to watch the news. Alek dreaded this part of the day, enforced to ensure they knew what glorious victories were being won by their comrades. If they fell asleep their neighbour had to do press-ups. Sounds of 'ouch, you fucker', punctuated the news as ribs were prodded and shins kicked to keep each other awake.

Something came on about flags being waved. Alek sat up when the camera paused on a dark-haired woman. Lena! The camera moved on but Alek was convinced it was his sister. *That had to be Lena. What was she doing outside a factory? I thought she was working for the Ministry of Information.*

His empty stomach felt even emptier all of a sudden. Alek realised that he missed his big sister. She had ignored him for the most part when they'd lived at home but she had come to watch him play rugby. And, after the war had started, she'd shown him how to manage his rations and do the laundry on her monthly trips up from Plymouth. *Will I ever see her again? Or Mum and Dad?* He had been too busy or too tired to think much about his family after his first night in the army.

Corporal Sanderson turned the TV off. 'That's all, folks,' he said. 'Right, listen in. We've had our orders. We shall be on the move in forty-eight hours. Make sure your kit is in order. We will do a night exercise this evening, practising your landing drills and advance to contact.'

The recruits groaned in unison.

'You'll sleep tomorrow.' Corporal Sanderson waved their moans away. 'Eat dinner now, assemble outside the accommodation at 23:00 hours, in light combat gear, belts and water bottles. Dismissed.'

Alek shuffled out with the rest. He felt sick. *In two days I could be dead.*

Swales sat beside Alek at the end of one of the tables in the canteen. Dinner was corned beef hash and instant mashed potatoes with peas floating in gravy. 'This doesn't make sense,' Swales said.

'What doesn't?' Alek said.

'Why we are practising jumping out of trucks for a parachute landing,' Swales said. 'The navy is supposed to be sinking all the enemy's ships – so why can't we go by boat?'

Alek shrugged and soaked some potato mash in gravy before pushing it around the plate; the thought of combat had dulled his appetite.

'I'm not getting shot for these fuckers,' Swales said in a whisper. He looked around to see if anyone was listening. 'I'm going to make a break for Kernow – do you want to come?'

'What? Are you serious?' Alek put his hand over his mouth. He lowered his voice. 'Isn't it too dangerous?'

Swales leant in closer. 'Dangerous? How long do you think we'll last behind enemy lines? That's why we're being pushed out of a plane.'

'But why us? We're only recruits.' Alek knew that he wasn't ready for war.

Swales shrugged. 'I don't know but I have heard of shock troops being used as decoys while the real soldiers regroup and re-equip.'

Alek put his fork down. 'Shit.' It was worse than he had thought. They might last minutes – not even hours. He didn't want to die. And if he escaped to Kernow he could see his parents; he'd do anything to be with his mum and dad again. To have home-cooked meals and listen to his dad's bad jokes. He would even put up with the lectures on historical buildings and literature if that meant he'd be with them and far away from the possibility of being shot. *Home at last. Away from this bullshit.* Lena would still be in Plymouth, but she'd seemed happy enough on the TV.

Alek looked around at the recruits, all busy eating, seemingly oblivious to their impending doom. *Risk an escape tonight or face certain death in two days.* He turned back to Swales. 'Okay, so how are we going to do it?'

Alek shut his eyes as the truck pulled out of the barracks, breathing in the cold night air tinged with diesel fumes. The hum of the engine and the rocking motion were newly familiar catalysts that induced slumber. If he had learnt one thing in uniform, it was that you should sleep when you had the chance.

An elbow in his ribs woke him and Alek realised they were no longer moving.

'It's time to make our break,' Swales whispered. 'Coming?'

Alek nodded. He was alert in an instant. The rest of his section were still asleep, exhausted but peaceful. He and Swales crept to the tailgate and swung a leg over the side. The engine rumbled and the truck lurched forward again.

'Now,' Swales said.

Alek dropped to the tarmac with a thud and rolled onto his side and up onto his feet again in one smooth movement, surprised at how well the technique worked. He felt light and agile. He patted down his body to check for injuries. *Nothing. So far, so good.* He watched the red tail lights disappear over the hill. There was no turning back now.

'Which way is south?' Swales said.

Alek pointed at the half-moon rising above the hedgerows that towered over the sunken road. 'That way.'

Swales nodded. 'We've come across the moor. We should be closer to the river. Let's go.'

The stars were out and the moon illuminated the hedges and road ahead. Their shadows stretched ahead of them as Swales set off at a fast pace. 'We'll get off the road when we hear a vehicle coming.'

Alek settled into a run he could sustain. The air was cold but fresh. The only sound was the noise of their boots briefly hitting the tarmac and their breathing. He smiled as he took in his surroundings, feeling fully alive for possibly the first time in his life. He felt in control of his destiny for the first time in weeks, if not months.

They reached a T-junction and Alek checked his watch: 00:40. 'They must have noticed we're missing by now.' He looked backwards but there was no sign of pursuit.

'I reckon so,' Swales said. 'But we can't worry about that. Which way now?'

'If we head west, we can reach the Tamar.' Alek pointed to the right. 'We should see signs for Morwellham Quay before we get there.' He had agreed to Swales' idea to cross the Tamar in a boat rather than trying to swim across. Swales had done some outward bounds courses near the quay and seemed confident they could sneak across the Tamar.

They ran along the wider road. Alek couldn't help but look over his shoulder every few steps, which slowed his pace. Swales was about fifty metres further on. Alek stopped, sure he'd heard an engine. 'Swales,' he stage-whispered.

Swales carried on running.

'Swales,' Alek shouted. He sprinted forward, adding, 'Something's coming.' He pointed back over his shoulder. 'We're going to be caught!' The engine noise was louder but there were no lights visible; the vehicle might have been using blackout lights or driving using the moonlight. There was the sound of gears crunching and then an engine idling. Maybe they'd stopped at the T-junction. *I'm not letting them get me. I'll fight if I have to.*

Swales was about twenty metres ahead, pointing at the hedge.

Alek nodded and looked for a gap for himself, but couldn't see any on this side. The engine noise got louder. 'Shit.' Alek looked around and saw a hole in the opposite hedge. He darted across the road like a stoat and slithered through the gap, ignoring the cuts and stings from the sprouting nettles. He could see a light on the road now and the sound of tyres squealing. Alek ducked his head to cover his face as a Land Rover whizzed past. He looked up and saw four soldiers holding onto the roof frame where the canvas soft top was rolled back.

Alek froze as the Land Rover squealed to a halt and reversed. The soldiers jumped out and ran to a five-bar gate on the other side of the road. Two climbed over it and stamped around. The other two waited. Voices carried over the night air.

'There's nothing there.'

'I thought I saw someone.'

'You idiot – you're chasing shadows.'

Alek held his breath and hoped that Swales was OK. He heard clanging as the soldiers climbed the gate and the Land Rover pulled away. Alek let out his breath and crawled forward to check the road. The vehicle had disappeared. He waited for a minute before scrambling through the hedge and running up the road.

'Swales?' Alek said. 'Swales?' He felt like he was calling on one of his cats for her supper. The only reply was a barn owl hooting. *Where is he?*

Alek walked up and down the road for ten minutes, whispering 'Swales' into the hedges. He looked over every gate and through every gap but there was no sign. He checked his watch every minute as if that was going to help somehow. *Shit.* Alek felt a gnawing in his stomach. *Has Swales left me behind? Or was he captured?* He suddenly realised how alone he was. *West. I need to head west. I'll stick to Swales' plan and hope he's doing the same. I've got about five hours before dawn*, he reassured himself, and then resumed his run to freedom.

Chapter 4

Lena stopped at the zebra crossing on her way home, hunkered under her umbrella against the onset of another shower.

'Lena Wasilewski?'

Lena lifted her umbrella to see the short blonde woman who'd called her name. Rain bounced off the woman's pigtails and down her grey raincoat.

'Yes, that's me,' Lena said.

The blonde woman smiled. 'I'm Tanya. I'd like to make you a cup of coffee and talk about your art please.'

Coffee. Lena salivated at the thought. 'Coffee? Where can you get coffee around here?'

The high street was littered with abandoned coffee shops. With them closed, along with the stores selling vanity gadgets and new clothing, the remaining city centre shops were scattered like cacti in a desert, desperate to survive. Most had names that included one of 'reused', 'recycled' or 'renovated'.

'I have some resourceful friends. Do you want some?' Tanya said. 'I also have some shortbread.'

Lena hesitated. *I will be missed at the flat. The girls might be suspicious. But shortbread? Where did Tanya get the sugar?* 'I don't know. Where would we be going?' She looked around to see who else was watching. She had heard of people being picked off the streets and taken for questioning for less than eating a contraband biscuit. *It could be a trap.* She could only see a few miserable pedestrians hunched into their coats.

'Just up the road,' Tanya said, jerking a thumb over one shoulder.

'Okay, just a quick one,' Lena said. *No risk it, no biscuit, as Dad used to say.* She was salivating before she'd finished crossing the road.

Tanya walked with a brisk, efficient step, avoiding the puddles that collected in the broken paving slabs, past the roundabout and towards the old university site. She took two side streets, each full of terraced houses that moulded themselves to the contours of the hill.

Lena was breathing hard when they came to a red brick single-storey hall with 'United Methodist Church' on the sign outside. She had expected an art gallery or a studio, not a church. *Do they have art displays inside? I hope they don't want me to paint Christian pictures.*

Tanya looked up and down the street before walking to the back of the building. She knocked twice on the glass door and a lock clicked. Tanya smiled at Lena as the door opened, saying, 'After you.'

Lena shook off her umbrella and entered a small corridor with a kitchenette on the right and two doors on the left. A large lady was standing in the kitchenette, wearing grey leggings, white and gold trainers and a black hoodie with the words 'Hot Stuff' stencilled diagonally across the chest.

Tanya said from behind, 'This is Chantelle.'

'All right?' Chantelle said while looking at her fingernails, finding something in them more interesting than Lena.

'Hello,' Lena said. She chewed on her lower lip. *These women don't look like a snatch squad but they must want something.*

Chantelle reached up to a cupboard and took out two mugs. Her hoodie rose to reveal a blue dolphin tattooed on the pale, white-lined flesh hanging over her leggings.

'I suppose you must be wondering what this is all about,' Tanya said.

Lena nodded. But foremost she was thinking: *Where's the shortbread?*

Tanya smiled. 'We like the posters you have been producing at the Ministry; they are very realistic. We also know that you used to go on holiday in Kernow, or Cornwall as it was known then, when you were a child.'

'How do you know all this about me?' Lena folded her arms. Now Tanya had her attention.

'Because you posted daily on Instagram before it got stopped. We're in contact with people in Kernow. Your mum and dad are there now, aren't they?'

'Yes.' Lena bit her lip and looked at her shoes. It was a risk asking about people who were labelled traitors, but she had to know. 'Have you heard from them? Are they OK?'

Tanya nodded. 'They are safe and well. They miss you and your brother.'

Chantelle poured boiling water into a cafetière, and the smell of coffee reached Lena.

'Milk, sugar?' Chantelle said.

'Erm, both, please?' Lena said. *They have sugar for coffee as well as to make shortbread? Then again, Chantelle doesn't look like she's on rations.*

Tanya continued, 'You might be able to help your parents.'

'Help them?' Lena paused. This was too good to be true. She didn't know these people. Any citizen suspected of helping traitors or sympathising with them was liable to be punished. 'My parents are traitors.'

'Your parents were lucky. Many people are unhappy with the war but unable to leave,' Tanya said.

'How are you in contact with people there? It's not allowed,' Lena said, 'and the phone lines are down.'

Tanya smiled again. 'We have ways of communicating that don't require the old British satellites.'

Lena looked at the door for a way out but Chantelle's bulky frame filled it. She put her hand up. 'Stop. This conversation could be reported and then I'll lose my job and be put in a Recreant Camp.' The camps were notorious for being a one-way ticket to oblivion. Rumours of gang rapes, murders and suicides circulated amongst the population. Lena didn't know whether they were true or not, but she was determined to avoid finding out. She'd rather be hungry and bored.

She turned to go; she hadn't said or done anything that would get her into trouble yet.

'No one here is going to report you. Stay and have your coffee first.' Tanya filled a mug from the cafetière on the worktop and carried it over to Lena. 'Here, there is no crime in listening.' She held out a small plate with two round shortbread biscuits.

Lena thought that listening to talk about Kernow might well be a crime: almost everything except flag waving seemed to be illegal nowadays. The bitter aroma of freshly brewed coffee wafted over Lena and awakened memories of a time before the war. Her stomach overruled her caution. 'OK, thank you.' She took the mug and put the plate on the counter. She dunked a biscuit and crammed it in her mouth whole, licking the crumbs and sugar dust off her lip and closing her eyes. She sniffed her mug and then sipped, savouring the warm, thick liquid.

'Good?' Tanya said.

'So good.' Lena cupped the mug in both hands, took another sip and felt a tingle in her brain and fingertips.

Tanya smiled over her coffee. 'Wouldn't you like to join your family?'

'Family? My brother is defending us from the Continentals and my parents are traitors.' *I'm not going to say anything treacherous. I can't be punished that much for just listening. I hope.*

Chantelle snorted and wiped some snot from her upper lip, 'Good one,' she said.

'Yes, yes, we know what the Party wants you to say – well done,' Tanya said. She smiled and added softly, 'We know your mum and dad are in Looe. We also know that your brother escaped from his unit.'

'Alek? Escaped? When?' *It's only been a month since he volunteered, so why has he escaped?*

'Two days ago – he stole a Land Rover,' Tanya said.

'How do you know this? Who are you?' Lena said.

'We are friends, Lena. We need your help so that we can get more people safely away. You won't be breaking any laws, just adding some details to the posters you already make.'

'What people; what details?' Lena took another sip of coffee. She was saving the second biscuit, letting the anticipation build so she could enjoy it more. Rain pummelled the window.

'People like you whose families are in Kernow,' Tanya said. 'Children who've been stranded and husbands and wives whose partners are on the wrong side of the Tamar. We would like you to include some boats in your next poster. Boats with two names on them.'

'Why?' Lena asked.

'The less you know, the better. Compartmentalisation keeps all of us safe. Your role is essential for us to succeed,' Tanya said. 'And we might be able to reunite you with your family.'

Lena frowned. 'Where is Alek if he's escaped?'

Tanya looked at Chantelle and then back to Lena. 'We don't know. He escaped with another recruit. He might be trying to get to your parents.'

Alek, what are you doing? Have you left me alone here? Was it because I didn't visit? That wasn't my fault. Lena felt as if she was falling from the ten-metre diving platform into the pool where she used to lifeguard – except there was no water and she'd crash to the bottom.

Tanya placed a small, clear plastic bag containing coffee granules on the worktop. 'You can take this as a gesture of faith. We will give you more if you agree to do the work. Chantelle here will be your contact from now on.'

Lena nibbled her biscuit. Contrary to her expectations, it was less enjoyable than the first because she had so much to think about now. Alek's whereabouts; seeing her parents; helping others escape. She drained the last of her coffee and picked up the bag of granules. *It's all very good having this coffee, but I'm more alone than ever.*

'All of this must remain between the three of us,' Tanya said. 'You can trust no one else. We'll give you twenty-four hours to think about it and then Chantelle will be in touch. Take the route home that you did today. Alone. If you follow the instructions, you will be safe.' Tanya escorted Lena to the door and said goodbye.

Lena put up her umbrella and stared around in the evening gloom, looking at the shadows, worrying that someone might be watching her. She set off for the apartment. *I'm not helping them. It's bad enough that my parents left me; now Alek has deserted too. My Soc-Cred score is going to be ruined and my rations will go down even further.* 'Thanks, Alek.' She felt the packet of coffee in her pocket. *Still, at least I have the coffee.*

27

Lena squelched her way to the top floor, feeling her way with the handrail; light didn't penetrate this building, even on a sunny day. *I wish I had bought that extra pair of shoes when the shops still had them.* It was a thought that came into Lena's head at least twice a day. But she had no money. 'Pay' was something that got talked about but never seemed to materialise in any tangible form. They'd given up asking Trevor for their back pay months ago. Not that there were any new shoes for sale – only an ever-decreasing number of second-hand pairs for increasing amounts of cash. The ATMs were restricted to £10 withdrawals in a futile effort to combat inflation. The black market was rampant despite the Party's efforts to crack down on it. Someone was making money in this economy, but not Lena, that was for sure.

She took off her wet shoes in the corridor and dumped them in her bedroom. She looked around for somewhere to hide her coffee granules. Alice had a habit of 'borrowing' things. The sorry-looking shoes might be the only things off-limits. Lena stuffed the plastic bag into the front of the left shoe and then took off her wet socks, hanging them over the end of her bed. Usually she preferred to sit and read on her own after work; living and working with the same women made her feel claustrophobic. But today she needed a distraction from her worries. She took a breath and decided to be sociable.

The living room had two small fake-leather sofas – one black, one beige – three easy chairs in various shades of brown and two coffee tables of different heights that were covered with magazines and empty glasses. A grey, oval stone with a red and white lighthouse painted on it lay on top of one pile of magazines, one of several painted stones dotted around the apartment. The women had tried their best to decorate their drab surroundings. But then their paints had run out.

Jane and Tamsin were draped across the furniture in relaxed poses wearing a mixture of pyjamas, leggings and hoodies. Neither looked up from their tattered paperbacks as Lena slumped into an easy chair. She rifled through the magazines on the coffee table; she had read them all but picked up a copy of *Good Housekeeping* anyway. She looked at the pictures of older women wearing floral dresses sitting on cast iron benches under flower-draped pergolas. *Was life really like that before the war?* The crackle of the radio broke her thoughts.

'Turn that down,' Jane said. 'We don't want to get caught.'

Alice fiddled with the dial and held up the wire antenna towards the window. The crackle faded and a song emerged. A disco beat with nonsense lyrics, but a song nonetheless. Alice started to dance, the antenna moving with her, bringing back the static. 'Anyone got any Blu Tack?' she said.

Jane put down her book and walked to the window. 'Stop dancing around – they could be watching.'

'Oh, don't be such a fuss pot.' Alice held up the wire, closed her eyes and waved her hands around.

'Alice, stop it,' Lena shouted, 'you'll get us into trouble.'

Alice opened her eyes and stopped dancing. 'You lot are no fun.' She coiled the antenna, turned off the radio, and hid it back under one of the sofa cushions. Jane sat down again and resumed her reading. Lena flicked through her magazine. The last thing she needed was a house raid and her Soc-Cred score taking a hit. She was already dreading the consequences of Alek's desertion.

'All right, brainiac?' Alice flipped up the cover of Jane's book. 'Whatcha reading?'

'A book,' Jane said. She was wearing thick black-framed glasses and a black polo-neck jumper. 'You might try it sometime.'

'Na, thanks, I tried one once.'

'Dinner's ready,' announced Beth, her head popping around the door. 'Did I hear music playing?'

'I don't know – did you?' Alice said.

Lena looked at the picture of 'Koftas with Broccoli Couscous and Zesty Yogurt' before putting the magazine down. She sighed at the thought of time spent wandering around Sainsbury's choosing items from the deli.

'No meat again?' she said to Jane when they sat down to eat. The extra walking had burned excess calories and, despite the two biscuits, her legs were trembling like a sparrow's heartbeat.

'Not until Ration Day on Thursday,' Jane said.

Lena suppressed a groan at the mention of rations. Alek's actions were bound to affect them all. If her rations were reduced then the rest of the women would resent her contributing less food to the pot – rather than sympathise with her. Things were desperate enough already.

After dinner and the clear-up, Lena hung back in the kitchen, thinking of her coffee. At least it was some kind of treat, even if she was always hungry. Her usual wake-up time was 07:00, and her bathroom slot was 07:20 to 07:30, but the first woman was in at 06:50. If she was going to make coffee it needed to be before then. She would set her alarm for 06:30. *Half an hour less sleep. Is it worth it? I think so. But how am I going to brew the coffee?*

Lena looked through the kitchen cupboards; as she expected, there was no cafetière, nor any filters. *But I could make my own… How do I make a cone from a sheet of paper?* She thought back to her art school days when they made collages. Something to do with making a square first and then cutting the bottom. *No, that's not it. I need to draw a semi-circle on the paper. And then what can I put the paper in to brew the coffee?* She pulled out a sieve and a pan. With a mug to drink the coffee from that made three things to wash up before anyone else rose.

She took a small plate from the cupboard to the privacy of her room. Her paper and scissors were stored in a desk drawer. She put the plate onto the paper and drew a semi-circle around the edge with a pencil. She was cutting it out when Jane walked in.

'Watcha doin'?' Jane said.

Lena waved the scissors at Jane. 'God, why are you sneaking around like that?' It was difficult to get any time to herself in the apartment.

'I wasn't sneaking; I was asking.' Jane spun the edge of the plate around on the desk. 'Are you doing some kind of art?'

'Yes – I thought about making some Easter decorations.' The lie slid off Lena's tongue. She didn't like lying to her best friend, but it was too risky to tell anyone about the coffee. Once one person knew, everyone would know.

'Good idea, let me help.' Jane sat on the desk.

The two women cut and coloured a series of cones to be used as table decorations. Lena only had a few short crayons stored in a wooden art box. She had worn out the pencils that she took from college. She had thought about taking some materials from work but the risk of getting caught was too high.

Jane drew two chicks and four eggs on the side of a cone. Lena made three paper crosses as she got into a creative flow. Drawing for her was a relaxing pastime and she soon forgot about her original purpose. Idly chatting with Jane while they crafted was a welcome distraction from worries about her family and her Soc-Cred.

Alice walked in, looked at the decorations, sniffed and lay on her bunk. She was the only one of the women without an art background.

'You're good at these,' Jane said. 'Where did you learn to do this stuff?'

'I used to go to craft fairs with my mum.' Lena smiled at the memory. 'She would sell them to raise funds for the TG. My brother always ate the leftover cakes.'

'What's the TG?' Jane said.

'Townswomen's Guild,' Lena said, then put her hand over her mouth. She had forgotten that the TG was a banned organisation.

Alice sat up. 'Your mum was a member of the TG?'

Lena held up her hands. 'Yes, but please don't tell anyone, Alice. I don't want my Soc-Cred to go down.' *Shit, shit, shit. Alice has a big mouth – she's bound to spill this to someone.*

Alice shook her head. 'I won't say anything. I just didn't know, that's all.' She lay back down on her bunk.

'What's the problem?' Jane said.

'Nothing,' Lena said. 'It's just the TG was banned for spreading unpatriotic ideas.'

'Like what?' Jane said.

Lena glanced at the supine Alice. 'Oh, you know. Women should be independent and that having a family was a choice, not a duty. That sort of thing.'

'Got to meet a man first, if you want to have a family,' Jane said. 'And there's little chance of that here.' She drew a chick and picked up the stub of a yellow pencil to colour it in.

Lena nodded. She didn't want to make a new family. She wanted her old one back.

Chapter 5

A tickling on his chin woke Alek. He stayed still, unwilling to scratch for fear of rustling the leaves he had hidden under. He had stumbled onwards until dawn, when his legs and brain had conked out. There'd been no sign of Swales anywhere on the road and he'd had enough cognition left to realise he needed to rest, choosing a deep ditch beside the road as his temporary bed.

His eyes crossed as he tried to focus on what was tickling his lip. A woodlouse! He pressed his lips tight together but the woodlouse crawled into his nose. Grimacing, he snorted snot and woodlouse over his mouth, and the itching stopped. The woodlouse lay on its back and wriggled its legs until Alek flicked it over and watched it crawl off his chest.

Alek opened his mouth again, listening hard. Nothing. He sat up and peered over the edge of the ditch. No sign of trucks or people on the road. *Time to move.* He wiped the snot off his mouth and chin and spat. Standing up was painful. His right knee was still sore and his legs had stiffened. The euphoria of escaping with Swales had disappeared. *Where is he? I'm alone, my body feels like it's been trampled on by a herd of cows and I need to take a dump.*

He shuffled across the road and broke into a trot, heading towards a gate in the hedge opposite the rising sun. *If I keep going west I'll reach the Tamar.*

Twenty metres from the gate, he stopped and listened. *An engine.* He bent forward and sprinted towards the gate as best as his boots would allow. As he reached the gate he saw a white pickup truck speeding around the corner. On its flat back, holding onto the driver's cab, stood a grinning Hulse.

'Shit!' Alek put his right foot on the first rung of the five-bar gate and bent over the top, reaching down on the other side with his left hand. Kicking both legs up and over, he landed softly in the field, wincing as his right knee absorbed the landing. He hobbled into the rows of corn, not daring to look back He heard the squeal of tyres and men shouting.

'Have you got him?'

'No, he's in there somewhere.'

'Right, let's get in there then and spread out.'

Alek crawled on his forearms and belly. He knew they would struggle to find him in this massive crop if he stayed still, but the fear of being captured drove him forward. His fingers shook with adrenaline and his mouth was dry. Guessing the soldiers would take the line of least resistance and edge downhill, he followed the natural line of the corn going uphill.

The dry weather had hardened the ground. His jacket and trousers had holes in the elbows and knees, every move making his grazes worse, but adrenaline numbed the pain. He hadn't drunk anything for hours. Parched from heat and dirt and unable to swallow, Alek picked up a small, smooth stone and wiped it on his sleeve. He placed it on his tongue and resumed his crawling. An old Apache trick he had learnt from watching Westerns with his dad. Breathing through his nose, sucking on the stone and moving quietly required all his concentration, just like Cochise.

Saliva returned to his mouth and he pulled the stone out, swallowing. Not as good as a hot bath, a mug of tea and a decent toilet, but it was a start. He could see the edge of the row of corn, he crawled forward.

'Come out, you Polish cretin – I can see you,' a familiar voice said.

Alek looked up and saw Hulse two metres in front of him, his red ears glowing in the sun, a thin sneer across his face.

No more running or hiding. This is it. Alek popped his feet under his torso like a surfer and charged at Hulse. Alek had never been in a fight before, so he did what he knew best: a rugby tackle. He drove his right shoulder into Hulse's midriff and wrapped both his arms around his left leg, picking it up and tipping him backwards into the stony ground. The weight of Alek's whole body crashed down on top.

Without thinking, Alek reached up for Hulse's face, fingers pushing down into soft flesh and squeezing, pressing down hard to lever himself up. As Hulse reached for his bleeding face with both hands and moaned, Alek kicked him in the side of the head for good measure. 'I'm not Polish, you idiot.' He turned and ran down the side of the field, ignoring the pain in his knee, corn stalks brushing his side as he sprinted for the gate. ,

Alek could hear the soldiers at the other end of the field. He jumped back over the gate and looked around. The Land Rover. He peered into the back; there was a body in grey combat fatigues, the blonde hair matted with blood. *Swales!* 'I'll get you out of here – hold on.'

Alek ran round to the front of the Rover. Seeing the keys in the ignition, he got in and started the engine, grinding the gears and driving past the empty truck. The engine revved as he accelerated, the Rover juddering as Alek changed from first to third, missing second gear. His only driving experience was two sessions in the Tesco car park with his dad, just before he and Mum had left. Changing gears and braking was all Alek knew. *It's all I need to get to Kernow.* The Rover picked up speed and Alek steered it west. 'Come on, come on!' Alek said as he checked the rear-view mirror. Soldiers were carrying Hulse's limp body to the truck.

Alek drove for two miles, grateful he didn't have to change gears, before he had to stop at a roundabout. The engine stalled. *Shit, clutch. Use the clutch.* The signpost said Plymouth, Tavistock and Morwellham Quay. Alek restarted the engine, turned left and followed signs to the quay, four miles away. He got up to fourth gear on this wider and well-maintained road. There was no sign of pursuit in his mirrors, but Swales had told him that drones would come; he had to ditch the Rover fast and get into cover. He started looking for a shed or barn, while his stomach grumbled and he squeezed his buttocks together to hold on.

Another sign read: 'Morwellham Quay 1 mile'. Alek spotted a cluster of farm buildings ahead and to the left. Slowing down, he remembered to use the clutch to change gears, and turned up the track. The recent drought meant the soil was loose, so he drove slowly to avoid causing a dust cloud that would attract a drone. Alek pulled up to the courtyard, parked between two large farm vehicles and got out with a racing heart. His bowels felt like they were going to explode.

Alek hobbled over to one of the milking sheds that formed one side of the courtyard and climbed through the metal bars. He shuffled down the empty concrete aisle, into one of the milking stalls, pulled down his trousers, held onto a bar and squatted. *Bliss.* The straw looked too prickly to use as a wipe, and there was nothing else to use, so he pulled his trousers up and waddled back to the shed entrance as if he were saddle sore. He knew that he had taken a risk pulling in here but he had to check on Swales before they went any further.

A tortoiseshell cat was dozing on a tractor tyre by the farmhouse but there was no sign of the farmer. Alek climbed into the back of the Land Rover. Swales' hair was matted brown with dried blood that streaked down past his ear. Remembering his ABC from his lifeguard training, Alek assessed his friend; Swales was breathing and he had a pulse. 'Yes, you're alive!' There didn't appear to be any other wounds apart from the head. Alek rolled Swales into the recovery position. 'You'll be all right, Swales – just a bump on the head. I'll get you cleaned up.'

Alek took his water bottle to a tap at the side of the house. Looking around and seeing no one, he filled up his bottle. The water was cool and fresh and Alek glugged it down without taking a breath. *Slow down, and take sips.* He stuck his head under the tap and rinsed his face, belched, and filled up his bottle again.

He looked up for drones and listened, but there was no sound. Stealing the Rover had seemed like a good idea, but now it was a burden. There were bound to be border patrols at the quay. If Swales recovered, they would have to move on foot – and at night. Alek looked at the farmhouse; food might be in there, but that would have to wait. He grabbed the door handle on the barn furthest from the house and leant back to slide the door across the concrete floor. The rollers squeaked. There was room to park the Rover in there; he just had to hope that if the farmer was around, he didn't check it that afternoon. It would give them a place to rest before they could continue at night.

Alek ran across the courtyard and started up the Rover. Getting into reverse gear was noisy; he winced as he crunched the gears and over-revved the engine. He managed to stutter backwards and then forward into the barn. Getting out, Alek looked from the back; he could see the other barn, but not the house or milking sheds. *That will have to do.*

A noise from behind startled him.

Swales was sitting up, rubbing his head. 'Where am I? Alek?'

Alek smiled at hearing Swales' friendly voice. 'We're on a farm near the quay. You've been out for ages.' He passed him the water bottle.

Swales took some sips, wincing as he tilted his head back.

'I'm so glad you're awake. I thought I was on my own there.' Alek punched Swales on the arm. 'I'm surprised they caught you. What happened?'

'That bastard Hulse had a pick axe handle.' Swales touched the back of his head. 'There's a big lump here.' He sipped more water. 'Where's the farmer? If they see us we're done for. We need to move.'

'We've got about six hours more daylight. My plan was for us to rest up here undercover. I didn't want to drive into a checkpoint at Morwellham. I think we should approach on foot across the country at nightfall.' Alek climbed into the back of the Rover and stretched out his legs. He rubbed his sore knee. 'Now we've got water, we just need some food.'

'I could murder a brew,' Swales said.

'Me too. And some fish and chips,' Alek said.

'A pasty,' they said together.

'You're on,' Swales said. 'We'll get one in Kernow. Have you still got your money?'

Alek reached down and pulled out the £5 note from his sock that Swales had told him to hide before they left. 'I hope they accept English money over there.'

'Who knows?' Swales said. 'Even if they don't, and we just get bread and water in a lock- up, it's better than being chucked into the front line.'

Alek nodded. His eyelids drooping, he lay down on the seat, using his hands as a pillow.

'Are we safe here?' Swales said.

'I haven't seen anyone on the farm,' Alek replied, letting his eyes close. Everything felt so heavy; even answering Swales was an effort.

'You rest then. I'll keep watch and if there's no one about, I'll see if I can get some food from the farm.' Swales shuffled to the tailgate and clambered out. The Land Rover wobbled as the weight changed. 'Shit.' Swales clung to the sidebar.

'Are you OK?' Alek said, opening one eye. 'I'll do it if you need to rest.'

'Just a bit dizzy. I need to get my balance back.' Swales let go of the sidebar and took a few tiny steps forward, his hands outstretched as if walking on a beam. The back of his head was a red and brown mess. 'I'm fine.' He pointed at the barn entrance. 'I'll see if I can get some scoff.'

Alek lay back on the seat and felt a wave of fatigue wash over him. He closed his eyes again and thought about eating one of his dad's Sunday breakfasts. *Pancakes, syrup and crispy bacon.*

The sound of the barn door sliding open woke Alek. *I can't feel my arm.* He sat up and shook his dead arm; it felt numb, unattached. Low sunlight streamed into the Rover. Alek held his working hand up to shade his eyes. 'Swales?' he said, his voice croaky.

Two hands grabbed Alek's collar and dragged him out of the Rover. 'What the—?' He winced as he landed on his bad knee and fell to the concrete floor. He saw four pairs of boots in front of him and, behind them in the courtyard, a four-tonne truck and an open-topped Land Rover. *Shit, shit, shit.*

Alek couldn't fight back as two of the soldiers lifted him by his elbows and hustled him out of the barn. He blinked to get the sleep dust out of his eyes and adjust to the sunlight. His platoon officer, Lieutenant Winslow, was talking to a red-cheeked lady wearing green wellies, jeans and a checked shirt with rolled-up sleeves. A body lay behind the officer.

'Swales!' Alek wrenched his arms free and ran stiff-legged to his friend. Swales' eyes were closed and his head lay sideways in the dirt. He cradled Swales' hand and brushed the blond hair matted with blood to one side.

'If he'd asked for food, I'd have given it to him,' the lady said. 'I don't want you doing no more killing on my farm.'

'No, Ma'am,' Lieutenant Winslow said. 'We're sorry for the inconvenience.' He saluted the farmer. 'Right, take this one away.'

Hands grabbed Alek's shoulders and pulled him up. He felt as limp as a sack of charity clothes, his legs buckling under him. Hands grabbing him under his armpits, he was dragged backwards towards the other Land Rover.

'Get in,' Hulse said from the back of the Rover. His left eye was swollen and a yellow bruise covered his cheekbone.

Alek had no satisfaction from seeing his handiwork – not after what had happened to Swales. He looked over his shoulder at Swales' body, knowing this time he wouldn't be waking up. Alek was shoved into the Rover by one soldier behind and pulled by another inside. He fell on the hard bench between two squaddies, opposite Hulse. Alek looked down at his feet. *No Swales, no Kernow, no Mum and Dad. It's over. What's going to happen to me now?*

'What's the matter – lost your boyfriend?' Hulse said.

Alek looked up at Hulse who sat there with a grin splitting his face from jug ear to jug ear. Alek didn't have the energy to fight now. He tried to swallow but his mouth and throat were dry again.

The Land Rover pulled away. Alek fell against the squaddie on his left who shoved him back. Two soldiers were picking up Swales' body. Alek leant back against the hard seat. The Land Rover bumped along the stony track, sending painful jolts through Alek's aching muscles and feet. He shut his eyes. *What's the worst they can do to me now? What's worse than pushing me out of a plane into enemy territory? At least you're at peace now, Swales.*

Chapter 6

Steam rose from the pavements where the sun struck the tarmac, little rainbows appearing in front of Lena as she walked to work. She had dreamt vividly and lost her night-time wrestling bout with the duvet, finding it on the floor in the morning. Her improvised coffee maker had been a success; the warm brew had tasted delicious and she felt a satisfying glow as the caffeine kicked in. *Finally, something to look forward to in the morning.* Even her hunger felt less severe.

'All right, Lena.' A large figure emerged from the shadows in the entrance of an old shoe shop.

Lena woke from her daydreaming with a start.

Chantelle's hooped earrings jiggled as she added, 'Made up your mind yet?'

Lena looked around before stepping into the doorway. 'No, I haven't – give me a chance.'

'Well, don't leave it too long.' Chantelle poked Lena in the shoulder. 'If you want to see your parents again, we need to get moving.'

Lena nodded and scurried up the street, looking over her shoulder and peering around the street corners. She felt like a shrew that had been patted by a cat.

The clock ticked behind Trevor's desk but the hands seemed stuck at 10:48. The sound penetrated the oppressive silence of the creative room. Lena tried to block it out but, like the earworm of a catchy pre-war song, she couldn't get it out of her head. She became aware of other sounds: pencils scratching rough paper, open-mouthed breathing and sniffling from the girls with hay fever, and squeaking chairs. *How can anyone concentrate with all this noise?* She chewed on her pencil. The familiar taste of wood and graphite did nothing to help ease her mind.

The clock hands limped their way to 11:00 – time to listen to the morning briefing. Trevor stood on the second step of the foyer and read from the yellow, A4 paper: 'The Royal Navy has sunk two more continental ships. Our heroic sailors have protected our ports.'

Lena tuned out. *With what?* She always asked herself this when she heard about the naval battles. Her friend Yasmin worked at the Met Office and, before the war had started, she'd told Lena about missiles being dependent on weather information provided by the European satellites. England had one weather satellite now, positioned in geostationary orbit above Exeter. *They must be using old-fashioned guns and torpedoes.* Lena looked out of the foyer doors towards the docks, where an aircraft carrier used to dominate the skyline. It had sailed months ago. Alice had said that it couldn't have gone far since the diesel had run out.

'Our Royal Navy is the envy of the world.' There was a murmur as the briefing ended and the staff ambled their way back to their workstations. Lena took one last look out of the glass front and trudged up the stairs. Her task this morning was to create a new recruitment poster: a cheerleading message to encourage younger teenagers to get involved in the war effort.

'Something green and ethical. Teenagers like that,' Trevor had said.

Plant a cabbage and save the country? Make love, not war? Lena shook her head – no, that wouldn't do; it was from a different era.

A knock on the door and the scraping of a chair made Lena look up. Trevor shuffled over to the door where another man was visible through the glass panel. There was some murmuring and then Trevor came over to Lena's desk. 'Please go with the inspector.'

Lena looked around the room; the other girls were staring, and she blushed. 'Why? What's happening?'

'Just go and answer his questions, will you? And be quick about it, we have work to do here.' Trevor was shifting his weight from side to side as if he needed to pee.

Lena walked to the door. *Have they found out about Chantelle and Tanya? Did someone report me?* She felt a bead of sweat running down her spine below her bra strap.

'Miss ... Miss Wa ... ?' The official made a face like he was sucking a lemon, if lemons had still been available. He left it at 'Miss Wa'. Dandruff lay on the man's suit shoulders and stubble rose in patches across his jaw like miscreant clover in a lawn.

'Wasilewski, yes, that's me.'

'Follow me.' He turned and led Lena to an empty classroom down the corridor. Tall stools were tucked under four rows of high benches. The inspector pulled one out and climbed onto it, gesturing for Lena to do the same on the other side of the bench.

He scratched at some stubble with a long fingernail and cleared his throat. 'Your brother, Alek, has deserted his post. He is a coward and a traitor. He has been named an enemy of the state.'

Lena clasped her hands to stop the trembling. *I hope he's safe. Maybe he's made it to Kernow? But that means it's only me left here now.*

'Well?' the inspector said.

'What?' Lena unclasped her hands and held onto the sides of the stool.

'Your whole family are traitors. The name Was … Wa …' The inspector shuffled his papers and cleared his throat. 'Your family name is tarnished. Your Soc-Cred will be deducted 1,000 points. We could put you into a Recreant Camp, but your supervisor spoke highly of you, so we will refrain for now.'

Lena gripped the stool tighter. No one came back from the Recreant Camps. Her rations would decrease because of her lower Soc-Cred score. *I'm already hungry all the time as it is. All because of my selfish family.*

'Of course, there is a way to redeem yourself,' the inspector said, smiling. It looked like an effort.

'How?' Lena filled the gap.

'You can marry a veteran,' the inspector said.

'Marry? I don't want to marry anyone.' Lena blushed.

The inspector pointed a stubby finger. 'It's not about you, it's about England. You can show your patriotism and marry an Englishman. Then your children will have English names too.'

Lena stared at the brown rim on the man's frayed shirt collar. He was either poor at personal hygiene or just poor. *Married? Children? I haven't kissed a boy for two years, let alone had sex.*

'Married to whom?' She couldn't believe she was even asking this.

'Oh, we have a list of suitable men. We are arranging a dance for you girls at the Derriford Rehabilitation Centre. There will be lots of heroic veterans of the war in attendance.' He smiled and the loose skin around his chin wrinkled.

The injured, the lame and the sick. Thanks a lot, Alek. This is all your fault. And Mum's and Dad's.

'Having strong English sons will be the best way for you to earn redemption.' He inspected a fingernail. 'Of course, we shall keep an eye on you still.' He looked up at Lena. 'Do you understand?'

Lena nodded, croaking, 'Yes.' Her mouth was dry. *What has happened to my life?*

When Lena returned, Trevor scowled and looked at the clock. She had been gone for ten minutes. She picked up her pencil and scribbled on the side of the jotter. Her stomach was empty but she felt sick. Doodles lay upon doodles on her rough paper. Her caffeine euphoria had been replaced by despair. *This time yesterday, my shoes and my stomach were my only problems. Now I've got a treacherous brother, reduced rations meaning less food and I'm being told to marry a stranger.*

Lena needed to talk to someone – but who? Her mum would have been the first person, and sometimes her dad. But that was impossible, now they were living in their second home, Puffins. The family had spent their last Christmas together there three years ago. Lena remembered sitting beside the tree and the candles in her favourite hoodie and thick socks, shaking her head at her dad as he walked in wearing his new 'Brussel sprouts farting' trunks over his briefs, his pale, hairy, skinny legs poking out. His jumper had a picture of Darth Vader knitted into it with the words, 'I feel your presents' underneath. Alek wore his new Plymouth Argyle kit and ate out of the tin of Celebrations, a small pile of plastic wrappers scattered around him. Her mum was in the kitchen, singing along with the radio. Meanwhile Lena moaned about being away from her friends as they posted filtered photos of their presents on Instagram.

That life was gone now. Instead, she could earn Soc-Cred points by getting married. That would lead to better food and a separate flat or even a house with a small garden. *That wouldn't be so bad, would it? At least I wouldn't be hungry again.*

Lena glanced at the girls on either side of her. They would be at the dance too. They'd have to marry and have children and be given a house. She bit her lip as a teardrop fell onto the jotter, smudging the pencil lines. *I can't believe I'm being forced into this.*

Thursday was ration card day, the last one before they'd be reduced. It was Lena's turn to visit the butcher's to collect the weekly meat ration. As she walked down the steep hill, she thought of her mother's bicycle, with its wooden basket on the front. She remembered her mother freewheeling downhill, legs out to the side, giggling as Lena held on behind, doing a backie. *I could freewheel down to the shops and then push back the bike with the groceries in the basket. That would save my shoes.*

A new butcher was serving behind the counter: young with dark hair that was combed back into curls above the collar of his white overalls. Lena pushed a strand of errant hair behind her ear and straightened her back. She stared at the meat under the glass counter, feeling the young butcher's gaze on her. The lady in front said goodbye and Lena stepped up to the counter.

'Good afternoon,' the butcher said.

'Good afternoon,' Lena replied and handed over the five ration cards, one for each flatmate. She pushed the loose hair back again.

The butcher looked through the cards and piled them on the wooden worktop. 'Would you like them all together?'

'Yes, please,' Lena said. She watched the butcher as he pulled out some cuts of meat and chopped them on the worktop, whistling the whole time.

Lena wet her lips. *What is that tune? Do they learn to whistle on the job or is it part of the interview process? They all do it.*

'Here you go, love.' The butcher handed over two parcels that were wrapped in shiny brown paper with pictures of the animals and the cuts of meat explained on it. He tapped his forefinger on the parcel and winked at Lena.

What's he winking at me for? Is he flirting? It had been so long that Lena had pretty much forgotten what flirting was like, especially from someone good looking like the butcher. She blushed, picked up the parcel and hurried out of the shop, head down, past the queue of customers. She turned up the high street and stopped at the corner to take a few breaths.

'Hold up!'

Oh no. The young butcher was running towards her. She tidied her hair again. *I haven't got any make-up on.*

'You forgot these.' He handed her the ration cards.

'Oh, right, thank you.' Lena took the cards.

The butcher grinned, adding, 'You left these on purpose so I would chase you.'

'What? No, don't be ridiculous.' Lena turned so he wouldn't see her blushing again.

'Enjoy,' the butcher said with a wink.

Lena walked around the corner. She could hear him whistling his way back to work.

The cheek! What a cocky man he is. She stopped as she finally recognised the tune. 'I got you' by Jack Johnson. Lena couldn't whistle a jot, but she sang the lyric as she walked up the hill that seemed less steep than usual on the way back.

Lena unwrapped the parcel on the kitchen counter, conscious of the time. Keeping meat fresh was a nightmare because of the unreliable power. In the summer, thanks to the solar panels, the fridge freezer could be used during the daytime, but it still defrosted every night. Trying to keep track of when meat had been frozen and defrosted was a waste of time. Steaks were okay to be kept cool but mince and sausage meat were dodgy; they had to be cooked first.

She counted out five sausages and five rashers of bacon from the first parcel and separated them into two piles, wrapped them back up and put them in the fridge. She unwrapped the second parcel, containing chicken, but there was an extra parcel inside that. *Strange – was that packed by mistake?* She took off the brown paper, revealing two pigeons. *Ah, that's why the butcher was winking at me,* it wasn't just him flirting. She smiled and put the chicken in the fridge and the pigeons in an empty saucepan, squashing them down so they would fit under the lid. The women would be excited at this feast and she could play a joke on Alice.

The radio was playing classic soul in the common room. Jane and Alice were lying on a sofa, tapping their feet. 'I've got the meat from the butcher's,' Lena said. 'You're on the rota tonight, Alice.'

Alice yawned, 'Really? Already?' She stretched her arms, revealing a cursive script of tattoos on the inside of her bicep. She was pescatarian before the war but her ethics had dissipated as the conflict progressed. Hunger made carnivores of them all, as mangoes, bananas and quinoa were no longer available to be photographed and posted, let alone eaten. The realisation that a lot of food came from foreign countries, rather than the supermarket, was a revelation to many young people.

'I've left the chicken in the saucepan for you,' Lena said, sitting down on the arm of Jane's sofa. She kicked her foot against it, out of time to the music.

'I guess it's chicken tonight then,' Alice said. She pushed herself up.

'I'll keep you company if you like,' Lena said. She nudged Jane's foot and jerked her head towards the door.

Lena and Jane followed Alice to the kitchen.

'I don't know why you put the chicken in the saucepan,' Alice said. 'I'm not going to boil a whole chicken.' She opened the lid and jumped back. 'Urgh, there are dead birds in there!'

Lena laughed and leant on Jane's shoulder.

'That's gross. You know I don't like dead animals.' Alice looked in the pan again. 'The poor birds.'

'No, but you were happy to cook the chicken,' Lena said.

'Get them out of here!' Alice said.

Lena took the pigeons out by their feet and dangled them in front of her housemates.

'Where did you get those?' Jane said.

'Oh, the new butcher gave them to me.' Lena wrapped the pigeons up in the butcher's paper, glad her back was to Jane.

'What new butcher?' Jane said. 'Your ears have gone red.' Jane turned Lena's shoulder and examined her face. 'You're blushing.'

'No, I'm not.' Lena put the pigeons on top of the fridge while she thought about how to cook them

'Yeah, you are,' Alice said. 'It's got awfully warm in here.' She grinned. 'And the oven's not even on.'

Jane laughed. 'Come on, who is he?'

Lena rolled her eyes. 'He's no one. He's just a bit younger than the rest, that's all.'

'A young man who's giving you extra rations?' Alice said. 'What did you do to get them?'

'Nothing,' Lena said. 'Don't be silly.'

'Well,' Jane said. 'Make sure you keep on his good side – we could do with the extra food and there's more meat on them than the sparrows.' The women sometimes resorted to capturing sparrows by placing a mousetrap and seeds on the kitchen window ledge.

'I can't cook with those dead things looking at me.' Alice pointed at the top of the fridge.

'Don't be daft – they're wrapped up. I'll cook them tomorrow, when it's my turn.' Lena was glad the subject had been changed. She didn't mind the joking, but it cut a bit too close to the bone. *Do I like the butcher? Why can't I stop thinking about him?*

She walked back into the sitting room. Beth was frowning at a piece of paper in her hand.

'What's up, Beth?' Lena prepared herself for another micro-drama. Beth was a lapsed hard-core vegan who managed to find the worst in every situation.

'Have you seen this invitation?' Beth waved the paper at Lena. 'To a veteran's ball?'

Lena's good mood deflated. The crushing weight of reality flattened the afternoon's fun. 'I know, but it's either that or the Recreant Camp, Beth.' *Bloody Alek! It's all right for you, but what about the mess you've left me in?*

Chapter 7

Alek woke with a twitchy leg, as if he'd been a dog chasing rabbits in his sleep. *I need to stretch.* He pushed up on one knee and stretched to the sloping ceiling of the disused office that was his temporary cell, taking a deep breath, vertebrae cracking. 'Gluck,' he said, his mouth dry. He smacked his lips in a vain effort to generate some saliva. Something smelt funky. *That'll be me.* He stood on tiptoes so his fingers reached the plasterboard and then bent forward to touch his dusty boots. He winced. His feet were sore from walking on the hard ground and his calf muscles felt as solid as cricket balls.

He slumped his back and shoulders, breathing out. *One, two, three, four.* He repeated the sequence five times until his back and hamstrings loosened. His mum had done this as part of her yoga routine, always wearing her stripy leotard and purple leg warmers.

'Sorry for laughing at you, Mum,' Alek said to the empty room. He could have been sitting with her now, drinking tea and eating a piece of her delicious cinnamon flapjack, if only he hadn't been captured.

Alek rubbed his wrists where the plastic grips had chafed his skin. He looked around the windowless room for a means of escape for the fifth time since being put in here. A desk, some metal shelves, a swivel chair and a red plastic bucket for a toilet were the only furniture. No toilet paper or hand gel. *Luckily I haven't eaten for a day.*

Alek's empty stomach groaned at the thought of food. He had opened all the desk drawers and run his fingers along the top of the dusty shelves. Unlike the movies, there were no convenient tweezers, calculators nor crocodile-clipped wires to fashion into a codebreaking door opener.

Not that they would have been any help; there was a solitary keyhole rather than a complicated electronic lock and Alek had no idea how to pick it. He had peered through the keyhole and seen stacks of '24-hour' ration boxes in a room on the other side. Three metres away, they may as well have been in France. He closed his eyes and thought of roast beef and then a Big Mac, both distant memories. Sardines, rabbit and the occasional chicken or pork were his diet now, more substantial than his time as a lowly college student, but still monotonous

'They're fattening us up for the slaughter,' Swales had said when Alek commented on the stodgy potatoes.

Alek missed his friend's streetwise knowledge. *Not that it did him any good. He's dead and I'm stuck in this cell.* He lay down on the floor and curled up like a dog. Sleep was his only respite from misery.

Alek was woken by the sound of a key turning in the lock. The door opened and Second Lieutenant Winslow walked in.

'Wasilewski,' the officer said.

'Yes, Sir.' Alek stood as straight as he could, his knee creaking.

'You've done something very stupid and your friend has paid the price,' the officer said. 'Normally you would be shot for deserting, but we are about to go into battle.' He pointed at Alek. 'We need every soldier ready for the glorious attack and we don't want to waste a bullet on you.'

Alek's heart was thumping. He took a slow breath in and out. Swales had been right; they were cannon fodder. No punishment was worse than being dropped into enemy territory from a great height, especially when he had missed the jumping out of the truck practice because of his escape attempt.

'Get yourself cleaned up, and pack your kit. The RSM is briefing you in twenty minutes.' The officer raised an eyebrow. 'What are you waiting for? Move.'

'Yes, Sir.' Alek shuffled out of the office and back to the barracks with leaden legs. He was in no hurry to comply even though time was limited. *What's the point?* He walked into the Nissen hut and found the rest of his platoon, in various stages of dress, checking their webbing or tidying their bunks. A wave of silence hit him as they stopped and stared at his bedraggled state.

Alek ignored the stares and walked to his bunk, conscious that Swales was not there to stick up for him now.

'What do you think you're doing, coward?' Hulse leant on Alek's bunk. Murdo and Trowbridge flanked him.

'I'm getting ready for the briefing,' Alek said. He looked around; maybe he could dive across his bunk to escape them?

'We don't want a coward in our ranks,' Hulse said.

'I'm not a coward. You're the one who had to use a stick to hit Swales,' Alek said.

'He got what he deserved – and you will too.' Hulse prodded Alek in the chest.

Alek took a step back and bumped into his wardrobe. 'Get out of my face, Hulse. The officer has told me to get ready.'

Hulse shoved Alek against the wardrobe. 'Just watch it, coward. Accidents can happen in battle.' He walked back to his bunk.

Alek took a towel and bar of soap out of his wardrobe with shaking hands. He had never felt as alone as he did now, surrounded by the rest of his platoon. He took his spare combats, a pair of pants, clean socks and a shirt, folded them under his arm and ran to the shower block. The two-minute shower in cool water was long enough for Alek to wash the grime away but too short to relax. He had gone from a top recruit in the orienteering exercise to a despised coward in forty-eight hours. *I hate this stupid army. We were so close to getting out of it.*

Regimental Sergeant-Major Thompson read out the official orders to the recruits who stood at ease in three tidy rows. 'You have a chance to help create a new generation of happy, loyal citizens. You will be donating...' RSM Thompson paused before adding, 'sperm to a bank.'

Some of the recruits sniggered. Alek frowned. He had been wallowing in self-pity and barely paying attention. Maybe he had misheard?

'You will each donate a sample that can be used in case you make the ultimate sacrifice for our glorious England. You will live on through your children.' RSM Thompson lowered the clipboard. 'What that means, lads,' he said, smiling, 'is that you get to have a wank for your country.'

The recruits around Alek laughed on cue. He hadn't misheard. *I don't want to help make a child. I'm only nineteen.*

The RSM let the noise die down. 'You will have five minutes to enjoy yourself and get your load into the pot before handing it sealed to your platoon corporals. They have kindly provided some materials for your viewing pleasure.'

The corporals each held up a handful of magazines with pictures of surprised-looking naked women on the front. Alek had never seen a porno mag before. Before the war, his gratification had come from online viewing. Pornography had been another casualty, one that never made the news. Half an hour ago, he'd thought he was going to be shot, and now this. He stood outside the toilet block shaking his head as grinning recruits handed their magazines to the next in line. *We're going to die and they're smiling?*

Two hours later and the recruits were lounging on the grass verge beside the aerodrome hanger, their stomachs full after they had emptied the tea caddy and eaten a round of powdered egg sandwiches.

Murdo belched and wiped his mouth. 'Aye, life's good. He pulled out a creased centrefold of a young blonde woman with huge breasts wearing only a Santa hat. 'I'm taking Miss December with me for company.'

The recruits laughed and asked to see her. Alek looked away as they started to boast about what they would like to do with the woman in the picture. His experience with girls had been very limited

– just some hand-holding and cuddles when he'd been in secondary school. The thought that he would die a virgin only added to his misery.

He checked his kit again to distract him from the upcoming trauma. They each had a light burden of a helmet, rifle and webbing that contained two water canteens, a 24-hour ration pack, mess tins and a hex-burner stove, a full magazine and thirty spare rounds of ammunition.

Trowbridge had asked for more ammunition at their briefing.

'You'll get more supplies when you land,' the officer had said. 'And sixty rounds means sixty Conts that you can kill.'

Alek doubted if Trowbridge could hit a tank, let alone a soldier. They'd had only had five rounds to practise with on the range. If Swales had been right, they wouldn't get a chance to eat their rations, so carrying more supplies was just a wasted effort. Alek was even more concerned about the lack of a map and compass; only the officer had one and if he went down, then they would all be lost.

'We are being dropped outside a village that has a church with a square tower and a clock on each side,' the officer had said. 'We need to reinforce our positions within the village. When we land we will form up and head for the village. If you are blown off course, make for the church tower.' He looked up. 'Understand?'

'Yes, Sir,' the platoon had responded. Everything sounded straightforward, but Alek doubted it would be. His failed escape had taught him that.

Alek watched as the Hercules C-130 taxied over to their position, its giant propellers menacing this close. Alek felt like a trapped mouse watching a cat approach. The Hercules' ramp lowered like a huge jaw, revealing the dark innards.

'Right, time to go,' Corporal Sanderson said. 'On your feet.'

Alek hefted his parachute onto his back and clipped the fasteners. He did his buddy check with Murdo; hardly reassuring with his fumbling and mumbling in his thick accent. *Swales would have done this better.*

The platoon lined up – Corporal Sanderson at the front; the officer who would be the first to jump at the back.

The RSM came to see them off, calling, 'Good luck, lads.' He saluted the officer and turned smartly, marching away with less starch in his back than on the parade ground.

Alek shuffled up the ramp and sat down on one of the benches at the back of the plane, rifle strapped to his chest. Opposite him sat Murdo, his helmet askew above his protruding brow, grinning like a Halloween skull costume. Alek forced a smile back. *I don't know about the enemy, but Murdo frightens the life out of me.*

A member of the aircrew, wearing green overalls with a blue pair of wings stitched to the chest, walked down the lines. 'It's about three hours of flight time,' he shouted above the droning engines. 'The buckets are there for when you feel sick.' He pointed to two buckets that were fastened on either end of the aisle.

The ramp closed and the Hercules rumbled forward, picking up speed. Alek felt his stomach lurch as the wheels left the runway. He gripped his rifle and braced his feet against the metal floor, his leg muscles stiff. He had never flown in a propeller-driven aircraft. The walls felt so thin and there was only one tiny window. As the plane banked he caught a glimpse of the green fields below and then a sparkle of sea. Alek strained to see the stretch of Cornish coastline beyond the sprawl of Plymouth. He blinked back a tear as he thought of his parents somewhere below.

The plane levelled and the clouds banked out in front, tinged with the orange glow of the setting sun. He thought about his great-grandpa, who'd flown in older planes across this same stretch of water when bombing the German industries. *I'm going to fight the Continentals. Even though I don't know why they are our enemy. I should have paid more attention to my Civics lessons. Listening to my dad and Swales has not got me anywhere except on a one-way ticket to death.*

The inside of the plane was dark except for the red lights at either end that gave an eerie glow. Alek regretted drinking that second cup of tea; peeing into a bucket while the plane flew low over the waves was more difficult than hitting a target on the range at 300 metres.

The turbulence increased as they flew above the Continental land mass, Alek's stomach lurching up and down. The egg sandwich came back up. He hadn't enjoyed it much the first time around either. Once Alek had puked, the rest of the platoon followed in quick succession, and the plane stank of piss and vomit within an hour of take-off.

The aircrewman walked down the aisle and tapped the officer on the shoulder to have a conversation. Standing up, the officer tapped the soldier next to him and jabbed this thumb up. The message to prepare to jump was passed down the line. Alek stood up and turned to the back of the plane where the two doors had been opened. He clasped the hook that held the parachute strap to the static line running above them to the doorway. His hands were trembling, his mouth still tasted of vomit and he needed another pee.

The green light came on. The officer jumped out, the soldiers hurrying their way to the opening. Alek felt the wind blow him back, the noise overwhelming. His turn soon came. He stood on the step holding onto the edge of the plane, unable to see anything below him. Closing his eyes and squeezing his teeth together, Alek jumped off the edge into blackness, his body immediately knocked sideways by the draught. He fell for what seemed an age before the parachute opened and he was jilted upwards. *Thank fuck for that.* He reached up and held onto the straps as tightly as he could, his eyes watering in the cold air.

The world was quiet up here now that the plane had flown away. There were no lights below, just darkness. Alek could see the falling shapes of the other soldiers around and stars shining through gaps in the clouds. He took a few breaths and felt at ease for some reason, enjoying the floating sensation and the peace.

Alek felt the ground rushing up to meet him rather than seeing it. His knees buckled and he rolled onto his side on hard ground. 'Oomph.' He couldn't breathe, the wind knocked out of him. He lay there for a second while the parachute collapsed around him, doing a quick self-diagnostic. *I'm okay. I'm not dead. Yet.* He sat up, unclipped the harness and rolled the parachute cords up, arm over arm like a giant cat's cradle.

Where are we? Alek had assumed that they would be dropped in old France but this ground was hard and barren, the field covered in rocks. The air was mild and smelt dry. He could see a couple of other parachutes being folded and two more floating down nearby. He patted the air out of his parachute, knelt on it to squeeze it down and then grabbed two rocks to place on top of the parachute. This was real. There was no point in feeling sorry for himself any more. No one could rescue him. There was no escape. There was only his platoon. He unclipped his rifle and crouched down, scanning the gloom for signs of the enemy, hearing only a few curses and stumbles as his fellow recruits joined him.

Chapter 8

Lena got up early to make herself another surreptitious coffee; she had enough granules for a few days. The aroma was still intoxicating; it filled the kitchen and threatened to seep under the door if Lena didn't open the kitchen window to let it out. She finished her coffee, washed out the mug and hid the grounds at the bottom of the food compost tub.

The pigeons stared at her from the saucepan. It was her turn to cook tonight and the extra meat would be welcome, especially as Beth and Tamsin had said they wouldn't touch them. Two pigeons between the remaining three women would be a feast. Lena salivated as she prepared the carcasses for cooking. They needed to be soaked in brine for flavour but salt was a rare commodity so she'd have to take a bucket down to the seafront to fetch seawater.

Lena smiled at the three anglers whose rods reached over the iron railings by the seafront. Two nodded back and one tipped his green cap in reply. The tip of a rod jerked and the angler in the cap reeled in a silver fish that folded itself in half and back several times.

Lena looked away as another angler raised a cosh, and she winced at the thud. She could eat almost anything now, and preparing dead animals for cooking was fine, but killing something herself was still too much for her. Lena remembered the first weekend she went home to see Alek and found a line of squirrel carcasses hanging inside their garage. Alek had been too squeamish to skin them. *We did have a great feast though.* 'I hope you are okay, baby brother, wherever you are. Even if you have dropped me in it.'

The puddles had evaporated, leaving the potholes uncovered in the pavements by the time Lena finished work that day. She dawdled up the hill, daydreaming that Chantelle or Tanya would approach her again. Helping them was risky but maybe she could bargain for some more food. She read the once-luminous fly posters advertising gigs for local bands, though they had been partially covered by 'sell-your-own-gold-and-silver' adverts now. Gigs with music, and alcohol and boys, going out with no plan other than just to have fun – they were all cultural casualties. Lena looked at her shoes; they were hardly dance-worthy, even if the gigs had still been allowed.

'All right, Lena,' Chantelle said from the shadows of the disused phone shop lobby.

'Jesus, will you stop doing that?' Lena looked around at the empty street before stepping into the gloom. *How does someone that big keep sneaking up on me?*

'Well?' Chantelle asked. She was wearing a sky blue hoodie displaying the words 'West Coast' in large bold letters and 'Miami' in small capital letters underneath.

'I'll do it. But I need to get some food. I can't stay this hungry for much longer,' Lena said.

'Right you are.' Chantelle passed a piece of paper to Lena. 'Memorise these names and put them on the boats.'

'*Chalfont, Lazee Dayz,*' Lena mumbled the names to herself.

'Make sure you get the spelling right.' Chantelle held her hand out for Lena to return the paper. 'Repeat them back to me.'

Lena did as she was asked.

Chantelle ate the piece of paper as if it was a piece of bread. 'Good girl. If you draft a copy and bring it to me, you can then paint it.'

Lena thought about that. 'It's going to be difficult to sneak a draft out. Why do I have to do that?'

Chantelle frowned, 'Duh! So I can check everything is okay before you do the poster for real. We don't want your spelling to be bad, do we?'

Lena bristled at the thought of her spelling being checked by someone who thought that Miami was on the west coast of the USA. 'And then you will you give me some extra rations?'

'Yes, once the posters are done, we'll get you something.' Chantelle pulled her hood over her head and stuck her hands in her pockets. 'Look for a plaster on the street sign outside your apartment in the mornings. That's my mark. When you see it, bring the draft to the church hall where we first met, at six that evening.'

'Yes, of course.' Lena looked up and down the street. A ginger cat was rubbing itself against a lamp post. 'What's the mark?'

'A sticking plaster on the post of the sign. I told you that already. Come on, girl, you've got to stay sharp.' Chantelle took a step back into the shadows.

'Sticking plaster – got it.' Lena cursed herself for forgetting. She had too much on her mind. *I can't afford to make mistakes.* Her idea of stress before the war had been having to choose which outfit to wear to college. Things had got worse in a hurry this week. *But at least I'm doing something positive now with a chance to get some food.*

When Lena reached her apartment, she looked up and down the street at the pedestrians. Two men in overalls, three boys in school uniforms and a young mum pushing a pram with a crying girl in tow. They all seemed occupied with what they were doing, so Lena bent down and pretended to tie her shoelace. She looked at the street sign with its flaky black paint and rust but no sticking plaster.

It's too soon; there won't be anything here yet.

She unlocked the entrance door and ran up the stairs. Deciding to help the Christians had been difficult but now she was desperate to start. Apart from getting more food, part of her excitement was the secrecy and part of it was tricking Trevor right under his nose. Her bedroom was empty when she dumped her satchel and took off her shoes and socks. There was a new blister on the ball of her left foot; she needed to make another masking tape repair.

Lena sang in the kitchen as she put the saucepan on the hob. She had an hour before the electricity was turned off. She reached over the sink to pull the tray of herb pots off the window sill – all they could grow in their apartment – plucked some sage and parsley and chopped them up with some withering celery stalks. After scraping them all into the pot, she turned it down to simmer.

'What are you singing about?' Jane said, leaning against the doorway. 'I'm so hungry I could eat a stray bird off the street.'

'Good one,' Lena said, smiling. 'Make yourself useful and get the plates out, will you?' She opened the bread bin and took out the half loaf of stale, crusty bread, cutting it into irregular, crumbly chunks with the serrated bread knife and placing one on each of the five plates.

Jane picked her piece of bread up. 'Stale. As always. We used to feed the ducks with stale bread.'

'Good luck finding a duck to feed,' Lena said. Ducks were another victim of the air rifle boom.

'It's a good job your boyfriend gave us these pigeons then,' Jane said with a mouthful of bread.

'He's not my boyfriend,' Lena said. 'Don't start that again.' Alek used to tease her like this when she was younger.

'Then why did he give you extras? I've never been given any,' Jane said. 'How about you, Alice?' Alice stood in the kitchen doorway. 'Have you got any extra meat from the new butcher?'

Alice shook her head. 'No. Anyway, have you heard the news?'

'No, what's happening?' Lena dipped a spoon into the saucepan and let the broth run into it.

'I've got some good gossip for you.' Alice prodded Lena on the shoulder causing her to spill the broth.

'Watch it! I could have been burnt.' Lena turned down the hob. It was hard to concentrate on the cooking when Alice was bouncing up and down like a Labrador puppy.

'There's a submarine coming in to dock and the sailors will be coming ashore this weekend.' Alice grabbed Lena's arm. 'They've been underwater for weeks – we can go and pull!'

'Is that it?' Lena said.

Jane held up a hand for Alice to high-five. 'Yes! Where do you think the sailors will go?'

Alice shrugged. 'A pub, as they can afford to buy beer, or even out on the Hoe. They'll be walking up and down in their uniforms with their bandy sea legs. Remember when that destroyer came in last year?'

Lena did. They had been taken out of work to wave and cheer on the dockside. They'd had to paint posters saying, 'Welcome Home' and 'Hello, Sailors' and wave handkerchiefs because there were no flags available. Rumours of the Party being embarrassed by the poor signage had flown around. The building of the flag factory had started soon afterwards.

'Have you no shame?' Lena said. 'It's undignified chasing after sailors. We're supposed to be independent women.'

That was what her mum had always told her. 'Let them come to you, love.' That had been good advice until one night on Union Street when a sailor had groped Lena in a dark corner of a nightclub. She had run out of the club and back to her college dorm. Drunk sailors on shore leave saw civilians in short skirts as a 'welcome home' gift that was waiting to be unwrapped. No matter how many times the women said, 'No.'

Alice shook her head. 'Don't be daft.' She pointed at her chest. 'They'll be chasing us.'

Jane laughed, 'Lena's not interested in sailors; she wants the butcher's meat.'

Alice held up her hand to be high-fived again. 'Good one.'

'Yuck, don't be so crude,' Lena said.

Jane reached for a crust of bread but Lena tapped her hand away.

'It's nearly ready.' Lena grabbed a ladle and dipped it into the saucepan. She took a sip of the broth. 'Okay, now you can grab a plate.'

The women took their plates into the living room to eat. The smell of the pigeon stew was too much temptation for Beth and Tamsin; they cleaned their plates like the others, dipping the stale bread into the sauce and licking their fingers at the end. Lena smiled even though she realised that the finger-licking was no longer a sign of a well-cooked meal. Hunger overcame politeness once again.

Lena looked around the grey, mundane office. Monday mornings were Monday mornings, war or no war. The glimmer of excitement when she'd spotted the round plaster on the street sign as she left the apartment that morning had gone. Now she felt the pressure to get the sketch finished by this afternoon – along with a spare draft to take to Chantelle. *Surely I can paint something more original than the cliffs of Dover?* She sketched the outline of two yachts leaning-to against a backdrop of white cliffs. She had never been to Dover but the bosses liked the overused iconic image. The problem was making the white sails stand out against the cliffs.

She doodled the outline of a bird above the cliffs while thinking of the tagline.

'Tis the hard grey weather
Breeds hard English men.'

Charles Kingsley was a change of tone but an apt quote when they'd been having so many spring storms. *I'd best add some clouds and a couple of men leaning into the wind too. Bugger.* Lena realised that her seagull looked more like a pigeon. *Friday night's meal must be in my subconscious.* She smiled, thinking of the relief she'd felt to have a full stomach after the meal. It was amazing what a little extra meat could do. It was almost fun. She counted on her fingers. Only another three days until they could visit the butcher's again.

Lena frowned at the sketch of the cliffs. It was clichéd and getting in the way of the message. She wanted to draw something more original but her memories of the coast were mainly of Cornwall and using that was strictly forbidden. She bit her lip. *Got it! Thurlestone Rock.* The arch was iconic and a good feature for the background. More importantly, it was the right side of the Tamar. She could use that.

Her family had spent an afternoon at the beach there before having dinner at the village pub to celebrate her graduation from sixth-form college. She had been embarrassed about her dad hugging her in public. He had picked her up and swung her around as if she was twelve, not eighteen. She hadn't been hugged like that since her parents had left. *I could do with a dad hug now.*

Chalfont and *Lazee Dayz.* Lena scribbled the names on the edge of her doodling pad and turned over a new sheet of paper to start again. Enthused, she sketched Thurlestone Rock and the small cove, adding two men standing on the beach holding pitchforks. No one used pitchforks now but the link to an agrarian past was always popular. The boats pitched towards the shore with the wind filling their sails. Lena imagined herself on one of the boats, snug in her waterproofs, the smell of the sea and the taste of the spray filling her senses as she sailed freely towards an unknown destination.

The clock struck one. The women downed their pencils and brushes. Lena trudged towards the cafeteria along the grey corridor that smelt of disinfectant and cabbage.

Once Lena had finished the second sketch of Thurlestone Rock and the two yachts, she looked up to see where Trevor was. He was scrutinising a folder and highlighting passages with a fluorescent marker. Lena curled the end of her rough sketch and rolled it as tightly as she could. *What if he sees it? What do I say if he catches me? I'm not cut out for this.* She looked at Trevor. His head was down. Lena lipped her spare hairband around one end of the tube and slid it down to the middle. She straightened out her left arm and pushed the tube up into her jacket sleeve. It was three minutes to five. She kept her arm straight out on her desk and roughly sketched a gull on her original draft to look busy.

She looked at the clock. *Come on, come on.*

The clock ticked to five and Trevor stood up. 'Right, finish time, ladies.

The women scraped their chairs in the rush to get out of the office. Lena kept her arm by her side with her hand cupped to steady the poster inside. She let the other women go out of the room first to avoid the jostling. They punched their time cards and strolled into the fresh air. One advantage of the lack of fuel for cars was the improvement in air quality.

Jane smiled at Lena. 'See you back at home.' They both liked to have a fifteen-minute respite from the crowd and Jane always took a longer route so that she could see the sea.

Lena said goodbye and headed for the church hall. The tape on her shoes was flapping by the time she reached Drakes Circus and she felt a blister coming on her right heel. Again. She checked over her shoulder at every crossing and stopped in front of several shops to look at her reflection. She couldn't see anyone who appeared to be suspicious. Not that she knew what she was doing. Her heel was raw as she walked up the hill towards the church hall. *I hope Chantelle has a spare plaster at least*, she thought, remembering the time when she had eight pairs of shoes. Half were in her wardrobe at her mum's house before it got commandeered; when her parents had left for Kernow, the council had taken over the property and sold all the items to raise funds for the war effort. Alek was allowed to stay there with two of his fellow students. Lena couldn't afford to go back and buy her clothes. She had worn out the other three pairs and these ones were at the end of their life now too.

With one last check over her shoulder, she walked down the alley. The back door was shut. Lena knocked. *We should have a code knock. I could be anyone.*

There was no answer. *Where is she?* Lena limped back down the alley and saw Chantelle's large frame wobbling up the slope, her face as red as tomato soup and her hooped earrings jiggling with every step. She coughed as she reached the top. Not a delicate, enter-stage-left type of cough but a hacking, rib-trembling, lung-bursting cough.

Lena squirmed.

Chantelle hawked and spat a globule of red and brown phlegm onto the kerb. 'Fuck a duck,' she said. 'That hill's going to kill me one day.' She straightened up. 'I need a fag.'

Lena looked up and down the terraced houses. *So much for being undercover and subtle. Everyone within a hundred-metre radius must have heard Chantelle.* Lena limped back down to the church hall entrance. 'Hurry up. If I'm caught with this sketch I could be charged with theft.'

'There's no one around. Don't panic. Come on inside,' Chantelle said as she unlocked the door.

Lena stumbled in and shut the door. She leant against it and took several deep breaths. *I'm not cut out for this secret agent business.*

Chapter 9

Alek had to lift his chin like a Pez container to look around because his helmet kept slipping down over his eyes. He hadn't felt this vulnerable since his scuba-diving foray around the Plymouth reef. He'd had a panic attack when he'd realised that sharks could attack him from above and below as well as either side and front and back.

He heard a rock scrape and then a, 'Psst!'

'Who's there?' Alek spun to see a silhouette against the stars. He pointed his rifle and flicked the safety off. With his mouth still tasting of vomit, he felt more bile creep up.

'It's me, Trowbridge,' the silhouette said, coming closer and crouching beside Alek. 'Who are you?'

'Wasilewski.' Alek switched the safety back on. 'Where are the others?'

'I've seen two more parachutes in this field, over there,' Trowbridge said.

Alek heard footsteps from behind, and he pivoted the other way. 'Who's there?'

'Murdo.' He squatted down by Alek. 'Is that you Hulse?'

'No, it's me – Wasilewski – and Trowbridge.' Alek hoped he wasn't going to have to repeat this all night. The confusion was farcical. He spat out a piece of carrot that had been stuck between his teeth, and smacked his lips. Taking a swig of water, he rinsed the vomit residue out of his mouth.

'Will you idiots keep your voices down?'

Alek spun and pointed his rifle for the third time, only relaxing when he realised it was Corporal Sanderson's voice.

'Form a circle and be quiet.'

They knelt in a circle, looking outwards. Alek was reassured by the clear command and relieved that Corporal Sanderson knew what he was doing. He felt more comfortable now he was on solid – albeit enemy – ground and his back was covered. Scanning the silent landscape, he watched the clouds break and a sliver of moon revealed above a row of stubby trees. A low wall ran along the ground below the trees, just like the ones on Bodmin Moor.

'There's a wall over there, Corporal,' Alek said.

'Right, let's shelter there, quietly.' Corporal Sanderson monkey-walked across the ground with silent ease, one hand for balance, the other holding his rifle. The three soldiers followed, kicking every rock and stone in their path.

'Quietly,' Corporal Sanderson said.

A head appeared over the wall, Hulse's ears sticking out under the helmet. 'Is that you, Corporal?'

Alek was pleased to see another member of their platoon but then remembered Hulse's threat about accidents. *I'm not going to turn my back on him.*

'Yes, Hulse. Have you seen anyone else?' Corporal Sanderson replied, crouching below the wall.

'I've got three more with me,' Hulse said.

'Right, and has anyone seen the officer?' Corporal Sanderson asked.

The soldiers shook their heads.

'What about the church?'

More shaking of heads.

'Fuck it,' Corporal Sanderson said. 'The officer has got the map. We don't know if we've been dropped near the village or miles away.' He peered above the wall. 'If in doubt, we make for high ground. Let's follow the wall up the slope.'

The soldiers walked either side of the wall, spread out to search for stragglers. Alek walked behind Murdo as the rear guard. He turned around every few steps to check backwards.

The ground rose to the edge of the field and then to another wall where six more soldiers were huddled in a corner. Alek could see a small hill ahead, and two farm buildings, but no sign of lights or a village. He felt better now that half of the platoon were together, even if they were lost. The soldiers bunched up for comfort and safety, forgetting or ignoring their training drills to keep their distance from each other.

'Listen in,' Corporal Sanderson said. 'We're crossing this wall and heading for the hill. That farm might have geese or dogs, so keep quiet. We're going to skirt wide left of it and, for fuck's sake, stay spread out.'

Alek waited until all the soldiers were over the wall before he lay on top and rolled to the other side. His nerves encouraged him to jog to catch up with Murdo but his mind knew he had to keep his distance. The sky was lightening to a dark blue and he could see further up the hill. Five figures were walking along the ridge, clearly silhouetted. The soldiers in front of Alek crouched down and Alek did the same. He pointed his rifle at the shapes on the ridge. *This is it. Our first contact with the enemy.*

Murdo crept back to Alek. 'You're wanted at the front.'

'What for?' Alek said.

Murdo shrugged. 'I dunno, just get up front.'

'Shit,' Alek said, monkey-walking past the line of hunkered-down soldiers, his thighs aching by the time he reached Corporal Sanderson.

'Idiots,' Corporal Sanderson said. 'They can be seen for miles.'

'Yes, Corporal,' Alek said. 'Are we going to shoot them?'

Corporal Sanderson grinned. 'They probably deserve it, but no.

They're on our side. You can tell by the shape of the helmets. Get up there and tell them to get off that fucking ridge. We'll meet at the top of the hill there.' The corporal pointed to the wood.

'Yes, Corporal.' Alek ran on a small trail that followed the slope of the hill, his eyes busy seeking out obstacles below and in front. *Why me? Because I'm expendable, probably.* His webbing felt tight against his heaving chest after a couple of minutes.

He slowed to a walk and took gulps of the dry air. As he reached the ridge, he heard an English voice ahead say, 'Are you sure it's this way?'

Alek smiled with relief. *Posh. That's our officer.*

'Sir,' Alek said from below.

The men stopped and turned their rifles towards Alek's voice.

'Don't shoot! It's Wasilewski, Sir.' Alek hugged the ground in case they were trigger happy.

'Ah, good, Wasilewski. Are you on your own?' the officer said.

Alek let out his breath, and rose to a kneeling position. 'No, Sir – Corporal Sanderson said that you can be seen for miles and to get down from the fucking ridge.'

The men dropped down like a chorus line, the officer following.

Alek suppressed a grin at the spectacle and said, 'We are to meet them at the wood on top of the hill, Sir.'

'Yes, of course.' The officer leopard-crawled down towards Alek. 'That's where we were going anyway.'

'Yes, Sir,' Alek said, though he knew the officer had been as lost as the rest of them. There was no sign of a village from the ridge, let alone a church.

A sliver of orange was visible above the eastern horizon by the time most of the platoon had made their way to the hilltop. They were on the edge of an escarpment that stretched out to the dawn light. Rows of evergreen trees had been planted behind a wire fence held by wooden posts driven into the dusty ground. Four men were missing from the platoon but there was no way of knowing where they were. The officer had checked his map for the escarpment but there was none marked. He had only been given a section that covered a five-mile radius of the village that was their target.

Alek listened as the officer explained the land to Corporal Sanderson, turning the map around and around.

Alek shook his head at the ineptitude. *That's not going to make a difference. Why on earth have we only been given a small map?*

Without any idea of where they were, or where they needed to be, Corporal Sanderson suggested that they dig in until they could see more landmarks. That was what the military book said. But they didn't have any entrenching tools. They were supposed to be reinforcing a defensive position in a village, not stranded on a hilltop. The platoon cursed the RAF for dropping them in the wrong place as they tore down branches to use as entrenching tools.

No wonder there are so many casualties in this war. Swales was right – it's a shambles.

Alek dug a shallow trench as best as he could. In half an hour, his fingers were raw and fingernails full of dirt. The ground was hard and the thick tree roots stretched their way into every space. Alek was partnered with Murdo, who, for all his faults, could work tirelessly and seemed happy building something resembling a cave. Sunlight poked through the trees, warming the digging soldiers who paused to take their jackets off.

The officer ran over, yelling, 'Put your jackets back on or you'll be on a charge.' He turned to Corporal Sanderson. 'Corporal, it's your job to keep the men in line. I've got to get in touch with Battalion HQ.'

'Yes, Sir,' Corporal Sanderson said. 'Jackets on, lads.'

After two hours of digging, most of the trenches were no more than knee-deep. The officer was still trying to make contact with Battalion HQ on his radio. Alek's shirt was heavy with sweat. Keeping their jackets on when digging didn't make sense to him. Nothing made sense. The more rules there were, the more they could be broken and the more they got shouted at. The purpose of the army seemed to be punishing its own soldiers rather than fighting the enemy.

Corporal Sanderson called a halt for a meal break. 'Not you, Wasilewski,' he said. 'You're going to go and keep an eye out for any movement. Take these.' He handed Alek the officer's binoculars. 'You'll get relieved once everyone else has eaten.'

Alek slipped the binos over his helmet and stuffed them down the top of his bulky combat jacket.

Hulse was grinning at him from his trench. 'That's what you get for being a coward,' he said.

Alek crawled forward to the edge of the escarpment, cursing the binos for the layer of discomfort they added around his head. It was hot in the sun and he was thirsty.

He lay beside a scraggy bush that cast a little shade and took the binos out. At least he didn't have to dig or listen to Hulse. He focused the binos and swept them from left to right. On the plain below, a river bisected a green meadow where three villages were set back from the flood area, surrounded by brown and yellow fields bordered with stone walls. None of the villages had a church with a square tower. A heat haze rose above the land and the two roads he could see shimmered. The odd civilian car passed by, and some farm traffic, but no military vehicles.

A whirring noise caused Alek to look up. *What's that?* He shaded his eyes and made out a grey drone against the clear sky, hovering above the hill. *Shit.*

'Hey, 'Ski, I've come to relieve you,' Murdo said as he walked across the open ground with his mug of tea in one hand, rifle hanging down in the other. 'What you looking at?' He looked up and squinted.

'Get down, Murdo! It's a drone,' Alek said. He took his binos off and laid them on the ground. 'I've got to let the corporal know.' He crawled back to the tree line and looked for Corporal Sanderson, finding him digging his trench. The officer was shouting into the radio a few metres away.

'Corporal, Corporal, there's a drone above us, Corporal.' Alek pointed to the tree line.

'Shit.' Corporal Sanderson looked up through the trees. The sky was visible in patches but the cover was good. 'Did it see you? What about any other signs of the enemy?'

Alek shook his head. 'I told Murdo to get down behind the bush. I couldn't see any military vehicles, Corporal. And no square church towers, either.'

'Good report, Wasilewski. Get yourself a brew.' Corporal Sanderson smiled. 'I hope you've learnt your lesson. We need all the good men we can get now.'

'Yes. Corporal.' Alek walked back to his trench and lit his hexi burner to boil water. He had been given two tasks by Corporal Sanderson since they'd landed and had done them well. It felt good to do a meaningful task rather than pointless exercises with imaginary bullets. If he was going to have any chance of survival, he would have to stick close to Corporal Sanderson who was confident and competent in the field. Alek made tea in his mug using powdered milk and a packet of sugar, then poured the remaining water into a foil pack of dried porridge. He sipped the hot drink and savoured the smell of tea and pine needles. This could be his last meal.

An hour after his breakfast, Alek's muscles were aching from digging. He stopped to inspect the newest blister on his palm.

Murdo looked over his shoulder. 'Got another one? Your soft hands not used to the graft?'

Alek picked up his stick and continued his scraping. 'I'd be all right if we had proper tools. We're supposed to have evolved since the Neanderthals,' he said to Murdo's back. There was no response. Alek prised a jagged stone from the dry earth and threw it onto a small pile at the side of their trench. He looked at the other soldiers; no one had got even waist-deep yet. *What's the point of this? We're stuck in the middle of nowhere digging holes!*

Alek heard a whistle and felt a rush of air. Whomp! He was thrown backwards as something exploded in the treetops. *What was that?*

'Take cover!' Corporal Sanderson ran past with one hand holding onto his helmet, the other gripping his rifle.

Whomp! Another explosion. Whomp, whomp. Trees creaked, groaned and banged as they crashed onto dry ground around the platoon. Alek tried to burrow lower into their shallow trench.

'Get off me!' Murdo said, kneeing Alek in the chest.

'Stay down,' Alek said. A tree fell over their trench, its branches crashing down onto Alek, pine needles sticking into his skin. The ground vibrated as shells landed around them. He hugged closer to Murdo, who stopped protesting. With every impact, Alek's teeth rattled and his muscles stiffened, the sound of the barrage penetrating every cell of his body. He struggled to hold his bladder and squeezed Murdo tighter, ignoring the rancid smell of stale sweat.

The ground stopped shaking.

Alek let go of Murdo and brushed a branch aside to look over the edge of his hole. Swathes of trunks lay across the paths and those that remained standing looked naked without their fallen branches. Sunlight streamed through the gaps in the canopy, contrasting with the dark areas where clusters of trees huddled together as if for protection. Stumps of trees had been eviscerated with a direct hit. Three craters now lay within their position. One was on top of a trench, where camouflaged body parts lay around the edge, a helmet perched on top of a branch. Alek was amazed that any of the trees in the woods were still standing.

Alek coughed in the smoke that tasted of grease and burnt flesh. The fresh scent of pine had disappeared with the trees. He pulled up Murdo's collar and looked into his wide eyes. 'Are you okay?' he said, but he could hardly hear his own words.

Murdo nodded and pointed to his ear, saying something that Alek took to be indicating his hearing was damaged too. They squeezed through the gap between the tree trunk and the ground, looking around. Corporal Sanderson was waving at them and they ran over to him, hurdling broken branches.

Corporal Sanderson handed Alek the binos, raised two fingers to his eyes and pointed towards the lookout position.

Alek nodded and regretted it. His head throbbed with the movement. His hands trembled as he walked past body parts and the upturned face of a dead soldier. He dry-heaved and staggered into the fresh air outside the tree line, inhaling deeply, glad to be out of the carnage. He thought of Swales and how pale he had looked in death. *A month ago I was at college. Now I am in a war and surrounded by bodies. All that life and hope and memories gone in an instant.*

He crawled towards the edge of the escarpment and took out the binos. Down on the plain, he could see a row of five self-propelled artillery vehicles with caterpillar tracks, their long barrels pointed towards him, and seven soft-shelled vehicles. Tiny figures moved around them. *So these are the dreaded Conts. They don't look so nasty from up here.* He did a quick count and then crawled back to report to Corporal Sanderson.

The officer was standing beside Corporal Sanderson when Alek returned. The officer's eyes widened when Alek gave his report, his hands shaking when Alek handed back the binos. Corporal Sanderson grabbed the officer's arm. 'What's your decision, Sir?' The officer seemed to shut down, his eyes glazing over. He interlocked his fingers and unlocked them again and again.

Corporal Sanderson patted the officer on the shoulder. 'Take a moment, Sir. I'll get the men moving.' He turned to Alek and said, 'Grab your kit – we're bugging out through the woods in five minutes.'

'What about the bodies, Corporal?' Alek said. The vision of the dead face was still with him.

'There's no time to bury them. Grab their weapons, ammo and rations. We'll need them,' Corporal Sanderson said. He shouted orders to the rest of the platoon to move out.

'Are we retreating, Corporal?' Trowbridge said.

'The English army doesn't retreat – we make fighting withdrawals,' Corporal Sanderson shouted so the rest of the platoon could hear. 'Now get a move on.'

Alek ran to his trench to pick up his webbing and then to the dead body outside the tree line. He turned the corpse over and retched again at the piece of shrapnel sticking out of its head. The sight of blood and brains brought bile into his mouth. He spat it out and held his breath as his hands struggled with the fasteners on the webbing pouches. The unavoidable smell was almost worse than looking at the contents of a skull.

'Hurry up, Wasilewski,' Hulse shouted.

'Come and give me a hand then,' Alek said to himself. He'd managed to open the two pouches and stuff the magazine and rations inside his combat jacket when he heard a whistle overhead. *Not again!* He sprinted into the tree line, shouting, 'Incoming!' at the back of the platoon.

Whomp! A treetop exploded, scattering branches and bark in a cloud of pine needles. Alek swerved and leapt over an empty trench. There was no need for him to waste breath warning the platoon; they were already fifty metres ahead, sprinting away from the bombardment.

Whomp! Alek was knocked to his chest by the concussive force.

He blinked, checked himself and got up to run again – even faster.

Chapter 10

Lena wiped her clammy hands on her jumper before following Chantelle into the cool air of the church hall. The room was the size of a badminton court but felt smaller with its low ceiling and piles of tables and chairs at the edges. Two noticeboards were covered with fading posters advertising clubs and activities.

Chantelle reached into the golden fake-leather clutch purse that was hung over one shoulder by a thin gold strap, and took out a key attached to a Disneyland Paris fob.

Lena scraped a line in the dust on the wooden floor with her floppy shoe. 'Is this ever used by anyone?'

'Yeah – the God squad come here on Sundays and there's a children's group three times a week,' Chantelle said. 'I bring my two here.'

'You've got kids?' Lena was struggling to imagine anyone having a relationship with Chantelle. She seemed so gross.

'Yeah, Warren and Brooke.' Chantelle smiled.

'Where are they now?' Lena said.

'At home – a neighbour looks after them for an hour while I do my errands.' Chantelle opened a cupboard stacked with toys in clear plastic containers. She bent down, revealing her bum crack over her leggings.

Lena looked away. *Errands? What errands? No one does errands now. Oh, she means the secret-agent work.*

'Anyway…' Chantelle shut the cupboard door. 'Whatcha got for me?'

Lena pulled out the roll of paper secured with her hairband. 'Here's my first draft.'

Chantelle held out her chubby hand. Her nails had immaculate white extensions.

Lena passed the paper, looked at her own stubby nails and put her hands behind her back. She shuffled from foot to foot and chewed on her lip while Chantelle held up the sketch to the dim light.

'Aww, this is nice. What do you use – charcoal?' Chantelle said.

'No, a 2B pencil. There's no charcoal left,' Lena said. 'Do you draw?'

'I used to at school. Now I help the kids with their crayons. What's left of 'em.' Chantelle shrugged. 'Tanya's hooked me up with a couple of packs but I can't bring them here cos I'll get asked where I got 'em from.' She held up the sketch again. 'This looks good. When are you going to paint it?'

'Tomorrow and Wednesday,' Lena said. 'I think I can get it finished by then.'

Chantelle pulled a pencil stub from her sleeve and squiggled a 'W' on its side on one of the yachts. She showed Lena. 'Make sure that goes on, too. It's a verification code,' She rolled up the sketch and passed it back to Lena. 'You're pretty good at this; you should do it for a living.' She grinned at her own joke.

Lena forced a polite smile. 'Thanks. I'd like to be able to sketch at home but I haven't got any pencils.'

'I'll ask Tanya to get you some next time I see her. Us girls have to stick together, right?' Chantelle nudged her elbow into Lena's ribs.

Lena winced; there wasn't much padding on her sides now. 'Ouch, and thank you.'

'You could do with a decent meal,' Chantelle said. 'You're too skinny.' She pinched a roll of flesh that overhung her leggings. 'But I'm too fat.' She prodded Lena in the chest. 'Between us we're about right.' She laughed. 'But it doesn't matter cos my boyfriend likes having something to hold on to.' She jiggled her bum and the hooped earrings clattered. 'If you know what I mean?' Chantelle laughed again.

Lena nodded. *I'm not going to get this image out of my mind. She must crush her poor partner like one of those spiders on the old TV documentaries. But if she has more food than she needs, she might give it to me.*

'Fancy a coffee? May as well while we're here,' Chantelle said.

'Yes, please,' Lena said. *She means well enough and she's right about me being skinny.* 'Do you have any more shortbread, please?'

'I'll see what I can do. If not, I'm sure we can find half a grape. That should fill you up!' Chantelle laughed and went to the kitchenette.

Lena hoped Chantelle was joking. She poked around the church hall, reading notices for old clubs that still hung from cork-boards: Pilates, bowling, u3a advocating 'live, laugh and learn', a 'move it or lose it' class for the over-sixties, and a men's breakfast club scheduled for 10:00 on Saturdays. *Alice and Jane would have loved to gatecrash that – if it was still running.*

Coffee aromas wafted from the kitchen and Lena walked in to collect her mug. There was no sign of any shortbread.

'Cheers.' Chantelle clinked her mug. 'Here's to some lazee days.'

'Cheers.' Lena took a sip, grateful that the mug hid her disappointment. 'Who names these boats?'

Chantelle shrugged. 'I dunno, the owners, I s'pose. We have to match them with the escape routes and make sure you get them in time. I don't ask about the names.'

'When do you tell the people who are going to escape?' Lena said.

'Don't ask questions like that. The less you know, the better.' Chantelle reached into her handbag. 'Here's your coffee.'

Lena took the freezer bag of coffee grounds. 'Thanks, but what I could really do with is some food. Tanya said she might be able to get me some.'

'Oh, yeah?' Chantelle shrugged. 'She didn't give me anything this time. You'll get it when the posters are published, I think.'

'Oh, okay,' Lena put the grounds in her pocket. *Are they taking me for granted? I'm not doing this unless I get food.*

'Don't worry, string bean.' Chantelle poked Lena between two ribs. 'I'll bring some biscuits next time.'

Lena stepped back and winced as her blister rubbed on her shoe. 'Ouch.' She lifted her left foot and peeled back the flapping sole. 'I need to tape these. Have you got a plaster?' She pulled down her sock and lifted her heel towards Chantelle.

'That looks nasty.' Chantelle reached into her handbag and pulled out a pack of plasters. 'Don't tell Tanya – these are s'posed to be for official business only.' Chantelle tapped her nose.

Lena took a plaster and put it on her heel. 'Thanks.'

'What size feet are you?' Chantelle said.

'Five and a half,' Lena said. 'Don't tell me you can get shoes, too?' She didn't know what she wanted more – shoes or food. If she could get both, then the risk of designing the poster would definitely be worth it.

'Five and a half? I'll see what Tanya says. They won't be brand-new shoes though. We don't want to make people suspicious.'

Lena looked at Chantelle's gleaming white trainers and her silver ankle bracelet. Inconspicuous seemed to be an alien concept to her.

Chantelle straightened her back, clearly noticing Lena's look. 'Yeah, well – I'm different, you know. I've got standards. I can't let the men down.' She winked.

Lena suppressed a shudder. 'A decent pair of walking shoes or black trainers to wear for work would be good. My feet are wet or bruised the whole time now.'

'I'm size nine, otherwise I'd lend you a pair of mine,' Chantelle said. 'You'd look like a clown if you wore them.' She laughed and her earrings jiggled.

Lena laughed too. Drinking coffee and laughing about nothing in particular was like old times; Chantelle's enthusiasm was contagious and distracted Lena from her thoughts about Recreant Camps and forced marriages.

The shadows were lengthening and a brisk wind blew from the north as Lena walked home. She was thinking about the poster again as she opened the apartment door. If she got it finished, it would be printed and sent out to billboards within a week. She would get a Soc-Cred bonus that might rectify her ration deficit but she would still chase Tanya for extra food.

Alice was lying on Lena's bunk, her wet hair spread over a towel on Lena's pillow.

'Hey, you'll make my pillow stink,' Lena said.

'All right, all right, no need to make a fuss.' Alice sat up and wrapped the towel around her hair into a turban.

Lena made a show of plumping the pillow and shaking it out. Several black hairs floated to the floor. 'Why don't you lie on your own bed?'

'You know I don't like heights. What's the problem?' Alice leant against the bunk.

Lena took a breath and let it out slowly. A tip from her mum's yoga. She didn't want to get into an argument with Alice.

'Help!' came a shout, along with running in the corridor.

'Fire!'

'Oh my God, what's happening?'

Lena opened their bedroom door and looked down the corridor, Alice leaning over her shoulder. Beth was waving her hands in front of her face, an acrid stink of burning filling the corridor. Lena ran down and looked into the kitchen. 'Who's burnt the cooking?'

'I was only making a cheese toastie in the sandwich maker,' Beth said, 'and now it's smoking.'

Lena took a breath, pushed Beth aside and used the knuckle of her right forefinger to switch off the sandwich maker at the socket. She opened the kitchen windows and let out her breath. Jane came in and wafted the smoke out with a tea towel.

'How come the smoke alarm didn't go off?' Lena said.

'No battery, I expect,' Jane said.

They looked at the sandwich maker. Globules of cheese ran down the side and onto the counter. Beth opened it up to reveal the blackened bread and the melted rubber-coated cable, the intertwined wires now visible.

'Oops,' Beth said. 'I think I shut the cable in with the toastie.'

'You muppet,' Jane said. 'We could have all been burnt to death.'

'What a waste of food,' Alice said.

Lena inspected the sandwich maker. 'It's buggered.' Life was now a little bit worse. The sandwich maker was one of the best ways of using stale bread and the hard bits of cheese rinds that were sometimes issued at the end of the month if the women were lucky.

'Sorry, everyone,' Beth said. 'I'll clear it up.'

Lena left the women talking in the kitchen and sidled into her bedroom. She put the coffee grounds into the base of her shoe. This sneaking around was stressful but she also felt a tinge of excitement. The greyness of her life had crept over her like an October fog coming onshore, and now she was just a corporate drudge. *It's a shame I can't tell anyone about the coffee.* The desire to share every minor detail of her life online was deeply ingrained. *What would I say in a post? It could be a series called 'The Undercover Artist'. Oh, I like that.* Her stomach rumbled as she day-dreamt, reminding her it was dinner time.

The smell of burnt cheese still hung in the air. *What a waste of food.* Heading back to the kitchen, she found Jane and Tamsin looking through the cupboards. Beth was sitting on a counter, her cheeks stained with dried tears.

'What's for dinner?' Lena said.

'Nothing at the moment – the cheese has all gone,' Jane said, staring at Beth.

'I'm sorry,' Beth said. Her shoulders shook. 'It was only the rind. It wouldn't have fed anyone else and I needed the protein.'

Tamsin put an arm around Beth. 'It's okay – it was an accident.'

Lena looked away. There was a tacit understanding amongst the women that Beth was gay. Lena thought that Tamsin was Beth's girlfriend but they seemed to have drifted apart. It was a delicate subject amongst the women who had to live and work together; the last thing they needed was a lover's spat on top of all the other friction. Besides, homosexuality, although legal, was frowned upon by the Party. None of the Soc-Cred points awarded for family life were given to same-sex couples. Nor were people who were openly gay promoted to positions of authority.

Lena's stomach rumbled again. 'Have we really not got any food?' Her ribs were poking through her skin and her bras were too big now. Chantelle's comments had only made her more self-conscious about it.

'There's no need to be so aggressive,' Tamsin said. 'We're all hungry.'

Lena thought back to the anglers she saw when she was collecting the seawater. 'How about we do some fishing?' They had to do something other than moan about the lack of food. They were good at complaining as a group but rubbish at doing anything constructive.

'What would we fish with?' Tamsin said. 'You need the right kit.'

'I'm not killing any fish,' Alice said as she walked into the kitchen.

'I thought you were a pescatarian,' Jane said.

'I was – I mean, I am.' Alice shook her head. 'But I don't want to kill them.'

'So you want other people to do the killing for you.' Jane winked at Lena.

'No…uhm…I don't know.' Alice shrugged. 'Life was a lot easier when you could buy everything in Waitrose.'

'Anyway,' Lena said, bored of the argument they'd had a dozen times before about eating meat. 'I think if we could catch some fish it would help us all. We just need to find out how and where to get the right equipment.'

'Why not ask the fishermen?' Jane said.

'Good idea,' Lena said. 'Anyone want to come to the quay?'

Jane shook her head. 'So this is the highlight of our week now?'

'We can't exactly go out on Union Street, can we?' Tamsin said. Their clubbing days were behind them now that the curfews and power cuts had shut their favourite venues.

Thankfully. Lena shivered at the thought of the hot and sweaty sailor groping her.

'Well, I guess it's better than staying inside and smelling the cabbage,' Jane said.

Alice wanted to go crabbing because, according to her, crabs looked more like spiders so she didn't mind killing them. She took their bucket and tied a double loop of string around it, putting two slices of bread inside. Lena went outside to jump up and down on the strip of lawn, soon delighted to catch three worms, which went straight in the bucket.

The women wrapped up in their jackets and walked down across the cobbled streets of the Barbican to the quay. Their combined fishing and crabbing knowledge was as empty as their stomachs. There were half a dozen anglers lined up by railings and across the Pilgrim Way footbridge beside the marina. A few couples were sitting on the wooden benches looking out to sea, the empty coffee stands boarded up behind them, the Italian and Greek names blacked out from the signs.

Tamsin walked up to one of the anglers and launched into a series of fishing questions. Going by the beam on his face, the old man seemed delighted to talk to a young woman. Jane walked around the marina, looking at the boats that were kept behind the locked footbridge. Lena stayed with Alice and the worms, lowering the bucket between the slimy green rocks and pulling it up every time they thought they had a crab. On the times they were lucky, they grabbed the crab by its body and held it at arm's length, dropping it into a tote bag.

'If we don't catch a big one soon, I'm going to eat the worms,' Lena said. Her hunger was made worse by the disappointment of not getting food from Chantelle.

'Yuck,' Alice said. 'Look we've got seven now.'

Lena looked into the bucket at the crabs; they were all smaller than her hands, with barely any meat on them. *They're skinnier than me.*

The women took turns as their hands grew sore from holding onto the string. Tamsin came back with a reel of information and the whereabouts of some second-hand tackle. 'The nice man will show me how to use it,' she said.

'Hold on,' Jane said. 'Are you telling us that some old man said he would show you how to use his tackle?'

The women giggled, and they laughed harder when they saw Tamsin blush, which didn't happen often. Tamsin pointed at the rustling tote bag hanging from the bike stand. 'What are we going to do with all of those?'

'Can we keep them as pets?' Jane said.

'We're supposed to eat them, remember?' Lena said.

Alice counted the crabs. 'Eleven. We might get a decent meal out of that.'

'I hope so,' Lena said. 'I'm starving.' Crabbing on holiday for fun was different from relying on it as a source of food. She counted on her fingers – three more days until their meat ration cards could be used. Three more days until she could see the young butcher. She smiled.

The women headed back home, discussing crab recipes and when they could get the fishing tackle. At least their talk had turned to action. Fresh fish would be a great addition to their diet. For the second time that day, Lena felt good about doing something positive. Even though she was hungry and her foot was sore, she felt alive.

'Look,' Alice said, nudging Lena in the ribs.

Two police cars and a van were parked outside their apartment, sending a wave of nausea through Lena's body. *They've found out about the coffee. Or the poster. Oh God, what have I done?*

Chapter 11

A whirring noise caused Alek to look up; it was the drone again. *I can't take another bombardment.* The platoon had been told not to open fire on it to save ammo despite it reporting their position and directing the artillery. Three of the soldiers had died in the last barrage, too slow to get their kit and bug out. Alek had ducked and weaved and run as if avoiding tacklers on the rugby pitch, overtaking the slower runners as they headed deeper into the woods.

He leant back against a tree trunk and clicked the rifle's safety button off. He took several deep breaths to recover, thankful now for all the running preparation they had done on Dartmoor. *One round will do it. The drone's bigger than a squirrel and doesn't bounce around as much.* He aimed at the hovering drone and remembered the lesson from the rifle range. *One breath in, half out, hold. Squeeze.* The recoil of the rifle pushed him onto a sharp stick that stuck out from the trunk. 'Argh,' he said as he felt the stab in his back.

'A hit, a hit,' someone shouted.

Alek checked his back and found no blood.

Hulse ran to the fallen drone. 'Who fired that?' he shouted. 'You'll be on a charge.'

Alek walked towards Hulse. 'It was me.'

'This will be the end of you, Wasilewski. You've disobeyed a direct order.' Hulse pointed his rifle at Alek.

'Hulse, stop!' Corporal Sanderson pushed the muzzle of Hulse's rifle down. 'You had best check that drone to see if it's still transmitting.'

'Yes, Corporal.' Hulse walked back, head down.

'Wasilewski!' Corporal Sanderson walked towards Alek.

'Yes, Corporal!' Alek stood to attention. *I'm in for it now. But it was worth it if means they can't pinpoint our position.*

'Relax, son.' Corporal Sanderson smiled. 'That was good shooting. But why did you disobey the order?'

'I didn't want to get hit by the artillery again, Corporal,' Alek said.

'None of us do, son.' Corporal Sanderson looked back to their old position. 'Was that a lucky shot or can you repeat it?'

Alek shrugged. 'I don't think so, Corporal. I mean, I don't think it was lucky.'

Corporal Sanderson grinned, turning the ends of his moustache upwards. 'Well, you've got my permission to shoot again. You may have bought us some time. You guard our rear.' He patted Alek on the shoulder.

'Yes, Corporal.' Alek beamed. *Fuck you, Hulse.* He kept an eye up to the sky as he waited for the rest of the platoon to move deeper into the woods along the escarpment, hoping to see another drone. Fighting back felt a heck of a lot better than getting bombarded. It might give them a few more hours to live, he thought, kicking the drone as he walked past it.

The half-light of the following morning revealed the hills ahead: black silhouettes silent against a grey sky. Dawn had yet to spread her rosy fingers. Alek sniffed as he walked; the air was always freshest before the day started, but he smelt something different now, something sweet.

The initial mission had been abandoned yesterday. The officer had nodded in agreement when Corporal Sanderson had given the orders to head west for the coast and reach their lines. Once they had outpaced the drone, Alek had been moved to the front; he had become the de facto scout, recognised for his sharpshooting and calm thinking. He remembered Swales' advice about putting effort into things. The time went faster.

As they moved this morning, Alek saw a few smallholdings ahead, each surrounded by a metal mesh fence. Civilisation was near. He held up his fist and signalled for quiet. A donkey brayed. Four fields became visible on their left, each surrounded by a low stone wall, unknown knee-high crops growing in three of them, and a stone shed with a corrugated iron roof in the corner of the fourth.

Alek followed the path that led past the single-storey buildings of the smallholdings. There were no humans visible, only signs of their everyday lives: jars, vases, bicycles and garden tools laid out on tables in front of the simple houses. Alek felt a temporary sense of freedom while the rest of the world slept, as if time had stopped and he was tiptoeing past a frieze.

A cockerel crowed. A thin black cat stretched on a low wall ahead. 'Hello, cat,' Alek said.

I miss my cats. I hope they're okay. That cosy world seemed a lifetime ago. *It's lucky that Mum and Dad took the cats away with them. Almost as if they knew what was going to happen.* Alek stopped. He felt a cold chill. *If they did, then they left me and Lena on purpose. No, that can't be right.*

He carried on walking through the settlement until he reached a set of stone steps carved neatly into the rock face of the hill. He led the platoon up the path that zigzagged along the hillside, taking long, steady strides to match each step. Stone huts with chicken coops beside them were scattered at intervals.

They reached the hilltop and paused below the skyline, sipping water and looking back down; still there was no sign of humans stirring. Corporal Sanderson sent Alek ahead to peer over the ridge, where he watched a yellow sliver of sun appear above the next hill, thickening like a yellow bubble that stuck to the top of the ridge and then, pop, it was free. He breathed in deeply, enjoying the cool air and the moment of solitude as he watched the sunrise. *We're on our way home. All I need is a nice mug of tea and a bacon sandwich and I'd be living the dream. If we reach our lines, wherever they are, then that's the first thing I'll do.* He sniffed his jacket. *And take a hot shower.*

He scanned the ground below, taking in the line of old stone huts standing in front of more plantations, then a river curving around the base of another tree-covered hill. The land seemed to be dry on the east of the hills and fertile on the west. He turned and waved the rest of the platoon up. There was no need to talk; they were familiar with the hand signals and procedures now.

Swales was wrong. We've lasted more than twenty-four hours. Most of us that is. Swales is dead and eleven others now. Alek watched as the remaining eighteen members of the platoon crawled up to the ridge, bellies sliding across the rocks, staying below the skyline.

Corporal Sanderson held up a fist and pointed at the bottom of the slope. Alek saw green figures emerging from the stone huts. *Conts!* The Continentals were spreading into a skirmish line, and Alek quickly realised there too many to fight. Thoughts of freedom and showers were gone. The enemy was in front of him. *Shit, there are so many of them!*

Corporal Sanderson jerked a thumb back towards the slope. 'Get back!'

Alek turned and crawled down from the ridge, knees and elbows pumping fast, ignoring the cuts and scrapes. *Why are the Conts hiding in the stone huts? How did I miss them? Did they see us?*

Corporal Sanderson signalled for Alek and Hulse to come closer, and the officer joined them. 'I think we dig in on this ridge. Those stone chicken coops provide some cover; if we try to run we'll be caught in the open. Thoughts?'

Alek and Hulse nodded, though Alek was wondering why he'd been summoned. The officer said, 'Where have they come from? There must be sixty Conts waiting for us down there.'

Corporal Sanderson put his hand on the officer's shoulder. 'No time to think about that, not when it's three apiece. Careful with your targets; we want to break through this lot and head for the next hilltop before more drones come.' He pointed left and right. 'Hulse, take Section One right. 'Ski, take Section Two left. Sir, you'll be with me in the centre.'

'Yes, Corporal,' Alek said, switching the safety off his rifle and crawling back down the path, one hand on the floor, the other clutching his weapon. Leading a section in an orienteering exercise that played to his navigation strengths was one thing, leading them in combat was another. Alek beckoned his section over and pointed to the left. As they followed him to just below the ridge top, looking for rocky cover, Alek heard a sound like a pork steak being tenderised with a wooden mallet and saw Trowbridge clutching the side of his neck.

'Get down!' Alek shouted, his voice croaking. There was no time to think, only time to react. Incoming rounds were hitting the rocks, spraying small splinters and dust over them. He saw Trowbridge fall, blood seeping between his fingers. Alek fired two bursts at the enemy below and looked back at Trowbridge, who was on his back.

'Man down!' he remembered to shout, but there were no medics to respond to the alarm. He fired two more bursts and then crawled to Trowbridge, grabbing his webbing straps. He dragged him to the shelter of the nearest stone coop where Murdo knelt. 'Murdo, get a dressing on Trowbridge.'

Murdo knelt on Trowbridge's neck to stem the blood while he fumbled for a field dressing. 'Shit,' he said, hunching his shoulders to stay low.

Whoomp! Alek felt the RPG rounds whizzing overhead as if he could touch them. Murdo had Trowbridge stabilised so Alek monkey-walked back to his section to check on them. He ducked under the first few RPG rounds before he realised the rounds were aimed high. The Conts were not yet in a position to hit them – unless someone stood up, as Trowbridge had.

Alek leopard-crawled the last few metres over the stones to join his section. He peeked over the ridge and saw the line of Continentals struggling up the hill. They were well-armed, but lacked cover – an ill-planned defence against a surprise encounter with English soldiers who were not supposed to be there. 'Aim when they're diving down; fire when they stand up!' Alek yelled. He slowed his breath as he realised he had time, and aimed several short bursts at the helmeted figures.

His rifle clicked empty. 'I'm out,' he shouted, going through his 'change-magazine' drill. He felt for his webbing, took out his remaining magazine and clicked it into place, grateful now for the endless repetitions he had done in training. Murdo was kneeling beside Trowbridge, his hands covered in blood, rocking back and forth.

'Murdo!' Alek shouted. 'We need you here.' He beckoned him closer with his hand.

Murdo picked up his rifle but didn't move.

Alek ran back to the coop, bent over from the waist. 'Get his ammo.' Alek pointed at the dead Trowbridge as incoming rounds skimmed on the stones. He rolled to the side before popping up and firing again. His only thought was the next shot in his mind. *Breathe. Aim. Fire.*

Murdo joined him and fired two wild bursts from the hip.

'Aim, Murdo, aim,' Alek said. 'We've got to make the rounds count.' *Breathe.*

Murdo fired from the shoulder this time. There were fewer targets, but closer now. An RPG hit the coop with a bang, and stones flew sideways and covered the section. Alek spat out dust and stone fragments as he crawled behind the half of the coop that remained, his ears ringing and his eyes weeping. *I can't see or hear!* He rubbed his eyes with his dusty sleeves and blinked to try to clear them, his head throbbing as he shook it to clear the ringing.

Two rounds ricocheted off stones near his foot. He tucked up his legs and peered around the coop. Two blurred shapes were on the ridge to their left. He took a breath and aimed but Murdo was up and running towards them, shooting from the hip. Murdo shot the loader but the rifleman fired, sending Murdo spinning to the ground. Alek blinked again to clear his eyes, took aim at the rifleman and fired, watching him keel over onto his buddy.

The ringing had either killed Alek's hearing, or the shots had ended. Moans and screaming, coming from the centre of their line, confirmed the firing had ceased. Corporal Sanderson shouted, 'They've pulled back. Check casualties and ammo.'

Alek gave a thumbs up and shouted back, 'Yes, Corporal,' his voice thick with dust and smoke. He took a sip of water and wiped some over his eyes before shuffling down to Trowbridge. Blood covered the bandage hanging off his neck. *Dead. You should have stayed low*. Alek took Trowbridge's webbing off and looped it over his shoulder. Murdo's corpse grimaced at him. *Poor Murdo.*

'One, two…' Alek counted the remaining members of his section. 'Two?' He carried the spare water and sparse ammo to them, so they could set up on the ridge to watch below. He tried to sound positive as he said, 'Get a drink, you've earned it. Stay sharp, lads.' The soldiers nodded, blinking out dust and shock from their eyes. Alek stumbled across the rocks, checking the dead bodies and noting their names. *Too many dead.*

Corporal Sanderson had a field dressing on his left forearm, 'It's a rock splinter,' he said when Alek raised his eyebrows. 'Report.'

'Two men left, Corporal. Eighteen rounds each. Some water; rations are gone,' Alek said as if he were reading out a shopping list, not relaying the news of dead comrades. He was working on autopilot, the shock of the firefight numbing his emotions.

'The officer's out of it, Hulse is down, and we've got seven men left, including us,' Corporal Sanderson said. 'We can't stay here; we have to move.' He pointed to the officer who sat against one of the stone coops. 'Get the compass from him – you can navigate our way out of here.'

'Yes, Corporal.' Alek knelt by the pale-faced officer as he stared ahead without recognition. *The poor bastard is not cut out for this. I know how you feel.* Alek felt in the officer's pockets, finding the compass and redundant map. The compass needle was loose and rattled inside the broken glass. *Useless.*

Alek heard a whistle and the air pressure changed. 'Incoming!' he shouted as he dived towards the shelter of the coop. The mortar round landed, sending stones flying around the coop as the officer sat outside. Alek reached for his collar and dragged him into the stone shelter. *Not again!* He curled into the foetus position and held his helmet. He lost count of the rounds that landed around him, one landing so close that the roof was blown off. Alek yelped as something hit his arm, realising a large rock had pinned his limb to the floor. Pulling the rock off his arm, he felt his bones move underneath. The next moment, he blacked out.

Alek woke with a mouthful of dust, a throbbing head and a sharp pain in his arm. The barrage had stopped but Alek didn't know whether that meant they were reloading or that an attack on foot was imminent. The officer beside him was half-covered with rocks, his head twisted, eyes open, staring into the void. His sidearm holster was still closed. He had never fired a shot.

'Corporal Sanderson?' Alek said. 'Corporal Sanderson?' There was no answer. Alek saw the Corporal's body that had been smashed in two. Without adequate cover, the platoon had been destroyed. Alek dropped to his knees, holding his wounded right arm. He felt sick. His head sunk to his chest. *I'm on my own. Why did you have to die, Corporal?*

Alek looked up at the scattered corpses. *Those fucking Conts.* Alek hefted his rifle with its empty magazine, crawling up to the ridge and ignoring the pain. There was no sign of the Continentals, except for the dead bodies that littered the hillside. Either they were hiding from the barrage or they had all been killed.

Time to retreat. I mean, make a fighting withdrawal. Well, I won't be doing much fighting with no ammo and a broken arm. First things first. He took the field dressing out of his webbing and held it to the cut on his wounded arm. His rifle, slung over his left shoulder, kept sliding down as he tried to tie the bandage ends. They were too fiddly for his left hand so he used his teeth to hold one end and made a messy knot as best as he could. He stuck his right hand into the gap between the buttons in his combat jacket to act as a sling, but he had no idea what else to do. His first aid course as a lifeguard had covered CPR and the recovery position but it hadn't touched upon gunshot wounds.

Alek checked his bearing by pointing the hour hand of his watch at the sun. It was eleven o'clock. *Halfway between that and noon is due south, so west is that way. Good old D-of-E.* He took a bearing on the line of trees on the far hill. That meant going down the hill and past the stone huts. There was still no sign of the enemy in front but the drones could be called in or more artillery. 'I've got to move fast or I'm done for,' he said to himself.

He took a last look around at his fallen comrades, feeling sick at their futile deaths, even of those he didn't like and the useless officer who hadn't even fired at the enemy. *Hadn't fired!* Alek scrabbled back down to the destroyed chicken coop and pulled the Glock 17 pistol from the officer's holster, shoving it into a pocket. It was better than nothing.

Alek inched down the hill, looking over his shoulder at the now abandoned position and up in the sky. Nothing but the wind, although he couldn't be certain because his ears still rang.

Alek held out his rifle as he skidded down the last part of the dusty track towards the stone huts. They appeared to be empty. *Thankfully.* He jumped as he heard a voice from inside the right-hand hut – a foreign language that he thought might be Spanish. The voice crackled and repeated the same phrase.

His body relaxed. *Just a radio! No one's answering, so they must be dead, but reinforcements will be on their way.* Alek looked back one more time at the ridge top where his comrades lay. *I'm on my own in a foreign country, surrounded by Conts. No one's going to help me but myself.*

He set off at a fast walking pace on a dirt path towards the next hill, tired, hungry, sore, wounded and with no idea of what lay in front of him.

Chapter 12

Lena's throat tightened as she approached the two police officers standing beside the street sign. Her eyes flickered towards the post but she couldn't see the plaster. *Have they taken it off? Do they know what the signal is?*

The female officer held up a hand towards the four women, her brunette hair tied in a bun poking out from under her peaked cap. She wore a flak jacket, a belt with several compartments and a pistol holster. 'Hold it there, ladies.'

The male officer walked behind them, dressed like the female, except his paunch strained the zip of his flak jacket.

Lena gripped the tote bag, feeling the crabs wriggling inside. Alice put the bucket on the pavement and asked, 'What's the problem, Officers?'

'We've had a report that you have been fishing without a licence.' The female officer pointed at the bucket.

'A licence? We didn't know we needed a licence.' Alice's flirty smile bounced off the officer's humourless face.

Thank God – it's not about the poster. Lena looked at the two police cars and van, then up at the apartment. *Where are the rest of the police though?* She felt a hand on her shoulder.

The male officer pointed at the tote bag. 'What have you got in there?'

'Nothing,' Lena said as if she had been caught stealing a cookie by her dad. A claw poked out of the top of the bag. 'Er, just some crabs.'

'Give it to me.' The officer held out his hand.

Lena passed him the bag and watched as he opened it.

'Yep, there are crabs in here.' The officer nodded to his colleague then spoke into his radio, giving his call sign and adding, 'Confirmation that we have the offenders with the evidence in front of their abode.'

Lena had never thought of the apartment as an abode; it sounded like somewhere Native Americans might live in. *Or is that adobe?*

'Have you got a fishing licence?' the female officer said.

The women looked at each other, shaking their heads and shrugging. Jane smiled and tilted her head. 'Sorry, Officer – we didn't know that we needed one.'

The female officer's face remained blank. Jane's attempt at charm was as wasted as Alice's had been.

Four more officers came out of the apartment then, surrounding the women. They moved closer together and Lena felt trapped. *My*

Soc-Cred is going to go through the floor if we get arrested. I might even get sent to the Recreant Camp. Shit, I can't let that happen. She looked up and down the street. *Can I make a run for it?* Lena glanced at her shoes. *Nope. Not with these and, anyway, where would I go?*

'Okay, let's get them in the wagon,' the female officer said and pointed to the police van. 'Names, ladies.' She pointed at Lena.

'Lena.'

The female officer sighed, 'Lena what? We need your surnames.'

'Wasilewski.' Lena spelt it out before walking towards the van where two large male officers held the back doors open. *Think, Lena, think.*

'Name,' the female officer said again.

'Tamsin.'

'Tamsin what? Come on, I already said – I need your surnames!' the female officer shouted.

Lena stopped at the back of the van, gazing up at the dark-haired officer whose face was as flat as a shovel: he looked like a boxer. She took a breath, tightened her fists, then breathed out and unclenched. Another yoga relaxation tip from her mum. 'Excuse me, Officer?'

He looked down, his eyes brown and sharp. 'Yes?'

'Is a crab a fish or a crustacean?' Lena smiled.

'It's a crustacean.' The officer shrugged. 'Everyone knows that.' He looked at his colleague who nodded.

'Then we don't need a fishing licence to catch crustaceans, do we?' Lena smiled what she thought was her sweetest smile.

The officer wrinkled his brow and bit his lip. 'I dunno – what do you think, Dave?'

Dave shrugged. 'I dunno, she might be right.' He turned towards the female officer, whose face was now red with frustration. 'Here, Sally – is a crab a fish or a crustacean?'

Sally frowned. 'What are you talking about, Dave? Quiz night is next week. Get these women in the van.'

'No – I mean, do they need a fishing licence for crabs when crabs aren't fish?' Dave said.

Lena held her breath while she looked at Sally, whose face had turned an even deeper shade of red. The female officer looked up at the apartment and then at the four women beside the van as they all stared in hope.

'Right, we will let you off with a caution. You'll be docked 200 Soc-Cred points for wasting police time.' Sally glanced up at the apartment again and shook her head.

'But,' Lena started to say, stopping when Jane pulled her arm. 'Ouch.' Lena rubbed her arm.

Jane was shaking her head, mouthing, 'Don't make things

worse.'

Lena nodded as they watched the police get into their vehicles and drive away. Being interviewed by the police and being released wasn't a criminal offence, but the 200 point deduction from their Soc-Cred scores meant their rations would be reduced further. The women would also be added to the list of citizens deemed 'persons of interest'. *We're going to have to find other ways to get food. Which is what got us into trouble in the first place.*

Lena carried the crabs into the apartment, cursing the unsuspecting crustaceans for causing all this trouble. She hoped the police would be slow in contacting the Soc-Cred department so she could get another week of meat. After that, things looked bleak, unless Tanya came up with the goods. *I'll have to get that poster finished tomorrow if I've got any chance of being given food.*

Warmth radiated off the concrete walls as Lena walked to the butcher's on Thursday afternoon. Daffodils strained their stems as they stretched towards the sun above a faded 'Plymouth in bloom' sign, which sat askew in the earth bank of the roundabout. The weight of the poster design was off her shoulders. Trevor had nodded his approval and sent it for publication.

Lena smiled at the two old ladies who were chatting at the top of the arcade. They stopped talking and looked up and down at Lena, tutting when they saw her shoes, before resuming their chat.

Lena ignored their disdain. It was all right for old people: they were given dead people's shoes by the Party as a gesture of thanks for their voting loyalty. A ginger cat sat on a car roof, washing itself with one leg up in the air behind its head.

'Hello, cat,' Lena said. *I hope our cats are okay; I miss them.*

The cat paused mid-lick, then continued its bath in the sun.

Lena joined the back of the queue that trailed down the street. As she shuffled along, she looked around the backs of the people in front to see if the young butcher was in the shop: he was. Lena checked her reflection in the window and tidied the errant strand of hair behind her ear. She looked down at her shoes, thinking, *There's nothing I can do about them. He probably won't be able to see them under the counter anyway. I'll stand close to make sure.*

As she reached the front, the woman ahead of her was asking about mince. 'Is that pork or lamb?'

'Neither,' the older butcher said. His hair was cut short at the sides and swept back under his white hat, his blue and white striped apron stretched over his stomach. 'It's beef, Mrs Ellicott.'

'Oh, how much?' The woman looked into her old-fashioned leather purse with two metal clasps.

Lena could only look on with envy. The old woman must have a

Soc-Cred score in the top decile to be able to buy extra meat.

The butcher put the mince on a piece of paper, lifting it onto the digital scales. 'That's a quarter of a pound for you.'

'What's that in grams?' the woman said.

'We're not allowed to sell in grams, Mrs Ellicott, remember?' He leant over the counter, adding, 'A hundred and twenty-five grams.'

'Thank you,' Mrs Ellicott said in a stage-whisper, heard by every customer, before she took her illegally weighed mince out of the shop.

Lena frowned at the rules being broken by the old woman who was going home with a large parcel of meat and no bad consequences. But with so many rules, who knew what was what? It was hard to step outside your door without breaking a rule. Lena moved up to the counter, placing the ration cards on top.

'What can I get you, love?' the elder butcher asked.

Lena looked at the new ration cards. The police had been too efficient in contacting the Soc-Cred department and the women's rations had been downgraded already, 'Three sausages and one pound, two ounces of mince, please,' she said in a hushed voice, embarrassed by the penalty.

The butcher checked the ration cards and then turned to his younger colleague.

'Rob, three sausages and one pound, two ounces of mince for the young lady,' he announced in a voice that could have been heard over a cattle auction.

Rob checked the order. 'Is that all?' He smiled at Lena.

Lena looked around the shop for a place to hide. Her reduced rations were being aired for all to hear.

Lena nodded and looked out of the window. She didn't want to have to explain why the rations had been reduced. *Rob. That's a nice name.*

'Never mind, dear. It's a nice afternoon now, isn't it?' the older butcher said. He stamped the ration cards with their pig-shaped ink stamp.

'Yes,' Lena said, meaning it for once. She couldn't understand why she was in a good mood today. Maybe it was just the weather. She hadn't admitted to herself that she was excited to see Rob.

Rob placed the parcel on the counter. 'Here you go.' He tapped the paper twice with his finger and winked at Lena.

With two other customers in the shop, Lena didn't know how to respond to Rob winking at her. She settled for a, 'Thank you,' and walked out, keeping her head down and trying to walk fast up the street without showing it. *He must think I'm an idiot. What did the finger-tap mean? Hopefully pigeons again.*

Lena strode up the street and round the corner. There was a large green disused broadband exchange near the pelican crossing.

A seagull landed on the box, its wings outspread, its grey claws grasping for purchase. Lena stepped back as the seagull screeched and its grey tongue poked up from its beak.

Lena clutched the parcel with both hands. 'Not today, greedy.'

Many of the locals had tried cooking seagulls early in the war but their flesh had been too acrid-tasting; without spices, the flavour was hard to mollify. Alek had shot two, but even he hadn't stomached their taste when Lena had cooked them. The seagull population was still below pre-war levels but those that were around were hungrier and meaner than ever.

The seagull followed Lena as she walked home, swooping from one piece of pavement furniture to another, forcing Lena to quicken her pace. The bird wouldn't give up, swooping over her head and onto a concrete bollard. Lena ended up jogging the last seventy-five metres, fumbling for her key while the seagull hopped along the low brick wall that bordered their vegetable plot beside the strip of lawn. Lena stabbed the key into the lock and stumbled inside the lobby, pulling the door shut behind her as the seagull pecked on the glass door, its black eyes gleaming.

I'm a prisoner in my own flat. Even the seagulls are getting desperate.

Lena ran up the stairs and into the kitchen. She unwrapped the parcel but there were no pigeons – just the mince and sausages. A postcard fluttered to the floor, displaying a picture of Sir Francis Drake's statue on the Hoe. Lena turned it over.

Written in a neat cursive script were the words: 'I hope these don't taste fowl.'

Lena smiled at the bad joke. This was the first time that a man had sent a handwritten note to her. The messages on her old phone did not count; the lines of ping-pong text that seemed so urgent but disappeared within seconds to be forgotten. Just like the boys who had dithered around her at college without summoning up the nerve to ask her out. That was the trouble with art students: they just wanted to be 'friends' and discuss their 'feelings'. Her last real boyfriend. Luke, had been at school, four years ago. They'd been together for nine months until school finished and they went to separate colleges. She hadn't heard from him since.

Maybe I should write a note back? Rob seems nice enough and if he's keen on me, we could go out – which would stop them from forcing me to marry a veteran!

Jane walked into the kitchen; it was her turn to cook. 'Well, did you get any extras?'

Lena slid the postcard under the brown paper before turning round. 'Sorry, no. Just three sausages and a little mince.'

'What did you do to upset him? Three sausages? What am I supposed to do with that?' Jane bent down to look in the cupboard for a pan.

Lena pulled out the postcard and held it behind her as she sidled out of the kitchen. 'I'll be back in a sec to give you a hand.'

She checked through the door hinge that Alice wasn't in their bedroom before going in. *What to write to Rob?* She didn't want to seem too forward, but she also didn't want to wait until next week to see Rob again. Not with the pressure of the veteran's ball approaching. She looked at the front of the card. *A walk along the Hoe is innocent enough. It's easy to get out of that if it goes wrong.* She only had a red pen – they had run out of blue and black – so she used that to write:

'Ha, ha. How about a walk on Saturday afternoon? See you at the lighthouse at 15.30. Lena.'

She thought about signing a heart or a cross but decided that would be too much. *I'll post this tomorrow after work – I can slide it over the counter.* Lena grinned to herself. *I'm becoming like Alice – a man-chaser.*

The women savoured the first bite of their dinner that evening, eating tiny mouthfuls, trying to make the meal last longer.

Alice inspected her sausage. 'Are you sure these are pork?'

'Pork and apple,' Lena said.

'Hmm, more apple than pork I think,' Tamsin said.

'Good,' Beth said. She scrunched up her eyes and took a bite.

Lena chewed slowly, counting to thirty as the sausage diminished. She looked down at her plate, too big for the tiny meal, remembering the food pics she'd once taken so much care over. *Not much to post about here. Something about child portions?* She'd shared pictures of her food with the world before the war – the world she'd thought would be at her feet once she left college. Instead, she had been drafted into the Ministry of Information as soon as she'd graduated. She gazed out of the window.

Food in my stomach is what matters now. And avoiding Recreant Camp. If I can get extra food from Tanya I might be able to think straight.

'Hey, dreamy girl, thinking about your boyfriend?' Alice said. 'Tell him we want more meat next time.'

Lena blushed. 'I was looking for the seagull that followed me home. It was this big.' She held her arms out to the side. 'I swear it knew I had sausages.'

'Sounds more like an albatross,' Tamsin said.

'Can you eat albatross?' Jane said. 'There's a lot of meat on them.'

'It's unlucky to kill an albatross,' Alice said. 'The sailors wouldn't like it.

'And you've got to keep the sailors happy, Alice,' Jane said.

Lena was glad that the conversation had turned away from her. She poked the cauliflower cheese around her plate. *I'm not telling this lot about Rob's note or me asking him out. They'd never let it go.*

Chapter 13

Alek walked as fast as his arm and the obstacles around would allow him, fearful of tripping with every jolt, his neck sore from looking up at the sky every few steps. The threat of the drones drove him on as the ground rose and he leant into the slope, his hamstrings aching by the time he reached the flat top. He took a moment to recover and to check his bearings. He was heading west – towards the coast. He figured that his side must be on the coast somewhere, no matter what country he was in now. *If only I had a proper map.*

He shook his head when he thought he heard something; his hearing was improving but still dampened from the firefight. Shouting, 'Bang!' in training was scant preparation for the noise of war.

There! Two green trucks and two armoured vehicles were driving towards the stone huts in the valley below. Alek threw himself to the floor and grunted as he twisted to avoid falling on his injured arm. He held his breath as he watched men disembark and enter the huts. Sharp voices carried indeterminable orders on the wind as a drone rose from between the armoured vehicles. It hovered over the huts before rising up the hillside towards the scattered bodies of Alek's comrades.

Alek lost sight of the drone against the grey clouds and decided to head for cover.

He hobbled to the woods and, when he was sure he couldn't be seen, sat on the gnarled root of a scruffy-looking tree. He held his canteen between his knees as he unscrewed the cap with his good hand. There was enough warm water for two sips, which he swilled around his mouth before swallowing. His arm was throbbing and every part of his unwashed, sweaty body itched. If he made it back to his lines, he might get a clean set of clothes and a hot shower. And a decent cup of tea. *I'm never taking a simple cup of tea for granted again.*

'Wishing isn't going to make it happen. Get up and move,' Alek said to himself. He stomped his feet to get the circulation going. *If only Swales were here.* 'Shit, I'd rather have Hulse than no one.'

He set off on the path through the woods that stayed level for another twenty minutes before descending to a stream. Alek smiled when he saw the fresh water and knelt to fill his canteen. They hadn't been issued purification tablets despite being told of their importance in the 'field hygiene' lecture. *I'll have to boil it to make it safe.* The air was clearer down in this valley, away from the dust. He took off his helmet and dunked his head into the cool water. *Nice place for a picnic – if I had anything to eat.* He closed his eyes and took a few breaths, listening to two birds competing in a song duel. *No time to forest bathe; must get on. I need to put more distance between me and the Conts.*

The western edge of the forest stopped at a single-lane tarmac road running parallel to the tree line. Fields stretched out beyond it, with scattered farm buildings on the sides of the low hills. The memory of Swales' pale face lying in the farmyard came to the forefront of Alek's mind. *I'm not going near any farms again.* Taking his bearings was more difficult with the sun lowering behind the trees; even so, he used the shadows as a guide to the location of the sun. A copse on top of a hill about two miles away was due west. *That will have to do for shelter tonight.*

Alek looked right then left before he scurried across the road and clambered over a gate; he was unable to vault with his injured arm and encumbered by his empty rifle. He crept alongside the hedgerows from field to field, looking up for drones and aircraft and around for farmers before climbing each gate.

By the time he reached the copse, his legs and back were aching and his right arm throbbed. The trees were gnarled and twisted with thick trunks and branches that hung low to the dense undergrowth. Alek forced his way through, getting stung and pricked by nettles and thorns before reaching a rise of huge stones covered in moss and lichen. Small bushes and plants grew in the gaps where soil and debris had accumulated over centuries. There was a space between two stones that leant against each other and Alek peered into the gloomy hollow. *This will do as a shelter. If I make a fire, no one outside will be able to see it.*

He took off his rifle and webbing, laying them in the hollow, then searched around in the worsening light for twigs and dried leaves to put in his pocket for kindling. He dragged several branches and larger sticks to the entrance, placing one end of a branch on a rock and stamping down on the middle. *Crack!* Alek looked around. *That was too loud.* He took the broken pieces and placed them on top of the kindling.

Alek crawled into the gloomy hollow and arranged the mess tins and hexi burner alongside two fuel blocks. Lighting the matches one-handed was the hardest thing; he had to place the end of the striking strip under a stone to keep it stable while he held the match in his left hand. He used one block of fuel to boil his water on the hexi burner and another to get the kindling going.

Alek crawled back outside to check that nothing could be seen from beyond the stones as the smoke drifted into the dark sky. *Safe enough.* Sitting with his back against the stone, he listened to the crackling of the burning wood, and inhaled the welcome smell of the paraffin fuel. *Luckily the drones don't have a sense of smell.* After ten minutes he poured the boiling water into his mug and let it cool at the entrance of the hollow. He dragged the branches into the fire so it would burn for longer.

He sipped the warm water and leant back against the warm rocks, his legs outstretched to prevent cramping, ignoring his rumbling stomach and the aches and pains in his body. With no immediate chore or threat of a barrage, Alek's mind drifted to his fallen comrades. Tears filled his eyes as remembered all the dead bodies, starting with Swales. His fingers trembled and tears left a salty path across his dirty cheeks. Corporal Sanderson had been a professional soldier, harsh but fair. Alek had earned his respect and felt pride from his praise. The rest of the platoon had been unfriendly but still he struggled to get the images of their young, dead faces out of his mind. Unlike the movies, a corpse didn't look like someone who was asleep: it looked like its soul had been eviscerated and only cold flesh was left to rot on a distant hill.

Alek finished his water and lay down on his left side with his back to the fire. Closing his eyes, he tried to think of the few good moments he'd had since he'd been press-ganged to get the death out of his mind. *Sitting on the grass bank looking at butterflies. So long ago.* His eyes closed as fatigue washed over him.

Alek woke with a yelp. He had turned in his sleep and jarred his arm. He shivered on the damp ground and saw the fire had gone out. He could hear birds singing their chorus outside. His muscles protesting, he crawled to the entrance of his cave and looked up through a gap in the canopy to see two stars visible against the dark blue sky. *Time to move.* He packed his kit into his webbing and swigged the last mouthful of water from his mess tin. *I need to find some more if I'm going to survive out here.*

The orange crown of the sun was rising above the dark landscape behind him. Alek stood at the edge of the copse and took a deep breath of the cool, sweet air. *A new day.* He took a bearing on a low hill opposite the sunrise and set off at an easy stroll to allow his stiff muscles to wake up.

From the low hilltop, as the light improved, he could see the fields flattening and the hedgerows replaced with stone walls. *I need to stay close to cover now it's daylight.* After half an hour he came to an empty two-lane road that headed west. He knew he would make better time on this surface but it wasn't worth the risk; he had learnt that from his escape with Swales. *The Conts must be somewhere along this road.*

But he could follow the road on the other side of the stone wall while keeping an ear out for traffic, and duck down to hide if he heard anything. It made sense; there was no other shelter in the dry fields because the crops were too low in the ground. The sun rose higher and Alek's pace slowed. *Where are all the cars? Maybe they have fuel rationing over here too.* His throat was parched after an hour of walking and there was no sign of water, not even a trough for animals. Climbing over the stone walls had left a dozen cuts on his hands and legs. *Is there no water in this shithole of a country?*

He looked across the shimmering dry fields to the rising hills in the north. Dust and heat rose together, making the air appear brown. A battered metal sign hung on the gate at the end of the field. Alek checked for cars before climbing over to read the sign. It had a picture of a smiling mechanic with a red rag in one hand and a spanner in the other, pointing west, with 'Servicio de Auto, 1km' written in green embossed lettering.

That's not French. I think it's Spanish. We could be near the Basque Country. He remembered from one of the lectures the officer had given that England had helped fund some of the Continental separatist movements, the Basque ETA being one of them. Rebranded from terrorists to freedom fighters, they were upheld as shining examples of democracy and individualism. They also held the port of Bilbao, which allowed the Royal Navy and Merchant Navy access to the Continent and a front that created a diversion from the besieged Gibraltar. Alek hadn't heard anything on the news about Gibraltar for months. But he had never paid much attention to news about places he had never been.

He felt a bit of grit in his mouth and tried to spit it out but he struggled to produce any saliva, and resorted to picking it out with his dusty left fingers. *If there's a garage, there's water. I might be able to find a tap somewhere. But I don't know if the locals are friendly. I might be wrong about the Basque being on our side.*

Alek climbed back into the field, blinking some dust out of his eyes and steadying himself. 'Come on,' he said. 'One K is manageable. Just put one foot in front of the other.' He walked across the field, stumbling twice on the stiff dirt ridges that had hardened since they'd been ploughed. Another stone wall blocked his path. Alek took a breath, stuck a boot into a small gap between stones to launch himself over the wall but stopped. He could see a T-junction ahead. *A roadblock. Shit! The Conts.* He crouched behind the wall and thought about how he'd get around it. It was too long to wait until nightfall. It had to be done now. *I'll crawl away from the road and cross the wall further up.*

Alek heard a vehicle approaching and peeked his head above the wall to look again at the roadblock. Two concrete posts were set in the middle of the road, with a pile of sandbags on one side protecting a machine gun and its crew of two soldiers. A green four-tonne truck pulled up behind them and four soldiers jumped out, wearing the same camouflage jackets as Alek. He watched as the guards changed. All of them were wearing the same uniform.

They're not Conts – they are friendlies! Thank God for that.

Alek scrambled over the stone wall, landing in a heap. He tried to shout out but his mouth was too dry and his tongue felt heavy and swollen. *Careful. Don't make any sudden movements.* He walked towards the gate at the end of the next field with his good hand above his head in the surrender position, desperate to reach safety but not wanting to get shot.

One of the soldiers saw him and, kneeling beside one of the concrete posts, he aimed his rifle. 'Advance and be recognised!' he shouted at Alek.

'Friend,' Alek tried to say. He forced himself to swallow and summon up some spit. 'Friend,' his voice croaked again. 'I'm with the Fifty-First Patriot Battalion.'

'Put your hands up – both of them,' the soldier said.

'I can't. My arm's broken,' Alek said.

'Then get your hand where we can see it,' the soldier said.

'Okay.' Alek stopped. 'I've got to use my other hand to get it out though.' He lowered his left hand and undid his jacket, lifting his right hand with his good hand and wriggling his fingers. 'You see, there's nothing in it.'

'Lift your arms up,' the soldier demanded.

'I can't. It's broken,' Alek said again. *How many times do I have to tell him?*

'Sergeant,' the soldier shouted, 'we've got a straggler.'

The sergeant was tall and lean. He walked up to the concrete post and squinted at Alek, saying something to the soldier before shouting, 'All right mate, come forward, and keep your hands where we can see them.'

Alek walked towards the checkpoint while holding his broken arm and lifting his left shoulder to stop the rifle sling from slipping.

'All right, son,' the sergeant said. 'Name, rank and unit.'

Alek gave his details, his voice croaking. He stared at the water bottle on the sergeant's webbing belt. His right arm was throbbing with pain and his left shoulder was aching from trying to keep the rifle from falling off.

The sergeant looked Alek up and down and then over his shoulder to the field. 'Where's the rest of your unit?'

Alek jerked his head backwards. 'Dead, Sergeant.' He nodded towards the sergeant's hip. 'Could I have some water, please?' He coughed for effect.

'Cozens!' the sergeant said, without taking his eyes off Alek.

A soldier ran forward. 'Yes, Sarge.'

'Get this man some water,' the sergeant said.

The soldier nodded, replying, 'Yes, Sarge,' and ran back to the checkpoint.

The sergeant waved his hand down. 'Lower your arm, son. How

bad is it?'

Alek slumped his shoulders and stuck his right arm back inside his jacket. 'I think it's broken.' He took a swig from the canteen that the soldier offered him. The water tasted metallic but cool. Alek glugged down two more mouthfuls and smiled at the soldier. 'Thanks.'

'Right then,' the sergeant said, 'what happened and where did you come from?

'We were dropped in the wrong place and got hit twice by artillery, Sergeant. Then, about twenty kilometres east of here –' Alek pointed with his thumb over his shoulder – 'we ran into a company of Conts and got pinned down by mortars and RPGs.' He looked at his feet. 'They're all dead now.'

'Stupid crab air,' the sergeant said, 'they're dropping blokes all over the place.' He put a hand on Alek's shoulder. 'It's all right, son – we'll look after you.' He clicked his radio and called for transport.

'Thank you, Sergeant,' Alek said, drinking drank more water. The checkpoint soldiers had lost interest in him now and were watching the road again.

'Is this your first action?' the sergeant said.

'Yes, Sergeant.' Alek was shaking. 'We didn't stand a chance on that ridge.'

'Did you see any of the Conts coming this way?' the sergeant asked.

Alek shook his head. 'No, Sergeant, we only saw the company we had a firefight with. We killed them all but then reinforcements came to their position with a drone.' Alek pointed upwards. 'I hid in the woods until daybreak, then kept walking until I saw you.'

The sergeant nodded. 'The drones are a menace. But, for the last few weeks, the Conts have laid low in their positions and we are doing the same. No point in causing a ruckus. You were unlucky to be dropped behind their lines.' He turned as a Land Rover pulled up at the crossroads. 'Here's your transport. You'll be looked after, son.'

'Thanks, Sergeant.' Alek climbed into the back of the vehicle. Inside were two soldiers wearing red berets. Alek hesitated as he saw 'MP' written on their white armbands.

Military Police.

One of the MPs shuffled down and pointed to the front of the seat. 'Give me your rifle and sit there.'

Alek squeezed by and winced as the Land Rover jolted forward, jarring his arm. He soon realised that the driver only took his foot off the accelerator as they neared corners. Alek was flung around like the last piece of pasta in a jar, the soldiers pushing him back when he fell into them. His adrenaline had gone; replaced by the pain from his arm and the trials of the last two days. But that was nothing compared to the trauma of remembering the eighteen pale, mangled bodies on the rocky hillside. *Swales was right. They were all dead within forty-eight hours. Except for me. Why am I still alive? I don't deserve it.*

Chapter 14

Lena changed her mind about what to wear on Saturday as the weather improved. It was grey and overcast to start, with a cold north wind that switched to a westerly as the sun broke through the clouds. Her mood changed inverse to the weather: from wild optimism at the hope of a date with a young man she found attractive to a sense of foolishness that she might be sitting by the lighthouse on her own. She left the apartment wearing her baggy jeans, a blue T-shirt and her favourite black sweatshirt that matched her shoes.

None of her roommates raised an eyebrow at her outfit as she left, absorbed in their Saturday afternoon reading, music-listening or napping. Lena was glad that they hadn't noticed her eyelashes; she had scraped out the remnants of her mascara. *It's the best that I can do.*

Lena took note of the scouts and guides walking in groups of four and armed with notepads. They stared at every citizen who was out for a walk, looking for Soc-Cred misdemeanours to mark on their pads. The streets had been litter- and dog-poop-free since the start of Soc-Cred; no one dared drop anything and there were fewer dogs overall because pet food was scarce and expensive. Lena made sure she waited for every green-man light at the crossings, even though there was minimal traffic. She didn't want a jamboree of diligent uniformed dobbers surrounding her and marking her down as a jaywalker.

She walked up the long flight of stairs that led to the Hoe. The sea was glistening under the afternoon sun, the swell rising and falling as if taking deep breaths. There were a few people walking on the Hoe but not the roller-bladers, skateboarders and joggers of old. Those strenuous pastimes were casualties of rationing; they expended too many calories. A couple of mums were pushing strollers, their toddlers wrapped in bulky all-in-one puffer suits with woolly bobble hats.

Military mums. They're the only ones who can afford those clothes. Lena felt self-conscious about her plain clothes, but the women walked past Lena without a glance, absorbed in their conversation about nap times.

Lena's heart beat faster as she saw Rob sitting on a bench beside Drake's statue, looking out to sea. *He's here, thank goodness. I'm not going to look like a total idiot.*

Rob was wearing light blue jeans and a black sweatshirt with black Dr Martens. Lena immediately thought that he hadn't made much effort but then looked at her outfit and awful shoes. *Oh no,*

we're wearing the same! I am going to look like a total idiot after all.
She walked behind him to hide her shoes and tapped his shoulder.

Rob stood. 'Fancy meeting you here,' he said, louder than was necessary.

'Oh, yes, nice to see you, too,' Lena said as if rehearsing lines for the school play. *He seems as nervous as I am.*

'Fancy a walk?' Rob said in his stage voice.

'I'd love to,' she said, her voice back under control.

They walked in silence past the red and white lighthouse and along the tarmac road towards the old lido. Now that Lena was on her date with Rob, she didn't know what to say. The anxiety of not knowing if he'd turn up had prevented her from thinking about what might happen if they didn't have anything in common. *Just be nice – ask him a question, you idiot.* She opened her mouth to speak but Rob beat her to it.

'Did you ever go swimming here?' Rob pointed at the empty pool with its walls covered in green algae.

'Yes, before the war. In my first year at college.' Lena remembered sunbathing and drinking cold lemonades from her mini-cooler with two of her classmates on weekday afternoons before the kids got out of school. The lido water had been cool and refreshing. Life stretched out ahead of her with no worries apart from how much sun cream to apply and when to turn over.

'Me too. What did you study at college?' Rob said.

Lena gave him her potted history. 'I was doing an extended degree in Illustration, hoping to get work in publishing, but then producing books was banned due to the paper shortages. I had good marks from my lecturers and was offered the job at the Ministry of Information. It's not what I had in mind, but at least I'm using my degree a bit,' she finished as they reached the end of the promenade. Justifying her job felt weak when she said it out loud.

'I'd like to see some of your drawings,' Rob said. He pointed to the east. 'Have you been to Devil's Point before?'

'No, what's that?' Lena said.

'It's a viewpoint that's quite nice, about a twenty-minute walk.' Rob looked at her shoes. 'If you can make that in those?'

Lena shuffled her feet. 'I was hoping you wouldn't notice. I might be getting some new ones soon.'

'Sorry, I didn't mean to embarrass you.' Rob grinned. 'I've had these for years.' He lifted a Dr Marten like a horse being inspected by a farrier. 'But they've still got some life in them. Where are you getting new shoes from?'

Lena looked at the sea. 'Someone at work.' Although Rob had given her contraband pigeons, she didn't want to tell him about Chantelle and the shoes because she hardly knew him. She waved a hand towards the steps. 'Shall we go?'

They walked into the town along the broad streets, passing empty Georgian hotels and guest houses whose dormer windows jutted out to give the residents a better view. Rob talked about his time at the University of Exeter, studying Environmental Sciences. He had graduated and returned to his uncle's butcher's shop when he couldn't get a job in his field; the environment was deemed too expensive by the Party to invest in.

So there's more to him than his muscles. He's got a degree and it's his uncle's business. Where are his parents?

They turned left and walked beside Millbay Park where four adults sat on benches watching four children playing football. 'What about your family?' Rob said.

Lena looked at the footballers, who were using orange cones for goalposts. 'They are all in Kernow.' She felt tears come, embarrassed to tell Rob about the shame they had brought on her. Even if it was unjustified, she was paying the consequences.

'Oh, so how come you're not with them?' Rob said.

Lena looked up at him. She was fed up with the whole situation.

'What's the matter? Do you miss them?' Rob put a hand on her shoulder.

Lena wiped away the tears. She hadn't thought about her parents for a few days, and life was difficult enough as it was. She forced a smile and replied, 'Yes, I do. But my parents are traitors and my brother is a deserter. I should warn you that my Soc-Cred score has been lowered because of them.' She put her hand on Rob's. 'You are taking a risk being seen with me.' She watched for Rob's reaction. *This date could come to an abrupt end now, but he seems too nice to lie to.*

Rob looked up and down the street before smiling at Lena. 'I can look after myself. I don't believe in guilt by association. Come on, let's enjoy the walk.' He squeezed Lena's shoulder.

His grip was firm but not harsh. Lena smiled as a wave of relief flooded through her. *I'm not being judged for my family's mistakes – at least not by Rob.* As they reached the end of Citadel Road, Lena looked at the grand four-storey stone building on the corner. It had a peaked tower with grey slates and a crenellated stone balcony at the top. Stone steps led to the main entrance, now boarded up. Plymouth's first luxury hotel was now barren.

'What are you looking at?' Rob said, followed Lena's sight line.

'Nothing, I just like old buildings,' Lena said. 'The architect of this had a good eye for detail.'

Rob squinted and seemed flustered. 'Oh. I see what you mean. Better than the concrete mess in the centre of town.'

Lena looked over her shoulder as they walked around the old ferry dock. The ferries had been seconded as troop carriers early in the war, never to return. Before that, Lena's family had made several crossings to Roscoff from here, starting their holiday with a drink on the deck as they watched the lights of Plymouth disappear, followed by watching a movie in the cinema. The decadence of sleeping in a cabin seemed unbelievable now.

She bumped into Rob, not realising he'd stopped. 'Sorry,' she said.

'Are you okay? You seem miles away,' Rob said.

Stop daydreaming, Lena, you're supposed to be on a date. He won't want to be with me if I look uninterested.

'Sorry, I was remembering our family holidays. I haven't thought about them for a while.' Lena looked around for eavesdroppers, 'I shouldn't talk about my family in case I get reported.'

'You can tell me about them. I don't think the Party should whitewash people's families out of existence.' Rob took Lena's hand. 'Come, we're nearly at Devil's Point and then I can listen properly.'

Lena felt a buzz of excitement as she held Rob's calloused palm. *He wants to listen to me talk about my family. He cares.* She tried to remember the last time that someone had held her hand. At least a couple of years ago – and that was only the soft hands of the artists on her course.

They walked up to the coastal path and gazed out across the water to Drake's Island in the middle of the harbour. Occupied by sailors and marines, they patrolled the entrance in their Rigid Raiders and two commandeered speedboats. The tide was out but a couple of hardy older people were swimming, their swim hats bobbing up and down like wrinkled seals by the yellow buoys. Rob led Lena along the narrow bricked path that followed the headland until it opened up onto a grassy bank with several boulders strewn around.

'Here we are,' Rob said. 'Let's sit over there.' He pointed to a low, flat-topped boulder.

A soldier was watching them from the top of one of the old bunkers dug into the side of the cliff fifty metres down the path, his rifle resting on his forearms. Beyond him were high rolls of barbed wire and the sparkling River Tamar with a line of pontoons blocking access to the wooded headland of Kernow. Rob nodded to the soldier, who nodded back.

'Notice which side of the wire the soldiers are on?' Rob said as they sat down on the cold rock.

'The other side from us,' Lena said. She took in the view of the glistening river.

'If they wanted to defend us, they'd be this side of the wire,' Rob said. 'They're keeping us in.'

'Oh,' Lena said. 'I'd never noticed that.' She looked up and down the long rolls of wire. No one was getting over that without being caught.

'Anyway, tell me how your family ended up over there.' Rob pointed to Kernow.

Lena gave the usual answer – one she had repeated many times over the last few years. The only change was adding Alek's desertion to the description. She hoped that he was okay, despite being angry with him. *He must be with Mum and Dad by now.* She looked at Rob and shrugged as she ended the story. 'That's it.'

Rob shook his head. 'I don't know why you refer to your parents as traitors. They weren't to know about the secession and Alek seems to have done himself a favour by getting out of the army. I mean, who would want to fight on the losing side in a war?'

Lena's mouth opened at Rob's treasonous words; he was mad to talk like this. She had called her parents traitors for so long when asked about them, she almost believed it. If she tried to defend them then she could be reported and lose more Soc-Cred points. Better to go along to get along, she'd told herself. Lena looked at the soldier on the bunker who had his back turned to them.

Rob seemed different to the others. Maybe he could be trusted. Talking to him felt easy – even about her feelings. 'I did think it strange that Alek left his BTEC at college to enlist and then deserted just a few weeks later.'

Rob snorted, 'Enlist? No one enlists any more! The military have to go into colleges and press-gang students. I'm only safe because I'm in an essential trade.' He shook his head. 'You shouldn't believe anything the Party tells you. They are so wrapped up in lies even they don't know what the truth is.'

'I don't believe everything,' Lena said. *Press-ganged? That makes more sense and explains why Alek has escaped.* Her little brother was not the enlisting type; he was too placid and would not have gone against their parents' wishes. 'Why do you think you know so much, anyway?' She prickled; she didn't come on a date to be told what to think.

'I don't.' Rob grinned and swept his arm around the seafront. 'Look about and take notice of what's happening. Ignore the newsfeed and listen for what's not said at your daily briefing.'

'How can I listen to what's not said? Is that a Zen thing like a tree falling in the forest?' she added, trying to lighten the mood.

'No, it's not.' Rob shook his head, appearing to miss the joke. 'It means that if the briefing mentions a change of territory, then think, *Why has it changed? Does it mean they've retreated?*'

'Hmm, I see.' Lena said, uncertain but ready to move on from this conversation, which was becoming heavy sledding for a first date. She had thought he might have put his arm around her at least by now after he had held her hand.

Rob stood. 'Do you want to see some fancy architecture?'

'Sure,' Lena said. So much for the cuddle. She looked over the

Tamar at Kernow. *Are you there now, Alek?*

They walked down the concrete steps that had once been white but were now discoloured with grime and lichen. They led to the Royal William Yard; Lena hadn't been there before. The old naval buildings had been renovated into luxury apartments occupied by hipsters. The magnificent stone buildings were a far cry from the 1970s office block eyesores that punctuated Plymouth's hilly landscape like exclamation points.

Rob pointed out some of the old bars and boutique shops that had opened to cater for the affluent residents. 'I used to do a quiz night here, every Monday. We never won because the middle-aged people got all the questions about music and obscure TV programmes right.'

They walked past a giant anchor and along the courtyard. Lena looked around at the people, young and old, couples and singles, who seemed to be consumed with their own interests and company. *What do they think about the war? Do they believe the newsfeeds too? I can't be the only one.*

Rob pointed to a stone arch at the western end of the archway, 'Look up there.' Two stone cattle heads were mounted on either side, looking down at them, like idols in an Egyptian temple rather than decorations in a naval yard.

'Cows? Why are there cows there?' Lena said.

Rob grinned and pointed to the courtyard. 'This used to be a cattle market. Farmers would bring their stock here and have it auctioned off and sold to the navy.'

Lena nodded. 'So you spend your afternoons off looking at old slaughter yards. Do you have any hobbies apart from beef?' She raised an eyebrow.

'As a matter of fact, I do. Asking pretty girls out on dates.' Rob smiled.

'Tart,' Lena said, while thinking, *I haven't been called pretty for years.* She linked her arm with Rob's as they kept walking.

Rob guided Lena to a wooden bench that sat against an ivy-covered wall. He picked up an England flag on a stick from the floor and waved it. 'I saw you on the news.'

Lena blushed. 'Stop. We were forced to do it.'

Rob spread his fingers out on his knees and then gripped them into fists. 'The old farts in the Party are sending us young out to die. And what are we doing?' He waved the flag again. 'We're making flags.' He looked at Lena. 'Don't you ever get fed up with it?'

Lena's bottom felt cold and damp in the shade. She shifted away from Rob and looked around the yard to see if anyone was watching. A pair of mums wearing trainers and matching tracksuits pushed their three-wheeled prams along the paving slabs.

'What future do you think those babies will have?' Rob said.

Lena shrugged. 'I hadn't really thought about it.'

'No, most people don't. They've stopped thinking for themselves and their freedoms have been eroded by stealth.' Rob pointed the flag at Lena. 'The Party has alienated everyone. All they have left are themselves and their informers.'

Lena stood. It was chilly in the shade. 'This is dangerous talk. Someone could hear you.' She jumped up and down on the spot a few times. 'Let's get moving.'

Rob got up. 'Back a different way?'

Lena nodded and they walked briskly under the cow arch and around the windy lane until they reached the coastal path. They turned left towards the Hoe, passing four guides sitting on a picnic bench outside an abandoned cafe, a clipboard on the table. Rob waved his England flag at them. One of the guides smiled and wrote something on the paper.

'Always good to keep them onside,' Rob said when they were out of earshot.

They walked in silence until they reached the smooth tarmac of the central promenade. Lena stopped by the railings and looked out across the harbour to the breakwater and the white lighthouse: the shining beacon that helped sailors come in to shore safely. *Where is my guiding light? I could do with Dad's advice now. He might agree with Rob.*

Rob leant on the railings and looked sideways at Lena. 'You know that the Party will have an informer in your flat, don't you?'

'What? Why?' Lena's brain was ransacking through her flatmates to figure out who it might be.

'Because the Party will pay someone or blackmail them to do it. They want complete control,' Rob said.

Lena thought about the girls. Beth and Tamsin seemed harmless, Alice was annoying, but Jane was lovely. 'Are you sure?'

Rob nodded. 'They have informers everywhere. It'll be someone whose Soc-Cred score is higher than it should be. Or they have access to something that you don't. Things like shower gel, deodorant, sugar or coffee.'

Feeling her face redden at the mention of coffee, she turned away.

'All I'm saying is, be careful.' Rob put his hand on Lena's.

'How can I trust you?' Lena looked at Rob. She didn't move her hand.

'I'm not telling you to trust me.' Rob gazed out to the sea. 'I'm just saying to be aware of your surroundings.' He squeezed Lena's hand. 'And there's no need to be ashamed about your family.'

Lena glanced away. The sky was pale blue above two great anvil-shaped clouds that rose above the sea, dark and solid-looking except for their tops, which turned peachy in the setting sun.

'I like watching the clouds above the sea,' Lena said. 'You can see the weather forming from miles away.'

'Yep,' Rob said. 'A storm's coming.'

Chapter 15

Alek felt sick by the time they pulled into the aid station. His arm had been jolted at every turn, but his stomach had nothing to throw up. He climbed down the rear step of the Land Rover as if he were disembarking a fairground ride. He held onto the tailgate and looked around while he regained his balance and his nerve.

Vehicles that looked like Portakabins on wheels were parked opposite a row of large, open-sided tents, all with red-cross markings on them. Steam rose from outdoor showers and a circle of metal cooking vats that were being tended by chefs. Alek smelt the stew and smacked his lips together; he had finished the canteen of water but was still thirsty.

A woman walked past and all thoughts of thirst and hunger were gone. Alek hadn't seen a girl since the moment he'd been snatched from the college canteen. But there wasn't just one girl: female soldiers of all ranks were everywhere, outnumbering the men by about three to one. Even in their baggy combats and berets, Alek's eyes were drawn to the women. Apart from his donation to the 'Patriotic Cause', he'd neither had the time nor energy to think about girls in his training.

A nudge from one of the MPs standing on either side of him brought his mind back to his current situation. The tall men escorted him to an open-sided tent that was the first in a neat row of many that stretched over one hundred metres. Alek stood to attention as best as he could in front of a table, behind which a corporal sat.

'A deserter picked up at Checkpoint Lima,' one of the MPs said.

'I'm not a—' Alek said but was cut off by an MP.

'Quiet!'

Deserter? Why did I hand myself in then? The sergeant was lying when he said I'd be looked after.

The corporal looked over his glasses. 'Name, number and unit.'

It wasn't a question. Alek gave his details, spelling his surname out.

'Fifty-First Patriot Battalion?' The corporal paused his writing. He reached over to a clipboard, ran a finger down the sheet of paper and tapped it. 'He needs to be debriefed ASAP,' he said to the MPs. 'Wagon six.' He handed an index card to Alek and added, 'Give that to the intelligence officer.'

Alek felt like he was going to the head teacher's office as he walked between the MPs to wagon six, in trouble for something he didn't do. Or like a pinball, bouncing from one NCO to the next. *Am I going to get shot? Not after all I've been through, please. I need to tell my side of the story.* He touched his left combat jacket; the officer's pistol was still in it. They had taken his rifle but not thought to check for sidearms. Soldiers didn't usually carry them. *I'll shoot my way out if I have to.*

One of his escorts knocked on the wagon door and walked back down the three steps 'In you go.'

Alek pushed the door open with his left shoulder, getting tangled as he tried to negotiate the narrow entrance with one good arm. Inside two soldiers sat with headphones in front of a row of radios and a captain was writing on a flip-up notebook at a desk covered in maps.

Alek stood to attention as best he could with an arm tucked into his jacket. He was tired, hungry, smelly, needed the toilet and his arm was getting sorer. *And I might get shot – if they believe I'm a deserter.*

'Who are you?' the captain said.

'Private Wasilewski, Fifty-First Patriot Battalion,' Alek said. He held out the card to show the officer.

'At ease, Private,' the officer said after looking at the card. 'Tell me why you are here and where the rest of your unit is.'

'I'm not a deserter, Sir. I escaped after everyone else was killed,' Alek said in one breath, waiting for the bollocking.

The captain smiled. 'Relax, Private. We know that your battalion was dropped all over the place.' He pointed to a map on the wall. 'We've lost contact with them all. You're the only one we've seen back here. Take your time and tell me what happened.'

Alek gave a stumbling account of the last three days; so much had happened in such a short time, it was hard to be concise and accurate.

'Do you have the map on you?' the captain looked up from his notes when Alek had finished.

Alek felt for it in his left pocket before remembering it was in his right. He fumbled with the button using his left hand.

'What's the matter with your right arm?' the captain said.

'I think it's broken, Sir. In the firefight.' Alek managed to get the pocket open and handed the greaseproof-paper map over, its markings shining under the artificial light.

'Haven't you seen the medics yet?' the captain said.

'No, Sir. I was sent straight here.' Alek felt dizzy. Hunger, fatigue and the horror of combat were swamping him.

'Sit down, Private.' The captain pointed to a chair. 'Stephens, get this man a brew, will you?'

'Yes, Sir,' one of the radio operators said and left the wagon.

Alek eased out of his webbing and slumped in the chair. He watched as the captain spent several minutes shuffling through maps and holding Alek's map up as if it were a jigsaw piece and he was looking for a place to put it. 'Can you read a map?' he said to

Alek.

'Yes, Sir.'

'Well, come and show me where this ridge was and your initial position.' The captain tapped his pen on a point on the map. 'We're here.'

Alek's first thought was how close they were to the sea, but the map was too large a scale to see in which country the coastline was. He leant over and traced his finger eastwards, looking for a tight band of contour lines and the flat plain. The stone tumulus where he had stayed last night was marked in a small patch of green. He followed the river up to the wooded hill and he saw the row of buildings at the base of the ridge. Alek moved his finger eastwards to the wooded escarpment and then south to a series of what appeared to be fields. 'There –' he tapped – 'I think that's where we landed, Sir, –' he tapped twice more – 'and that's the two places where we were attacked.'

The captain leant over and wrote down the grid references. 'You travelled that far on your own? How did you find your way here?'

'Yes, Sir. I did.' Alek lifted his sleeve and explained how he had used his watch to navigate.

'You left that bit out of your report earlier,' the captain said.

'Sorry, Sir. A lot has happened.' Alek's chin sunk onto his chest. He felt a wave of dizziness and held onto the table for balance.

'Sit down, Private.' The captain guided Alek back to the chair. 'If what you say is true, and we've lost the rest of your platoon, then you're either very lucky or you have some impressive skills that got you back here.' He tapped his pen on his notebook. 'Of course, we have to verify your story, although how we do that, I don't know.' He smiled. 'In the meantime, drink your tea and then you can get yourself fixed, fed and some kip. Oh, and for God's sake take a shower and find some new combats.' He wrote a note on Alek's card and handed it over. 'Report back here in four hours; I'll know by then what to do with you.'

A young, chubby-faced nurse with her hair in a tight bun underneath her beret was sitting at a flimsy desk in the triage tent. 'Name, rank, unit, injury?' she said, glancing at Alek.

Alek gave the answers, spelling his name out before being asked. His escort had grunted when he had shown him the card with the captain's notes written on it. Alek was free to walk around the aid station now, and relieved that someone trusted him.

'We'll X-ray you first, then get you sorted.' The nurse smiled. 'Would you like a brew while you wait?'

'Yes,' Alek said, 'please,' he remembered. If he wasn't going to be shot for desertion, he might as well drink as much tea before they patched him up and sent him back into combat.

'The tea mob are in tent four.' The nurse made a snake action with her arm for directions. 'Grab yourself a mug and then wait outside wagon three. That's where the X-ray is.' She smiled again and handed Alek the notes. 'Take this with you.'

'Thanks.' Alek followed her directions to the tea tent. This was his first experience of being with any unit other than his training platoon and he was relieved not to be shouted at all the time. His fatigue prevented him from thinking clearly and following an order to get a cup of tea was all he felt he could manage right now.

Soldiers in various states of dress sat on benches and upturned ammo boxes, nursing their large mugs of tea. Some had helmets and rifles and webbing, others were just in combats and field dressings. Three middle-aged ladies in green overalls, their hair tied up under white cardboard hats, were manning the metal urns, stacking mugs and washing up in two plastic bowls. The ladies were chatting amongst themselves and to the waiting soldiers who quietly handed over their mugs, with some collecting two mugs – one on behalf of a comrade. There was no other chatter in the tent.

'Tea, my darling?' one lady asked Alek as his turn came.

'Yes, please,' Alek said.

'Hurt your arm?' the lady asked as she poured the black liquid from a large metal teapot that required two hands to lift.

'Yes,' Alek said and took the mug.

'Never mind, lovely. The milk is over there, and some sugar too.' The lady smiled and pointed to the next table.

'Thank you.' Alek smiled back. It was almost like being at home with his mum looking after him. He added milk and sugar and stirred before going to sit on a canvas stool outside wagon three. Soldiers and medics, most of them female, walked past. There was no parade ground saluting or shouting here; everyone was quiet and efficient. *Maybe that's because the women calm things down?*

The doctor, a middle-aged lady with a belly pushing over her combat trousers, leant out of the wagon and said, 'Are you waiting for an X-ray?'

'Yes, Ma'am.' Alek stood up.

'Come on in.' The doctor smiled. 'You can bring your tea.'

Alek followed the doctor. She smelt of soap and disinfectant, which made him more conscious of his own smell. He stood as far away from the doctor as possible inside the pristine X-ray wagon. Another woman was organising the X-ray while the doctor wrote notes.

'I don't think you've broken it,' the doctor said once Alek had been scanned. She held up the finished picture. 'But it's badly sprained and bruised. We'll put you in a cast to protect you from further injury when you travel. The journey can be a bit rough. You can get a shower after the nurse has put it on.' She held her nose and winked. The radiologist grinned.

Alek reddened and mumbled, 'Thanks,' before hastening out of the wagon. His first contact with women for months and he was smelly, tired and the subject of their jokes.

The orthopaedic nurse in the wagon next door was the most attractive woman Alek had seen in the camp. She was a tiny brunette with freckles and a smile that warmed Alek more than the tea. She propped Alek's arm up and got the materials out for the cast. 'Don't let your tea get cold,' she said.

Alek slurped his tea. He could feel the body heat of the nurse as she set the cast, realising he hadn't been this close to a woman since college. But that was only friendly hugs with the college girls at parties; this woman oozed sexuality.

'There, all done,' the nurse said. 'That'll be good as new in a couple of weeks if you keep it out of harm's way' She put her hand on Alek's shoulder. 'Let's hope we don't see you back in here.'

Alek felt a tingle down his back. 'Thanks very much.'

As the nurse put a sling around his injured arm, Alek felt her body leaning against his and closed his eyes. For a second, he imagined he wasn't in the army and could hug this nurse.

She tapped Alek on the knee with his notes. 'Take these down to the discharge tent. They'll get you sorted for the trip back home.'

Home! Thank goodness it's not the front line. But what is home, now? Alek carried his kit to the tent and gave his notes to the clerk, who yawned. 'Sorry, mate, it's been a long day.'

'Tell me about it,' Alek said.

The clerk looked up. His moustache was flecked with grey. 'Right, sorry, of course.' He smiled, adding, 'You'll be on a plane home soon enough.' He pressed a wooden stamp into an ink pad and stamped Alek's notes, blowing on the card and shaking it before handing it to Alek. 'You can go to the QM stores beside the shower area now.'

Alek managed to scrub away the grime, sweat, blood and stress in his three-minute shower with one hand, the cast covered with a plastic bag. He was issued with a fresh pair of combats, a shirt, socks and pants, and he felt the best he had for a week or more. Alek ate his stew alone and in silence at a table in the mess tent. There was meat in the stew, with vegetables, and a thick, crusty white roll that soaked up the sauce. He wiped the mess tin clean and brushed the crumbs from his clean jacket. *That was the best meal I've ever had.*

Thoughts of battle returned to him as he looked around the injured soldiers. Those deemed fit to fight again had been marched off, carrying what equipment they could, including Alek's rifle. He felt empty and vulnerable without it. *Strange how quickly I adapted to that.* He felt the pistol in his pocket for reassurance.

Four soldiers who had shot themselves in the foot had been patched up and sent back to fight; the army didn't want to waste bullets on cowards. But Alek didn't judge them; if he had to face another artillery barrage he might do the same. He was glad he was heading back to Plymouth, rather than the front, but he didn't know what to expect there. Probably wait until he had recovered and then sent back to fight. *I'm too tired to think straight.* He thought of his platoon still lying on that ridge, their corpses left to rot in the sun. Alek felt tears well up, and his shoulders shook as he wept into his hands.

Alek heard the table creak and felt it move as someone sat opposite him.

'Mind if I join you?' a female voice said.

Alek peered through his fingers, seeing the freckly nurse. He wiped his eyes with his palms and shook his head. 'No – go ahead.'

The nurse put a hand on Alek's arm. 'Oh, I'm sorry. I didn't realise you were upset. What's the matter?'

'Nothing,' Alek said.

'Suit yourself.' The nurse took a mouthful of stew. She pointed at Alek's cast with her spoon. 'We're good at fixing broken bones and tendons but not so great at helping soldiers deal with the trauma of war.' She ate another mouthful before adding, 'I'm Sarah. If you want to chat about it, I'm happy to listen.' She looked at her watch. 'For fifteen minutes.' She grinned.

Alek smiled back; a pretty woman's smile had a magical healing effect. 'Thanks, but I think I'd rather talk about anything else other than the war at the moment.'

The trucks rattled along the dusty roads and Alek tucked his face into his jacket to use it as a filter. He had a full stomach, clean clothes and was heading in the right direction, away from the war. The intelligence officer had verified Alek's story and told him to expect further contact back in Plymouth where he would be doing his rehabilitation.

His lunchtime chat with the nurse, Sarah, had been the best fifteen minutes he'd had since being press-ganged. A proper conversation about music, sports and places they had been on holiday; all the things that they couldn't do now. She had left with a wry smile on her face and an enigmatic, 'See you later.'

Alek groaned when he saw a row of Hercules C-130s lined up at the airfield to transport the soldiers home. He regretted eating the second portion of stew, now percolating in his stomach. Once he was strapped into his seat he closed his eyes and let the drone of the engines lull him to sleep. *At least this time I'm heading away from the danger.*

Chapter 16

Lena stood in the office lobby listening to Trevor read out the daily news. Monday morning briefings were a chance to stretch and daydream. Listening to the list of glorious victories had become monotonous after a month. Now, two years into the war, there was barely a town left in Europe that hadn't felt the might of the English army. She gazed out at the clouds moving inland at a walking pace and thought back to the kiss on the cheek that Rob had given her at the end of their date.

Rob was nice; he seemed supportive of her family and that made Lena question her own thoughts. But he did lecture too much – saying things that she should have known for herself was annoying. She had been duped like the rest of the country.

She looked at Trevor. *How can we be winning all these victories but never getting anywhere?* Her face tightened and— *What was that?*

'The sixty dissidents had been trying to escape to Kernow, but our heroic Royal Navy sank the boats and stopped them.'

No – please don't tell me that's the boats on the poster? Lena chewed on an errant hangnail, the pain as she tore it off distracting her for a moment. Sixty dissidents. *What went wrong? Was it a coincidence or did someone betray them? If the escapees were betrayed, then someone knows about the poster and that will lead to me!* Lena felt her chest tighten as she struggled for breath. She grabbed Jane's shoulder as her vision blurred.

'What's wrong?' Jane said.

'Come on, ladies,' Trevor said, clapping his hands. 'No talking.'

Lena closed her eyes and took a breath in for a count of six and then out for a count of four. She let go of Jane and looked at Trevor.

'Heroic soldiers of the Fifty-First Patriot Battalion have defeated an enemy force in a hard-fought battle, against superior odds, on the Continent,' Trevor read.

Lena gasped. 'That's my brother's battalion,' she said before putting her hand over her mouth.

Trevor lowered his paper and looked over his glasses. 'What was that, Lena?'

Lena looked around at the faces staring at her. 'Sorry.' She gave a slight shrug and a half-smile. 'My brother was in the Fifty-First Patriot Battalion.'

Trevor looked down at the paper and back at Lena. 'I wouldn't talk about that if I were you.'

Jane put her arm around Lena and whispered, 'Lucky for him that he escaped.

'Ahem, may I continue, now?' Trevor peered over his paper at Lena and Jane. He didn't wait for an answer. 'Congratulations to Beth for earning twelve Soc-Cred points for her painting of the dockyard.'

The women clapped at the end of the briefing and trudged back to their offices.

Lena felt a hand on her back. 'Are you all right?' Jane said.

'Fine,' Lena said, 'I've just gone a bit dizzy. Must be low blood sugar.' She took a few breaths and pulled herself up the stairs. The news about the boats being sunk had sent Lena's mind into overdrive, her brain rattling around like an old washing machine on a tiled floor. She drew, erased, drew, erased and finally scrumpled up her draft. She needed to see Chantelle or, better still, Tanya, but she didn't know how to make an appointment. *Perhaps if I leave a plaster, they might get in contact?* She looked at the clock that never moved when she wanted it to, and counted down the minutes until lunchtime. Not that cabbage would ease her guilt.

Chantelle was wearing a grey hoodie and black leggings when she let Lena into the church hall after work on Tuesday. Lena's idea of putting a plaster on the street sign had worked; another plaster had appeared the next morning.

Lena had slept fitfully the night before; dreaming of drowning people reaching out to her, and she was unable to save them. Unlike the time at the leisure centre when she had rescued an elderly man in distress, towing him to the shallow end and performing CPR until her colleagues got the defibrillator. Saving one man's life had been worth all the training. She was never going to forgive herself for being the one who'd caused sixty people to drown.

'All right?' Chantelle said with a tilt of her head.

'No, not really. I need to see Tanya,' Lena said. 'I'm not happy that sixty people drowned trying to escape. They were on the boats I painted on the poster, right?'

Chantelle shrugged. 'Yes. I saw that, but it was just a coincidence. They would get through normally.' She hitched up her leggings. 'It's not your fault that they sailed right into a warship.'

Lena chewed on a nail. 'I still want to see Tanya. She owes me some food. Our rations have been cut and I did the poster like she asked.'

'Tanya's a busy lady,' Chantelle said. 'I'm supposed to be your contact.'

'I know, I know.' Lena crossed her arms. 'But I need what I was promised. I'm not going to do any more painting until I see Tanya and I get my rations.' The guilt of sending sixty people to their deaths, plus her hunger, made Lena more assertive than usual. She had no patience to be messed around.

Chantelle shrugged again. 'All right, I'll have a word, but she won't be very happy.'

That didn't bother Lena; it was the least of her problems. This grief wasn't worth a few cups of coffee. She said goodbye and left Chantelle setting out chairs. *I need a hug from Mum. Or Dad. Or maybe Rob.*

Lena walked to work on Wednesday morning with her head down, tired after a guilt-ridden sleepless night. She jumped sideways like a startled cat when Chantelle appeared from the shadow of a shop porch.

Speaking from the corner of her mouth Chantelle said, 'The old aquarium, this evening, 18:00. Got it?'

Lena repeated the instructions and watched Chantelle merge back into the shadows.

She mumbled the appointment details to herself as she continued to work. She couldn't write anything down in case it fell into the wrong hands, especially now she thought one of her flatmates might be an informer. Her diary used to be full of coffees, haircuts and art exhibitions, but now the only appointments she had were in her head: Tanya, Rob, Chantelle and work. She'd been excited about having more to her life than just work when Tanya had offered the chance to help people escape, but now that was wearing off and she felt angry at being used.

After work, Lena looked at her sparse wardrobe; she had time for a quick change. *What shall I wear? I need to be unobtrusive.* She could wear her hoodie and say she was going to watch the fishermen. Her hair was hanging down over her eyebrows. *Tanya's hair is so bloody perfect, I can't see her like this.* She rummaged in her sparse make-up bag for nail scissors and trimmed the fringe. She blew the hair strands away and wiped her brow.

Jane was reading in the sitting room. 'What have you done to your hair?' she asked, looking over her book.

'Really? Is it that bad?' Lena flicked her fringe to tidy it up.

'It looks like the Himalayas.' Jane pointed at the raggedy edges. 'Did your butcher boy do it?

'Ha ha! And he's not my butcher boy.' Lena blushed despite the denial, though it did feel nice to have him referred to like that.

'I'll tidy it up for you if you like.' Jane swung her legs off the sofa and gave a theatrical stretch: her knees bent, back arched, arms behind her head. 'I've told you before to use my hair scissors.'

The other women filed in once they saw Lena sitting with a towel over her shoulders and Jane snipping. They formed a disorderly queue that draped itself over sofa arms and chairs. Beth was asking for a cut and blow-dry, Alice wanted her curls straightened and Tamsin was keen to have her eyebrows waxed. Lena brushed herself down once Jane had finished and left the women chatting. The impromptu salon distracted the girls and Lena sneaked out of the apartment unnoticed.

Lena walked along the cobbled roads of the Barbican to the quayside. The air was crisp in the shade but pleasant in the evening sunshine. Lena's neck grew stiff from checking behind her. She strode as fast as her shoes would allow, thinking that if anyone was following her, they wouldn't be able to keep up. Two old ladies were sitting in silence on one of the benches. Resting and gazing out to sea was one of the few pleasures left for old people. *I used to love coming here to sketch.*

The footpath across the harbour gates was empty and so was the restaurant with faded 'Rockfish' lettering on the chipped wooden fascia.

Lena thought back to her fourteenth birthday, when her family had gone out to dinner at Rockfish in Exmouth. They'd had a table by the window that overlooked the grey, choppy sea. She couldn't remember what she'd eaten; the highlight of the evening was watching a middle-aged couple struggle to bring their dinghy inshore to the causeway. The boat pitched and rolled and Lena's family hoped that someone would fall in, for further entertainment. After ten minutes of drama, the couple managed to get the dinghy's painter wrapped around a bollard and the man jumped out in his deck shoes and rolled up chinos, getting soaked to his knees as he clambered up the causeway to get the trailer for the dinghy.

Eight years ago! I wonder if they managed to escape in their boat. Probably not. They were poor sailors.

Tanya was sitting on a wooden picnic bench, her back to the table. She was wearing a black trouser suit, black low-heeled shoes and a grey silk blouse, her hair perfectly in place like a Lego person. She was reading a hard-covered book with a picture of an oil painting on the front.

Lena felt drab in comparison to Tanya. *How did the Christians get all these nice clothes?* 'Hello,' Lena said as her shadow fell on Tanya.

'Good evening.' Tanya closed the book and peered around Lena. 'I couldn't see anyone following you.'

Lena looked around. 'No, I don't think so.'

Tanya patted the seat, which was covered in dried bird shit. 'Sit down – it's warm in the sun.'

Lena lowered herself onto the cleanest spot and crossed her legs, mirroring Tanya, but saw her shoes and tucked her feet under the bench. She sat on her hands to hide her scruffy nails and looked at the boats.

Tanya cleared her throat. 'Now, about the unfortunate incident with the boats. It was very upsetting.' She shook her head. 'Such a tragedy.' She held her hands up. 'But there was nothing we could do.'

Lena had rehearsed what she wanted to say about the drownings but her anger was dissipating under Tanya's contrition. 'How did the navy know they were there?' she said. 'If they were informed and they read the poster, they could trace it back to me.'

Tanya shook her head again. 'It's just an unhappy coincidence. The navy do these patrols and the skippers should have taken a different route. Instead, they sailed straight into the channel where the ship was waiting. As for the boats, I don't think anyone looks that closely at the names on posters, do you?'

Lena shrugged. 'I don't know. If they do then I'm in trouble.' Lena wondered if she could scribble the names out on all the posters displayed in Plymouth. But she'd need a marker pen and could be arrested for vandalism, meaning even more trouble.

'I think they would have found you by now if that was the case, don't you?' Tanya said. 'Besides, the navy has better things to do than read propaganda posters.'

Lena shifted her weight on the bench and placed her hands on her lap. She looked towards the empty sea. *Where is the navy now? If Alice is right, and they only have a few ships, the capture was a massive coincidence.* 'But sixty people have drowned, Tanya. Was it worth the risk?'

Tanya patted Lena's hand. Lena could smell her autumnal perfume of cinnamon and apples.

'We'll make sure this doesn't happen again,' Tanya said. 'We need you to do another poster and we shall brief the skippers to take a different route.'

Tanya's cold hand felt nice despite its temperature, reminding Lena of her mum when they sat together on the benches beside Exeter Cathedral.

'Fine,' Lena said, 'but only if I get some food now. I can't keep going on with this hunger.'

Tanya nodded. 'Of course. We need to get this batch of escapees away and then we can look after you.' She squeezed Lena's hand. 'You are invaluable to the Resistance. The families will be eternally grateful.' She lifted a finger to her lips, adding, 'But until then, we can't tell them who helped. We'll have to be happy in our thankless tasks, with their safety as our reward.'

'I'd rather have food,' Lena said.

113

'Yes, yes.' Tanya sounded annoyed at the request. 'You said that. I'll get it to you.'

Lena looked at the boarded-up aquarium that she'd enjoyed visiting as a child. The turtles and the sharks had swum carelessly in the big tank and the rainbow fish in their little tanks. She'd never been able to look at starfish the same way after the young aquarium assistant had explained their mouth and anus used the same hole. 'Yuck,' she had said to her dad. 'They eat where they poop!'

'Poop mouth, poop mouth!' Alek had taunted Lena for the rest of the week.

The tanks had been drained years ago, the fish and mammals gone to who knows where. Hopefully back to sea. They couldn't keep the generators running nor protect the tanks from the risk of drone strikes. One more piece of Plymouth culture eroded.

'I have some news about Alek,' Tanya said.

Lena turned and grabbed Tanya's arm. 'Is he safe? Is he with my parents?' She thought about her family squeezed into Puffins, her heart aching at the thought of them being together without her.

Tanya nodded. 'Yes, he's safe.'

Lena puffed her cheeks and blew out the air. 'Thank God for that. Did your contacts in Kernow tell you that?'

Tanya squeezed Lena's hand. 'Kernow? No. Didn't you know?'

'Know what?' Lena's throat tightened. 'Where is he if not there?'

'Sorry, I thought your supervisor would have told you. He was captured after his escape and sent with his battalion to fight the Continentals.'

Lena pulled her hand away and stood. 'Oh my God.' She crossed her arms in an attempt to hug herself and started pacing up and down in front of the bench. 'They were in the news briefing on Monday – they've been in a battle. Is Alek okay?'

Tanya waved a hand. 'A flesh wound, nothing more. He'll be fine.'

Lena wiped away a tear, thankful that he was alive. 'This stupid war. It's broken up my family and I don't want my little brother killed.'

'Shh.' Tanya patted the bench. 'You will be docked Soc-Cred points if someone hears you. And you wouldn't want that would you?'

Lena sat and stretched her legs out in front of her. *'Shit, I thought Alek was in Looe with my parents. I've been worrying about my shoes when he's been at war.* She wriggled her toes and a piece of masking tape fell off. 'Chantelle said you can get me some more shoes. Can you? You can see how bad these ones are.'

'They are a mess. I'll see what I can do. What size are you?' Tanya said.

'Five and a half.' Lena reattached the masking tape, only for it to unwrap, as if for emphasis.

'Yes, yes, of course. Chantelle did mention it.' Tanya stood and looked around the quay, half now in shadow. 'Take care to stay here for a few minutes after I leave. If anyone asks, we were chatting about art.' She pointed to the book on the bench. 'You can keep that, and I've got these for you too.' She pulled out a packet of pencils graded from 12B to 6H and walked away without saying another word, along the quayside towards the multi-storey car park.

'What about my food?' Lena said to Tanya's back. 'I can't eat this book.' She picked up the book – a glossy guide to pre-twentieth-century British artists. She opened it and ran her fingers over the smooth pages. A lavish photograph of a famous painting was on each right-hand page and a biography of the artist and description of the painting on the left. The index page was stamped with 'Plymouth College of Art' in red ink. Lena lost herself in the book until the shadows crawled up the bench and over the pages. She shivered, realising the sun was below the Barbican and the lights were on in the old buildings, silhouettes inside moving around doing their evening chores. She thought about sketching this scene and how it would look in pencils or charcoals.

Her stomach rumbled. *Tanya has fobbed me off without any food. She knew I was desperate but didn't bring any. Is she all talk? I'm not doing another poster until I get what I really need. I'm taking a lot of risk with not much reward.*

A pair of guides walked in step across the footbridge, clipboards under arms, the sound of their shoes clanking carrying across the water.

Lena closed the book and walked the long way around the quay to get back to her apartment block. She didn't want to be questioned by some uniformed pre-teens about why she was still out so close to the curfew. Even a minor infraction would dock her more Soc-Cred.

Lena had forgotten to ask Tanya where Alek was now. *Is he still on the Continent? I should have paid more attention to the news briefing.* Her shoes flapped on the cobbles. *I've still got crap shoes and I'm still hungry. So much for being assertive. Thank goodness it's ration day tomorrow. I can see Rob and get some extra meat. I can talk to him about Alek, too.*

Chapter 17

Alek walked down the ramp on giddy legs and took a deep breath of the damp morning air tinged with a hint of diesel. *Home*. He had been out of the country for less than a week but it seemed like a month. The return flight had been as turbulent as the outward one but, without the anxiety of imminent combat, he'd kept his food down.

The soldiers were dispersed into three green buses according to injury severity and other unexplained criteria. Alek's bus drove down the A38, a familiar trip from his childhood, over Haldon Hill and past the bleak tors of Dartmoor. Alek pressed his nose against the window, noting each landmark, remembering the comments from his dad that Alek had dismissed as boring as a young kid.

But, instead of going home, he was being driven to an army camp north of Plymouth. His future was uncertain; the reprieve of a wounded arm was only temporary. He could recover and then be sent back into combat. His mouth was set in a grim line, feeling utterly alone despite being on a bus full of soldiers.

A tall sergeant stood with a clipboard in hand as the wounded soldiers limped or walked off the bus and lined up in two ranks. Alek stretched and cracked his back, emitting a yawn.

'You there!' the sergeant shouted. 'Boring you, am I?'

'No, Sergeant. Sorry, Sergeant,' Alek said.

'Straighten yourself up, you sorry excuse for a soldier.' The sergeant tapped his clipboard. 'Name?'

'Wasilewski, Sergeant,' Alek said with his back as straight as a fencepost.

The sergeant made a tick on his clipboard. 'Step forward. You're to go to the officer's mess.' He shook his head before giving Alek directions.

'Yes, Sergeant.' Alek frowned as he recited the directions in his head. *Take the first left past the parade ground, then the second right until I reach the end of the tarmac road. Why am I going to the officer's mess?*

'Fall … out!' the sergeant barked out the order.

Alek turned to the left, marching as smartly as was possible while wearing webbing and a sling. He felt like a duck waddling away from the bus.

The officer's mess was a large brick building covered with ivy. Two small iron cannons were mounted on stone plinths on either side of the front door. Alek walked up the paved path and read the brass plaque. Alek looked around – there was no one to be seen. He rang the doorbell and stood back.

He was about to ring it again when the door opened inwards, pulled by an elderly man whose speckled scalp was adorned with a white strand of hair. He wore a white jacket and blue trousers with highly polished black shoes.

'Good morning, Sir.'

'Oh? Me?' Alek said, confused by the politeness. 'Good morning. I was told to report here.' He handed the porter his well-stamped card.

The porter squinted at the card. 'I haven't got my glasses. I'll take your word for it.' He stepped back. 'Come in, Sir.'

Alek walked into the dark entrance hall that became even gloomier once the porter had shut the front door. Wooden panels covered the walls, adorned with portraits of soldiers and watercolours of battles from the last few centuries, all in ornate frames with engraved brass plaques detailing the medals or campaigns pictured. Alek tiptoed across to the wooden counter, unwilling to break the silence as if he was in a church or a library, where an open ledger lay next to a ballpoint pen attached to a stand by a piece of string.

'If you could sign in here, please, Sir.' The porter tapped the ledger.

Alek signed with his left hand as best as he could. He couldn't remember the last time he'd had to write anything with a pen.

'Take a seat in the coffee room, Sir. Captain Maguire usually comes in for 10:30.' The porter pointed to a walnut-panelled door that displayed a wooden sign with 'Coffee Room' engraved in gold letters at eye level. 'You'll have to leave your webbing in the cloakroom, there.' Another door, another sign.

'Yes, of course, thank you.' Alek didn't want to ask who Captain Maguire was. The porter seemed to think everything was normal, but Alek was confused. The cloakroom had two rows of benches with hooks above them, reminding Alek of a rugby dressing room. An open door led to the toilets and two sinks. He hung his webbing on one of the hooks and took out his wash kit. He checked his face in the first mirror he had seen for a week; his eyes were sunken and bloodshot, skin flaked around his stubble and he had a white line around his forehead.

Helmet tan!

He washed, shaved, cleaned his teeth and patted his straggly helmet hair down with warm water until he looked less undead. He felt better after removing the taste of travel from his mouth.

The coffee room's tall windows let beams of sunlight pour onto the long dark tables, dust dancing in the rays and settling on the old chairs and sofas. A row of thin news sheets hung on wooden poles in a rack; scarcity of paper and advertisers had reduced their bulk. An open cabinet beside the far wall housed a jumbled collection of paperbacks and old hardback biographies. A silver coffee pot with a long, thin spout sat on top of an electric heating pad beside a matching milk jug and a silver bowl full of sugar cubes. A dozen of the smallest coffee cups Alek had ever seen lay upside down on saucers with teaspoons.

Alek poured out some coffee and added a splash of milk; there was no room for more. He sipped and smiled; he hadn't had coffee for years. The grounds left a sludge at the bottom of the cup. He looked around; no one else was there, so he poured himself another thimbleful, making the most of a good thing while he could. The army was full of long bouts of tedium punctuated with moments of extreme peril, and all that underlined with massive uncertainty about the future. For now, he would drink and enjoy the coffee.

The door opened and a petite captain walked in, wearing a light green beret, her combats pressed and starched.

'Alek?' she said and held out her right hand.

'Yes, Ma'am.' Alek put the cup on the saucer on the coffee table and extended his fingers through his sling. He was surprised to see a female officer in the barracks; he thought only the medics were female.

The captain swapped hands to shake Alek's left. 'I'm Captain Maguire, Intelligence Corps.'

Alek shook her cold left hand, soon hoping she would let go. He was unused to handshakes, let alone left-handed ones with a strong woman. He'd always tested weaker on his left side in the college grip-strength tests and never seen their relevance. Until now. *Outdone by a woman.*

Captain Maguire released Alek's hand and poured herself a coffee. She gestured towards a two-seater sofa. 'Let's sit down, shall we?'

Alek sunk into the soft cushions, his knees higher than his waist. Captain Maguire sat on a high, firm-backed chair opposite. She sipped her coffee before putting the cup and saucer on the low coffee table next to an old *Horse and Hounds* magazine.

'So, Captain Stephens sent me your debrief, but I'd like you to tell me yourself what happened over there.' Captain Maguire took out an A5-sized tablet from her pocket and tapped on the screen with a stylus.

Alek described his journey, repeating himself when required, the details already fading but the emotions provoking a lump in his throat. So much had happened in less than a week. The sun moved around the room and beams fell on his face, making him drowsy; he hadn't sat on anything this comfortable since being press-ganged.

'Hmm.' Captain Maguire tapped her tablet and scribbled with the stylus. 'I've spoken to the colonel about this. We're looking for a good news story and you're it.' She smiled, looking up. 'There could even be a medal in it for you – maybe a promotion too.'

'What?' Alek was struggling to keep his eyes open. 'I mean, yes, Ma'am.' *How can my whole platoon getting killed be good news?*

'You did well to get out of there alive. We are looking for people who can think and can read a map.' Captain Maguire shook her head. 'You wouldn't believe the number of officers who get lost.'

'No, Ma'am,' Alek said. *Like ours did.*

'Would you be interested in becoming an officer?' Captain Maguire swapped her tablet for her coffee cup and saucer. 'There's a short-conversion course and then you would be assigned to our unit. We let the posh, dim ones go to the combat arms: infantry, artillery and tanks.' She smiled.

Alek smiled back and then looked around at the coffee room: the soft furnishings, the tiny cups and silverware, the paintings. This was better than the barracks of the training camp and he wouldn't be going into a combat arm either. He thought of the intelligence officer at the aid station, with his warm office, surrounded by nurses, cups of tea and hot food on demand. If Alek couldn't escape the army, then he could at least be comfortable. There was nothing for it but to say, 'Yes, Ma'am. Thank you, Ma'am.'

Captain Maguire waved a hand. 'You can dispense with the formalities now – call me Tanya.'

'Yes, Tanya.'

'You'll have to go through rehab first, but we can assign you as an officer cadet in the meantime. You can stay here, in the mess accommodation.' Tanya smiled as she stood.

Alek struggled to his feet, his legs stiff from the plane and bus and sitting in the low chair.

'I'll get the porter to assign your room and mess card,' Tanya said. 'Your rehab starts tomorrow – a bus leaves from here at 08:30 I think. There are a few of you going. You'll need to go to the QM stores to get your PT kit issued.' She held out her left hand.

Alek shook it, prepared for the grip this time. 'Thank you.'

Alek stepped outside the mess and blinked like a lizard in the sunshine. The air was still and heat radiated off the concrete. He walked along the neat lines of roads, swinging his good arm, his back upright. The mild exercise and the caffeine kicking in woke him up.

The crisp shouts of a sergeant drilling returning soldiers pierced the air, every syllable perfectly enunciated and compact. The crunch, crunch, stamp of marching boots came to a halt in unison, an echo rolling around the buildings before silence returned. A grey squirrel sprung up a trunk and paused. It turned 360 degrees before scampering along a branch. Alek smiled.

What would Swales say about me getting a promotion? He was a pragmatist but also hated the officers.

He paused mid-step. It didn't matter. Swales was dead. So was everyone else. If Alek wanted to stay alive he would have to be smart. Surviving two barrages and a firefight had surely drained whatever luck he might have had. That was enough combat for a lifetime. And the promotion meant he could stay in the rear. Swales would have to agree that was a good thing. Or maybe not. 'They're not using me; I'm using them,' Alek said to his dead friend's memory, as if speaking it aloud might make it true.

Alek was assigned a room that he shared with Mike: a tall Irish captain with curly black hair and a hooked nose who oozed professionalism and confidence. He'd broken his ankle abseiling from a helicopter – all the details he'd given. Alek knew better than to ask for more.

Alek had a single bed, a bedside table and lamp, a small wardrobe for his new kit, a desk and a chair. There was a painting of a fox hunt on one wall and the windows looked over the parade ground. The toilet block at the end of the hallway was next door to the shower room, housing four showers. Everything was comfortable, but without frills. Alek lay on his bed at 19:30 hours and was asleep within a minute, fully dressed.

For the first time in weeks, he woke up in the morning without a sense of fear or anxiety. Either the sound of Mike snoring or the gentle light streaming through the curtains had roused him from sleep. Alek stretched and got out of bed, considering the fact he'd been awake for five minutes yet no one was shouting at him or shooting at him. *I'm lucky to be here.*

Breakfast was a formal affair compared to Alek's recruit meals. A menu sheet was folded in half and propped up as a table setting, which showed the three items that he'd selected the night before: toast, poached egg and a glass of pear juice. Alek sat next to Shane, a friend of Mike's, whose broad-shoulders and short hair that stuck to his head made him look like he had been carved from stone. Alek was adjusting to his new surroundings and was grateful that Shane was as taciturn as a statue so that small-talk was avoided.

They had been driven to the rehab centre in a green bus with green leather seats and filed into the sports hall. Alek watched the Royal Navy Physical Training Instructor walk up and down the polished floor on his hands, his muscles straining through his pale skin that matched his white vest. The PTI paused, turned 180 degrees and brought his white plimsolls down onto the floor with a slap.

Alek tilted his head upright so he could make out the red logo on the vest: two crossed clubs. The PTI brushed the moustache that hung down past his lips before addressing the two lines of injured servicemen. 'Those of you with leg wounds can still get around if you try hard enough.' He grinned and revealed a gold tooth. Alek wondered when a cutlass or parrot might appear.

Show off. Alek had never been able to do a handstand and he had no chance now with his injured arm.

The PTI divided the injured into three groups: Uppers, Lowers and Advanced, depending on the type of injury and the stage of rehabilitation. Alek was put in the Uppers. His arm throbbed and itched as he sweated through the warm-up exercises – skipping, jogging, jumping and running. They spent the morning doing a mix of physical drills and playing a modified game of volleyball, where they were allowed five touches instead of three on each side. Lunchtime was called when Alek's team was losing 17–19. The pain in his arm had been drowned by adrenaline and Alek found he didn't want to stop. 'Wait, Staff. Can we play for five more minutes?' he asked.

All the PTIs were called Staff, no matter their rank – for some reason unknown to Alek. His request was denied and he followed the group outside, to a set of picnic tables and benches. He sat beside Mike and Shane, mulling over the game. *Five more minutes and we could have won.*

They had been issued a plastic water bottle and a white paper bag that contained two sandwiches wrapped in cling film, two biscuits and an apple. 'Horror bags,' Shane called them. Unwrapping a sandwich, Alek saw it was filled with a creamy brown paste. He peeled aside a corner of the bread and sniffed the filling. 'Tuna?'

'Who knows? It might be dolphin or dogfish.' Shane shrugged, eating half a sandwich in one mouthful.

Alek nibbled the sandwich before taking large bites. Hunger beat taste and he needed the calories after all the exercise. He devoured the rest of the lunch and inspected the bottom of the horror bag, but there were no hidden treats. He sipped his water and stretched out his legs, letting Mike and Shane's conversation wash over him. It was mostly about what sports the officers had played at their schools. Alek hadn't heard of half of them: sculling, fives, real tennis. *Is that different from normal tennis?* They called rugby 'rugger', and they seemed to be experts in it, confidence dripping off them; neither of them seemed to have played football.

Alek had enjoyed playing rugby and football at school, and later for college, but didn't think he was anything special. He just liked playing sport with his mates. The PT that morning had been more like his course at college than being in the army. The work was hard without feeling like punishment. *I could get used to this.*

121

He felt a tapping on his foot, realising Mike was kicking him. 'Wake up young 'un – we want to know if you're coming out with us on Saturday?'

'Saturday? What day is it today?' Alek said. His next thought was about what they would wear out. He hoped it wasn't civvies, because he didn't have any.

'Wednesday, of course,' Shane said. 'We always do volleyball on Wednesdays.'

'It's a chance to meet some girls,' Mike said. 'They like a man in uniform.'

'Sure, thanks,' Alek said, relieved they'd all be wearing uniform. *I won't be embarrassed about my clothes. But I don't have any money to buy a girl a drink.*

Alek spoke to Mike after dinner that evening – or supper as they called it in the mess. 'Erm, Mike, about Saturday?'

'Yes?' Mike was lying on his bed, wearing jeans and a T-shirt, reading a paperback.

Alek thought about the best way into this conversation. 'Are we allowed to wear civilian clothes off-duty?'

Mike raised an eyebrow and pointed at his jeans.

'Yeah,' Alek said. 'I thought so. But I don't have any.'

'You can get some in the NAAFI shop,' Mike said without looking up.

'I can't – I haven't got any money,' Alek said.

'Spent it all on beer?' Mike said.

'Ha,' Alek said. 'No.' The chance would be a fine thing; not that he had drunk beer before he was in the army either. 'I haven't had any money since I was press-ganged— I mean, since I was recruited. We handed our wallets in to the corporal and I haven't been paid, so I have zero cash.'

Mike lowered his book. 'Where's your corporal? Can you get your wallet back?'

Alek thought of Corporal Sanderson's face staring up at the sky where he left him on the ridge. 'He's dead. Caught in a firefight with the Conts.'

Mike got off his bed and put a hand on Alek's shoulder. 'That's tough. I'll put a call in to your old unit to get your things sent over and have your pay sorted.'

'Thanks,' Alek said, grateful to have one small part of his civilian life returned. Mike seemed like a decent man and a decent officer. They weren't all as useless as Swales had made out.

'Come with me to lost property,' Mike said. He led Alek to an old whitewashed concrete single-storey building. Inside was a cross between an old school gymnasium and a department store, filled with racks of clothes sorted by size and type.

Alek's jaw dropped. He could have spent an hour in there but Mike gave him ten minutes to stop procrastination. He left with two pairs of trousers, two T-shirts, two shirts, a sweatshirt and a coat – plus his favourite find: a pair of hardly worn white New Balance trainers with a green trim.

'Happy now, young 'un?' Mike said.

'Yes, thank you,' Alek said. Life in the mess was a world apart from recruit training or combat. *I could get used to this. Maybe Swales didn't know everything after all.*

Chapter 18

Lena's routine at the office seemed more mundane without having a secret name to leave on a poster. The clock moved slower and the propaganda quotes were cornier. For about the twentieth time, she told herself that tonight was meat night, something to get her through the day. After the morning news briefing, Trevor waved a piece of paper in front of the women.

'Here are the details for the veterans' ball this Saturday. You will be picked up at 19:00 hours from your accommodation. Attendance is mandatory. You will be debriefed on Monday and asked which veteran you wish to see again.'

Jane leant into Lena. 'You might get lucky and be debriefed on Saturday night.'

'Yuck.' Lena punched Jane in the shoulder. 'Speak for yourself.'

'Have you got something to say, Lena?' Trevor said.

Lena looked around the atrium and down at her shoes, fuming that Jane had got her into trouble again. 'Er, yes, actually.' She bent down and pulled off a shoe. 'How can I meet Prince Charming if this is my glass slipper?' She pulled the sole open and waved the shoe to make a clacking noise like a castanet.

Jane held up a shoe too, along with half a dozen of the other women, waving them in the air, complaining about sore feet and not being able to dance. Lena felt like Spartacus. *Dad would be proud that I remembered that scene from the movie.* Trevor looked at the rebellious women and pushed his glasses up his nose. Holding his hands aloft, he waved the paper down, a token surrender.

'All right, all right. I'll see what I can do. You do make a reasonable point.' The women quietened down. 'Now, can you please go back to work?'

Lena put her floppy shoe back on and flip-flopped up the stairs to their office. Her victory glow had diminished by the time she sat back at her desk. *Which veteran will you see again? I don't want to be forced to see any. I have Rob, so I don't need anyone else – as long as he stays keen on me.*

At home, when Lena walked into the living room, Beth was scrutinising the rota on the cork board.

'What you got this week?' Lena said.

'The toilet.' Beth made a face like a sad clown.

'Unlucky,' Lena said.

'Yeah,' Beth said. She ran a finger down the column. 'Oh, you've got the butcher's. Again.'

Jane looked up from her magazine. 'Want some company?'

'No,' Lena said, a little sharp. 'Thanks – I've got it, you stay comfy.'

'All right.' Jane smirked and resumed flicking through the pages. 'I'll leave you lovers on your own.'

Lena taped up her shoes, changed into her jeans and hoodie, used the new 4B pencil to shape and colour her eyebrows, and brushed her hair before heading out. She was desperate to unburden her worries with Rob: Alek being in a battle, the veterans' ball and, of course, the need for extra rations. *I can't lead with that – he'll think I'm using him. I can't tell him about the boat casualties either – that would be too careless.*

Two elderly ladies wearing knee-length winter coats and headscarves stood by the pedestrian crossing at the corner of Vauxhall Street and Hoegate Street. Lena looked at their well-heeled solid shoes that she would have scorned a few years ago. *How are they still so good? Maybe they don't walk as much as I do. I wonder if they have any spares they'd give me? Anything would be better than mine.*

'Good afternoon,' she said as she passed, deciding she wasn't ready to beg from strangers yet.

'Oh, good afternoon,' the ladies replied, looking grateful for a kindly greeting, before resuming their conversation.

Lena checked they weren't following her, now suspicious of pretty much anyone now. They were still at the crossing but looking at her. She glanced away and walked as fast as her shoes would allow her to the butcher's. The days had dragged on until now. *Slow down. Stay cool. I don't want to seem desperate.* She looked at her reflection in the window and straightened her hair before walking inside the butcher's.

The shop was empty except for the smart older butcher behind the counter. He was wiping globules of red meat and scrag ends of fat off a thick wooden chopping board. 'Good afternoon, love. What can I get you?' His redundant phrase was a holdover from more prosperous times.

'Hello, just the usual, please.' Lena handed over the ration cards. She peered over the counter to see into the back room. There was no sign of Rob. Lena frowned.

'He'll be out in a minute, love.' The butcher winked at Lena. Winking and whistling were either hereditary or mandatory in the butcher's.

'Oh, right.' Lena popped her head back down faster than a meerkat. She blushed at being caught peeking, tapping her fingers as the butcher whistled. She had never been able to whistle, or sing in tune.

The butcher placed a brown paper parcel on the counter. 'There you go, love.'

'Thanks,' Lena said. Her heart beat faster as Rob walked in.

'I'll leave you two to it,' the butcher said, winking at Lena again.

'Hello,' Rob said.

'Hello,' Lena's voice squeaked. She coughed and added, 'Hello,' in her usual voice.

'Would you like some eggs?' Rob sounded as if he was talking to any other customer rather than offering extra food to a woman he had dated.

Lena nodded. 'Yes, please.' *What's wrong? Why's he being so formal?*

Rob put a carton with a dozen eggs beside the brown parcel. 'I've nearly finished up – would you like to go for a walk?' He smiled. 'Just a short one to save your shoes.'

Lena smiled back. 'Thank you. I'll wait outside.' She put the parcel and eggs into her tote bag and walked outside. Her hands trembling, she gripped the bag tighter. *What's the matter with you? Get a grip before he sees you.* She took a deep breath and counted to five as she breathed out. *That's better.* She walked down the street to a bench underneath a tree that had the first signs of blossom buds along its lower branches.

The next five minutes felt like an aeon for Lena. She repeated a cycle of sitting, standing and chewing on a hangnail while looking at the butcher's until she told herself to stop. The nerves of seeing a man for what might be classed a second date were getting to her. She had more to lose if it went wrong now.

She smiled when Rob sat on the bench beside her. He smelt of soap and something else. *Fridges? Can anyone smell of fridges?*

'Hey,' Rob said, 'how have you been?' He leant in to kiss her on the cheek.

Lena turned her head and they clashed cheekbones. 'Sorry.' She got it right the second time and he kissed her just below her cheekbones. She felt his stubble scratch her cheek. *That was terrible – I'm out of practice.*

'Where do you want to start?' Lena said. 'It's been a mad week. My brother isn't in Kernow – he was in a battle on the Continent.'

'What?' Rob put his hand on Lena's. 'Is he okay? I thought you said he escaped.'

Lena felt a tingle in her arm at Rob's touch. 'I did. That's what I was told. But I found out this week that he was captured and sent over to the Continent to fight. Apparently, he's safe.' Lena shrugged. 'I don't know though. I'm worried about him.'

'Wow.' Rob shuffled on the bench. 'It must be tough not knowing.'

Lena looked up and down the street. 'There's something else.' She looked at Rob. 'I have to go to a ball on Saturday where single women are going to be matched with veterans.'

Rob removed his hand. 'What do you mean, matched?'

'I don't know exactly, but on Monday we have to give the name of the veteran we want to see again. It's horrible.' Lena bit her lower lip. 'I'd rather put down the name of someone that I liked to keep the inspector off my back.'

Lena waited for Rob to say something but he was looking the other way. The two old ladies Lena had seen at the crossing were walking towards them.

Rob stood and held out his hand. 'Let's go and see the sun set over the sea.'

Lena took his hand and put her bag over her shoulder. *This definitely counts as a second date.* They walked down the shopping arcade and across the High Street towards the Hoe. *But he hasn't replied to my hint about putting someone else's name down. What's going on? Did he hear me?* They walked up the steps to the promenade, the knot in Lena's stomach growing tighter. She decided direct action was best. 'Can I put your name down on Monday, please? It won't mean anything except that I won't have to go on a date with a soldier.'

Rob tilted his head to the side and held his hands up. 'Sorry, but if you put my name down, they'll come and investigate me.'

'So? Do you have anything to hide?' Lena clutched his forearm. She waited for an answer but Rob was silent. He looked out at Drake's Island where passengers were disembarking from a small boat. Large crates were piled on the small jetty and the people were sidling past. He turned to Lena and put his hands on her waist. 'I don't want to be investigated and I don't want to get into trouble.'

'Why would you get into trouble?' Lena felt the strength in his fingers and slipped her hands under his jacket, onto the hard muscles of his lower back.

'I can't say, Lena.' He smiled. 'I would if I could, but I can't. He bent down and tilted her chin upwards with his finger and kissed her, his lips gentle on hers.

Lena kissed him back and for a few moments forgot about everything else except this kiss. She felt safe and warm and happy and wanted all at once. She stopped and hugged him, laying her head on his chest, feeling his arms wrap around her.

'We need to get out of here,' Rob said.

Lena squeezed Rob's hand. 'I know. There's something I need to tell you.' She led him to an empty bench. 'I want to join my parents in Kernow. I might be able to get there on a boat.'

Rob pointed towards the shrubbery at the western end of the promenade where two girl guides were sitting on a bench. 'I meant, we need to get away from the Hoe – we're being watched.' He nodded his head towards the city centre.

Lena walked with Rob, away from the guides, her face reddening. *I'm such an idiot.* They walked down the concrete steps and past a tall, derelict hotel, before turning right. Pedestrians carrying half-empty grocery bags were heading home an hour before curfew. Rob looked over his shoulder. 'Okay, tell me about the boat. It's harder for people to eavesdrop when we're moving.'

Lena looked around her before explaining how she'd made contact with a local girl who gave her coffee. The rest of her story about the posters, escape boats and the Christians poured out; the tension eased from her shoulders and the knot in her stomach unravelled. She hadn't planned to spill everything, but she felt safe in Rob's arms. They had been the key to unlocking the secrets that had been churning inside Lena.

Rob kept quiet until she finished the story.

Wow!' Rob said. 'So you're a secret agent?' He bumped Lena's shoulder.

'Don't be silly,' Lena said, bumping him back. 'I'm just helping people escape. I thought it was a Christian thing, but Tanya said it was part of something called the Resistance.' She felt Rob stiffen.

'What's wrong?' Lena said. 'Is it because of the people who drowned?'

'Nothing,' Rob said. 'I was just thinking where would that leave your friends and the old and the vulnerable?' Rob held Lena's hand. 'And Alek? How do you know you can trust these people? The Party have eyes everywhere. You're taking a massive risk by being involved.'

Lena bit her lip. She had taken a risk by telling Rob but had hoped he'd be supportive. Getting out on a boat seemed the only way to escape the clutches of a state that wanted her married off. Especially if Rob wouldn't let her put his name down as an official boyfriend. She was running out of options.

Two scouts were stood beside the mini-roundabout, one of them looking at his watch.

'Here's trouble,' Rob said. 'We've got twenty-five minutes until curfew. Keep quiet until we pass.'

They smiled at the scouts as they walked past them, Lena clutching her bag as she scurried to keep up with Rob's long strides. The scouts were still looking their way as they reached the Theatre Royal.

'Over there.' Rob grabbed Lena's hand and strode across the pedestrian crossing.

Lena was out of breath. 'Slow down.' Her feet were sore.

Rob glanced down the street and then led Lena up a side street lined with tall sandstone buildings. He pulled her into a doorway. 'Let's have a quick kiss before we have to separate.'   Lena reached up and kissed him on the cheek. 'Are you sure I can't put your name down? I don't see what the problem is.'

Rob shook his head. 'I can't.' He tried to kiss her back on the lips but she offered her cheek instead. 'We can talk more on Sunday if you'd like to meet up then?'

Lena stepped out of the doorway and folded her arms. 'Sure. If I'm not engaged by then.' *Why won't Rob let his name be put down?*

Rob put his hand on her shoulder, but she shrugged it off.

'Same time, at Drake's statue?' he said.

Lena shrugged, too annoyed to reply.

Rob leant down and whispered, 'Be careful not to tell anyone what you told me. Remember that there are informers everywhere. I'll go first and try to draw the scouts off.' He walked away and waved after he crossed the road.

Lena watched him go. She felt better after unloading her secret but was annoyed at Rob's lack of practical help. *The kiss was nice – but kisses won't help me get out of here. I need to chase Tanya about getting on a boat. As well as food and shoes. Food!* Lena looked in the tote bag at the eggs and parcel. *Maybe Rob isn't so bad, after all. He's given me more food than Tanya has.* She took a look down the street and saw no one. She checked the doorway to see that she hadn't dropped anything and noticed the stone engraving in the block above the door: the letters 'TG'. Lena stepped back into the street to look at the whole building.

'Huh, that's funny, I wonder if Mum ever came to this one?' She turned and walked towards the High Street, taking one last look over her shoulder. *Wait! Did that curtain move?* 'Stop it, Lena. You're getting twitchy,' she said to herself and then hurried home as fast as her sore feet would let her.

Lena listened to the commotion in the living room, the women fuelled by an omelette that even the vegans had enjoyed.

'I'd shag anyone for a decent pair of shoes,' Alice said.

'You have already,' Jane said.

'Will they have vegetarian snacks?' Beth said. 'I hope they do.'

'It's just a mixer,' Tamsin said.

'But still, there will be food, won't there?' Beth said, looking at Alice.

'Well, they do have food in the navy mess, so I'm sure they'll have something,' Alice said with a serious face. It was unusual for her to be asked for advice but she was the default expert on military social matters.

'Ooh, scram! Do you think they'll have a dance card?' Jane said.

'I don't think so – it's not the American South. You've been reading too many romance novels,' Lena said.

'Why, Lena, whatevah makes you think such a thing, sugah?'

Jane fanned her book in front of her face and fluttered her eyelashes.

'I hope they're not too scarred,' Beth said.

'You'll be fine with the lights off,' Alice said.

'Yuck,' Beth said.

Lena wondered if Alek had any scars from the battle; she thought about him missing a limb or suffering with burn scars.

The doorbell rang. The women ran to the window to see a white electric van parked by the kerb. Whoever had rung the bell was hidden under the porch.

'Delivery!' Lena ran out of the living room, down the hall and out of the door, skipping down the stairs two at a time. She won the race to the lobby door by a short nose ahead of the other women arriving in a bunch. They jostled for position behind Lena as she tried to open the door but fumbled the lock. She managed to unlock the door on the second attempt and waved the women back with her free hand to get room to open the door. The delivery driver was a middle-aged lady in a brown set of overalls, with a black cloth sack beside her feet.

'Delivery for Was, Vas…?' She peered at her clipboard.

'Wasilewski!' Lena was hopping from one bare foot to the other.

'Yes, that's it. Sign here, please.' The driver handed the clipboard to Lena.

Lena snatched the pen and scribbled her name. 'Thanks.'

The driver pointed at the sack. 'It's all yours – have a good evening.'

Lena picked up the heavy sack and carried it into the lobby.

'Open it. Open it,' Alice said.

'What's in it?' Jane said.

Lena ripped open the seal and reached into the bag, pulling out a black lace-up shoe and grinning. The other women pushed Lena aside and pulled more second-hand shoes out of the bag. They tried them on in the lobby before walking up the stairs to the apartment, the excited chatter drowning out the sound of clicking heels echoing around the staircase.

Lena waited for them to go before checking the note on the sack. The shoes were from Trevor. He had listened to their demands and delivered. Lena smiled at the irony. After receiving no help from Tanya, she now had escape-worthy shoes from a member of the Party. At least she didn't have to rely on Tanya for everything. Lena would get a decent meal at the ball and Rob had given them extra eggs. *I can now bargain for just my escape with the next poster. That can't come too soon. I'll get some much needed extra Soc-Cred points too.*

Chapter 19

The days passed quickly for Alek as he settled into the rehabilitation routine. He enjoyed this new environment with zero bullshit and a clear timetable of what was happening when, and for how long. There was no vagueness, no trickery and the shouting was half-hearted and good-natured. Ab-sprints were the PTI's favourite punishment: lying on your back and touching opposite knee to elbow with the other leg extended above the floor. A thousand a day was common for those who forgot their water bottle or wore the incorrect T-shirt.

The only intrusion into the training was the daily news briefing from a naval officer at 11:00 where everyone had to stand or sit to attention. On Thursday he had announced, 'Our supreme forces have secured another victory on the continent. A heroic force held a position near Rivabellosa in the Basque Country, fighting to the last man against a superior number of the enemy. The Conts were defeated thanks to our valiant soldiers. The sole survivor, Private Wasilewski, will be decorated and promoted.'

There was a breakdown in discipline as Alek was patted on the back and congratulated. The naval officer folded his sheet and smiled.

'You kept that quiet,' Mike said.

Alek shrugged. He hadn't wanted to relive the experience by relaying it to his new friends, and he also felt like an imposter amongst the older men who had seen far more combat than he. Alek felt lucky rather than brave. The position had been lost and he had run away as soon as he could. He could have as easily been facing a firing squad.

Training finished at 16:00, followed by tea in the mess at 16:30. Biscuits and cakes were laid out alongside miniscule cups; the only thing worse than recruit training where at least they had large mugs for their tea. Alek washed his hands before gulping down his first cup at the table and refilling. Mike beckoned Alek to join him on one of the doze-inducing soft armchairs at the far end of the lounge. It was where he and Shane sat, keeping themselves apart from the rest of the officers.

Alek sat beside a low bookcase between two tall French windows. *Patio windows*, he corrected himself, since they weren't allowed to call them French any more. He sipped his tea and looked at Mike and Shane over his cup. These men were proper officers; they exuded professionalism and confidence and Alek felt privileged to be asked to sit by them.

'I didn't see your name on the sign-up sheet for the ball on Saturday,' Mike said. 'Are you going?'

Alek frowned. He didn't read the noticeboard in the mess; it was full of orders of the day and general notices aimed at people with actual responsibilities in the military. Unlike him. 'What ball?'

Shane laughed. 'The veterans' ball. It's a chance to meet local single women. After all, you're not going to find any here. The deadline to sign up is 19:00 tonight.'

Alek looked around the tea room at the men chatting or reading as if there was no war. It was all so different from his basic training and the horror of combat. Going out to meet a woman had not been on his mind at all, survival was his only thought. He was out of practice; not that he had been any good at it when women had been around. Except with the nurse. She'd been easy to talk to. *I wonder if Sarah is single?* Alek closed his eyes and pictured himself going out with the pretty nurse, allowing himself a smile.

Laughter from the other end of the room stopped Alek's daydream. The men laughed again. One of them was pounding the arm of his chair.

'Fucking RAF,' Shane said.

'Exactly,' Mike said. 'That's why we sit over here.'

'What's wrong with the RAF?' Alek said.

Mike looked at Shane, who shrugged. 'One of the reasons we're in the shit is because they keep fucking up,' Mike said to Alek. 'You should know – you were dropped in the wrong place. Your muckers might still be alive if you'd been dropped properly.'

Alek hadn't thought of that. He looked over at the RAF officers, feeling sick to his stomach. *My mates could still be alive…*

Shane tapped Alek on the knee. 'They dropped you in the shit and then flew home to their comfy beds. The navy guides their ships using stars, the army sleep under the stars and the RAF choose their hotels using stars.'

'Eh?' Alek said, not understanding the phrase.

Shane shook his head. 'Hotels used to have stars to rate how good they were. The RAF live it up far from the front line.'

'Oh,' Alek said, feeling conscious of how little he still knew about the military and its in-jokes.

Mike nodded. 'We're in a stalemate over there. The big bosses don't want to lose any more of their precious planes so they don't give us proper air cover, let alone casevacs.'

'Casevacs?' Alek said. *I'm learning more here than I did in training.*

'Casualty-evacuation,' Shane said. 'You aren't the only one who had to make their way back through enemy lines.'

Alek listened as Mike and Shane launched into a softly spoken diatribe against the general staff and their lack of strategy. He was surprised to hear them speaking so candidly; he'd thought that they were war heroes but this talk was treacherous. Mike told his story of being left to hobble down a stone valley after a helicopter ignored his distress signal. Shane's company had been overrun by enemy tanks, his men scattering before regrouping and fighting their way to safety.

The lack of a clear plan, an exit strategy, failed equipment and communications, along with a reliance on the bravery of the men was common to their stories. They spoke without boasting but it was obvious they were brave and cared about their men.

'But I thought we were winning,' Alek said when both the men had finished talking.

Mike laughed, 'Ha!'

Shane leant forward. 'Did it look like we were winning when you were over there?'

Alek looked out of the window at the low grey clouds. *So many people have died. It can't have been for nothing. Swales said we were being used as cannon fodder to help the veterans regroup. Sounds like he was wrong. It wasn't just us.*

'But what did my platoon die for?' he said.

'It was a heroic last stand defending our freedom against the Continentals,' Captain Maguire said from behind Alek.

Alek fumbled with his cup and saucer, pushing himself out of the deep chair. 'Yes, Ma'am.'

'Relax, Alek.' She waved him back to sitting. 'And call me Tanya, remember.'

Mike and Shane stood and introduced themselves.

'Yes, I know who you are.' Tanya tapped her Intelligence Corps cap badge before shaking hands with them. 'How is your ankle?' she said to Mike.

'Sore after all the rehabilitation, but on the mend, thanks.' Mike looked over Tanya's head towards the tea table. 'Would you like some tea?'

Tanya smiled. 'Yes, please. Easy on the milk.'

'I'll get some too,' Shane said, limping towards the tea table behind Mike.

Tanya waited until the men left before taking Mike's armchair and leaning forward. 'How are you settling in here?'

'Fine, thank you,' Alek replied.

'Hmm, not too posh for you?' Tanya pointed to one of several paintings of fox hunts.

Alek shrugged. 'It's okay. Mike and Shane are all right.'

'Good.' Tanya pointed a finger at Alek. 'You're getting your medal tomorrow at 11:00 hours, so I'll pick you up at 10:30, here. Wear your number two uniform.'

'Right, thank you.' Alek slumped in his chair. He was going to miss the circuit for this medal ceremony, and then the volleyball game, and he'd been hoping to get even with the other team. 'Can I go to rehab when it's finished?'

Tanya laughed. She took the tea from Mike who looked at his occupied seat and then for a spare. 'You are keen, aren't you? I think I've made the right decision.' She sipped her tea.

Alek thought about his unworn dress uniform in his wardrobe and his brown shoes. He was going to have to spend the evening getting them ready. *This medal better be worth it. I could even wear it to the ball and impress the girls.*

Mike and Shane were talking with Tanya about the quality of new recruits, the two men sitting on the edge of their seats. Alek had not seen them so formal before. He didn't know why; they were all captains so rank wasn't the issue. The vagaries of mess etiquette were lost on Alek. There had been none of this in the college canteen. He'd hung out with his group of friends on the BTEC course, following them from class to class, down for lunch or to the tiny gym. *Where are Callum and the others now? Dead or about to die, I expect.*

Tanya stood, and the three men copied her. 'Right, I'll see you tomorrow, Alek. Goodbye, gentlemen.' She nodded at Mike and Shane.

Alek stood to attention until Tanya had left the room.

Mike collapsed into his chair. 'Thank fuck she's gone.'

'Yep,' Shane said.

'Why?' Alek said. 'She's been very helpful to me.'

Mike looked at Shane, who shrugged and said, 'Tell the kid.'

Mike leant forward. 'Be careful of what you tell anyone in the Int. Corps.'

Alek felt his throat tighten. He thought back to the conversations he'd had in the debrief at the aid station and then with Tanya. 'I don't think I've said anything bad. I just told them what happened,' he said.

Shane tapped his nose. 'It's not what you've done. It's how you might sound if you criticise the RAF for dropping you in the wrong place and then your platoon commander breaking down. They don't like anyone pointing out what a shit show the war is.'

'But Captain Maguire has been good to me. She said I could be an officer – that's why I'm here,' Alek said. 'Aren't we supposed to be on the same side?'

Mike and Shane exchanged glances. 'Be careful,' Mike said, 'that's all. If you say the wrong thing then you could get arrested – maybe your family too.'

Alek nodded. 'Okay, thanks.' He didn't want to let the older men know his parents were labelled as traitors, which might affect his chances for promotion. *I don't want to get Lena into trouble either. Lena! She's in Plymouth. I might be able to see her now that we're so close.*

The medal ceremony was held inside the Guildhall in the city centre. The grey stone building had an impressive glass door entrance that sat underneath three curved arches, linked together like waves. Alek walked in with Tanya, his neck constricted by the tie that Mike had shown him how to wear after breakfast. Alek had only worn clip-on ties at school and this was the first time wearing his smart brown 'number-two' uniform. Tanya wore a skirt and a peaked cap, her left breast was covered with four medals – not as many as some of the infantry soldiers and sailors. Alek counted eight medals on a white-bearded sailor who also had several gold bands on his sleeves.

Alek felt even more insignificant when they walked from the atrium into the Great Hall; gold chandeliers hung from the high ceiling, and half a dozen high-arched, stained-glass windows lined each wall that led to a stage. TV cameras and an array of wiring were set up between the stage and the rows of blue chairs, which were filled with service personnel. *Everyone here must have done something to help their comrades too.* Alek sat in the third row from the front, next to an airman with an artificial lower leg. He was glad to be separated from Tanya; mindful of Mike's warning, he had been monosyllabic in his conversation on the way here.

Alek had an overwhelming urge to pee but he didn't know where the toilets were and the hall was full. If he got up now he would have to walk past hundreds of people and then be late for the start of the ceremony. He clenched his fists and studied the painting above the stage. It was a montage of different people in the city: pilgrims, Sir Francis Drake, sailors and craftsmen. Alek had no idea what constituted good art. He wondered what Lena would make of the painting. *Where is she now? She might be close by. I could have invited her if I knew where she was. I'll ask Tanya if she can help me find her.*

Alek shifted his whole body to look around the audience, unable to turn his neck. He had a vague hope that Lena might be there anyway, or his parents, despite the lack of invitation. Rows of unknown faces stared back at him. This was the first time he would receive an award without a member of his family watching. No one would be there to hug him and congratulate him afterwards. He felt alone in a room of 600 people.

Alek was glad when the tedious ceremony was over. He followed a line of servicemen to the toilets, their nailed boots clattering on the tiled floor, and fumbled with the stiff fly that seemed to be designed to hamper any easy access.

'Congratulations,' Tanya said once Alek walked outside the Guildhall and into the sunshine.

'Thanks,' Alek replied. Two uniformed strangers patted him on the back. Alek stood tall and felt more pleased than he'd expected. Being recognised and being part of something bigger than himself was nice. He looked around at the medals and uniforms. *There are a lot of good men and women here. I don't understand why Mike and Shane slate the other units; we're supposed to all be on the same side.*

'Come with me,' Tanya said as the crowd dispersed.

Alek marched in step with Tanya towards a row of benches sitting underneath a line of saplings that bordered the large, paved square beside the Guildhall. He sat down after her and inspected the medal on his chest. *It's a shame Mum and Dad couldn't see this, I hope they'd be proud, even if they don't like the war.*

'Right, young Alek,' Tanya said. 'Now you've got your medal, you need to get ready for some real work.'

'Yes, Ma'am.' Alek was confused. He thought the medal was for real work.

'Part of our role in intelligence is to find out what the enemy is thinking and anticipate what they are going to do next,' Tanya said. 'Some of the information we need we gain from reports from the field, but sometimes we need to find information ourselves. Clear so far?'

'Yes Ma'am.' Alek swallowed. 'Am I being sent back to the Continent?'

Tanya pointed at Alek's cast. 'Not with that thing on. No. I'm going to get you gathering information here, in Plymouth.' She swept her arm from left to right.

'Oh,' Alek thought for a moment. 'I don't want to spy on my friends, Ma'am.'

Tanya frowned. 'Friends? Do you mean in the officers' mess?' She shook her head. 'No. I mean here. The enemy is not just on the Continent you know. Starting on Monday, I will give you a few tasks to get you trained up. We'll start simple and go from there.' She pointed at the medal. 'That is unless you want to go back to the infantry?'

'No Ma'am.' Alek was certain of that. He had seen too many injured veterans at the medal ceremony. Walking around Plymouth sounded much safer. *But what did she mean by the enemy being not just on the Continent?*

#

Alek had to visit the medical officer after Tanya dropped him off at the rehab centre. The middle-aged, portly and balding medic held Alek's arm and asked him to make a fist and then stretch his fingers.

'We can take that cast off now –' he looked over his glasses at Alek – 'and put something lighter on. They are pretty brutal in the field hospitals.'

'Thank goodness for that; it itches like a bastard.' Alek covered his mouth, adding, 'Sorry, Sir. I mean, it itches a lot.'

'That's all right, son.' Corporal Dillon will sort it out for you, she's next door. I'll sign a chit to continue the rehab. You're in the right place to get stronger.'

'Thank you, Sir.' Alek walked out into the corridor and along to an open door where he stopped at the entrance. Inside the medical room, a short woman wearing a grey uniform dress with a white cardboard nurse's hat was sorting small packets into different coloured plastic boxes.

Alek knocked on the door frame. 'Excuse me – the MO said that I could get my cast removed here. Are you Corporal Dillon?'

The nurse turned and smiled at Alek, her freckles dancing, her brown eyes glinting. 'Yes, I am. Come in.' She pointed at a chair by her desk.

'You?' What are you doing here?' Alek kept his mouth wide open. It was Sarah.

'I work here.' She rolled her eyes.

Alek reddened. 'Sorry. I mean, I saw you at the medical station on the Continent. He held up his cast. 'You put this on.'

'So I did. Take a seat.' She opened a drawer and took out a pair of medical scissors bent at the top at a right angle. She snapped them open and shut them to see if they were working. 'Right, put your arm on the rest and hold still.'

Alek did as he was told. He felt a buzz as Corporal Dillon placed her left hand on his elbow. She smelt of coconut. He watched as she cut up the cast and then peeled off one side, revealing his scrawny, blotchy arm with grey bits of skin peeling off. 'Yuck.' He tugged some skin off and it fell to the floor.

'Don't scrape that off in here,' Corporal Dillon said. 'You can do it in the sink over there.' She pointed to the metallic sink sunk into the counter.

'Sorry, Corporal.' Alek ran the water and stuck his arm under the tap. The skin fell off like scales from a fish, accumulating into a sludge in the drain. Taking the nail brush, he scrubbed more skin off until his arm was pink and shiny like a baby's. He wiped the sink around with a paper towel and cleaned the nail brush. 'All done,' he said, holding up his arm as if he had won another medal.

Corporal Dillon was looking at her notes. 'Well done for washing yourself.' She shook her head.

Alek dried off his arm. The only impression he was making was that of an idiot. 'So how come you're here now?'

Corporal Dillon looked up from her notes. 'We're on a rotation: six weeks in the field; six weeks back here; two weeks off. We see a lot of you here that we treated over there.' She smiled, adding, 'The patients smell better here.'

Ah, so she does remember me! Alek sat still while she applied a lighter fibreglass cast on his arm. She was quick and efficient, which only made her more attractive to Alek. Captain Maguire was the only other woman he'd spent time with since being press-ganged, and she was as cold as stone. Sarah was warm and friendly and her coconut scent was intoxicating. Thoughts of war and promotion went out of his head, replaced by something more primordial, like most normal nineteen-year-old men.

'All done.' Corporal Dillon patted Alek's shoulder.

'Thanks, Corporal.' Alek smiled, already thinking of an excuse for how he could get back to the med centre as soon as possible.

Chapter 20

Lena pushed her lumpy mashed potato around the plate with her fork, mopping up the runny gravy and trying to capture the last four peas. The canteen cooks had excelled themselves today: making the simplest meal bad. This never bothered Lena – her stomach welcomed any type of food – but she was distracted from the taste today. She had seen a plaster on the street sign this morning and she was worried that she had said too much to Rob. *What if he betrays me?*

Jane and Tamsin were talking about the veterans' ball.

Jane wiped some gravy from her chin. 'It's not that bad – we get to meet some fit men and have a free meal.'

'That's not the point,' Tamsin said. 'The point is that we don't have a choice.'

Jane held up a lump of potato with a black eye in it. 'Surely you want to eat something better than this for a change?' She pointed her fork at the news feed on the canteen TV. 'Look – some of those soldiers are quite handsome.'

Lena followed her gaze. A dozen servicemen and two women were lined up in front of a short, red-faced man in a brown uniform with a peaked cap and medals on his chest. A banner headline ran across the bottom of the screen:

'Medal ceremony for our heroic service personnel in Plymouth Guildhall.'

Lena remembered visiting the impressive building for a college project. They'd had to sketch a stained-glass window and then replicate the effect with plastics back at college. She put her fork down and squinted at the TV. 'Stop talking,' she said, she was reading the banner:

'Alek Wasilewski, awarded the Patriot Medal for bravery under enemy fire.'

'That's my brother.' Lena clutched Jane's arm. 'He's in Plymouth!'

The canteen went quiet and Lena felt all eyes on her as the TV reporter read out the details.

'Private Wasilewski displayed excellent marksmanship skills under fire. He shot down an enemy drone and several enemy soldiers while defending two different positions in the space of twenty-four hours. This action, in the face of overwhelming odds, helped defeat the Conts and keep the position from being overrun.'

Lena watched as Alek stepped back and gave a clumsy salute with his arm in a cast. Her baby brother looked so different: his hair was short and he was in a smart uniform. Apart from his arm, he looked unhurt.

'Ooh, a war hero,' Tamsin said.

'He does look handsome,' Jane said.

'All right, switch it off now, please.' Lena looked out of the window. She was relieved that Alek was safe but frustrated that she had missed him in person. The Guildhall was less than a mile away. *He must be stationed close by. But how can I reach him? If I'm going to escape, he can come too. We can start afresh together.*

Lena wore her coat despite the sunshine; she needed pockets to stash the food she hoped was coming from Chantelle. She scurried out of the apartment after work before Alice came back. Rob's comment about an informer in the apartment still rankled. She didn't know who to trust – including Rob. Every corner and street crossing was an opportunity to look over her shoulder, every one of the few shops that still had glass windows an opportunity to look at the reflections. No one seemed to be following her, but she knew her limitations and stayed vigilant.

Chantelle was wearing a grey hoodie with 'Pineapple' written in pink across her chest at an angle. She wore matching grey jogging bottoms and a pair of white Nike Air Force trainers. 'All right?' she said after Lena knocked on the church hall door.

'Yes, hello.' Lena closed the door.

'Were you followed? Chantelle pointed her chin at the door.

'I don't think so, but I'm not a trained spy like you,' Lena said.

Chantelle grinned. 'Good one. I'm just like James Bond, me.' She held up two fingers and blew away imaginary smoke from their tips. 'Coffee?'

'Yes, please.' Lena followed Chantelle to the kitchen and looked around the shelves for signs of a food parcel. It didn't look good; the shelves were empty.

'Here are the two names we need on your next poster.' Chantelle handed Lena a scrap of paper once the coffee grounds were brewing.

Lena looked at the names. '*Terracotta* and *Champney Flower*? They are worse than the last ones!'

'I know – all these sailing boats are for posh people. What about us workers?' Chantelle said.

Lena didn't point out Chantelle's lack of a job. She memorised the names and handed the paper back to Chantelle. 'Actually, sailing boats might go well with the motivational quote I have to use next week – it's from Wordsworth.' Lena thought of two sailing boats on a lake, pulled out of her memories of reading *Swallows and Amazons* as a young girl. She'd never been to the Lake District but had been camping at Stithians Lake in Cornwall. She could use that for inspiration.

'What's Wordsworth?' Chantelle handed Lena a mug of coffee.

'Thanks. Not what, who.' Lena smiled. 'He was a poet.' She recited the verse she had been given.

'I travelled among unknown men

In lands beyond the sea

No, England! did I know till then

What love I bore to thee.'

Chantelle snorted and a bubble of snot appeared out of her left nostril. 'Who comes up with these quotes? Thee!' She prodded Lena in the chest. 'Would thee like your coffee? Look, I'm Chantelle Wordsworth – thee rhymes with coffee.' Her earrings jangled as she laughed. 'Maybe I should write this stuff?'

Lena laughed too. Chantelle's raw love of life was refreshing. Lena could be herself; Chantelle wasn't going to inform on her, not as a member of the Resistance. 'You could be on to something – we could do real-life England instead.'

'A couple of tins of cider on a park bench.'

'Kids playing in an abandoned bus stop.'

'Graffiti in school toilets.' Chantelle prodded Lena again. 'There you go. You could put the boat names in some sort of graffiti writing.'

Lena shook her head. 'Somehow, I don't think they want us to paint reality.' She finished her coffee and put the mug in the sink. 'Chantelle,' she began – it was time for business. 'Have you got that food parcel for me?'

Chantelle slapped a hand on her forehead. 'Fuck a duck! Sorry, I forgot it.' Her forehead had a white mark on it now. 'I'll bring it next time.'

Lena groaned; she hated confrontation but she couldn't let this go. 'Tanya promised me some food. We're on low rations because we went crabbing and because Alek deserted.' She folded her arms. 'I'm not doing the next poster with these new names until I get the food.'

Chantelle moved her lips in and out and side to side like a ruminating goat. 'Hmm, I could drop it off at your apartment. How's that?'

'Yes, that would be great, thank you,' Lena said, her stomach rumbling at the mention of food again. 'When will that be?'

'The next couple of days, I expect.' Chantelle handed Lena a bag of coffee grounds. 'Trust.'

Lena said goodbye and walked home with an empty stomach. She liked Chantelle but was getting annoyed at having to chase the Christians for the food they promised. *If they can't deliver food, how can they get people out on a boat?*

\#

Lena fixed her morning coffee on Saturday, drinking it in a welcome silence in the kitchen. The other women liked to lie-in, even though none of them went out on Friday nights. The illusion of having a weekend was important. The caffeine fuelled Lena's creative urge and she decided to use the new box of pencils from Tanya. She set up in the living room, using an A4 ring binder as an angled board for her paper.

She sketched the quay from memory with the aquarium in the background. It was the closest landmark to her and she had stared across the footbridge enough times for it to be familiar. She added a woman holding a child's hand in the foreground.

Fisherman. I should add a fisherman after seeing them at the quay the other day, but where? She outlined a single lonely face silhouetted in a window overlooking the bay, watching the world go by. It was hard to put that into detail on this small piece of paper, and she hunched over with tongue stuck out to aid her concentration.

Jane walked in and perched on the sofa's arm, looking over Lena's shoulder. She yawned. 'You're up early – what are you drawing?'

'Just the quay,' Lena said.

'Am I in it?' Jane said.

'No,' Lena said. She waved her pencil at Jane. 'You're blocking my light.'

'I think I should be in it,' Jane said and stuck her nose upwards to the side. 'It will sell better and we'd be rich.'

Lena laughed.

Jane smiled and stood. 'Rich, I tell you!' She twirled around the room. 'We'll have diamonds and servants and…coffee!' She stopped and sniffed an imaginary cup. 'Hot, fresh coffee and servants to make it.'

Lena winced at the mention of coffee. She hoped that Jane was only imagining the smell.

'What would you buy?' Jane said.

Lena bit on the end of her pencil, happy to change the subject. 'Hmm. A decent shampoo and some make-up. Oh, and a box of paints with some canvas.' The things that she took for granted only a couple of years ago were now beyond her reach.

'Boring, old Lena.' Jane sat down. 'But you're right. You don't realise how much of a luxury toiletries are until you don't have them.' She rubbed her foot. 'At least we have new shoes.'

'Remember when we used to buy shoes because they looked nice?' Lena said.

'Ha, the fools that we were,' Jane replied.

They both fell silent, and Lena carried on with her sketch. She added shade to the left side of the aquarium and the figures, deciding this would be an evening scene.

'Lena,' Jane said, 'can I ask you something?'

'Sure.' Lena lowered her voice to match Jane's.

Jane leant forward. 'When do you think the war will be over?'

Lena bit her pencil. This could be a trap. Talk of the war was forbidden unless it was linked to the glorious victory. She shrugged. *Surely Jane isn't the informer? Even if she is, I can't be arrested for shrugging.*

'It's been two years now,' Jane said, 'and they said it would be over in five days.'

Lena sighed. 'I know. I can hardly remember a time before the war.'

'Me neither. I know we had no choice and all that but I'm tired of it.' Jane looked out of the window. 'I wish we would hurry up and win.'

Lena put down her pencil, the moment lost. 'Me too.' *It's not illegal to hope for victory is it?*

Jane peered at the sketch. 'That little girl – is that you?'

Lena looked at the figure. 'I hadn't thought about it, but yes, I think you're right.' She missed the times when she held her mum's hand. She felt tears well up in her eyes. Jane bent down and hugged her. Lena let the tears flow.

Once she stopped crying, Lena wiped away the tears. The little girl in the picture looked lost and lonely, just like Lena felt. *I've been painting my subconscious. I miss my mum. She would like this sketch. She got me excited about art at the TG craft fair.* Lena put down her pad, overwhelmed by a sudden desire to connect with her mum. The TG building she had seen yesterday might be it. *That will take my mind off the stupid ball tonight and stop my stomach from thinking about food.*

Lena decided to break in her new shoes with the clunky heels along the High Street. She felt taller than usual and her calves ached by the time she reached the old Derry's department store on the corner. *I'm glad I didn't wear these to work.* On either side of the street were boarded-up shop windows and doors. She stopped and looked around; there were plenty of people out at this time on Saturday morning, even if there was nothing to buy. It was hard to tell if she was being followed.

She walked down the side street and took her time scanning the TG doorway. The smooth sandstone looked old, and the two large wooden panelled doors even older, but the round brass handles seemed modern. And polished. The buildings on either side were concrete horrors of the 1970s. Lena tried the door handles but they just revolved in her hand, with no click. She took a step back and looked up at the high windows on the first floor.

Lena turned around, sure there'd be informers in the crowds. She couldn't hang about here aimlessly. She walked away from the High Street and turned left. Moving was less suspicious; walking fast, with an apparent purpose, even less so. She'd appear as if she had to be somewhere on time – busy and productive.

Lena reached the end of the road and, her curiosity unsatisfied, decided to see if she could find a back entrance to the building. She saw a narrow alley behind the line of buildings. It was empty except for a line of wheelie bins and portable skips overflowing with rubbish. Lena walked past the rubbish that smelt of urine and the acrid aroma of rotting fruit until she saw a wooden gate set into a stone wall about a head taller than she was. Lena looked back down the alley; all was quiet. Pushing the gate open, she peeked into a small courtyard that was knee-deep in weeds, nettles and brambles that overflowed from neighbouring walls. A bird table with two hanging mesh baskets stood next to a stone bird bath with a sparrow splashing in it. *It looks deserted; I'll never get inside. This was a waste of time.*

Lena closed the gate and saw two old women at the end of the alley. 'Bugger!' she said under her breath. She crouched down and peered around the line of wheelie bins.

The women were walking down the alley.

'Bugger, bugger!'

Needing to hide, Lena opened the gate again, wading quickly through the weeds of the courtyard, avoiding the nettles and thistles, towards the laminated black door. Two brown rats scuttled past her. She jumped and stifled a scream, then stomped her way forward, hoping to scare off any more wildlife that might be lurking. She looked up at the windows but nothing could be seen behind their closed curtains. The PVC door had opaque glass that prevented Lena from seeing inside. She took one last look over her shoulder before trying the handle.

To her surprise, the door opened – into a large room with a stone floor, piled with swivel-back chairs, desks stacked on top of each other and five grey filing cabinets. Two black plastic dustbins were overflowing with office detritus: flip chart paper, old computers, keyboards and calendars with Townswomen Guild logos. Lena wiped a finger across one of the desktops and left a line through the dust. *Why did I do that? What if they fingerprint it? Idiot. And if the door is open, then someone might be in here. I'm trapped!* She regretted wearing her clunky new shoes as she tried to move quietly across the room to the first of two doors set in the far wall.

The door led into a long corridor with a faded red carpet illuminated by two lights that glowed a dull orange. Three doors were set into the right-hand wall and a stone staircase faced the front entrance doors. Voices came from behind her, sending panic through her bones. She tried the first door handle and it opened into a dark room. Lena bundled inside and clicked the door shut, holding her breath. Her heart was beating hard; she was sure it could be heard outside the room.

The voices got louder, though she couldn't make out any words yet. Lena closed her eyes. She felt light-headed from holding her breath.

The voices passed and Lena could hear footsteps on the stone steps; she breathed out and counted to ten. She opened the door a crack and peered down the corridor. It was clear. Tiptoeing onto the carpet, she looked up at the ceiling. The voices that came through were a murmur and Lena still couldn't distinguish any specific words. *What is going on here?* She moved to the stairs, put a foot on the first step and gripped the bannister.

'Can I help you?'

Lena leapt and turned around, her muscles trembling. A middle-aged lady with grey streaks in her black hair stood in the doorway nearest the staircase. Wearing a flowery pinny, she held a duster in one hand and what looked like a can of furniture polish in the other.

'God, you made me jump.' Lena put her hands on her chest. The lady looked familiar.

'Sorry, dear, but this is a private building and you shouldn't be in here,' the lady said, smiling without any humour.

'Yes, I know.' Lena's chest tightened further. Trespassing was a serious offence; if she was reported she would be sent to the Recreant Camp for sure. She took a breath and decided to come clean. 'I saw the TG sign on the front door and I thought I'd come and have a look.' She shrugged, adding, 'My mum was a member.'

The lady looked Lena up and down and then towards the back of the building. 'Are you alone?'

'Yes,' Lena said.

'You said your mother was a member of TG. What happened to her?' The lady lowered the furniture polish.

'She moved to Kernow before the border closed. My brother and I were left behind.' Lena explained who was who in the family and where they had lived before the war. She hoped to gain the lady's sympathy.

The cleaning lady listened without interruption and was silent for a few breaths when Lena stopped talking. 'Well, I'm afraid there's not much to see here now,' the lady said. 'It all got closed down when the TG was banned by the Party.' She wiped the duster over the inside of the front door. 'I come every week to keep things tidy.'

Lena thought about the dust in the room at the back. Either the lady was a bad cleaner or a bad liar. 'That's a shame; my mum was a proud member.'

'What was her name?' the lady asked.

'Emma Wasilewski.' Lena saw a flash of recognition in the lady's eyes. A noise like a chair scraping came from upstairs.

'Rats,' the lady said quickly, 'they're everywhere now.'

Lena knew rats couldn't move chairs but she didn't want a confrontation.

The lady held out the duster towards the door. 'I'll see you out.'

Lena looked at the doors in the corridor as she walked past. Something was happening here, but she didn't know what. As they reached the back room, Lena remembered where she had seen the lady before.

'You go to the butcher's,' Lena said.

'Goodbye, dear,' the woman said.

Lena knew she was being fobbed off, but not why. She was sure the lady had recognised her mum's name and the rat story was ludicrous. She tiptoed away through the courtyard, stopping at the gate to take a last look at the building. *Maybe the TG is still going in secret? But why take the risk for some crafts and cakes? There must be more to them than that. If only I could ask Mum*

Chapter 21

Alek's mind was on the nurse, Sarah, during the bus journey to the veterans' ball. He had been thinking about her all day. She was about the nicest woman he had met, though from an admittedly small sample size. The officers around him were talking about the prospect of meeting available women at the ball, but Alek tuned them out. It all sounded a bit too much like a game to them. He had his sights on Sarah and was planning to sit in a corner at the ball, keeping himself to himself.

They drove through the city, the bus lurching down the hills with its gears grinding, until they got to the high walls of HMS Drake. A sailor in dress blues and a gleaming white hat opened the door to the bus. He stood to attention, eyes fixed ahead with a smart salute, as the officers filed past.

Alek nodded to the sailor, and said, 'All right,' since he wasn't an officer yet. He ran a finger around his tight collar; for the second consecutive day he was wearing his smart khaki.

Alek followed Mike and Shane, who saluted in return as two more sailors greeted them outside the entrance to the mess. It was housed in a grey-stone building topped with towers and minarets and an old clock tower at the far end. The sailors opened the large wooden doors and Alek bumped into Shane who had stopped at a table in front. Despite two overhead lamps, it was dark in the entrance. The wood panels, high ceilings and narrow windows could have been there a hundred years ago – maybe even two hundred.

A row of sticky labels was laid out on the white tablecloth next to a cluster of permanent marker pens. Another sailor was sitting behind the desk, her hair in a neat bun that poked out behind her small cap. Alek didn't realise that the navy had female sailors; he had heard they had been removed from the ships after the Party deemed it unpatriotic for women to fight in the front line. The sailor smiled and asked the officers to write their first names clearly on the label, then stick it on to their jackets. She pointed them to the hall and a row of flutes filled with sparkling wine on the end of a table. 'Take a drink, gentlemen, and go on through.'

Alek took a flute that Mike handed him. 'Here you go, young 'un.'

'Cheers.' Shane clinked Alek's glass. 'Here's to finding a suitable girl for you.'

Alek sipped his drink and then coughed as the bubbles went up his nose, making Mike and Shane laugh.

Alek wiped his nose and walked through the double doors into the ballroom. He felt uncomfortable enough in his uniform in this formal environment without being laughed at by his friends.

The ballroom had a high ceiling with two sets of windows above each other, as if the builders had forgotten to put the second storey floor in. A long banner hung between two of the windows, with the insignia of each military branch in the corner and 'Veterans' Ball' written across the middle. A dozen round tables with white tablecloths and hard-backed chairs were placed in four neat rows around the empty dance floor. Men were sitting in groups of homogenous blue, grey or khaki uniforms, their heads turning like a Wimbledon crowd watching a return of serve as a group of women entered the hall from the toilets.

A long buffet table stood under the banner and a semi-circular bar was tucked into the corner. Two women and an older man, all in black and white civilian uniforms, served drinks. A low stage was set up beside the dance floor, with two pairs of huge black speakers on either side of a turntable desk. The DJ had a goatee, thick black glasses and wore a floral short-sleeved shirt. Alek watched as he pulled a vinyl record out of its sleeve, flipped it over by the edges and placed it on the turntable before lifting the needle onto the groove.

Alek felt the bass vibrate through his feet from a dance tune that was new to him. He tapped his fingers against his thigh and realised his head was nodding too. Someone grabbed his arm and he turned to shake them off.

'I'd recognise that bad rhythm anywhere,' a woman said.

Not any woman – it was Lena.

Alek stood up, his mouth open. 'What!'

'You still can't dance, baby brother.' Lena smiled. She held her arms out and stepped forward. 'I'm so glad you're safe.'

Alek lifted up his good arm so that Lena could wrap hers around him. His ribs squeaked as he rested his chin on her hair. It smelt of soap.

'I can't breathe,' he said but still squeezed her back. His big sister was here and in his arms. It was hard to take in; there were times on the Continent when he thought they would never see each other again.

'You've grown,' she said, releasing him.

'You haven't – you're like a sparrow. What are you doing here?' Alek gestured around the room.

Feeling a tap on his shoulder, he turned and saw a blond RAF officer with a red face holding a pint glass. Another officer, taller and wider, was standing behind him.

'You're holding up our ladies,' the blond officer said.

'Yes, come on over. We've got you another drink,' the dark-haired officer said to Lena.

Alek looked at his sister, who gave a tiny shake of her head. Another woman, tall with long, straight brown hair, was now beside

148

Lena.

'I don't think so, Sir,' Alek said. 'They seem to be happy here.'

'We saw them first – they're ours,' the blond officer said, pushing his glasses up his nose.

The other officer stepped past Alek's right side and reached for Lena's elbow, but Lena twisted and the officer lost balance, spilling beer down his uniform.

'Look what you made me do,' he yelped, wiping the beer off his jacket.

'It's your fault for trying to grab me,' Lena said, linking her arm into her friend's, like two second rows preparing to scrummage.

The officer's face went red. 'What?'

Alek stepped in between them. 'They don't want to be with you, Sir.'

'Back down, soldier, or I'll put you on report.' The blond officer stepped up to Alek.

Alek took a breath, reckoning that if he could beat Hulse, he could beat this wallflower – even with one arm – but then that would mean a court martial. And the officer knew it. A change of approach was necessary. 'For what, Sir? Protecting my sister from being groped?'

The airman stepped back at the word 'sister'.

'Come on, Henry.' The dark-haired airman grabbed his colleague's arm. 'There're better-looking girls here.'

'Yes, you're right,' Henry said, 'and they're not frigid, either.'

Alek felt the iron knots in his shoulders ease as the airmen walked back to their table. He tilted his neck left and right, and ran a finger around his collar, glad that he hadn't started a fight. His dad had made him watch *Bad Day at Black Rock* one Sunday afternoon – a film where a one-armed Spencer Tracy defended himself using judo against Ernest Borgnine. But this was no movie and Alek might end up in the brig. He smiled at the memory of the wet Sunday afternoons when his dad would fall asleep in front of old movies – which seemed to always star Borgnine.

'What are you smiling about?' Lena disturbed Alek's reverie.

'Oh, nothing. Are you all right?' he said.

'Yes,' Lena replied. 'Thanks for stepping in. They bought us a drink and then thought they owned us. This is horrible.' Her hand was as light as a ladybird as she touched Alek's arm.

'I can't believe you're here!' Alek said. Lena looked so fragile compared to the last time he had seen her. 'Let's move away from this lot.' Alek pointed to a space beside the buffet table. They walked past the dance floor, where a woman with wild, curly hair was standing between two sailors, a glass in each hand. The DJ was inspecting a record and nodding to the beat, the music dampening any conversation beyond one metre. Alek looked back at the RAF table; the officers were still staring. He stood with his back to the wall so he could keep an eye on them.

'Alek, this is my friend, Jane. Jane, my brother, Alek.' Lena waved her hand back and forth.

Alek held out his left hand. 'Nice to meet you.'

Jane shook his hand, her grip warm and soft. She was taller than Lena but just as skinny, her blue eyes sparkling in the lights.

'How did you hurt your arm?' Jane said.

Alek lifted up his new cast. 'This. Oh, it's nothing serious. Just a bad sprain.'

'What are you doing here?' Lena prodded him in the sternum. 'I saw you on the news yesterday.' She pointed at the medal ribbon sewn onto his jacket.

Alek prodded Lena back in the shoulder. 'What are you doing here?'

'She's here to meet her future husband,' Jane said.

Lena elbowed her. 'Shh! Don't say that. They don't need any encouragement!' She looked around the room to see if anyone had heard. Alek followed her gaze and saw two women at a nearby table shrinking into their seats, surrounded by marines.

'But it's true – we've been brought here in order to meet veterans,' Jane said. She pointed her glass at Alek. 'You should know that; you must have been told that women would be here.'

Alek shook his head and held up his hand, 'Yes. I mean, no way. I was told this was a dance for wounded veterans and that local civilians wanted to welcome us back.' His lie covered the guilt he felt about his sister being one of the women paraded for the veterans. He looked down at his sister who was inspecting her shoes. 'What's going on?'

'Jane is right.' Lena looked up with tears in her eyes. 'They promised us more food, more clothes and our own houses if we meet someone. And we're pretty desperate. You don't know how hard it is to get by.'

Alek clenched his teeth, looking across the room. He could see it now. Groups of men hanging around the young women. The dance was just a sideshow; the men's attention lay elsewhere.

'Oh my God,' he said. 'I'm sorry. I had no idea.' He realised that he wasn't the only one who'd suffered since their parents had left. *Maybe I was too hard on her, thinking that she left me.*

'It's not all bad though.' Jane smiled at Alek. 'We might meet a handsome man and we get a decent meal.' She pointed at the buffet table, covered with a white tablecloth. The staff were laying out white plates containing dishes of barbecued chicken drumsticks, breaded goujons of unknown variety, three different types of quiche, vegetable sticks arranged in circles around small pots of pink, white and green sauces and bowls of crisps. Four cake stands held pieces of cake on three tiers, while small pastries were lined up in multi-coloured rows, glistening with glaze and syrup.

'I'm here for the scram,' Lena said. 'All I care about is when we can eat.'

'Do you want a drink first?' Alek said.

'No.' Lena pointed to the food. 'Let's get it now.'

'I think there is some type of etiquette about going first,' Alek said. 'I bet it will be an officer who has to start.'

'Well, have a word, will you? I haven't seen a feast like this since my eighteenth, and my stomach is literally eating itself right now.' Lena leant over the table.

Alek looked at the two tables of soldiers in khaki uniforms. They would be on safer territory there. One was full of officers, including Mike and Shane, the other with NCOs.

'Lena, let's go to the army table. I'll ask Mike about the food,' Alek said.

Lena looked at Jane. 'Wait – have you seen Beth? She's surrounded.'

Jane rolled her eyes. 'All right – I'll go and sit by the marines and rescue Beth.' She patted Alek on the arm, adding, 'The things I do for my country.' She smiled and Alek felt a warm glow. He grinned back and watched her walk over to the marines. *An opportunity missed.* Thoughts of Sarah had disappeared at the sight of another attractive woman. He winced as a knuckle caught him between the ribs.

'Put your tongue back in,' Lena said.

Alek snapped his mouth shut and looked at Lena. *Burnt.* 'I don't know what you're talking about.' He rubbed his ribs. He had forgotten how much of a prodder Lena was.

'Yeah, right.' Lena grinned. 'You can't lie to me, little brother. Your eyes always move.'

Alek led her between the tables and introduced her to Mike and Shane.

'Nice to meet you both.' Lena shook their hands after they stood. 'When can we eat?'

Alek nudged her. 'Sorry,' he said to his friends.

'I was thinking the same thing myself,' Mike said. 'I'm pretty sure it's whenever we want.' He looked at Shane. 'I think we're senior enough.'

Shane nodded. 'I'll get some drinks – what would you like?'

Lena asked for a lemonade and Alek the same. He felt tipsy enough after the one glass of champagne.

'Follow me,' Mike said.

Alek watched Lena pile up her plate at the buffet table. 'Are you going to climb that or eat it?'

Lena balanced a cocktail sausage on top of a piece of quiche.

151

'Ha, ha.'

Alek watched her navigate the oncoming rush of women as if she was in the school egg-and-spoon race. He grabbed half the amount of food that Lena had and followed her back to the table. He was used to eating fast but was a laggard compared to Lena. When he looked around all the women seemed to be devouring huge plates of food. *They must be starving. No wonder they are all so skinny.* He glanced at the ravished buffet table and the untidy plates of food remnants.

Lena licked her fingers, wiped the corner of her mouth with a napkin and eyed Alek's unfinished plate. He pulled it closer to him. 'Hands off.'

Lena stifled a burp with her palm. 'Excuse me.'

'Are things that bad?' Alek pulled his chair closer to Lena.

Lena leant forward. 'Worse. But not as bad as you've had it.' She patted his cast.

Alek shrugged. 'I'm okay. But everyone in my platoon is dead.'

'What about Callum? Did he join the army with you?' Lena said.

Alek chewed his lip. 'I don't know. He was put in a different platoon from me.' Alek checked that no one was close enough to hear over the music, except Lena, before he recounted his experiences. He started from being press-ganged to being sent to fight and then returning home, listing the people who had died, starting with Swales.

Lena sniffed and wiped away a tear. 'Have you got a tissue?' She hugged Alek and he held on to his sister, feeling her heart beating against his chest. Tears pricked his eyes and his throat swelled. He had not been held like this since his parents had left.

'You poor boy. What would Mum say about this?' Lena said.

Alek sat back. 'She wouldn't say anything; they abandoned us for a bloody house.' Resentment about being left alone came uncorked. He took a sip of lemonade.

Lena was shaking her head. 'Oh, Alek, don't say that. They weren't to know that the border would close and they couldn't get back.'

Alek shrugged, 'Maybe, but then why did they take the cats? They must have known something. But, it's done now, so why bother thinking about it?' He put his hand on Lena's. 'I am glad to see you, even if you are annoying.' Thoughts of home had helped him during his escape on the Continent, but now he was a war hero and potential officer, he couldn't afford to be so soft.

A ghost of a smile formed on Lena's mouth. She glanced around the table. 'I don't want to lose you, Alek. This war has done enough damage.'

'Don't worry about me. I'm safe for the next few weeks and then I should get promoted.' Alek sat up straight. 'I'm going to help defeat the Conts who killed my platoon. I'm more worried about you. I don't want you being forced into a marriage.'

'Me neither – I'd rather be artificially inseminated,' Lena said.

'Yuck,' Alek said, 'why would you think that?'

'I've heard that you can get Soc-Cred points by going to a sperm bank,' Lena said.

Alek sucked his lower lip inwards and looked around the room, feeling bile rise at the thought of his semen sample being used by Lena. He shivered. 'Promise you won't do that. Please?'

Lena sat back and folded her arms. 'Fine. I don't want a baby anyway. But I'm not marrying one of this lot.'

Alek thought about how he could look after Lena. Maybe he could set her up with one of the decent blokes, like Mike or Shane. She would be safe and well fed. Then he could concentrate on his rehab and training. It would be good to have her close by in a military house.

Alek put his arm around Lena. 'Mike and Shane are nice – how about having a dance with one of them?'

Lena pushed his arm off. 'Bloody hell, Alek, didn't you hear what I just said? Besides, I'm seeing someone else.'

'Oh, sorry, you didn't say,' Alek said, taken aback.

'You didn't ask,' Lena said.

Alek thought for a second. 'You're right, sorry.' He put his arm around her again. 'Tell me about your boyfriend,' he said, putting air quotes around the word 'boyfriend'.

Lena elbowed Alek in the ribs, smiling. 'Piss off.'

Alek laughed and listened as Lena told him about her work, her low Soc-Cred, without mentioning his desertion being one of the causes, and the need for extra food. She described Rob and how he had given her extras. She started to say something else but stopped, looking around. 'Not here, Alek. Not now.' She stood and held her hand out. 'Come on, let's dance. I don't have to worry about you groping me.'

'Ugh,' Alek said. 'Okay then, but I won't be able to bust my best moves with this.' He tapped his cast. Alek followed Lena onto the dance floor, where Jane and another woman were already dancing with Mike and Shane. Alek loosened his collar as he warmed up. Within minutes he had lost himself in the music and dancing and laughter with his sister and their friends. He was glad to see his sister happy, even for a short time – but he knew he had to help her, whatever it took.

Chapter 22

Lena staggered to the table, supported by Alek, and collapsed in a chair. Three glasses of champagne were more than she had drunk in two years and, despite a full stomach and the dancing, she was feeling it. She pulled off her shoes. 'My feet are killing me.' Her ankle socks were too thin to provide adequate cushioning.

Alek sat down beside her, wafting a napkin in front of his glistening brow. 'At least you don't have to wear all this.' He waved his hand over his uniform. 'My back is sodden with sweat.'

Lena looked over at the now sparse buffet table. She wished she had a handbag to smuggle the remaining food out but she hadn't carried one for years. There was nothing to put in them. Alek had called her 'Lena the locust' after she'd finished his leftovers. It was good to have him around. She tapped his shoulder and leant forward to speak over the music. 'Hey. Where are you based, now? Can we meet up again soon?'

'I'm at the barracks at Bickleigh, about eight miles away. What about you?' Alek said.

Lena gave him her address and directions. She chewed her lip and then said, 'Eight miles? That's a long way. Can you get into town at all? I need to speak to you properly.' *He's grown up a lot in such a short time – and I can trust him more than anyone.*

Alek looked around the room before replying, 'I don't know. I might be able to get a lift from someone. I'm free tomorrow but I'll need to ask a favour. I don't know when I could get to you.'

Lena tried to come up with a solution but the champagne and loud music made thinking difficult. 'I'm free too, except for the middle of the afternoon. I'll be in the flat if you can come – try, won't you?' She squeezed his good arm.

'I'll do my best.' Alek squeezed her arm back.

Lena's endorphins from dancing and the elation at seeing Alek had dissipated by Sunday morning. Instead, her body was tense, thinking about the meeting with the dishevelled inspector tomorrow. She felt more miserable than ever. She did not want to give the inspector a veteran's name – unlike most of the other women in the apartment, who could talk about nothing else. Every conversation, look and touch by a man had been dissected and discussed by them. Alice had snagged the attention of two sailors and caused a fight, Jane had bruises on her legs and buttocks from being pinched, Beth was traumatised by the whole experience and Tamsin had met a decent marine, but was playing it cool.

Jane sat beside Lena. 'Can I give your brother's name tomorrow?'

'Yuck, no!' Lena pulled a face.

'Why not?' Jane said.

'Well, he's too young for you and he's my brother.' Lena slapped Jane's leg with her book.

Jane tapped Lena on the arm. 'I'm not asking you to date him; I'm asking if I can date him.'

Lena pulled another face. 'Why would you want to do that?'

Jane raised her eyebrows. 'Really?'

Lena made an 'O' with her mouth. 'Yuck again. That's disgusting.'

Jane laughed. 'No. What's disgusting is an old man sucking diarrhoea out of a sock.'

'Yuck.' Lena slapped Jane again. 'What's the matter with you?'

'Nothing that a decent Sunday roast wouldn't cure. Seriously though – I don't want to be paired with any of those other idiots,' Jane said.

'How can you be hungry?' Lena patted her stomach. 'I feel like a python that's eaten a goat.' She thought about the choice – or lack of choice – of men she had. Every time she pictured a man in uniform, Rob popped up in his stripy apron. The whole situation was mad. They were normalising the pairing off as if the women were choosing apples at the grocers – not being forced to date. She shuddered. She didn't want Alek to be one of the men, either. 'What about his friend, Mike? He was all right, wasn't he?'

'Well, you can have him then.' Jane prodded Lena. 'I'll have your brother.'

Lena stood. 'I'm not putting anyone's name down.' *But if I don't, I'm going to be sent to the Recreant Camp. I've got to persuade Rob.* She looked at her watch; she was due to meet him in three hours. She was fed up with the women's chattering but she had to wait around in the apartment in case Alek came. She picked up her book and went to her bedroom. Reading *The Shipping News* on a Sunday morning felt like a return to normal life pre-war.

Lena checked the street sign but doubted a plaster would be there on a Sunday. She was right. She looked up and down the street, in case Alek was arriving. *He might come later.* She eased her way over the cobbles in the Barbican, her balance worse in the new shoes, before striding out around the headland, past the deserted ice cream shop and up the tarmac slope. Although she was meeting Rob at the same place, she wanted to take a different route in case she was being followed. Lena pulled her cardigan tighter as she felt the wind come in from the sea. Rob was sitting on the bench looking the other way when she arrived.

'Hello,' Lena said as close to Rob as she could before he noticed her approach.

He jumped from the bench. 'Jesus, don't do that.' He bent down and kissed her on the cheek, his stubble scraping her skin.

Lena grinned. 'Bit jumpy aren't you?' She felt relaxed in his company. It was nice to be appreciated by a man without feeling like a cow at a market auction.

Rob stuck his hands into his jacket pockets and rolled his shoulders like a boxer stepping into the ring. He looked around to check for eavesdroppers before lowering his voice. 'There's something I need to tell you.' He held her forearm, 'But you mustn't tell anyone else.'

Lena nodded. What was he going to say?

Rob pointed to the deserted lido and held out his hand. 'Let's go over there.'

Lena held his hand, feeling the callouses on his palm. Her palm sweaty with nerves, she let go and linked her arm in his instead. They walked down the steps towards the once gleaming white pavilion, its walls now flaked and chipped with a green fungal growth creeping upwards. Two windows were broken and the main door had a plywood plank nailed over it. Lena looked down into the lido that was empty of water, laughter and play. A few leaves were caught in a vortex, circling around themselves, unable to escape the confines of the lido.

She followed Rob down another set of steps until they reached a metal railing that overlooked the rocks. Sea-spray licked their faces.

Rob checked the empty path behind them before looking at Lena. He took a breath, closed his eyes and said, 'I've been checking into what you told me about the women who asked you to help them.'

'The Christians?' Lena said. 'Why did you do that?'

Rob held Lena's hand. 'They're not Christians. Well, they may be, but that's not the point. The church hall is a cover. We think they are Russians working to undermine the Resistance rather than help it.'

Lena took her hand away and leant against the railings, the steps before her a blur. *Russians?* Her parents had told her what the Russians had done to their family and their homes in Poland in 1945. 'What are you talking about? There is no way Chantelle is Russian – she's a Janner through and through.'

Rob put his hand on Lena's shoulder. 'You might be right but she's working for the Russians. We think Tanya is a sleeper agent and is masterminding the operation.'

'What? No? She's helping people escape on the boats.' Lena gripped Rob's jacket sleeve.

Rob held up his hands. 'Look what happened to the last two boats. Think about it. Instead of helping people to escape, they're sending them to be captured or sunk.'

Lena considered what Rob was telling her. She had acted in good faith and been told the tragedy was an accident. She felt sick as she realised how wrong she had been. She leant over the railings and retched up acidic bile, spitting it into the ocean. A string of it hung down her chin and blew sideways in the breeze like a cobweb. She wiped it away and rubbed her hand clean on the wet railing.

'How do you know all this?' Lena said. 'You're just a butcher.'

'What's wrong with being a butcher? Anyway, that's not the point; I'm part of a Resistance group that is trying to overturn the Party. We think that if we can get rid of them, we can make peace with the Europeans and stop the war.' Rob paused.

Lena gripped the railings until her knuckles turned white. It was difficult to process this new information. As if life wasn't hard enough already, now her boyfriend was also a member of the Resistance. But now his lectures about the Party made sense. She shook her head. *One thing at a time.* 'I can't believe that Chantelle is a Russian agent. Have you met her?' *Chantelle is an uber-Janner but she has a decent heart.*

Rob shook his head. 'Chantelle is just a dupe who's trying to earn money to help her kids. She probably thinks the same as you do – that she's helping people escape. Now, we need you to tell us what is happening next, and when.'

'So you think I'm a dupe, do you?' Lena shoved Rob. Helping sixty people die was bad enough; being called a dupe was insufferable. Guilt fuelled her anger. 'Why didn't you tell me this sooner?' *Maybe he's been using me to get information?*

Rob put his hand on Lena's shoulder. 'It's not your fault. They are trained to manipulate people.'

Lena shirked Rob's hand off her shoulder. 'Why do they want to do that?' Lena held up her hands. 'Why are we only talking about Russians now? Why didn't you tell me this on Thursday, or before? And how do you know about Tanya?' *If this is true then that might explain why she's procrastinated on giving me extra rations. Shit! There's no way she's going to get me on a boat out of here either.*

'I had to check that you were working in good faith rather than undermining the Resistance deliberately. Tanya is a very clever woman.' Rob reached for Lena's hands but she folded her arms. 'I don't want you getting hurt, nor married off to a soldier, but we have to think of the whole country,' he said.

Lena looked out to sea. *I thought I was helping people to escape but what if I've been making things worse?* She turned to Rob, who was leaning against the iron railing watching her think. *What if Rob is lying? This whole romance thing could be a farce.*

He smiled. 'Now do you understand why you can't put my name down tomorrow? I can't let them do a detailed background check on me.'

'I suppose so,' Lena said, disenchanted by Rob's smile. 'But do you know that I have to give someone's name?' Lena said. 'My Soc-Cred is in the toilet and I need to get my rations back.' The thought of the Recreant Camp caused her to lean over the railings again and retch.

'Are you okay?' Rob said.

'Does it look like I'm okay?' Lena wiped her mouth. 'If I don't put someone's name down I could be sent to a Recreant Camp.'

'That's awful.' Rob shook his head. 'I can't bear to think of you being with anyone else.' He put his arms around Lena. 'We'll work something out.'

His smell of fridges was familiar and reassuring; she felt secure in his strong arms despite the revelations about the Russians and the Resistance. Lena held on until the waves of nausea had subsided. 'That was nice,' she said.

'I would kiss you, but you know.' Rob pointed to a string of bile on Lena's cardigan.

Lena punched him on the shoulder. 'Stop it. It's your fault I feel sick.' She wiped the bile off on the railing.

'Sorry, I know – none of this is our fault. It's the Russians and the Party and their stupid war,' Rob said. 'But hopefully, we can do something about it.'

'What do you mean?' Lena said. 'I thought I was already doing something to help. I now feel terrible that I helped send those poor people to their deaths.' *And what about the poster I'm supposed to paint tomorrow?*

Lena looked out at the sea, noticing the wind had changed and was now coming from the east. White-topped wavelets were moving across the harbour, buffeting the small boats. She stuck her hands into her cardigan pockets. At the far side of the harbour were the dark hills of Kernow and, beyond them, her parents. If what Rob said was true, then she needed an escape plan to get there with Rob and Alek, safely and soon. She was tired of only reacting to events. She wouldn't be a dupe any longer.

'Okay,' she said, 'supposing you're right, we need to warn the escapees – or the skippers – about the boats being a trap.' She prodded Rob. 'And we need to come up with a plan to get us out of here. Including my brother.'

Rob held his hands up. 'One thing at a time. We can't blow our cover. There's too much at stake.'

'Well, I'm not putting their stupid boats on any more posters,' Lena said. She wasn't having anything to do with more innocent people being sent to their deaths.

Rob put his arm around Lena. 'You'll have to keep putting the boats on the posters. Otherwise they might suspect something's wrong.'

Lena chewed her lip, feeling uneasy. The information was overwhelming. Part of her wished she'd never been approached by Tanya, nor met Rob. Jane and Alice seemed a lot happier bimbling along talking about the men they had met at the veterans' ball. She shook her head. *Stop it. You were sleepwalking into a trap of conformity. Snap out of it.*

'Tell me about the Russians – why do you think they want the war to continue?' Lena wanted to understand what was happening and why.

'The Russians were weakened after the war in Ukraine. The central European countries had diversified their fuel sources to avoid being reliant on Russian gas, which ruined the Russian economy. When the separatist movements, emboldened by Ukraine, had started to move from rhetoric to rebellion, the Russians had seen a way to weaken European unity. Funding the Eurosceptic politicians in the UK and their special interest groups was a cheap and easy way of creating a crack in European unity. Manipulating the social media algorithms to feed anti-European sentiment onto the British phones widened the crack. This method was used to help the ETA, the Basque, the Cornish, the Scottish, the Flemish and half a dozen other splinter groups.

Once England decided to go to war to defend the 'Freedom Fighters' on the Continent, the crack became a chasm. The Russians were playing a long game. They didn't want the war to end yet; they wanted resources and personnel to be exhausted. Then they could offer aid to the countries most in need. Tanya's role is to stop those English people with the tenacity and bravery to escape from linking up with those already in Kernow.' Rob's words lingered in the cold sea air.

Lena looked at the piece of skin hanging from her index finger and chewed it off. The same questions kept popping into her head. *Who can I trust? Am I letting my feelings for Rob influence me? How am I going to get out of here now?* Lena looked over at Kernow. Her mum and dad were so close but unreachable, yet she needed them more than ever.

'That's a lot to process,' she finally said. 'I need to think this through.'

Rob smiled. 'I know. Just be careful – remember that the Party will have an informer in your apartment.'

'I know that! You've told me already.' Lena pushed off the railings and ran up the flight of stairs. Tears were in her eyes. The thought of one of her flatmates betraying her was unbearable. What if it was Jane?

Rob caught up with her by the lido. 'I'm sorry, Lena. I just don't want you to get in any more trouble.'

Lena carried on up the next flight of stairs. She wanted to be alone now. Away from Rob – away from all thoughts of this stupid war and the deaths.

'I'll see you Thursday?' Rob's voice carrled on the wind.

Lena didn't answer but ran across the Hoe, racing down the steps on the other side. The movement felt good, adrenaline and anger coursing around her body, hastening her strides. She turned away from the apartment on the High Street; she couldn't face the girls right now. Past the Guildhall, where Alek had been only on Friday, past the theatre, until her chest was heaving and her ribs ached. She slowed to a walk and crossed the street, a habit to avoid being followed, although it was hard to know who was following her with so many Sunday afternoon strollers around.

She paused at the Robert Dyas shop, closed on Sundays, like all the rest. She was at a loss for where to go now. Her thin reflection stared back. *I need a plan to get out of here.* She walked past Derry's department store and looked down the street to the TG house.

Whenever her mum talked at home about the Townswomen's Guild, Lena had ignored her or told her to go away. It'd seemed like boring adult stuff at the time. She tried to remember what her mum had done in the TG. She knew that it was run by fiercely independent women who fought for equality. Its time was limited after its efforts to provide affordable housing for young women had been deemed as 'socialist' by the news sheets; a word that was synonymous with 'traitor'. Her mum had left before the TG was declared a breeding ground for insurrectionists and disbanded early in the war. *Maybe that's why she was in a hurry to leave? What are they up to now? Maybe Alek had listened to Mum and will be able to tell me more about the TG.*

'Alek! Bugger.' Lena headed home, hoping her brother would be there or on his way.

Chapter 23

Alek sat in the mess tea room on Sunday morning. He had woken early, despite his late night, and got up for breakfast before realising that it wasn't served until 08:00 on Sundays. There was no one else up so he'd found a paperback Western from the communal bookshelf and read for an hour.

Mike joined him, stretching out his long legs, a cup and saucer perched on his stomach. 'Good morning, young 'un. What's the name of your sister's friend?'

'What friend?' Alek said without looking up from his book.

'The hottie – you know the one.' Mike sipped his tea.

'I'm sorry, I can't remember – I was too busy talking to Lena,' Alek said. 'Why?'

Mike shrugged. 'I need to put down a partner to be on the list for the Easter Sunday lunch. We get roast lamb. Didn't you read the notice?'

Alek shook his head. 'You know I don't read those.' Roast lamb sounded good though. He heard laughter and looked at the three RAF officers at the other end of the lounge.

Alek thought about his confrontation last night with the RAF officer. *What would have happened to Lena if I wasn't there?* She seemed beaten down by poverty and hunger until the buffet. He had never seen her eat so much. 'Mike,' he said. 'Could I get a lift into town at some point today, please? I need to see my sister.'

'Sure,' Mike said.

Shane slumped into an armchair next to Alek. Particles of dust rose and drifted towards the window. He pointed at Alek's book. 'Are you reading my autobiography?'

'Eh?' Alek said. 'Oh, no. It's a Western.'

'I know, you idiot.' Shane rolled his eye. 'I've had the book read to me and watched the movie countless times with my dad. Why do you think I'm called Shane?'

'Really?' Alek said. 'It's a good book.' He smiled. 'Could be worse – he might have liked *Maleficent*.'

'That's after I was born, young 'un,' Shane said.

'How about *Willow*?' Mike said. 'If your dad had liked fantasy you'd have been in trouble.'

Shane laughed. The reference went over Alek's head but he smiled anyway.

Shane tapped Alek on the knee. 'Young 'un, do you think your sister would come to the Easter lunch with me?'

Alek shrugged. *If she agrees to go to the Easter lunch with Shane, then that would be another decent meal for her. There's no need for her to be so obstinate about dating a man like Shane.* 'I can ask her if you like? I'm going to see her today. Mike said he'd give me a lift.'

After breakfast, Alek walked outside the mess to help clear his thoughts. Mike had offered a lift for lunchtime and a return mid-afternoon.

'You there!'

Alek jumped at the sound of the sharp voice, the hair on his skin standing up. He turned to see an NCO marching with a pacing stick in one hand, a clipboard in the other, wearing a khaki number two uniform. His forage cap was pulled down so far over his nose that he had to tilt his head backwards to see forward.

Alek stood upright and brought his feet together. 'Yes, Sir,' he said, spotting the sergeant-major's insignia on his sleeve.

'What are you doing?' the sergeant-major said, his voice lowered to a few decibels above normal.

'I'm just going for a walk, Sir.' Alek pointed to the line of trees.

'Right, well, you can walk your way to the guard house. We're a man down due to sickness.'

'Oh, okay. I mean, yes, Sir,' Alek replied.

'What's your name and unit?' The sergeant-major pulled out his clipboard.

'Wasilewski, Sir. I was with the Fifty-First Patriot Battalion but now I'm in the rehab unit.'

The sergeant-major paused writing, looking confused. 'Which barracks are you in?'

Alek pointed down the avenue. 'The officers' mess, Sir.'

The sergeant-major looked at Alek then the barracks, then the officers' mess and finally back to Alek. 'Oh, sorry, Sir, I thought you was an enlisted man.' He tucked his clipboard under his arm with his pace stick and saluted.

Alek looked at his trainers. 'Er, I'm not an officer, Sir – not yet. I'm just staying there until I finish my rehab.'

The sergeant-major took off his forage cap and scratched his furrowed brow as he processed the information. The wrinkles eased away and he put his cap back on. 'You're not an officer?

Alek shook his head. 'No, Sir.'

'But you are enlisted?' the sergeant-major said.

Alek nodded. 'Yes, Sir.' He lifted his arm. 'That's how I got injured. On the Continent.'

The sergeant-major smiled. 'Good, then you can do the guard duty.' He looked at his watch. 'Report for duty in combats in fifteen minutes, at 09:00. Shaven.'

'But, Sir…' Alek realised what had happened – he couldn't see

Lena if he was on guard duty.

'Sharp, soldier.' The sergeant-major turned his back and marched away.

Alek yawned and rubbed his chin, feeling the slight stubble there. 'Shit!' He cursed, running to the mess.

Guard duty was a mixture of boredom, fatigue and frustration for Alek. He was put on a two-hour-on and two-hour-off rota, alternating between gatehouse duty, where he had to sign visitors in and out and check their vehicles, and patrolling the perimeter of the camp with another soldier, armed with rifles containing no ammunition.

Mike had shrugged when Alek had moaned about being collared by the sergeant-major and being unable to see Lena. 'That's the army, young 'un.'

Alek leant on the gatehouse window shelf cursing the army and everyone in it. He'd had become complacent over the last week with everything here: hot meals, a comfortable bed, a medal, fun physical training and games, meeting the nurse again – even a ball where he had spent time with Lena. *Complacent or soft?* He scratched his wrist where the cast rubbed. *Apart from this, it's as if I had never been on the Continent. So much for getting revenge for my comrades.*

Alek's daydreaming was interrupted by the next car waiting at the barrier. The driver was the blond RAF officer. 'Wake up, Private,' the officer said, emphasising the rank.

'ID, please, Sir,' Alek said. He checked the photo and handed the card back.

'I'm glad to see you're in the right place today. We don't need other ranks stinking up the mess with their uncouth habits.' The officer grinned at his passenger.

Alek's gripped his rifle tighter. He thought about smashing the butt into that grinning face. Instead, he turned to his colleague in the gatehouse. 'Okay, let them through.' He saluted as the car drove off.

He kicked the concrete curb once the car had gone. Everyone else was free to come and go and here he was stuck on guard duty. Nothing seemed to be in his control. The stupid army and its stupid rules. *I'm fed up with being bossed around. Especially by idiots like that RAF knobhead. It'll be different once I'm an officer.*

Alek felt nervous as he followed the rest of the guard to the NAAFI for lunch; he had only eaten in the officers' mess since being posted here. They entered the single-storey brick building via a covered porch that led to a set of double glass doors. Alek picked up a plastic tray and chose pie and chips with peas and gravy for his lunch that brought back memories of his recruit training. He looked around the canteen: a dozen square tables were occupied with soldiers, mostly in civilian clothes, sitting on the plastic chairs. Next to them was a bar with beer dispensers and rows of bottles on glass shelves. Two men were playing pool at a table next to a small polished square of wooden floor, a row of coloured lights above it. *A dance floor in a barracks?*

Alek chose an empty table; he was in no mood for company. He ate without tasting the food and pushed his last chip around the plate while he thought about how he was going to see Lena now.

'All right if we sit here?' Corporal Dillon plopped her tray down opposite Alek before he had a chance to answer. She was with a taller woman whose black hair was piled up on top of her head like an iced gem.

'Sure.' Alek sat upright. *Wow. Today might turn out okay after all.*

'As long as you've showered that is,' Corporal Dillon said. She nudged her friend. 'I've met him twice and he's smelt each time.'

Alek reddened. 'Yes, of course I have. But I've had a reason for smelling – either I'd just escaped from the enemy or I'd been exercising.' He was used to banter from soldiers and his BTEC classmates but it was different when a woman was doing the teasing. Especially one who wore a tight T-shirt and jeans and smelt of coconut.

'Well, you missed a part when you showered.' The tall woman tapped her chin.

Alek felt his chin and saw brown liquid on his hand. He rubbed around his face until he was sure the gravy was gone. 'Thanks,' he said, his ears reddening.

'How's the arm?' Corporal Dillon pointed a chip at Alek.

'Fine, thanks,' Alek said, adding, 'Corporal,' when he remembered. He put his knife and fork together, deciding the last chip would have to stay on his plate. It was too messy to eat in front of two women.

'Sarah,' she corrected him, grinning and making the freckles dance on her face. 'You can call me Sarah in here.' She waved another chip. 'This is Chloe.'

'Hi,' Chloe said, with a mouthful of pie. 'This pie tastes of piss.'

'I thought that too,' Alek said. 'What is it?'

'It's supposed to be steak and kidney pie.' Sarah cut off a piece of pie and nibbled it. 'What are you doing in here? I thought you were in the officers' mess?'

'I got put on guard duty and we have to come here for lunch,' Alek said.

Sarah looked around, leant forward and put the back of her hand at the side of her mouth. 'Guard on Sunday? Unlucky. Sucks to be you.'

Chloe laughed. 'Are you sure you don't mind slumming with us folk?' she joked, her vowels flattened.

Alek shifted in his seat, feeling the eyes of nearby tables on him. He was sitting with the only two women in the canteen. 'I'm not like that,' he said.

Chloe poked her fork at Alek. 'I bet you play polo or go hunting. Have you killed any foxes?'

Alek shifted in his seat again, but he kept slipping on the plastic. 'No, of course not. I'm not like those officers. Anyway, I'm not even an officer yet.' He realised he sounded defensive.

'What are you then?' Chloe said. She was blunter than a mallet, her questions more penetrating than a bullet.

'I don't know,' he said. 'I'm nothing, really. I'm supposed to be going on officer training but I can't do that until my arm's healed.' He lifted it. 'I don't even know where I'm supposed to eat – I just followed everyone here.' He pushed the chip around his plate, making a pattern in the gravy. 'All I know is that I'm stuck on guard duty all day.'

'Ah, poor Alek.' Sarah smiled. 'Welcome to the army.'

Alek frowned. 'I wish people would stop saying that to me. Anyway, you're here, but you're not working. Don't you ever go out?'

Sarah and Chloe looked at each other before Sarah said, 'We would do but there's nothing to do in town except fend off the locals. We're better off here where we can get a cheap drink.'

'Oh,' Alek said, realising he might have an opening. He could ask Sarah for a drink – but he was skint. He'd have to ask Mike what was happening with his pay. Despite her teasing, or maybe because of it, he wanted to get to know Sarah more. But not when Chloe was around.

'What time do you get off duty?' Sarah said.

'19:00, I think,' Alek said. 'Why?'

'Well...' Sarah looked at Chloe. 'We could come back here and have a drink then.' She smiled. 'As long as you shower beforehand.'

Alek shifted again. 'I'd love to but I'm skint. I haven't been paid yet.'

'Join the club,' Chloe said. 'We're supposed to get paid, but it's not money. We get credits that we can spend in approved stores like that one.' She pointed with her fork to the shop on the far side of the canteen. 'By the time they take our food and accommodation out, there's not much left. But the drinks here are cheap.'

Sarah nodded. 'We can stand you a drink or two, can't we, Chloe?'

'Sure, but he only needs one.' Chloe pointed a chip at Alek. 'He looks a bit of a lightweight.'

Alek finished his chip. 'That's nice of you. Thanks. I'll pay you back.' *Finally, something to look forward to.* He was pretty sure it wasn't his imagination; Sarah seemed to like him too.

Alek sprinted to the mess after his last shift on duty. It had dragged and dragged. He bundled out of his uniform, showered and dressed into his civvies.

Mike walked into their room and sat on his bed. 'Where are you off to, young 'un? It's too late to see your sister now; she'll be under curfew.'

Alek paused in mid-shoelace tie. 'Shit, I forgot about that. She's going to kill me.' He moved his feet. The trainers felt springy – better than the army issue ones. He checked his hair in the mirror and brushed it tidy. He could see Mike watching him. 'I'm going to meet a couple of the soldiers I was on duty with,' Alek said. .

Mike yawned, 'Well, don't stay up too late – it's a school night.'

Alek ran back to the NAAFI, slowing down when he felt a bead of sweat; he didn't want to smell again. He was surprised to see how many people were in there even though Sarah had said the Sunday-night-bop was a new tradition. He took a breath before going inside. This was his first time out with women that weren't classmates and he felt as nervous as he did before rugby matches.

Sarah was sitting beside Chloe and two other women. Alek swallowed. *Here goes.*

'Hello,' he said.

'Hello,' Sarah said. 'You've had a shower, then?' She pointed at Alek's damp hair.

'Ha ha.' Alek was glad she noticed.

Sarah patted the empty seat beside her. 'Take a load off.'

Alek sat down, relieved that she had left space for him. One beer later and he had forgotten the petty grievances of the week – even thoughts of war and promotion. Two beers later he was on the dance floor with Chloe and Sarah, bumping into them as thirty soldiers tried to squeeze into the small space. He was sweating within five minutes, but so were the women, and Sarah wasn't making any comments about him smelling. Alek enjoyed dancing much more in civvies than in his uniform at the veterans' ball. The crowd gave him an excuse to dance close to Sarah.

As the night wore on, and the squaddies drank more, Sarah suggested she and Alek leave before the fights broke out. Chloe had sidled her way over to the rest of the women, dancing in a tight circle for protection like settlers on the Oregon Trail.

Sarah led Alek by his hand to the back of the canteen. Alek hadn't kissed a girl since college, and never gone further than that. But it didn't bother him; his animal instincts took over. They kissed under the stars beside the row of wheelie bins, the stench of discarded food and refuse doing nothing to cool Alek's ardour.

Sarah stopped the kiss and put a hand on Alek's chest. 'You know that officers can't fraternise with other ranks, don't you?'

Alek grinned. 'It's a good job I'm not an officer then.' He lifted Sarah's chin with a forefinger, brushed an errant hair from her eyes with his other hand and kissed her again. *I don't care about the stupid army rules anyway.*

When they broke for air, Alek grinned again. 'When can I see you again?'

Sarah grinned back. 'What makes you think I want to see you again?'

Alek's smile disappeared and his shoulders slumped.

Sarah put her arms around his waist. 'You're like a scolded puppy.' She squeezed him closer. 'We have to be careful, that's all.'

Alek smiled. He stayed smiling all the back to the mess, as he undressed and as he fell asleep.

Chapter 24

Lena waited to be debriefed by the dishevelled inspector on Monday morning. She had chewed her hangnail down to a bloody stub while Jane and then Tamsin were out of the office. No solution had come to her during a night of fitful sleep. Alek had let her down by not coming to see her yesterday and Rob had let her down by not allowing his name to be used. It seemed she was on her own.

The inspector entered the office with a clipboard and a sense of urgency. He beckoned to Lena, who blanched, then followed him down the corridor to a small side room. She watched while he ticked a box and scrawled something on his paper. His ear hair was hanging down over his lobes.

'So, Miss Wasi... Miss Waz...' the inspector tried, giving up. 'Miss W, all the other women have given me a veteran's name, so who is your choice?

Lena knew this from the chat the night before. Jane had chosen Mike, despite asking for Alek again, Tamsin a marine and Alice was struggling to choose between the two brawling sailors. Even Beth had relented and decided she'd put down a slight RAF officer.

Lena looked around the bleak room but found no inspiration. 'I don't know,' she said. 'There's too many to choose from.' The lie came easily.

'Come on, Miss W. I need to know the name, rank and unit of a serviceman you might be interested in so that I can arrange your visit on Easter Sunday.' He pushed his glasses up. 'Hopefully, it matches up with a man who's put your name down. Otherwise, you'll have to take what's given.' He smiled. 'You get roast lamb for lunch.'

Lena's stomach grumbled at the mention of food, even though it was six days away. As there was no other way to avoid the Recreant Camp, she closed her eyes and gave Shane's name. *Thanks very much, Rob. I've still got a week to get him to change his mind.*

'Good.' The inspector wrote down the details. 'Make sure you wear a nice dress; the servicemen don't like seeing women in trousers – it reminds them of their colleagues.' He grinned, his teeth as crooked as a row of Victorian gravestones. 'I'm sure you'll agree that this is much better than the artificial insemination programme.'

Lena gripped her chair seat. She felt a wave of nausea at the thought of being inseminated against her will, visions of cold metal tubes and syringes filling her mind. She came out of the interview room wanting a shower.

Lena inspected the turnip soup, letting it trickle back into the bowl from her spoon. 'At least we ate well on Saturday,' she said to Jane before risking a mouthful. It was bland but warm enough to keep her stomach from complaining. 'How did they get so much food for the ball?'

'I don't know.' Jane looked around the canteen and then leant over her bowl. 'But I know now why we're being rationed. It's to feed the military. It has to be.'

'Shh.' Lena felt like tapping Jane on the nose with her spoon. 'You'll get us in trouble.'

Jane slurped the thin soup and shook her head. 'Well, if it means getting fed, I'm happy to marry one of them.'

'Are you serious?' Lena looked around the canteen. The women and the odd man who was too old for active service were slumped or hunched over the tables. An almost tangible pall of misery cloaked them.

'It's okay for you.' Jane jabbed her spoon at Lena. 'You've got the butcher boy to get you food. Did you put him down as your boyfriend?'

Lena gripped her spoon until her knuckles whitened. 'No, I didn't.' She thought about telling Jane why Rob was reluctant but held back. Rob's comment about the informer was still relevant even if he had let her down.

'Really? Who did you put down?' Jane said.

'Shane,' Lena sighed. 'Alek said that he was nice. It keeps them off my back for another week and out of the Recreant Camp.'

'What if Shane puts you on your back?' Jane laughed.

'Don't!' Lena said. 'We're being put aside like cattle to be bred. I may as well have a plastic tag on my ear.'

Jane frowned. 'It's not that bad. Shane's a good-looking guy.'

Lena told Jane about the inspector's insemination comment.

Jane stopped eating. 'Yuck! That's disgusting.'

'Shh.' Lena signalled for Jane to lower her voice. 'I know.' She looked around the canteen before saying, 'But think about it. He said the lunch was better than the insemination programme. That means they want us to have babies, so if we don't do it with the veterans, we'll get inseminated.'

Jane sat back in her chair. 'Shit. I thought we were just doing this to keep the veterans happy after being in the war.' She looked over to another table where Tamsin and Beth were sitting. 'Well, I'll bet they'll love that.'

Lena nodded.

'Poor Beth might prefer the artificial insemination rather than being forced to have sex with a man,' Lena said, realising there was someone in a worse position than herself. *What am I thinking? The whole situation is a mess. Why am I trying to rationalise it?*

She poked her spoon around the thin, brown soup, searching for a crouton. 'Crust,' she said aloud. Crouton was another forbidden word.

'What?' Jane said.

'Sorry, I found some crust in my soup.' Lena lifted the cube out of the bowl with her spoon.

'Well, if we get married, we can move into better accommodation and get more rations,' Jane said. 'If we marry someone high-ranking we might even get moved to the South Hams.'

'Why do you say that?' Lena said. The South Hams was rumoured to have avoided rationing because so many of the Party members had moved to Salcombe and the surrounding areas at the start of the war. When the panic about being bombed by the Continentals had proven unfounded, the wealthy evacuees had remained there.

Jane lifted some soup and let it dribble back into the bowl. 'Because the Sunday lunch is being held at the swanky Thurlestone Hotel, in the South Hams. If I'm going to have a family, I'd rather do it sooner and get the perks than wait around and starve.'

Lena ate some soup while she thought about their conversation. Her dad would be fuming that one of their favourite spots was being used by the military. Jane seemed too comfortable with the matchmaking situation. So did Alice, but she was always talking about sex, so maybe she really was happy with all of this. *Why is Jane so complicit? She's not the informer, is she?*

A new wave of distress bubbled up inside Lena. She switched the conversation to safer ground and asked what clothes Jane was going to wear on Sunday.

Lena spent the afternoon designing her Lake District poster, but she hesitated about putting the names on the boats. If Rob was right, then she could be sending more people to their deaths. If she left the names off, and Rob was wrong, then she would be stopping people from escaping. *But if I leave them off, then Tanya will get suspicious? What if Rob is wrong? Then I could get out on one of the boats!* The knot in her stomach twisted and tightened all afternoon as she kept changing her mind. She needed to speak to Alek but had no way of getting in touch with him.

When the time came to put their pencils down, Lena's shoulders felt as stiff as teak. *I need to walk.* She set off at an arm-swinging pace uphill from the office and kept going until her the arches of her feet groaned: her heeled shoes were not designed for this terrain. The tension had eased from her shoulders as she slowed down on a level street lined with terraced brick houses. She walked along until she got to a junction and looked left towards the sea. The water was flat and grey and unforgiving. Lena thought about the phrase that said the sea was a reflection of the soul – or something like that. You could find what you wanted by looking at it hard enough. She certainly felt flat and grey right now. The sun broke through the clouds and bathed the lighthouse in a warm and soft early evening light. *I wish I had my watercolours to paint it. Painting helps put things into perspective.* She smiled at her pun.

Lena took a deep breath and inhaled the sea air, thinking through what she needed to do, and in what order. *Get hold of Alek. How can I do that? I need a car to reach him – there's no way I could walk eight miles. Who's got a car? Rob's uncle has the butcher's van!* Maybe Rob would be good for something after all. *I'll go and see him now, before curfew.*

Lena strode across Armada Way where she used to sit and sketch the trees in her unhurried lunch breaks from college: where her only concerns were shooing away squirrels and pigeons from her Tesco meal deal picnic. Her sketchpad and pencils had been company enough, ignoring the hipster office workers with their pointy brown shoes and pointy beards, mismatched suits and no ties, leaning over her shoulder, dropping crumbs from their pasties like brown snowflakes onto her coat.

Now, the magnificent old trees were gone, tender saplings growing in their place. The council chief who had ordered the destruction of the trees was long gone but the memories continued to hurt. Lena scurried across the barren concrete; there was no blossom, no shade to dawdle under, no birds or butterflies and no squirrels. No hipsters, either; they were all enlisted or dead.

She walked past the Theatre Royal and the giant statue of Messenger. Lena walked around the statue, never feeling comfortable enough to walk under it in case it fell on her. Derry's department store was opposite. She remembered the TG building. *There had been something more than cleaning going on in there. Maybe one of those ladies can help me see Alek if Rob can't?*

Lena arrived at the butcher's shop red-faced and breathless. She was determined to get Rob to help her; he was good at picking fault with the Party but it was time for him to be useful. The shop was closed with its shutters down. Lena checked her watch, she had taken longer than she thought to get here. There was a black door at the side of the shop, with a round brass doorbell. Lena pressed it, hearing a chime, and shuffled from foot to foot. Two scouts walked around the corner.

Lena pressed the doorbell again, this time hearing footsteps from inside.

Rob opened the door. 'What are you doing here?' He looked over Lena's shoulder at the scouts who were watching them. 'Jesus!' He grabbed her by the wrist and pulled her closer, bending down to kiss her.

Lena's surprise melted away as she kissed him back, his stubble tickling her chin.

He let go. 'Sorry,' he whispered. 'We need to get rid of the scouts.'

Lena took a breath. Her heart was racing. The kiss was better for being unexpected. Looking around the street, she saw the two scouts walking towards them. 'We need to kiss again, quickly.' She reached up to Rob's face and pulled him closer to kiss him. She meant it this time, losing herself in the moment before pulling away.

'They're gone,' Rob said. 'Public displays of affection make people uncomfortable.' He held the door open wider. 'Come in, quick, before they come back.'

Lena followed Rob up a narrow flight of brown carpeted stairs that smelt like an old attic in the summer. They walked into a square sitting room containing a two-seater brown leather sofa, a three-bar electric grill set into a stone fireplace and a green fabric armchair with scratches on the arms. The walls were lined with a brown floral wallpaper and the thin carpet was a beige cream.

Rob drew a net curtain aside and peered out of the window. 'It's clear. What's the drama? You could get us both into trouble by coming here.'

Lena flapped her T-shirt away from her stomach to cool off her back. 'Do you live here on your own?'

'My uncle moved out a year ago to be with his girlfriend. He owns the shop below.' Rob gestured with his hand around the room. 'It's just me and Terry the cat.'

Lena struggled to believe that the mastermind of the Resistance or, at least, one of its key operatives, lived in this dingy flat. But then again, where else were people supposed to live? And it kept people from nosing around she guessed. 'I've had a shit day and I need your help. Could I have a glass of water, please?'

Rob took another look out of the window before gesturing to the sofas, 'Okay. Take a seat. Do you want a cup of tea? I have some milk.'

'Milk? Yes, please!' Lena collapsed onto the sofa and took her shoes off, rubbing her feet. She could hear Rob clattering in the kitchen. The power would be going off at curfew time for an hour.

She took the mug of tea when Rob returned. 'Thank you.' She sipped the tea and closed her eyes. *Where to start? I need him on my side before I ask the favour.*

Rob sat next to Lena. 'Okay, tell me what's happened.'

Lena recounted the morning conversations, finishing with, 'I'm not going to be married off and bred like a mare on a stud farm. If you won't put your name down then you can at least get me to Alek.

He will help me.'

Rob shook his head. 'I don't understand their rush to get you pregnant. They'll have to wait eighteen years for any baby you have to be any use. The war will be over.'

'I bloody hope so,' Lena said. 'But I'm not having a baby; I'm going to get out of here.'

Rob ignored her prompt. 'But what about your friends? They'll be having children. What are their futures? Haven't you heard? They're bringing back the eleven-plus exam. The top ten per cent will carry on with their education, the next forty per cent will go to a technical college and the bottom half will be put onto civic duties from the age of thirteen.'

Lena shook her head. 'What? That's not fair.'

'Of course it's not fair. Best hope your children aren't stupid then,' Rob laughed.

'That's not funny. Or kind. Or helpful.' Lena pushed herself off the sofa. He was making light of a bad situation. *He said 'your' children – so he's not interested at all in settling down.* She put on her shoes.

'Where are you going?' Rob said.

'I need some fresh air.' Lena gulped down the rest of her tea and looked at Rob. 'Are you coming?'

'Yes, hold on.' Rob put on his Dr Martens.

Lena walked down the stairs and outside into a brisk breeze. She folded her arms and took two breaths. *Stop getting cross about things that are out of your control.* Her mum had always told her that.

Rob put his arm around her. 'What's up?'

Lena scowled at Rob before reminding herself that she needed him. She checked that no one was in earshot before saying, 'I can't stay here any longer – I need to get away, with Alek. Can we use your uncle's van?' She shrugged in an effort to appear nonchalant. 'You can come too if you want.' She was uncertain that she wanted him after his unkind comments. He seemed too caught up in the abstract and politics of the breeding and didn't understand the human tragedy, including her own.

Rob shook his head. 'I can't leave.'

Lena grabbed his arm. 'I thought you cared about me. I guess I was wrong.'

Rob waited to reply as a young couple pushing a baby in a stroller walked past. He smiled at them. They looked back with the ghostly stare of sleep-deprived parents.

Rob carried on with a lower voice. 'That's not true; I do care about you. But I can't leave because of the Resistance.'

'Well, why won't you tell me about the Resistance and what they do?' Lena lowered her voice too. Two teenage girls were walking from the shopping centre towards them, huddled together against the wind. 'Can they help me get out?'

173

'It's all to do with compartmentalisation. If you don't know, then you can't betray us,' Rob said.

'Betray? Why would I betray you?' Lena's voice rose again. The two teenage girls stopped at the bench under the tree and looked towards Lena, one of them giggling.

'If they arrest you and interrogate you, then you will betray us if you know too much. Everyone does.' Rob stepped closer to Lena and bent down to whisper in her ear. 'We can't talk here, like this. We're drawing too much attention. Come back to my flat.'

Lena scowled again. 'I don't care. Can you help me get to Alek or not?'

Rob nodded. 'Okay. Let me speak to my uncle about getting the van. If you come round after work again, I'll let you know.'

'Fine,' Lena said. 'I'll see you tomorrow.' She looked at the teenage girls and saw an older woman standing behind them.

Rob held Lena's arm and whispered again, 'We have to divert their attention. I'm going to squeeze your bum and then you slap me and walk away. Everyone will think we're having a lovers' row.'

Lena said, 'Okay.' She felt Rob's hand on her backside and then let loose a slap that started from her feet, went through her twisting torso like a discus thrower and landed on his cheek with a loud smack.

The onlookers gasped. Rob staggered to the side, holding his cheek. 'Ow, that really hurt.'

Lena shook her stinging hand and walked past Rob. The two teenage girls smiled at her and clapped. Lena nodded and smiled back at them.

That felt better.

She strode onwards to the Royal Parade, mulling over Rob. He might realise that she meant business now. It seemed like him coming with her was out of the question until he understood what it meant to her. He was either being selfish or was too ideological. But she wasn't going to stay here in this environment being secretive, with no food and the threat of Recreant Camp hanging over her. It was escape or nothing. He could come with her if he liked but if he didn't want to commit, then that was his loss. She would take her chances with Alek. *If I can get hold of him.*

Lena stopped at the pedestrian crossing at the bottom of the parade. The city council hadn't changed the timing of the lights to match the lighter vehicle traffic and heavier pedestrian traffic, so she dutifully waited with a couple of other pedestrians for the green man.

Lena glanced at the woman who joined them at the crossing, doing a double take as she recognised her: it was the cleaning lady from the TG house.

Chapter 25

Alek grinned as he walked over to the med centre, holding his left arm after a session of his new boxercise hobby had come to an abrupt end. Staff Farquharson had shown him how to jab, hook and cross, as well as how to hit the bag hard with his wraps and gloves on. Alek had thrown a few combinations before punching the bag as best as he could with a left hook and immediately yelping. He'd made it look real enough to fool Staff Farquharson and get him sent to see Sarah, but it didn't hurt at all.

He climbed the three stairs and opened the door to the reception area. A civilian woman wearing a black cardigan, with a pair of glasses hanging from her neck, was sitting behind a sliding glass window. She took Alek's details and told him to take a seat. He sat down in the empty room and looked at the posters that exhorted him to 'stay hydrated', 'use a condom' and 'check your testicles regularly'.

The three-minute wait seemed to last an eternity. Alek's mouth was dry as he thought of what to say to Sarah.

'Private Wasi…shoe?' a scrawny, ginger-haired corporal said from the doorway, her face screwed up as she read from her clipboard.

Alek put his hand half-up, even though he was the only person in the waiting room. 'Wasilewski – that's me, Corporal.' *Where is Sarah? Isn't she working today? Maybe that's why she had those drinks last night.*

'Right, come with me then, Private.' The corporal led the disappointed Alek to the nursing room.

Alek trudged back to the gym, his ears red, dismissed in seconds by the corporal who'd established nothing was wrong with his wrist that a good dose of common sense wouldn't fix.

'Oh, and here's a bottle of "man-up" pills for you,' she'd added.

He reported back to his group and joined in with their leg exercise circuit. The lunges, squats, jumps and step-ups were not enough to tire Alek out, and he overtook some of the other participants, pushing in front of one of the RAF officers to get to a bench first. It was the same guy who'd been trying to pull Lena.

'Watch it,' the officer said.

'Move faster, Sir,' Alek said while jumping over the bench and back. He raced around the rest of the circuit and sat with his chest heaving, waiting for everyone else to finish.

When break time was called, Alek sat outside next to Mike and

Shane and sipped his water.

The RAF officers were sitting on the neighbouring picnic bench. Two had burns on their faces, one had three fingers missing from his left hand, one was in a wheelchair and the one that Alek had overtaken had no visible injuries; he'd cracked his ribs pranging his jet. Alek eavesdropped as the pilot explained the crash in detail and how he'd managed to save the plane with only one engine working. One of the burns victims followed this by talking about an incident at the aerodrome involving the wing commander and the station mascot – a black goat. The other officers laughed loudly and banged the table.

'God, they're worse than doctors,' Mike said. 'They talk about themselves non-stop and think they are the most important people on earth.'

Shane nodded. 'I don't know how they'd manage to fly a paper aeroplane, let alone a jet, they're so weedy.'

Alek stared at the RAF officers, wondering what they had so much to be happy about when they had been so grossly disfigured or injured. *Better than being dead, I s'pose?*

'What's the matter, Pongo?' the officer with the missing fingers said. He looked like he had a permanent suntan, with thick black eyebrows that merged into one.

'Nothing,' Alek said. 'I just wish you'd be a bit quieter.'

'Ah, what's the matter, Pongo? Is it time for your nap?' Monobrow said. The others laughed.

Mike laid a hand on Alek's forearm. 'Ignore them, Alek. They get their kicks from picking on the younger and weaker.'

Alek wrenched his arm away from Mike. 'I'm not fucking weaker than them.' He turned to Monobrow. 'My name's Alek, not Pongo.'

'Yeah?' said Monobrow. 'Well, wherever you soldiers go, the pong goes too.' More laughter and table banging.

Alek resisted the urge to smell his armpits. He knew he smelt okay because he had showered last night. 'That's only because we do all the work.' He pointed at Mike and Shane.

Shane tapped his water bottle on the table. 'That's enough, kid.'

One of the officers with facial burns stood and leant over Alek, pointing to his scars. 'You do all the work, do you? Just because you've got a medal, doesn't give you the right to put us down.' He tapped Alek on the shoulder. 'Stand up when an officer's talking to you.'

Alek looked at Mike and Shane. Mike nodded. There was an unwritten rule that rank was ignored in the rehab sections, and rarely mentioned in the mess. People were on first-name terms or would at least use a generic 'Sir'. But Alek realised he had gone too far. He stood and looked at his feet, feeling the eyes of the injured servicemen on him.

The officer continued, talking loud enough for his colleagues to hear. 'In the army, the officers send the men into combat. In the navy, the officers sail into combat with the men. In the RAF, the men send the officers into combat.' The servicemen laughed; it was an old joke but one that eased the tension. The officer leant closer to Alek and whispered, 'And I've got the scars to remind me of it for the rest of my life.'

Alek's face reddened; he knew the officer was right. He looked around, seeing everyone staring at him, including Mike and Shane. This was the second time this morning he had been laughed at. Shane gave a slight shake of his head.

'Sorry, Sir,' Alek mumbled. He picked up his water bottle and stormed over to the gym, heading for the punchbag. *The sooner I become an officer, the sooner I stop getting pushed around.*

Alek hovered in a dark corner of the mess lobby until the coffee room emptied. His afternoon had dragged due to a painful few hours of self-exclusion; he knew he was behaving foolishly but rage or pride or both stopped him from joining in with the banter. He dashed in to the coffee room before the catering staff cleared up.

There were two Rich Tea biscuits left on a plate and half a pot of cold, stewed tea. It was better than nothing. Alek snapped the biscuits in half and dunked them into his tiny cup, sucking the soggy remains.

Captain Maguire walked into the room wearing a pair of blue chinos, a long-sleeve grey T-shirt and a pair of blue suede casual shoes, her hair in a tight bob. She made a beeline straight for Alek who was standing up, his mouth full of biscuit.

'Ah, there you are,' she said.

Alek swallowed his biscuit to reply, 'Good afternoon, Ma'am.' She seemed smaller than before and he could smell apples and something else. *Cinnamon? She must be wearing perfume with her civvies.*

'How's the arm?' Captain Maguire pointed at the fibreglass cast.

'It's better, thank you. This is just a precaution,' Alek said. 'Ma'am, can I ask you something?'

'Yes, Alek.' She poured a cup of tea, took a sip and put it down.

'When can I start officer training?' Alek said.

Captain Maguire narrowed her eyes. 'Why do you ask?'

Alek shifted his feet. 'Well, I want to make a difference.'

Captain Maguire stared at Alek as he shuffled his feet again. 'Keen, aren't you? You need to get that arm fixed first, but I've got an important job that'll keep you busy in the meantime. Get changed into civvies and I'll explain in the car. Meet me at the front of the mess in five minutes.'

'Yes, Ma'am.' Alek looked at his tea, then at Captain Maguire, who was already by the door. *Shit.* He gave up on the tea and took the stairs two at a time, flinging open his bedroom door.

Mike was sitting at his desk, writing in a notebook. He startled and looked at Alek. 'Jesus, you made me jump.'

Alek nodded and said, 'Hello.' He switched from tracksuit to civvies, conscious of his stale sweat and a ring of salt under his armpits, but there was no time to shower.

'What's the rush, young 'un? Got a hot date?' Mike said.

'No. I'm doing an important job for Captain Maguire.' Alek tied his shoelace.

'Ah, so you're Maguire's errand boy now?' Mike smiled

'It's not an errand –' Alek tied up a lace – 'it's a mission.' He tied up the other lace.

'Ha!' Mike shook his head. 'Be careful, young 'un – you don't know what she's up to.'

'Yeah? Well, it gets me off the base,' Alek said as he moved to the doorway. He ran down the stairs before Mike could reply. *How dare he give me advice? He was siding with the RAF officers this morning and slating them the other day. They all seem to blame each other for the war going badly.*

Alek found Captain Maguire at the wheel of a black Honda Civic outside the mess. He got into the low passenger seat and buckled up. The car smelt of lemon that overpowered the perfume. It pulled away quietly and Alek realised he'd never been in an electric car before, the lack of sound strange to his ears. They drove through the security gate with a casual wave at the guards and turned towards the city centre – the same route that the bus took every morning to the rehab centre.

'So, what's the plan, Ma'am?' Alek said.

'Tanya, Alek, remember?' she said.

'Sorry, Tanya. But I'm confused about the ranks because I'm technically a private still.' The morning's confrontation with the officers still rankled.

'Yes, you are. But you have a chance to earn your promotion,' Tanya said. 'Starting this evening.'

They had reached the city outskirts. Tanya put the windows down as they slowed to thirty miles per hour. 'It pays to follow the rules, Alek. Breaking them arouses suspicion. We want to avoid that so we blend in. That's your first rule of surveillance work.'

'Yes, Ma'am,' Alek said. *So this is a surveillance mission!* He took careful notice of his surroundings as they drove past Plymouth Argyle's abandoned football ground and down the hill towards the city centre, turning left into the train station car park. Two cars with missing wheels were jacked up on bricks and an overturned shopping trolley had two fluttering plastic bags tied around its handle. *Nothing unusual here.* 'Why are we at the train station?' he said. 'Am I going on one?'

'No. This is the drop-off point. You're going to walk down the road until you get to the roundabout, cross that and walk due south along Armada Way – a footpath through the green areas – and then you'll reach the Royal Parade. Turn right there and walk until you see Derry's department store, opposite the Theatre.' Tanya paused. 'Got that so far?'

Alek repeated the instructions. He visualised himself walking along the streets and ticking off landmarks.

'Good,' Tanya said. 'Once you see Derry's, walk down the side street and take note of anything unusual about the buildings.'

'What am I looking for?' Alek said.

'We don't know. We've had a report of suspicious activity.' Tanya tapped the dashboard. 'Now, this is the important part. You're a new face, so you won't be on any of the traitors' watch-lists, and we want to keep it that way. Walk around the block and then take a break on one of the benches by the theatre. You can see the side-street from there.'

Alek nodded. 'Okay. But I still don't know what I'm looking for.' This all sounded too vague to him.

'This is just a recce, Alek. You are doing a casual walk-by. Take your time and look for anything that doesn't fit.' Tanya smiled. 'You'll be fine. You've got a good brain. Details are important. Names, times, numbers and places are our bread and butter. Intelligence work is crucial to help us win the war. It's our job to collate, analyse and interpret information gathered from different sources before presenting likely scenarios to the senior officers.'

Alek sat straighter. 'Yes, Ma'am.' It was nice to be praised. Someone thought he had some worth. After they had synchronised their watches and arranged to rendezvous in two hours, he clambered out of the low seat of the car and followed Tanya's directions at a brisk pace. When he was out of sight of the car park he broke into a jog. *If I spend ten minutes doing this surveillance, I can use the rest of the time to go and see Lena.*

Alek sat on the bench outside the Theatre Royal with his arms and legs outstretched. He noted the different buildings and shops, the statues and signs. Plymouth wasn't that different from Exeter, just a bit wider and with more space. He kept glancing across the street, not wanting to mess up his first job.

Alek watched the people walk past, with their furrowed brows and sloped shoulders, looking for anything out of place. Office-type workers were common, older people less so; they usually did their errands in the morning. The only teenagers were the guides and scouts who patrolled in pairs, and Alek. He realised that he might be conspicuous if he sat on the bench doing nothing. *I can't do my job if I'm being questioned by young zealots.*

He stood and stretched, revealing a pale stomach under his sweatshirt. His short haircut, blue jeans and trainers were the uniform of an off-duty young soldier. Hopefully, the scouts would realise that. He walked up the steps of the theatre and looked at the black and white flyers in the window advertising the bands who performed for local troops and those citizens who could get tickets. Alek tilted his head to peer into the theatre lobby and shaded his forehead with his hand. He could see a concessions desk, a bin, three benches and a flight of stairs. There was nothing unusual or exciting in there.

Alek walked back down the steps and stood behind the bench, stretching his calves; an unconscious action to ease the normal aches from his rehab. Nothing was happening in the buildings beside Derry's department store either. Alek's initial excitement was waning. There was scant activity to make a report for Tanya and there was no point walking down the side street to look at some boring buildings. It was time to see Lena.

Two guides stood beside the theatre looking at Alek. When he stopped his stretching and smiled at them, they looked at each other and then at their clipboard. Loitering was an offence that was vague enough in its description to catch many people out; non-uniformed teenagers had been punished heavily until they learned to stay inside. Or join up.

Alek walked past the guides to the pedestrian crossing, smiling at them again. They stared back with eyes as black and unblinking as two trout, following him as he crossed the road as if he were a tasty fly floating down a stream. He walked past Derry's and glanced down the side road, scanning the tall buildings that stood lifeless. A middle-aged woman wearing a blue head scarf and carrying a beige tote bag over one shoulder walked towards Alek.

That's unusual. I haven't seen anyone that age with a head scarf before.

She stopped and took off the headscarf, putting it into the tote bag before pressing back her black hair that was tied in a bun.

Alek realised that he was staring and walked towards the Robert Dyas shop. He looked in the shop window at the products on sale; the pen knives and multi-tools caught his eye. He loved how they could fit so many things into a small space. Two were on offer and he was tempted to buy one to replace the knife that was still back at their house in Exeter, but he had no cash. *I haven't got my wallet back yet.*

He saw the reflection of the woman with the tote bag walk past him, along the Royal Parade. She moved fast and left a smell of lemon in the air behind her. It reminded Alek of something but he couldn't think what. He watched her go about thirty metres before he decided to follow her on instinct, rather than having a reason, aside from the lemony itch that he wanted to scratch. *What is that smell?*

Alek lost sense of the time and forgot about Lena as he followed the woman down the parade and up the slope of the wide shopping arcade that was punctuated with items of street furniture: benches, flower pots, trees, advertising boards, a map of Plymouth and cycle railings. Alek zigzagged his way up the arcade behind the furniture like a damsel-fly moving between lily leaves on a pond. *I can put this in my report to Tanya!*

At the top of the arcade, the woman stopped in front of a shop window and straightened her hair again. Alek tied his shoelace on a bench. The woman turned right and disappeared from view. Alek jogged up the side of the arcade and stopped at the corner, kneeling and peered around it. The woman was sitting on a bench that circled a large tree, the tote bag resting on her lap. She looked over her left shoulder and then checked her watch.

Alek ducked back. *She's not doing anything. I've wasted my time when I could have gone to see Lena.* He checked his watch. *An hour until the rendezvous.* He brushed the dirt off his knee and looked around the corner one last time. The woman was looking over her shoulder. Alek followed her gaze, but saw nothing except two teenage girls who were braving the loitering laws and a young woman in earnest conversation with a tall, dark-haired man. *She looks like Lena.* The woman slapped the man and walked away in Alek's direction. *It is Lena.*

Alek was about to wave when he saw the woman in the headscarf follow Lena. *Something's not right.* Alek ducked into a shop porch and blended into the shadows, his heart racing.

Chapter 26

The green man lit up and Lena crossed with the throng of pedestrians. The cleaning lady turned right down the Royal Parade towards the Townswomen's Guild building.

Lena skipped to catch up with her, calling out, 'Excuse me.'

The cleaning lady kept walking but said, 'Don't talk – just keep your distance.'

Lena stood still, ignoring the tuts from pedestrians who had to walk around her, uncertain if she was supposed to follow the cleaning lady or avoid her. She could see she'd stopped and was looking in the window of a haberdashery.

Lena decided to follow her, keeping twenty metres behind. She crossed the Royal Parade again, and turned right onto the street with the TG building. Lena lost sight of her at every corner but guessed where she was going now: to the back of the building. The alley was empty and Lena checked over her shoulder one last time before pushing open the gate.

The cleaning lady was standing beside the bird table. 'Were you followed?' she demanded.

Lena shook her head. 'No.'

'Good. Your bust-up with your boyfriend was very loud and very public,' the cleaning lady said.

'He's not my boyfriend.' The words came out quicker than Lena had expected. She hadn't realised that she felt that way but he had made his feelings clear by refusing to leave with her.

'Hmm, well, you fooled me and that means you should have fooled the Party snoops.' The cleaning lady smiled her humourless smile. 'That's a good thing.' She held out a hand. 'I'm Wendy.'

Lena shook hands. Wendy's grip was firm and bony. 'I'm Lena.'

'I know. We've been watching you since you first met Rob,' Wendy said. Her eyes were green and piercing.

Lena realised Wendy was more intelligent than she had assumed. 'Why were you watching me? And who's "we"? The Townswomen's Guild?' Lena didn't need anyone else watching her, especially with her plan to escape.

'Yes, to your second question. As to the first...' Wendy walked past Lena and opened the courtyard gate a crack. She looked down the alley before shutting the gate. 'It's safe. What has Rob told you about the Resistance?'

Lena thought before speaking. She remembered what Rob had said about compartmentalisation. Although he had not let her put his name down, and wouldn't leave with her, she still didn't want him to get arrested. She didn't know Wendy at all. She could be working for the Party. Or the Russians, if that was still a thing.

'Well, at least you've learnt to keep a secret,' Wendy said. 'You're right not to divulge information to a stranger.'

'How do you know about Rob and me?' Lena said. There was no point denying that she knew him.

Wendy gestured inside. 'Let's have a cup of tea, shall we? There's a lot to explain.'

Lena needed to find out why Wendy was watching her – and why her relationship with Rob was deemed worthy of scrutiny by strangers – so she followed Wendy, through the storage room, into a kitchenette. She watched Wendy boil the kettle and make the tea in two green mugs.

'Here you are, love.' Wendy passed Lena a mug. 'We've confirmed that your mum was part of the TG. It took some time because communication between here and Exeter is difficult. At least, keeping it confidential is difficult.'

'But what about Rob?' Lena said. *How much else do they know about me? And why?*

'We were watching Rob because of his role in the Resistance and wanted to see how you fitted in. Let's just say that we like to keep an eye on what everyone else is doing.' Wendy sipped her tea. 'We don't want to tread on each other's toes nor blunder into something unawares.'

'So are you part of the Resistance too?' Lena said.

Wendy shook her head. 'No, love. The Resistance is run by men – it's like a giant boy's club, with a few token female agents. They've attempted active acts of sabotage, as well as trying to help people escape, but the last part hasn't been working so well in the last three months. Escapees are being captured by the navy or, worse, their boats are being sunk.'

Lena gripped her mug and took her time sipping some tea to cover her face. The steam dampened her brow. *Does she know that I was involved with that? It doesn't sound like she's aware of the Russians. Maybe Rob is wrong and it was all an accident? But then who is Tanya working for?* Lena rubbed a temple; she had come here for clarity, not more confusion.

'So what do you do then? I thought the TG was banned?' Lena said.

'It is but someone has to stay and look after the vulnerable.' Wendy patted Lena's arm. 'It's all well and good being dashing and brave and plotting escapes, but the poor children and elderly that are left behind suffer.'

'What do you mean, "plotting escapes"?' Lena said. *Does she know I want to leave or is she talking about the Posters?*

'People like your boyfriend have helped thousands of people escape – usually those who have money or resources to help them get away. People like your parents.' Wendy waved her mug at Lena.

'My parents? They left before the borders came down,' Lena said, jumping to their defence. 'They didn't escape on purpose.' *I'm not letting anyone else drag their name through the mud.*

'Yes, love, I know that's what they told you.' Wendy put her hand on Lena's arm. 'I was using them as an example of the brain and money drain. All that's left are the wealthy, members of the Party, uniformed services and a vast number of starving people in the deprived areas of the city.'

Lena nodded. This matched what Rob had said and what she had realised over the last week. She had been thinking about herself for so long that she had forgotten there might be those worse off. Everyone was hungry. At least she had a job and a place to live. For the moment.

'Why are you telling me this?' Lena said. 'Are you trying to get me to break up with Rob?'

'No, goodness, no.' Wendy held up a hand. 'We're not trying to ruin your romance. We know that you are being forced to go to the Easter Lunch with a veteran and you know where that's leading.'

Lena shivered. 'Don't remind me.' She frowned. 'But how do you know about that? I've only told Rob and my flatmates.'

Wendy smiled. 'We have our sources, love. But don't worry about that – we could help you if you like?'

'Help me?' Lena felt a tingle of hope. 'Help me escape?' she blurted out before considering any sense of confidentiality.

Wendy shook her head. 'Not escape, no. But we could help you relocate to another city and then work with us.'

Lena's shoulders sagged; it sounded like the same old shit but in a different place. Talking about her mum had made her even more desperate to see her parents. For them all to be reunited. *I need to get to Alek so we can go together.* Still, she decided it was nice to be asked and Wendy's heart was in the right place. 'I'll have a think about it.' She put her mug on the counter. 'Thanks for the tea; I need to get back before curfew.'

Wendy showed her out. 'Be careful, love and keep your chin up.'

Lena nodded.

She was nearly at the end of the alley when she saw two guides standing at the corner.

Shit. Have they seen me come from the TG? I don't want to give Wendy away.

Lena threw herself into the shadows, pressing herself against the dirty concrete wall. It was about a nine-minute walk back to her apartment if she went directly. If she ran, she might get there in five. There was no way of getting past the guides without being seen. She would have to brazen it out. She walked fast and turned right out of the alley.

'Excuse me!' a girl's voice called out.

Lena walked faster.

'Excuse me!' the voice called out again.

Lena turned right at the end of the road towards the main street and ran halfway down it before slowing to a fast walk. She looked behind, seeing the guides at the corner.

These bloody shoes. Why are the heels so clunky? My old shoes would have been better for running.

The long high street was ahead, and Lena looked left towards the direction of her apartment. Two scouts were outside the old council building, blocking the pavement. Lena crossed the road back towards Armada Way, so she could take the coastal path back home.

'Stop!' the girl guide shouted.

Lena saw the two scouts look up. She wouldn't be able to outrun them in these shoes, so she had to hide. *Where?* She ran through the saplings and turned right, then right again through a covered shopping arcade, looking for a place where she couldn't be seen. There was an ornamental garden to one side. *There!*

Lena leapt onto a wooden bench, jumped over the low brick wall and lay down in the woodchip bedding. She heard the clatter of feet, light then heavy, go past her. She waited for three breaths before looking over the wall. There was no one in sight. Pushing herself out of the dirt she clambered over the wall, running back the way she'd come onto Armada Way and then walking back to the High Street.

The light was fading; the curfew would be underway in minutes. If she got caught out after that, she would be arrested and charged. The apartment was about eight minutes' walk away, but she couldn't risk going directly with the guides and scouts running around.

Argh! I thought my day couldn't get any worse.

The only other way home was to head uphill through the shopping arcade and around Drake's Circus. *Shit.* Lena power-walked around the streets and then jogged down the hill to the back streets near their apartment. The narrow alleys were dark, the last remnants of the dusk unable to penetrate the tall buildings. Lena crept close to the brick walls, the sound of her breathing seeming as loud as the waves crashing on the rocks in the Sound.

When she saw the darkness lighten, she knew she was on her wider road. She took off her shoes and sprinted across the road as silent as a cat. Her chest heaved as she fumbled with the apartment lock.

'Lena.'

The male voice behind her caused Lena to shriek. She turned with the key between her fingers, making a fist, just as her dad had shown her for self-defence. She breathed out when she saw who the man was. 'For fuck's sake, Alek – you gave me a heart attack.'

Alek grinned. 'Sorry, sis. A bit jumpy, aren't you?'

Lena shoved his chest. 'Of course, I'm jumpy, you idiot. You don't know what I've been through.' She looked up and down the street. 'What are you doing here? It's nearly curfew.'

Alek gestured to the door. 'Can we go inside? It's unsafe to talk here.'

Lena considered it for a second; it was against the rules, but then what wasn't? Her Soc-Cred was already in the toilet. 'Okay, we can talk in the lobby.' She opened the door and let Alek go ahead. It was gloomy inside; there would be no lighting until an hour after curfew when the power came back on. Here they'd be hidden from outside eyes and ears. Lena sat on the mail desk and swung her feet underneath, Alek joining her as if they were sitting on the swings in the park near their childhood home.

Lena put her hand on Alek's tapping hand. 'It's good to see you, little brother, but what happened to you on Sunday? I needed to talk to you then.'

'I'm sorry – I've had a bad couple of days.' Alek explained about his guard duty. 'I've had to leg it here during a mission to see you before I get picked up.' He looked at his watch. 'In twenty-four minutes. How about you – what's been going on?'

'Oh, Alek, I'm in a mess.' Lena explained about the forced marriages and putting Shane's name down for the Easter lunch, so she'd avoid the Recreant Camp.

Alek shook his head. 'That doesn't sound too bad. Remember when we had lunch at the pub there? Shane's a decent man and you get to have a decent lunch at a posh hotel.'

Lena stood and kicked Alek's shin. He yelped and rubbed it.

'How could you say that? I'm your sister. I'm not being forced into a relationship with someone just to have an easy life.' Lena jabbed her finger at Alek.

Alek held up his hands. 'Okay, okay, I'm sorry.' He stood and put his hands on her shoulders. 'I'm just trying to help.' He smiled. 'Can I ask another question, please?'

Lena nodded. 'Sure, as long as it isn't about pimping me out for the Party.'

'What were you doing with that old lady in town?' Alek said.

'What old lady?' Lena folded her arms. 'Wait, were you following me?' *Bugger! I've given it away.*

Alek shook his head. 'Not initially, no. I was on my way here when I saw you with your boyfriend. What's up with that? Are you all right? Do I need to have a word with him?'

Lena patted Alek's hand. 'Thanks, but no, it's fine. That was done to fool anyone watching us.' She grinned. 'It worked, didn't it?'

Alek nodded. 'But why did you need to do that? And why did you go with that old lady?'

Lena chewed on her lower lip. Alek didn't seem to understand her desperation to escape; he was even more chipper today, as if it was all a game. She decided to tell him what had happened with Tanya and Rob. He needed to understand how serious it all was.

She finished with, 'I'm responsible for the deaths of sixty people.' Her eyes were hot and prickly with tears.

'Wow,' Alek said. 'And I thought you were just leading a boring civvie life.'

'You use that word as an insult,' Lena said. 'The army is brainwashing you.'

'No they're not,' Alek said. 'I'm sorry – I'm trying to understand what is happening.' He laid his hand on her arm. 'You weren't this rebellious before – what's changed? How do you know that this man, Rob, is telling the truth?'

'About what?' Lena said.

'About anything? I'm just thinking that all of this talk of the Resistance and Russians and escape is dangerous. It's also betraying our country. It's hard enough fighting the Conts without having people at home undermine what we do.'

'Our country?' Lena said, tilting her head to one side and raising one eyebrow. 'Our country? Wake up, Alek. Mum and Dad have gone; our grandparents are dead. It's me and you left, and they're trying to get you killed and turn me into a baby-making machine.' She rested her hand on his chest and spoke in a softer voice. 'We need a plan, Alek. I've got to get out of here. We can go together. You don't want to be sent back to the Continent, do you? You might not come back from another battle.'

Alek blinked. He put an arm around Lena. 'I'm sorry; it must be hard for you. But don't worry about me – I'm out of danger.' He lifted his cast. 'At least while this is still on.'

Lena wiped a tear away. 'I don't want to leave without you. Your army training must be of some use – surely if you can escape from the Continentals, you can escape from a few girl guides?'

Alek laughed, 'Well, if you put it that way.'

Lena wrapped her arm around him and put her head on his chest. It felt good to be together again, even if Alek seemed to be unconcerned about what the army was doing to him. She let go. 'Rob's looking to get us some transportation – a van – and then we can go tomorrow.'

Alek shook his head. 'Rob? Is he in on this?' He checked his watch. 'Shit, my pick-up is in nine minutes. I've got to report back.'

'Report back?' Lena said. 'What do you mean?'

'Nothing,' Alek said. 'It's just a phrase.' He stood from the table and straightened his jeans.

Lena's brow wrinkled. 'Hmm. We need to work out a way of getting you tomorrow. Are you allowed visitors?'

Alek laughed. 'Don't be daft. It's not Butlins – it's an army base. You have no idea.' He looked at his watch again and stepped towards the door. 'Don't do anything hasty.'

Lena stood, uncertain about what to do the next day. Getting Rob's van might be a one-off event and Alek was being elusive. 'Listen, I'll try to get to your barracks tomorrow night. Is there somewhere we can meet?'

Alek looked out of the door window and then back at Lena. 'Fine, there's a lay-by about seventy-five metres south of the entrance. What time?'

Lena took a guess. 'Nine o'clock?' It was after curfew but darkness was necessary to escape. The roads would be quiet and getting out of Plymouth was easier by vehicle than foot. If she could persuade Rob and if he could get the van.

'Okay.' Alek opened the door. 'But don't let Rob make you do anything stupid. We can talk it through tomorrow. Bye.'

'Bye,' she replied, watching him go. Lena walked up the stairs thinking she had the beginnings of an escape plan. But it was dependent on two other people. *If we could all escape together, we'd have a new life in Kernow – much better than what we have here. How can I persuade them both?* The question whirled in her mind, and Lena was still thinking about it when she fell asleep.

Chapter 27

Alek ran the mile to Union Street in less than six minutes, gaining the attention of two scouts and a guide en route who tailed him. He saw Tanya's car parked in the parking zone outside a row of abandoned shops and sprinted to the passenger side. He was breathing hard and sweating in his jeans when he opened the door, the scouts and guide just a few metres away.

'I've got trouble,' he gasped, wiping the sweat off his forehead with the back of his sleeve.

The scouts and guide stopped beside Alek, breathing even harder than he was. One of them waved his clipboard at Alek.

Tanya stepped out of the car. 'This man is with me.' She held up an ID card. 'He's on official army business.'

Alek leant with his hands on his knees and sucked in the cool air, gulping it down like a goldfish out of its bowl. He hadn't thought about showing his ID in his haste.

The scout with the clipboard walked over to Tanya to look at the ID. 'Sorry, Ma'am,' he said. 'We thought he was a dissident, running through the city centre like that.'

Tanya smiled at the scout. 'Well done for being vigilant. You've all done a good job. Keep it up.'

The scout straightened and walked back to his peers. Tanya kept smiling until the enthusiastic youths reached the Royal Parade. She turned to Alek. 'Get in.'

Alek did as he was told. They drove back in silence with the windows down. The cool breeze dried Alek's sweat and he shivered as they went along the smaller roads, passing through grey concrete housing estates, past clusters of brick houses and into the countryside, marked with stone farm buildings. He was thinking of Lena spouting careless treacherous talk, after traitors had persuaded her to act recklessly. *She's lost the plot.* He had only seen Rob once but he didn't like him. Shane was a much better man and Lena would be better off with him, even if she didn't know it yet. She might be his older sister, but he needed to protect her. He would have words with Rob tomorrow night if they did come to the barracks.

Tanya slowed the silent car to a halt at the guard hut of the barracks. She showed her ID to the soldier and Alek did the same. The soldier saluted and waved them through.

Alek glanced at the NAAFI as they drove past. *I wonder if Sarah is in there?* His stomach rumbled and he realised he had only eaten two biscuits since lunch. *I'm starving.* They pulled up outside the officers' mess. It was 18:55 – five minutes until supper. Alek looked at his trainers, realising he wouldn't be able to wear them; he would have to change and take a quick shower before he could eat.

'Right, follow me,' Tanya said and walked into the mess before Alek had a chance to reply. She was short but her legs moved fast. Alek struggled to get out of the low seat; his legs had seized up after his day of exercise and then the sprint to the pick-up. His knees creaked as he bent and stretched them to loosen up before following Tanya.

'Hurry, up, Alek. We need to do the debrief now.' Tanya was holding the door open to the snooker room.

Alek squinted as his eyes adjusted to the gloom of the dark-panelled room he'd never entered before. A full-size snooker table covered with a beige cloth sheet dominated the room. Several high-back chairs were lined up on either side under portraits of moustached soldiers, wearing red jackets with bands of medals on their chest. A pair of armchairs were at the far end, next to some heavy red curtains. Tanya brushed past Alek and sat in one of the armchairs.

Alek took the chair opposite Tanya. His stomach rumbled again. *I hope this is quick. I don't want to miss supper.*

'Right, let's do this properly.' Tanya pulled out a notebook and pencil.

Alek stifled a groan and directed his thoughts to his surveillance; it was less than an hour ago but seemed like yesterday.

'So, how did it go?' Tanya smiled with her pencil poised.

'Good, thank you, Ma'am. It was nice to spend time doing something interesting.' Alek hadn't realised how much it meant until he said it. His brain had been engaged and he had some freedom to operate on his own. That was rare in the army.

'That's nice.' Tanya shook her head. 'But I meant, have you anything to report?' She tapped her pencil. 'Details, Alek. Details.'

'Oh. Yes, Ma'am. Alek thought about what he could say without getting Lena into trouble. He gave an overview of his observations and a description of the woman he'd tailed and the old building that she'd entered. He left out any mention of Lena. He was confused about was going on but he didn't want to get her into trouble.

Tanya continued writing after Alek had finished and then raised an eyebrow. 'Did you notice any markings on the building? Or did anyone else go in or out?'

Alek thought back. 'No, Ma'am.' *She seems interested in that specific building. Maybe that's why I was sent there?*

'Hmm. Why were you running when the scouts saw you? That was pretty careless,' Tanya said.

Alek shifted his weight in the armchair. 'I was late Ma'am – I didn't realise the time and when I did, I had to run back. They saw me sprinting and thought I was up to something.' That was close to the truth and therefore the best form of a lie.

Tanya looked at her notes. 'When was the last time you saw your sister?'

Alek jumped at the question from nowhere as if had touched an electric fence. This was no coincidence. *How does she know about Lena?* 'I saw her at the veterans' ball on Saturday.'

Tanya stared at Alek, one eyebrow raised.

Alek shifted again. *She knows. How does she know?* He slapped his forehead. 'Silly me, sorry. I bumped into her while doing the surveillance. I saw her walking down the high street with her boyfriend.' He grinned and shrugged, trying to keep cool.

'Boyfriend?' *Tap, tap, tap.* 'Who is this boyfriend?'

Alek felt the temperature drop as if a cold wind had blown in from the east. *Shit. I shouldn't have told her that. If I get him into trouble then Lena could be implicated.* 'Er, I don't know who he is. She just said "boyfriend". I could find out if you like?' Alek held his breath. He needed to play it safe. He wasn't used to all this lying. Maybe Intelligence wasn't his thing, after all.

Tanya made a note. 'That sounds like a very good idea.' Her smile, if not exactly warm, was at least tepid. 'We wouldn't want your sister to be mixed up with the wrong people, would we? That could affect your chances of promotion.'

'No, Ma'am,' Alek said. *Why is she so interested in Lena? Has she been following her? Or was it Rob? Shit. Lena could be in trouble.*

'Now then.' Tanya smiled her lukewarm smile. 'You have given me some good information but you also forgot about your sister and her boyfriend and were careless about running back and giving away our pick-up position. Forgetful and careless are hardly the watchwords of good Intelligence gathering.' She left the statement hanging there.

Alek squirmed in the silence until he had to fill it. 'No, Ma'am. I mean, yes, Ma'am.' *I thought she was on my side. God help the enemy.*

'You have to realise, Alek, that we are facing an enemy on two fronts.' Tanya pointed her pencil at him. 'The Continentals that you know about and the unpatriotic dissidents on the home front. Our work is important to help defeat both. You have some skills that can be used to help defeat the dissidents. You work well independently and have a good brain...when you remember to use it.'

Alek's mouth was dry and sweat trickled down his spine. He nodded and tried to get some saliva in his mouth before saying, 'Yes, Ma'am.' Maybe Intelligence was his thing.

Tanya smiled. 'It would be a shame to have you wasted in a futile attack on a well-defended enemy position.' Tanya stood, indicating the debrief was over.

Alek struggled out of the armchair; his legs had stiffened again. Tanya's compliment had contained an implied threat. She never wasted words. He was being given a choice: help her or be sent back to the infantry.

'You had best shower before you go and eat. You can't go into the mess like that,' Tanya said.

'I'll have missed supper,' Alek said. He was thirsty, hungry and fed up after running around Plymouth.

'You can go to the NAAFI to get something – they're open until 2000 hours,' Tanya said.

'Thanks,' Alek said. 'But I haven't got any money.' He looked at Tanya, adding, 'Still.' The least Tanya could do was to get him some food.

'Payday won't be until the end of the month,' Tanya said. 'I'll lend you five pounds. That will be enough for tonight.'

'Thanks,' Alek said.

'I'll see you again later this week,' Tanya handed him a fiver. 'I want you to stay out of trouble in the meantime.' She pointed at Alek's chest. 'No arguing with the officers. Do you understand?'

'Yes, Ma'am.' *How does she know about that?* Alek shivered as he watched Tanya walk out of the snooker room.

Alek walked up the neat pathway towards the NAAFI, thinking of what he wanted to eat and drink. A cold lemonade and something stodgy like chips or a baked potato with beans and cheese. If they were still serving hot food. It was 19:14. *Hopefully.*

Alek opened the entrance door and stepped back as two women in civvies were leaving. It was Sarah and Chloe. *Yes!* Alek was pleased he had taken a quick shower rather than just changing his clothes.

'Thanks,' Chloe said and walked past.

'Thanks,' Sarah said. 'Oh, it's you – what are you doing here?'

Alek grinned while thinking of something clever or useful to say to keep Sarah from leaving. 'I'm getting some food.' *Argh, idiot.* He hadn't had a chance to develop his flirting skills with any women, let alone one as attractive as Sarah. He couldn't exactly practise on his sister or Captain Maguire.

'Oh, I see,' Sarah said. 'Well, enjoy.' She took a step towards Chloe, who was waiting on the footpath.

'Erm, I looked for you today but you weren't at the med centre,' Alek said.

Sarah stopped and turned. 'Really? I thought your arm was feeling better?'

Alek looked at his cast and then back at Sarah. *Why is she making this difficult? I thought she liked me.* 'Yes, it is. I just wanted to say, "Hi."' He felt his ears burn.

'Ah, sounds like he missed you,' Chloe laughed.

Alek shuffled his feet; he didn't need Chloe interjecting.

Sarah smiled. 'Did you? Miss me, I mean.'

Alek looked at Chloe, the ground, the door and then at Sarah. He shrugged. 'Yeah. We had a nice time last night.'

'Go on, Sarah, don't leave him hanging, the poor boy.' Chloe waved at her friend. 'I'll see you later.' She walked up the path towards the female accommodation block.

Sarah gestured inside the NAAFI with her chin. 'Come on then. I'll keep you company while you eat.'

Alek grinned. He'd have wagged his tail if he had one. His day was going to finish on a good note after all.

'Alek, wake up,' a female voice said.

Alek stirred, brushing a hand off his ribs. 'What?' He felt the warmth of another person under the duvet.

'You need to get out of here.' A hand shook his shoulder.

Alek turned over. Waving his hand towards the noise, he felt a face. 'Sarah?'

'Yes, you idiot – who did you think it was?' Sarah gave him a prod in the stomach. 'Come on. Reveille is in fifteen minutes. You need to be out of here before anyone sees you.'

Alek stretched out and tottered over the edge of the bed, grabbing Sarah to stop him from falling out. He remembered that he was in Sarah's accommodation and that was a serious offence. She was entitled to her own room because she was a corporal. *I'll just stay here for one more minute.* He reached down and gave a good scratch under his trunks, rearranging his constricted testicles.

Sarah pushed her foot into his leg and shoved.

'Ouch.' He rolled onto the floor with a thud. His mouth was dry and his voice raspy. Standing on one leg, Alek hopped around as he put his jeans on. 'When can I see you again?'

'Later.' Sarah sat up on the bed, her long white T-shirt tucked over her knees, her hair hanging down onto her shoulders. Alek was mesmerised. *I can't believe I slept beside her.*

'You've got to go now.' She pointed at the door, softening the command with a smile.

Alek put his hand on the door handle but then remembered his manners. He skipped across to Sarah and kissed her, before saying, 'Goodbye.'

She shooed him out.

He closed the door and tiptoed down the grey corridor in his trainers. The door at the end of the corridor was locked from the inside. Alek unlocked it with a click and pulled the door with another click before slipping out to the stairwell. He was on the first floor; no female soldiers were ever accommodated on the ground floor where open windows invited trouble.

Alek heard an owl hoot as he crept outside. He crouched down beside the door to let his eyes adjust to the darkness. The clouds in the east were lightening and he could make out the silhouettes of the buildings after a minute or two. He squinted up and down the path and listened for any footsteps. *Nothing.* He decided to risk it and walked down the path, taking care to roll his feet across their edges to be silent. As his vision improved and the dawn approached, he could see the end of the path and the officers' mess. There was no one else around. He grinned as he recalled last night's dinner, conversation and then snogging before Sarah suggested they sneak into her room. That was as close to having sex as he'd been and he hoped the real thing would come soon. *As long as I don't mess it up.*

Alek was still smiling to himself when he walked into the mess for breakfast. He poured himself a coffee and sauntered over to where Shane and Mike were sitting.

'Well, looks like you're in a better mood now,' Shane said.

'What happened to you last night?' Mike said. 'You must have come in late.'

Alek chewed on a piece of toast. 'I told you, I was helping Captain Maguire.'

Mike nodded. 'Yes, the mission. How did it go?'

Alek shrugged and grabbed another piece of toast. 'Good, thanks.' He ripped the toast in half with his teeth and shoved a piece into his mouth. Food was his substitute for the sex he had been so close to experiencing for the first time. 'I was doing important work to help us defeat the dissidents.'

Mike glanced at Shane. 'Maybe Intelligence should be focusing on what the Conts are doing and helping us beat them instead of spying on civilians.'

Alek stopped chewing. 'We have to do both. We can't win the war if people are undermining it at home.' Mike and Shane were great soldiers but they didn't get the big picture like Tanya did.

Mike smiled. 'So it's "we" now, is it? Maguire's got you hooked. Listen, young 'un, the citizens get disgruntled when we lose battles and they see injured soldiers coming home. If we have better Intelligence about the Conts, we can formulate better plans and then win the battles. The public loves to cheer victories.'

Shane nodded. 'No one likes being on the losing side. Everyone loves a victory parade. Don't punish the people for being upset; think about how we can win. It's a much healthier perspective.'

Alek drank some coffee and pondered what his superiors had

said. They made good points but they also made it sound like Intelligence was not doing its job properly. They had said that about the RAF too. *None of this brings back my comrades.*

He looked around the breakfast room at the various servicemen. *We're on the same side but they bicker about each other all the time. If we're going to win, we need to work together.* He would have to explain that to Lena tonight, if she came, and get her to drop that boyfriend who was a bad influence on her. He finished his toast and coffee before picking up his horror bag.

'Hey, Shane.' Alek ran to catch up as they boarded the bus to the rehab centre. 'I saw my sister yesterday – she's put your name down for the Easter lunch.'

Shane's smile looked out of place above his square jaw. 'Thanks for letting me know.' He put his heavy hand on Alek's shoulder. 'I'll make sure to look after her.'

Alek nodded. 'Thanks.' If he could get Lena to the lunch, then she was bound to change her mind. Once she was happy, they could settle down near each other. Life would be good. All this talk of escape was futile and unnecessary. *I know. I've tried it and failed already. It's not worth the risk.*

Chapter 28

Lena walked past the church hall on Tuesday afternoon before crossing the road, looking left and right, wary of any eyes that might belong to informants. There was no one else around. She had a draft of the poster rolled up her sleeve ready to show Chantelle. The plaster on the street sign this morning had been inconvenient because she had enough on her mind but Lena wanted to keep the Christians onside to avoid any unnecessary interference with her tentative escape plans.

Not Christians – Russians according to Rob. But I hope he's wrong. She had pencilled the names of the boats and winced at the thought that it could lead to more deaths. *I still can't believe Chantelle is working for the Russians. If she is, then so am I, and what does that make me? The sooner I get out of here, the better. I can't wait any longer.*

Lena walked past two more houses and then recrossed the road back to the church hall. She didn't know who might be following her, or which side they might be on, but she was being doubly careful ahead of this evening's venture. Rob had slipped her a piece of paper when she had popped into the butcher's. Written in a neat cursive script was: '20:30: the aquarium car park'. Lena had nodded, careful not to show her excitement.

Chantelle opened the door with a, 'Where have you been?' She was wearing a pair of black leggings and a black hoodie that had the words 'Free Hugs' printed above a picture of two female wrestlers grappling.

'Sorry, I was making sure I wasn't followed.' Lena squeezed past Chantelle and into the kitchen that smelt of fresh coffee.

Chantelle stuck her head out of the door before closing it. The cafetière was ready and Chantelle poured two mugs. 'We've got two boats ready and we need to get them out.' She glanced at the clock on the wall.

Lena took her mug. 'Thanks.' She looked at the clock too. 'Are you in a rush?'

'Sort of – I have to pick up the kids in half an hour, so we need to get on with it.' Chantelle added milk and sugar to her coffee and stirred it. 'Have you got the draft?'

Lena pulled the paper out of her sleeve and gave it to Chantelle. She sipped the coffee and savoured the taste. This was worth the trip even though the caffeine would stoke the firepit of stress in her stomach.

'This is nice,' Chantelle said. 'Makes me want to visit the Lake District. I could do with a holiday.' She marked a T on one of the boats before handing back the poster. 'Once this is printed and up, we can help the next group escape.'

'Have you thought about getting out yourself?' Lena said.

Chantelle shrugged. 'Yes. But then I'd have to take the kids. What am I going to do in Cornwall?'

'Kernow,' Lena corrected automatically.

'Whatever. No one wants to employ a single mum with two kids. As long as I help out here we have enough to live on and a few extras.' Chantelle took a sip of her coffee. She brushed a loose hair behind her ear and looked out of the window.

That sounds genuine. Maybe there is a chance to escape on the boats? She reached across and touched Chantelle's arm. 'Can you ask Tanya if I can get out on one of them?' She explained to Chantelle about the arranged dates and the danger of the Recreant Camp, hoping this would gain her some sympathy.

'Oh,' Chantelle said. 'Are you sure you don't want a hunky soldier giving you some loving and getting fed?' She prodded Lena in her scrawny ribs.

'Don't you start,' Lena said. 'That's what everyone keeps telling me. What's wrong with wanting to choose the person I have a relationship with? Can you ask Tanya about the boat for me?'

'All right, I'll ask her later.' Chantelle shrugged. 'It's good to be an independent woman.'

'Thanks.' Lena rubbed Chantelle's arm. 'I'll miss you if I go.' As she spoke, she realised she meant it. Chantelle was Chantelle but she was a breath of fresh air. If you liked your air loud and turbulent. *A human tornado.* Lena smiled.

'What's funny,' Chantelle said.

'Nothing.'

'G'wan. I need a laugh.' Chantelle prodded Lena on her tiny collarbone.

Lena stepped away. 'I thought of a wrestling nickname for you: "Chantelle the Tornado". She pointed at Chantelle's hoodie. Lena's dad had been a WWE fan and made her watch the SmackDown events, celebrating the victories with chest bumps while her mum had rolled her eyes and told them to watch a real sport, like Wimbledon tennis. Her dad's response had been to strip down to his black trunks and chase her mum around the house before lifting her onto his shoulders. Except he had sprained his neck and Lena had been told to get an ice pack from the freezer.

Chantelle bit one of her fingernails. 'Hmm, not bad.' She screwed up her eyebrows. 'But if I was going to be a wrestler I'd be Chantelle the Destroyer.' She grinned. 'What would you be? Lena the Pixie? Come on...' Chantelle dropped into a crouch and rolled up her sleeves, revealing a blue tattoo of a butterfly resting on an ornate dagger. She held up her hands and moved sideways, crab-like.

Lena didn't know what to do. She backed up against the cabinets and put her mug down. Chantelle pounced and wrapped her arms around Lena's waist, picking her up. Lena felt her ribs move and her head touch a ceiling light. Chantelle let go and Lena's legs crumpled when she landed on the tiled floor.

'Whatcha scared for? I'm only joking?' Chantelle helped Lena back to standing. 'You know, I bet I'd be good at wrestling.'

Lena's heart was beating as fast as a hummingbird. She rearranged her twisted knickers through her skirt and pulled her blouse back down. 'You're not wrong,' she said after a few deep breaths.

'Let's have another coffee, shall we?' Chantelle filled Lena's mug. She feinted a grab and Lena jumped back.

Chantelle guffawed and Lena laughed with her, all thoughts of matchmaking and mating gone, along with the stress in her stomach. Chantelle had that effect on Lena.

As she walked home, Lena decided that there was no way that Chantelle was a Russian spy. Rob was either wrong about the whole thing or he was right about Chantelle being duped. *Like me. It's a shame she doesn't want to leave. Maybe I can still persuade her to come on the boat with me if we can't get out in the van?*

What the…? Lena struggled to make sense of the scene ahead of her as she turned the corner onto her road. Two police vans and two police cars were parked opposite their apartment building. Two male police officers were standing behind a line of yellow tape that was stretched across the road. Jane, Tamsin and Beth stood on the other side, their arms crossed.

Lena walked up the pavement until a police officer standing by a stop sign held up his hand. 'Hold it right there, please.' He was tall with a saggy face and flecks of grey in his moustache.

'What's happening, Officer?' Lena peered around him at her flatmates. There was no sign of Alice.

'We're doing a search,' the officer said.

'Another one?' Lena said. 'It was only searched last week.'

'How do you know that?' the officer said. 'Do you live here?'

'Erm, no. I live over there.' Lena pointed down the opposite street.

The police officer looked at his colleague – a broad guy of medium height, his head sticking out of his body armour like a tortoise looking out of its shell.

'We'd like to ask you a few questions, anyway,' the tortoise officer said as he walked over.

Lena looked at Jane, who shook her head. Tamsin was biting a nail and stood closer to Beth, who was looking at the pavement.

Lena took a step backwards and looked behind her. *This isn't good. I can't get caught here now – not when I'm so close to getting out.*

'Hold it there.' The tall officer walked around the sign and grabbed Lena's shoulder.

Lena pulled it free. 'I've got an appointment.'

The tall officer grabbed her arm and tightened his grip. 'That can wait. You need to answer our questions first.'

Lena winced as she felt his fingers dig into her skinny arms. 'Let go, you're hurting me,' she said.

'Come with me,' the tall officer said, dragging Lena towards the apartment.

'Let her go.' Jane reached for Lena's free arm. 'She's done nothing wrong.'

'Really? Then why did she try to move away?' The tortoise officer grabbed Jane's arm now too. He jerked his chin towards the top of the apartment block. 'Look up there. You're in trouble for listening to illicit broadcasts.'

Lena looked up. The only thing she could see was the metal aerial that was pointing westwards. *What's wrong with that?* She turned to the nearby buildings. *Shit.* Their aerials were pointing east or north. *At least it's not about me, it's about the radio.* She relaxed in the officer's grip as he led her and Jane towards the police van. Tamsin and Beth followed in silence, accompanied by the tall officer.

Inside the van were two rows of black leather seats, all torn and frayed. A wire grill separated the passengers, or prisoners, from the driver. Lena was hoisted up, tumbling onto the lumpy seat. She looked out over the small crowd that had gathered, their faces blank.

A scout ran up to the tall officer shouting, 'Sir, Sir, look what I've found.' He held up a black shoe held together with masking tape, pulling out a small clear plastic bag containing brown granules.

Lena groaned.

The officer opened the bag and sniffed. 'Contraband,' he said. 'Whose shoe is this?'

Lena put her hand up. There was no point denying it given the rest of the women would recognise her shoe and she didn't want them to get into extra trouble.

The officer took her name and wrote it in his notebook. 'So you do live here. I'll add wilful deception of a police officer to your charges.' He shut his notebook with a flourish. 'That's not the worst of it. You lot make me sick.' He walked away, leaving another officer standing guard outside the van.

Lena folded her arms and bent forward, feeling sick. *What else do they know? About me going to the TG? Seeing Chantelle? Or Rob? Bugger. That's tonight's plan ruined now.*

'I can't believe you had coffee and didn't share it,' Jane said.

'Yeah,' Tamsin said. 'How much of it did you use?'

'Where did you get it from?' Jane asked.

Lena held up her hands as if her palms could ward off the questions. 'I'm sorry – I didn't want to get anyone else in trouble.'

Jane and Tamsin stared at Lena until she looked away. Beth was sitting with her feet on the seat, hugging her knees, head down. Lena moved over and put her arm around Beth. 'Don't worry – I'm sure it will be okay.' Her words sounded unconvincing even to herself. They were all going to be docked Soc-Cred points for this and that meant even the Easter lunch might not be enough to save her from the Recreant Camp.

Lena looked out of the back of the van. The tortoise officer was standing with his back to them. Lena leant forward and whispered, 'We'd best get our story straight about the antennae and the radio if we've any hope of getting out of this mess.'

Jane nodded. 'Where's Alice?'

Tamsin shrugged. 'I haven't seen her – she didn't come home after work.'

Lena chewed on her lip. *That's strange. Alice is usually resting on my bed by now.*

'Anyway, the officer said that it wasn't the worst of it,' Jane reminded them. 'What else are we in trouble for?'

Lena looked at the floor.

'I haven't done anything wrong. Nor has Beth.' Tamsin pointed at her stricken friend as she looked up with red eyes.

Jane held up her hands. 'Me neither.' She looked at Lena. 'You're always late coming home now. I heard you talking to a man downstairs last night. If you brought your boyfriend back after curfew, that could be the real reason the police came here.'

Lena shook her head. 'That wasn't my boyfriend, it was my brother. And what do you think you're doing eavesdropping? Have you snitched on us?'

'N-No, I'm haven't,' Jane huffed, stumbling over her words. 'How dare you call me a grass. I'm not one of them.'

Tamsin stood between Lena and Jane and waved her hands around. 'Calm down, will you? This isn't helping.' She pointed to the tortoise officer, who was now staring at them.

'Sorry, Officer,' Jane said.

The officer turned his back.

Jane moved forward and whispered, 'Listen, none of us know what's going on. But look who's not here.' She pointed to the empty seat beside her. 'That's who's grassed us up.'

Lena glanced at the seat. *Is Alice the informer?* She closed her eyes and thought back to any conversations they'd had that might have been incriminating. Alice could have found the coffee in Lena's shoe. She would have known when Lena was coming in late. *If she's told the police this then I'm doomed.* Lena banged her head against the van's wall a couple of times. 'Bugger, bugger, bugger.'

'Here, you, stop that,' the police officer said. 'I don't want you damaging my van.' He slammed the doors shut.

Lena groaned as she heard the bolt clank. The engine started and they pulled away. Lena was jolted around the back of the van like a stray coin in a tumble drier as they drove along the cobbled streets of the Barbican. The gears crunched as they navigated a steep, narrow street, and Lena slid against the back door. It didn't take much to make her feel travel sick. She tried to think about what she'd say to the police when she got to the station.

Lena tasted acidic bile in her mouth and her stomach felt like she had eaten a dodgy hamburger. Like the one at the surf festival where she'd been surrounded by dope-smoking public schoolkids wearing their Jack Wills uniform of oversized sweatshirts and jogging bottoms. She'd been sick four times from that burger and left alone by her friends to stagger back from the hedge and clean herself up. That was the last time she'd eaten a burger from a van and the last time she'd been to a festival. *Three years ago.*

The van finally stopped and Lena righted herself. The door opened and the tall officer, with the face like a bloodhound, held out his hand to help the women down to the cobbled car park. Lena's knees were wobbling as if she had come ashore from a ship, rather than driven a mile in a van.

Why does Plymouth have so many cobbles?

She looked up at the stone building with a blue lamp outside and the word 'POLICE' written on a blue sign above the door. She felt tiny and vulnerable and petrified about what was going to happen inside.

She looked around her: five patrol cars and another van were parked nearby. A dozen officers were either walking in and out of the station or standing by the vehicles. Lena wondered if it was usually this busy; she rarely saw police out on the streets since the war had started. They had the guides and scouts to do their observation work for them and the younger, fitter officers had been drafted into the military. Her dad had told her the quality of policing was going downhill now that only those men with personal connections to help them avoid the draft were left. Her mum had disagreed because the female officers were still in the force.

She followed the tortoise officer and the other women into the station, the bloodhound-officer behind them. The foyer walls were painted sky blue and adorned with posters listing various crimes and how to report them: Encouraging homelessness, Anti-Party Hate Speech, and Being Economically Inactive. Three teenagers were sitting on a dark wooden bench seat, wearing ubiquitous black jeans, threadbare jumpers and black make-up, with multiple piercings in their ears, tongues and noses.

Their Soc-Cred scores must be awful. They're hardly the type of new citizen that the Party wants me to draw on their posters.

'Four for questioning, Sarge,' the tortoise officer said, his chin barely reaching the high desk counter.

The sergeant behind the plasti-glass screen was a middle-aged thin lady with a wizened face, her silver-blonde hair tied back into a bun. Her thin fingers flicked open a large desktop binder. 'Name, please?' she said to Jane first.

Lena watched her flatmates being escorted to various interview rooms until only she was left. Lena gave her name, knowing what was coming next. She watched in disappointment as the sergeant wrote down Lena's name without asking how to spell it. *How does she know that? Has someone told them my name? The informer!*

'Okay, interview room three.' The sergeant banged on the plasti-glass and crooked a finger at the teenagers. 'You three, over here, please.'

The goths shambled over to the desk as meekly as cows going to the shed at milking time.

Lena swallowed. As she began to follow the bloodhound officer, she heard the buzz of a walkie-talkie.

'Hold on, Pete, we've got a logjam,' the crackly voice said.

'All right, Dave, let us know when you're free,' the bloodhound officer said. He turned to Lena. 'Sit down there and don't move.' He pointed to the bench seat vacated by the teenagers.

Lena did as she was told. She chewed on a hangnail and looked around. The foyer was empty except for the teenagers talking to the exasperated desk sergeant, forcing her to repeat her questions – along with the bloodhound officer, who was now talking to a female officer.

'Fancy making me a brew, Shaz?'

'Make it yourself, you lazy git.' The female officer nudged the bloodhound officer with her elbow.

'All right then – fancy one too?' he said, walking through a side door.

'Go on then,' she replied, following him. 'I haven't had one since this morning.'

Lena rocked forward and back, clenching her hands.

The desk sergeant licked her finger and searched through a large blue binder, eyes screwed up and lips moving as she mumbled to herself.

Lena took a breath and stood. The desk sergeant carried on reading. *Can I do this? I'm never going to get a better chance.*

Lena walked towards the front door in what she thought was a casual fashion, her eyes closed as she reached for the handle. She took another breath and then stepped outside. *Look normal.* She walked down the steps and smiled at two police officers as they walked towards her. *Keep walking.* She got to the entrance of the car park and turned left. She chanced her first look back; there was no sign of anyone yet. She ran.

Chapter 29

Alek bit his biscuit and dunked the remains into his tea. The low sun warmed the mess lounge like a greenhouse and caused Alek's eyelids to droop. He looked at his watch: 16:30. *Four and a half hours to go until I'm supposed to meet Lena. I might be able to see Sarah in the NAAFI before then.*

'Watch out,' Shane said. 'Here's trouble.' He and Mike stood.

Alek looked up to see Captain Maguire in her combats and green beret. He pushed himself up. 'Ma'am.'

'Gentlemen,' she said. 'May I borrow this young man for a minute, please?'

'Of course,' Mike said, 'as long as you don't get him into trouble.' He placed a hand on Alek's shoulder as he passed and Shane nodded at him.

Captain Maguire waited until they had left earshot before sitting down in an armchair that dwarfed her tiny frame. Alek sat back down.

'I've got bad news,' she said. 'Your sister has been arrested.'

'What?' Alek said, forgetting etiquette. 'What for? Is she okay?'

Captain Maguire waved the back of her hand as if shooing a fly away. 'Yes, she is okay. She's been mixing with some bad company, which means she will miss the Easter lunch and the chance to boost her Soc-Cred points.'

'Shit,' Alek said. He looked over to where Shane was now sitting. *I know she didn't want to go to the lunch but this is too much. Why are you always causing trouble, Lena?* 'But what's she done to get arrested?'

'She's been listening to illicit radio stations in the apartment,' Captain Maguire said. 'All of the women living there have been arrested. Their Soc-Cred will be reduced.'

'Oh,' Alek said. *Is that it? That's ridiculous. Shit, she might be sent to a Recreant Camp.* He frowned, 'Is there anything I can do to help her?'

Captain Maguire nodded. 'We think her boyfriend might be the problem, leading her astray.'

Alek nodded back. 'Yes, I thought that too.'

'We need evidence against him – ideally without your sister getting into more trouble,' Captain Maguire said. 'Here's what I was thinking…'

With the curfew imminent, Alek approached the butcher's from the north. Captain Maguire had warned him not to get chased by scouts again. He was to observe the butcher's and tail Rob if he saw him. If Alek got caught watching, he had an alibi that he was coming to help Rob. Alek was wearing his civvies and as the light dropped he regretted how white his trainers were, standing out against the grim architecture of Plymouth: the pebble dash brown walls, concrete blocks and acres of grey paving slabs. He ducked into a side alley that had a good view of the butcher's, and knelt behind a grey metal bin. A red canvas blind was pulled down behind the shop window.

A stench of rotting nappies caused Alek to look for the source. He felt an ooze through his jeans and saw a dark stain on one knee. 'Shit!' He duck-walked backwards and looked around for something to wipe off the undetermined liquid. Surveillance and Intelligence seemed far from glamorous right now.

He heard a door slam and looked across the shopping centre. A woman was standing outside the door to the left of the shop. She turned, looked left and right and then walked away from Rob.

Lena! But how? She's supposed to be in police custody. Alek ran over, ignoring his damp knee, to catch her up. She looked over her shoulder as he approached, her eyes widened.

'Lena.' Alek stopped. 'What are you doing here?'

'Oh, Alek, thank goodness it's you.' Lena hugged him and then let go. 'We can't stay here – I'm on the run from the police.'

'I heard you'd been arrested!' Alek looked around at the shopping centre. 'We need to get off the street.' Two guides walked around the corner. 'Now.' He tucked his arm through Lena's. 'Pretend we're a couple – it's less suspicious.' He led her away from the guides but Lena pulled back.

'No,' she said. 'I need to head the other way.' Lena nodded her head towards the guides. 'We'll go past them.'

Alek let Lena lead him past the guides, down the shopping centre towards the sea. He recognised the wide paved avenue across the street that led to the Theatre Royal. They walked faster once they were on the Royal Parade and turned right.

'What's going on?' he said as they walked past Robert Dyas. He'd forgotten about his mission from Tanya to observe Rob, all thoughts now on his sister.

'Sorry, Alek. We're nearly there and then I'll explain.' Lena led him past a series of sandstone buildings, down a deserted alley between them.

The alley that Alek had seen her go down on Sunday. *This can't be a coincidence. Does Captain Maguire know that Lena is here? What is this place?*

'In here,' Lena said as she opened a dilapidated wooden gate that led into a courtyard.

Alek looked behind him, but there was no one there. He followed

Lena through the courtyard and inside the cool, dark building. Lena closed the door behind him and gave him another hug.

Alek felt her chest heave and heard her sob. He hugged her back. 'It's okay. I'm here.'

As his adrenaline faded, he remembered his mission. *I'm going to be in the shit with Captain Maguire for not following Rob.* He felt Lena push away. The last light was disappearing outside and he could just see Lena's outline.

'You stink of shit,' she said. 'What have you been doing?'

Alek sniffed. She was right. 'I think I knelt on an old nappy.'

'Ew,' Lena said, 'that's disgusting.'

'I know,' Alek said. 'But what on earth are you doing on the run from the police? And what is this place? Why are we here?'

Lena filled him in on her arrest and escape. She had run to Rob's, but he'd had told her to leave in case she was followed. They were going to meet up later at the van and drive to see Alek.

Alek was dumbfounded when he heard about the TG. He couldn't imagine that the boring organisation, and the tedious events that his mum had dragged him to, were part of an underground movement. *What has Lena got herself into? That explains why Captain Maguire had me watching the street. She knows about this building.* 'But why did you run? That's just making things worse!'

Lena squeezed Alek's arm. 'Haven't you been listening? What's worse than the Recreant Camp? I'm so scared of it – don't you understand? I can't go back to my apartment in case they're watching. I've got nowhere else to go. I've got to get out tonight!'

Alek thought about the problem. He had to meet Captain Maguire in an hour and he had better tell her something. He couldn't let Lena be sent to a Recreant Camp, but if she escaped then his career would be in the toilet. He kicked a table in frustration. 'Argh, it's a mess.'

'I know, but Wendy might be able to help us,' Lena said. 'Let's go and see if she's here.'

Alek followed Lena up the stairs, using the bannister to feel his way in the darkness. He needed time to think.

Lena knocked three times on a dark wooden door. It opened a crack and a soft glow of light came onto the landing. A face was visible behind.

'Alice!' Lena said. 'What are you doing here?'

'Lena? What the…?' Alice opened the door wider. 'Who is that?' She pointed at Alek.

'It's my brother, Alek,' Lena said. 'Do you remember him from the ball?'

'Jesus,' Alice said. 'What have you brought him here for? Get in here, quick.'

Alek walked into the large, musty room, where the tall windows

206

were covered by thick green curtains Several watercolours hung on the light-green walls, four high-back armchairs and two sofas were arranged around two low, heavy-looking coffee tables. A single standard lamp gave the room a cosy feel even without heating.

'Were you followed?' Alice said to Lena.

'No, at least I don't think so.' Lena looked at Alek.

'No, we weren't. I'm better at this than Lena – she didn't notice me on Sunday,' Alek said.

Lena scowled at Alek, then looked back at Alice. 'Did you know we were all arrested earlier? I managed to get out but everyone else is in a police cell. Except you.'

Alice put a hand on Lena's shoulder and gave a gentle squeeze. 'You aren't the only person whose mum was a member of the TG.'

'What?' Lena looked at Alek, who shrugged. He was still coming to terms with his mum's cosy crafts organisation being some sort of underground resistance.

'There's more to life than chasing men, you know,' Alice said.

Lena hugged Alice. 'Why didn't you tell me this before?'

'I couldn't trust you,' Alice said. 'When you told me that your mum was a member, I started to do some background digging. That's when we began to watch you.'

Alek shook his head. 'I'm confused – who is watching who? And how did the police know about your radio?' He thought for a second. *Hold on, Captain Maguire told me that Lena was arrested but not that she escaped. Something's not right.*

Lena held up a hand. 'I'm sorry, Alice. I thought you must be the informer because you weren't there when we got arrested.'

Alice smiled. 'It's okay. I walked up the street just as you were put in the police van. I hid until you left, went back to get my things and came here.'

'But who's the informer then? There must be someone for the police to know about the radio,' Lena said.

Alice shrugged. 'I think it's Beth. She's been blackmailed for being a lesbian.'

Lena closed her eyes and took a breath. 'The poor girl – no wonder she's seemed on edge.'

'Yes, it's unfortunate,' Alek said, 'but the damage is done. We need to get you out of here.' He looked at Alice. 'Can you help?'

Before Alice could answer, the door opened and in walked the middle-aged lady Alek had seen with Lena. She was carrying a cardboard box and smelled of lemon.

'What's he doing here?' the lady said.

'He's my brother, Alek,' Lena said. 'Alek, this is Wendy – she's one of the TG.'

Before Alek could answer, Wendy said, 'He shouldn't be here, Lena. He could bring us all down, even if he is your brother. We're compromised.' She put the cardboard box on a coffee table.

'I'm sorry.' Lena linked her arm through Alek's. 'But we're in this together, Wendy. We both need to get away.'

Alek remained silent; he was going to have to help Lena but he wasn't going anywhere himself. Not to mention he had to get back to be debriefed by Captain Maguire.

Wendy shook her head. 'He's in the army.' She pointed at Alek. 'He's one of them.'

Alek felt his neck redden. 'One of who? What do you mean by that?'

Lena patted his hand. 'He's not, Wendy. He's here to help me, aren't you?'

Alek looked at the three women. He didn't know what to think. *What are they doing here? Why is Captain Maguire interested in them and why didn't she tell him? Argh.* 'I don't know what you mean by "them". I just want my sister to be safe and to stay out of trouble.'

'It's too late for that, young man,' Wendy said. 'We're all in trouble if they find out we're here.'

'Can someone please tell me who "they" is?' Alek said. He was getting tenser by the minute.

Lena waved her hands up and down. 'Let's all take a breath. We should all be on the same side here.' She looked at Wendy. 'Can we have a moment together, please? I'll get him up to speed and then we can plan our escape.'

Wendy nodded. 'Five minutes. Then you have to go.' She picked up the cardboard box. 'Come on, Alice – we've got to get this stuff out of here and away.' She looked at Alek. 'And, for your sister's sake, I suggest you keep quiet about this house and us.'

Alek bristled at the command. 'Yes, I know.' He waited for Wendy and Alice to leave the room before turning to Lena. 'Who does she think she is? How many different parts of the Resistance are there? This is all a right mess.'

Lena put her hand on Alek's arm. 'I know. It's so hard to know who to trust.' She squeezed his arm. 'Except you.'

Alek looked down at his older sister. He'd never seen her look more vulnerable. She was going through a lot and it seemed too much for her to take. *She needs someone to look after her and the butcher isn't cutting it. He's leading her astray instead. She'll be much better off with Shane. Maybe there's a way to get her out of this...* 'Thanks. Now, let's confirm the details for tonight. I think I know where we can go. An old comrade of mine told me about a good place to cross. I'll guide us there if your boyfriend drives, okay?'

Lena hugged Alek. 'Yes – thanks so much. You'd best go now before Wendy gets cross, and be careful about not being followed. I've got to get a few things from the apartment before I meet Rob.'

Alek put his hands on Lena's shoulders. 'Be careful; it's after curfew now and they'll be watching.'

Alek took his time to get to the rendezvous point at the railway station, careful not to be followed or to run into any patrols. He opened the passenger door and sat down, five minutes ahead of schedule.

'You stink – get out of my car!' Captain Maguire waved a hand in front of her nose.

'Do I?' Alek said.

'Yes, get out. Now!' Captain Maguire pushed Alek's shoulder.

He almost fell onto the tarmac in his scramble to get out. 'Sorry,' he said.

Captain Maguire walked around the back of the car and stood with her arms folded. 'Have you been crawling through a sewer?'

'No, Ma'am. I knelt in something when I was observing the butcher's.' Alek looked down at the encrusted stain on his knee, surprised at how quickly he'd become accustomed to the stench.

Captain Maguire opened the car boot and pulled out a sheet of plastic. 'Here – sit on this so you don't get it on my upholstery.'

Alek took the sheet and mumbled, 'Sorry, Ma'am.'

'Get in and tell me what you saw, and remember all the details this time,' Captain Maguire said.

'Yes, Ma'am.' Alek got in the car. As they drove off Alek asked, 'Do you have any more news on my sister, Ma'am? Has she been charged?'

Captain Maguire looked in her rear-view mirror before answering, 'No, I haven't. But if you want to keep your chances of promotion, you'd better hope she isn't mixed up with the butcher.'

Alek looked out of the open window. *She either doesn't know that Lena's escaped or she's hiding something from me. Is this a test?* He decided to give Captain Maguire a null report, even if that was a disappointment, hoping she was unaware of the truth. That would give him a chance to rectify things with Lena in a couple of hours.

Alek discarded his stinky jeans, showering and changing back into his tracksuit before heading for the NAAFI to see if Sarah was there. Intelligence work was making him hungry. He had missed supper again and the soggy digestive biscuit at tea time had done little to keep his appetite at bay. The sooner he got paid, the better. He hadn't wanted to ask for another loan from Captain Maguire, which meant he'd have to wait until breakfast for his next meal.

He peered through the NAAFI windows and saw a dozen off-duty soldiers sitting around or playing pool. There was no sign of Sarah or any other of the female soldiers. Alek knew he couldn't risk going to the female accommodation. 'Argh,' he said as he walked away. 'How are we supposed to see each other if I keep getting sent on missions?' Captain Maguire and Lena were messing with his love life. *I hope Sarah isn't too annoyed. I'll have to try the med centre tomorrow and apologise. Bloody hell, Lena, I hope you appreciate what I'm doing for you.*

Alek waited until Mike had gone to the bathroom before he slipped his combat jacket over his tracksuit. Mixing uniforms was against the rules, and he could be charged if caught by an NCO, but he needed the jacket pockets. He reached into the bottom of his wardrobe and took out his one souvenir from the Continent – Lieutenant Winslow's Glock 17 – and stuck it into his jacket. He tiptoed along the corridor down the mess stairs and out into the darkness. Thoughts of food and romance had vanished as adrenaline pumped through his body. His fingers trembling, he took a breath of the cold air to calm himself.

Alek felt his way in the gloom towards the main fence. It was three metres high with a roll of barbed wire on top. He took off his combat jacket, slung it over a shoulder and climbed up the wire. The fingers in his cast arm ached, and he was afraid of falling, but he reached the top and held on with his good hand, throwing his jacket over the wire with his weak hand. The barbed wire collapsed under his weight as he lay across the roll and reached for the other side of the fence. His fingers slipped and he tumbled to the ground outside the camp, remembering to tuck and roll. His jacket was left hanging on the wire. *Shit.* He crouched and listened for any signs of alarm. *Nothing.* He shook off his hands and climbed back up to get his jacket, his muscles screaming at the top. The jacket ripped as Alek jerked it off the wire and threw it to the ground. He let go of the wire, fell and his foot slipped on the jacket, jarring his knee. *Shit.*

Alek rolled over and hobbled to the road, turning left towards the lay-by. After a minute of painful walking he could see the white outline of the van from ten metres away.

He tapped on the bonnet and the passenger door opened, the internal light revealing Lena and Rob.

'Thank God you're here, we were worried,' Lena said. 'Get in.' She pointed to the back of the van.

Alek sat on an upturned plastic crate, holding onto a strap hanging from the van's side as Rob pulled away. Lena introduced them to each other.

'All right, mate?' Rob said, to the rear-view mirror.

'Where's your stuff?' Lena asked Alek.

'I've got everything I need in my pockets.' Alek patted his combat jacket. He saw a signpost for Tavistock flash past. 'Keep heading along the road until you see signs for Morwellham Quay – it's about thirty minutes from here.'

Rob looked in the rear-view mirror, 'Morwellham Quay? Isn't there an army company stationed there?'

'I don't know,' Alek said. He was basing their escape route on what Swales had told him. He needed to persuade Lena to change her mind and give her a chance to get her Soc-Cred back up to a healthy level, and there was only one way to do it. He hoped that it worked out better than it did for poor Swales. It seemed like years since he and Swales had headed for this same spot, not just a few weeks ago. *Poor Swales. But if we had made it, I wouldn't have been able to help Lena.* He looked over to see her hand resting on Rob's. *She's confused, the poor girl. And it's entirely his fault.*

Chapter 30

Lena gripped the dashboard as Rob swerved around a lane. Her legs were throbbing, she had blisters forming on both heels, and a layer of dried sweat was beginning to smell after running around Plymouth in her heeled shoes. Her nerves had been overworked during the previous three hours as she waited for Alice to collect a few things from their apartment and then hid in the shadows of the aquarium waiting for Rob. The pressure had eased once she saw him arrive with the van. He had come good.

'Slow down a bit, will you?' She put her hand on top of Rob's. 'We don't want to crash before we get there.'

'Sure,' Rob said. 'I love getting instructions from non-drivers.'

Lena looked over at Alek. He sat staring straight ahead, his eyes glazed as if in deep thought.

'Are you okay, Alek?' Lena said.

He looked up. 'Eh? What? Oh, sure.' He tapped his temple with a finger. 'I'm just thinking about the route.'

Lena nodded. 'Good.'

They sat in silence for twenty minutes while they drove down the narrow lanes past Buckland Abbey and towards the Tamar. Lena thought about the people she was leaving behind: the surprising Alice, Jane in prison, and even Chantelle and her two kids. *I can't help everyone.*

Rob switched off the headlights on the open road when the moon came out from behind the clouds. Lena saw a brown sign that pointed to Morwellham Quay. Rob pumped the brakes as they descended towards the river.

'Lights!' Lena pointed at a row of vehicle headlights ahead.

'I know, I know,' Rob said. The beams rose and fell as they followed the road before disappearing behind a slope. 'They must be on this road – look for a turn-off, quick. This van stands out like a barn owl at night.'

'Who chose a white van for a getaway vehicle?' Alek said.

'Don't have a go at me – you're lucky to be getting away.' Rob slammed the brakes and reversed.

Lena braced herself as they drove down a farm track, jolted by the rocks and potholes, her teeth rattling. The trees glowed white as the headlights came closer.

Rob braked and cut the engine. Lena heard Alek being slammed into the back door.

'Quiet,' Rob said. Two Land Rovers and four trucks rumbled past the lane and disappeared.

'Are you okay?' Lena said.

'No, I'm bloody not.' Alek clicked his head side to side and rubbed his neck. 'I'm fed up with being tossed around in the back of a vehicle. I'm not a bloody lettuce.'

Lena laughed and then covered her mouth. 'Sorry, I know it's not funny.' She pointed at the road. 'It looks like Rob was right about the army being here. What are we going to do now?' She turned to Alek

Rob jerked a thumb at Alek. 'His idea is going to lead us straight into the arms of his mates.'

'Fuck off, mate,' Alek said. 'What are you talking about? I didn't know there was an army base here.'

'Oh, yeah?' Rob said. 'Then why did you choose this spot?'

Lena looked at Alek, who was shaking his head. 'I chose Morwellham Quay because of my friend, Swales. Remember I told you about him?'

Lena nodded. 'Yes, I do. Was this where you were headed with him?' Alek looked tearful and she felt bad; his old psychological wounds must have opened up.

'Yeah,' Alek said.

'I'm sorry that your friend died, but what are we going to do?' Lena said. 'We can't just sit here – we'll have to go down the river a bit.'

Rob put his hand on Lena's thigh. 'One of our escape routes is close. I didn't want to say anything until I knew we were clear.'

'Really?' Lena squeezed Rob's hand. 'That's amazing. How do we get across?'

'There's a gap in the fence a mile downstream where two boats should be moored – you can take them across,' Rob said.

Lena shifted in her seat to look at Alek then back at Rob. 'Please come with us. There's room at our parents' house and you will be away from all of this. You'll be safe.'

Rob shook his head. 'No, you know I can't, babe. If I go missing my uncle will be put into a Recreant Camp. I can come and join you when things settle down.'

Lena folded her arms. 'Fine. Let's go then.' If he didn't want to come, that was his problem. She would be safe with Alek; her brother mattered most.

Lena got out of the van and opened the back door. 'Pass me my rucksack,' she said to Alek. It contained her few possessions, randomly thrown in by Alice. She glanced at a wooden noticeboard in the middle of the lay-by; a faded infographic poster had peeled half off. *In happier times, we might have come here for a picnic.*

'This way,' Rob said. He walked across the road and climbed over a stile.

Lena followed and lumbered over the stile, hampered by the

ungainly weight of her rucksack. She heard Alek tut. He had always moaned at her for being slow on family walks. She traipsed through the long grass that soaked her bare legs and heard the river gurgling and bubbling before she saw it glistening in the moonlight. An electric fence barred their way.

'Don't soldiers patrol this?' Alek said.

Rob looked at Lena. 'The fence runs the length of the border with substations every four hundred metres and guard posts every mile. This footpath is halfway between two stations in this mile sector. Patrols are supposed to check the two substations on either side of their posts.' He grinned at Alek. 'But, soldiers being soldiers, they take shortcuts.'

Lena saw Alek clenching his fists and stepped between him and Rob before anything could happen. Rob's mansplaining was annoying but she didn't want any fighting.

Rob crouched by the fence and held up a section. 'We bypassed the circuit by adding this extra loop.' He pointed to a thin, green plastic wire.

Lena took off her rucksack and then crawled under the wire, her woollen jumper absorbing the dew. *Yuck, I'm soaked.* She took her rucksack from Alek and waited for him to crawl through. *So this is a flaw in the defence plan. It's impossible to secure the whole border.*

'The boats should be here.' Rob pushed past Lena to the water's edge where rows of weeds rose like sentinels. He slipped on the mud and fell into the shallows with a splash that echoed across the water.

'Shh,' Lena said. 'You're making too much noise.' She looked up and down the river; she could see the outlines of trees but no people.

Rob waded through the reeds. 'I've got it.' He pulled something towards him and shuffled back to the bank.

'That's not a boat – it's a kayak!' Lena said.

Alek bent down and helped turn it side on. There were two paddles in the seat deck and a set of elastic cords embedded on the stern. Lena hefted her rucksack onto the kayak and secured it with the cords. She pointed at the seats. 'Front or back?'

Alek shook his head. 'Neither. Lena, I'm not going across.'

'What are you talking about?' Lena said. 'I know we'll need to paddle, but it's not far.'

'Hurry up and get in, you two,' Rob said from the river, 'so I can get out of here.'

Alek took a breath. 'I don't want to have to do this.' He reached into his pocket. 'But it's for your own good, Lena.' He raised a pistol with his left hand and pointed it at Rob.

Lena shivered as she saw the moonlight reflecting off Alek's weapon; her shoes were sinking into the mud and her feet were wet but she was scared. Her hair felt as if it was leaving her scalp. She wriggled her toes to get purchase but that made things worse. 'What are you doing, Alek?'

'I'm stopping you from making a mistake.' Alek's voice was shaky.

'Where did you get that from?' She had never seen a weapon this close before, let alone one that was being pointed at her. Or rather, being pointed at Rob. 'What on earth do you think you're playing at?

'Nothing. I'm not playing.' Alek grabbed the stern of the kayak with his right hand. 'I'm not leaving England. My future is here, and so is yours – with me.'

'What are you talking about?' she said. 'There is no future here, except more misery for me and maybe death for you.' She pointed across the river. 'We're nearly there and we can see Mum and Dad.' She heard Rob move in the water behind her.

Alek raised his pistol. 'Hold it there, Rob, where I can see you.' He stepped to the side and spoke to Lena while watching Rob. 'I'm not going to be a traitor like them. I have a chance to help win the war here. I'm going to get promoted. We just need to stop people leaving and joining the enemy.'

'We? Who are "we"?' Lena's voice carried across the water. 'It's us, Alek. Me, you, Mum and Dad – and then it's them. Can't you see that?' She couldn't stop the tears rushing to her eyes. Was Alek really doing this? Ruining their chance of being together as a family again?

'Mum and Dad are traitors! But you can still stay and be part of the victory. He's playing you along.' Alek waved his pistol at Rob. 'You can settle down with a decent bloke, like Shane, and have your own family to look after. I can help. Please, Lena, stay.'

Lena looked across the water and back to Alek. She could hear the grit in his voice and knew he was serious. He had changed so much. 'So you were never really going to escape with us?'

Alek shrugged. 'Escape to what? What am I going to do there? I can't get revenge for my dead comrades by sitting around in Looe.' He nodded at Rob. 'Captain Maguire will be very happy. We've found the traitors' pipeline.' He held out his free hand. 'We are heroes now, Lena. I'll say you came and showed me the escape route and you'll get loads of Soc-Cred. You'll never be hungry again.'

Lena took a step back, into the water. 'Alek, I think you've been brainwashed like I was once. You're too clever to be this stupid. Think about it. We can have a new life together, without worrying about all this war crap.' Lena took another step back, feeling the kayak against the back of her knees. 'Come on – put the gun away.'

'No! I want you to stay here, with me.' Alek leant forward and pulled the kayak towards him.

Rob waded towards them. 'Alek, you're wrong. We're not traitors. We're normal people who want their normal lives back. The Party is keeping the war going for its own purposes, using people like you. Can't you see that?'

Alek pointed the pistol at Rob. 'Stay where you are. Lena, he's wrong. You've got to come with me.'

'Don't be stupid, Alek! I'm going without you then.' Lena pulled the kayak back. Alek lost balance and slipped over, falling on his bad arm. Rob leapt past Lena and dived onto Alek, grabbing his gun arm and forcing it under the water. Lena didn't know what to do, confused by the thrashing water and the two men turning each other around. 'Stop, stop!' She moved towards them but slipped in the water and her head went under. The cold water and the darkness caused her to panic; she flailed and swallowed a mouthful of river. When she surfaced she saw they were still grappling over Alek's gun arm. Rob swung a right hook at Alek, who ducked his chin and took the blow on his cast. Rob yelped before punching Alek in the stomach three times in rapid succession. Alek grunted and slipped forward. Rob lifted his fist and smashed it down on Alek's back, reminding Lena of him chopping meat on the butcher's block.

'Stop!' Lena waded towards them.

Alek threw his cast up and under Rob's chin. Lena heard the crack of contact. Rob staggered before launching himself at Alek, his long arms encircling the shorter Alek.

Bang!

Lena had never heard a gunshot. It was louder than she'd imagined. Rob slipped into the water. 'Rob!' She grabbed his jacket as he floated head down, pulling him towards her, grunting as she tried to turn him over.

'Leave him, Lena, he's dead.' She turned to see Alek had his pistol pointed at her.

'What have you done, you psycho?' Lena hugged Rob's floating body. She was soaking wet and tears poured down her face. 'Rob, Rob!' There was no response. 'You've killed him. He was helping us and you've killed him.' She shoved Alek, not caring about the gun.

'I'm sorry, Lena, but he attacked me.' Alek put the pistol in his pocket, 'Come, let's get you dry.'

Lena looked at Rob's body and then across the water. Her hopes of escaping with them both seemed so foolish now. She didn't know this version of Alek. Her younger brother was gone. A killer stood in his place.

'Fine.' Lena put her hands on the bow of the kayak. 'Have it your way.' She shoved the kayak into Alek's legs as hard as she could, turned and dived into the river. Kicking her legs she moved deeper under the water, pulling four strong breaststrokes with her arms, not wanting to open her eyes in the cold. She didn't think Alek would shoot, but she had to do everything to avoid it if he might. Her chest was tight but she kept kicking and feeling for the bottom of the river until her head pounded.

Anger and desperation gave her strength.

She pulled for the surface and gasped for breath as her head came clear, turning around to see where Alek was. There was no sign of him. The current had taken her downstream and she was about halfway across the river. Filling her lungs with air again, Lena did a sidestroke to avoid lifting her arms out of the water and make any splashes that might alert Alek to her position. She did not want to end up like Rob. *Poor Rob! How can he be gone?*

Lena's legs felt heavy with the shoes, her arms burning by the time she could touch the stony riverbed, her feet scraping along the rocks. She waded towards the bank, crouching down on it, looking back across the river towards where she thought they had been. The cawk of a moorhen made her jump.

Lights appeared on the road near where they had parked the van and the sound of engines carried across the water. *The army?* Lena dragged her legs through the weeds and fell onto the grassy bank.

I'm in Kernow.

She lay there, chest heaving for a minute, until she recovered from the effort of her swim. Only then did the realisation wash through her: she was alone, her boyfriend was dead, killed by her brother. She rolled onto her side like a foetus and sobbed. *All of this and I'm alone.*

The cold water and river slime permeated her clothes and shoes, making Lena shiver. *I can't lie here and get pneumonia.* She took off her ruined shoes and poured water out of them, then took off her socks, twisting them tightly and squeezing as much water out as she could before holding them by their end and spinning her arms rapidly. It got blood flowing into her shoulders at least. She put the damp socks and shoes back on.

Lena looked up at the stars. She could make out the W shape of Cassiopeia; she hadn't seen it for years because of the curfew. Taking a breath of the damp air, she thought about Rob and how she wouldn't be able to look at the stars with him. *Oh, Rob, I cared for you more than I realised.*

Lena shivered. She rubbed her arms to get warm and then squelched her way through the grass, looking for a road to somewhere. Anywhere. It didn't matter where. Every step was a step closer to her parents.

But every step was leaving Rob further behind.

The stars were fading as the sky turned from black to azure and Lena stumbled along the road, searching for somewhere warm and dry. Her jeans clung to her legs, her pale skin visible on either side of her black bra: she had taken off her wet jumper and blouse.to reduce the chance of hypothermia. Knowing the moon set towards the west, Lena walked with it on her right. Devon was less than a mile away but the countryside was different on this side of the Tamar. The hills were longer and lower, the hedgerows shorter. The lanes wound around the hills, making her feel like she was getting nowhere. Yet the urge to see her parents drove her on, fuelled with determination to make the most of her life that seemed so precious now that Rob had lost his.

Finally, she reached a crossroads. Lena knew that Looe was in the south but the narrow lane in that direction looked unsafe to walk along in the gloom. She headed west on the bigger road, hoping it would lead to a settlement of some kind and help. The hedgerow dipped, giving her a view of a flat area on her left: a golf course with its neatly manicured lawns and lush fairways. The opulence seemed ridiculous compared to the poverty she had left behind.

Lena heard a car approaching and panicked, realising she was half-naked. She put her jumper back on and waved at the car – but, instead of stopping, the driver waved back and carried on. *Idiot!* The sky lightened but there was still no warmth from the low sun.

Lena tried to flag down several more cars until a red estate pulled over. The driver lowered the passenger window. 'Where are you going, maid?'

Lena saw the driver was a middle-aged man with red cheeks and greying hair, wearing a checked shirt under a green gillet. 'Looe. Could you take me there, please?'

'You're in luck – I'm headed that way. Hop in.' The driver beckoned with his hand.

'Thank you.' The car was toasty and the leather seat was soft. Although the driver seemed happy with silence, Lena closed her eyes to ward off questions.

Lena woke with a jolt as her head nodded forward. She felt the drool on the side of her mouth and realised she'd been sleeping with her mouth open. She recognised the windy part of the road to Looe with the river and meadows on her right and the small, wooded hills on her left. Memories of family car trips came back. *I'm nearly there.*

'You were snoring,' the driver said.

Lena wiped the drool off her chin and smacked her lips. The inside of her mouth felt dry. They turned the corner and Lena saw the familiar houses on the outskirts of Looe.

'Could you drop me off at the car park there, please?' Lena pointed at the pay and display sign next to a small brick building beside a bridge that crossed the river.

'Are you sure that's close enough?' the driver said as they waited for the oncoming traffic to pass.

'Yes, it's easier to walk along the narrow streets.' Lena smiled. A knot in her stomach grew as she realised she was nearly home. They pulled in and the driver wished her good luck.

'Thanks ever so much,' Lena said as she unbuckled. 'I don't know your name.'

'Roger.' The driver held out his hand.

Lena shook it. 'Thanks, Roger. It was lovely to meet you.' She stepped out of the car and waved goodbye. Although it was still early, several shops had lights on, dog walkers were up and two ladies were jogging in matching sweatshirts and leggings. Lena walked down the tiny high street and was amazed at the rows of fresh pasties, rolls and cakes that lined the bakery windows; the smell of the fresh pasties and cinnamon buns wafted over her like a warm blanket. She closed her eyes and inhaled, feeling fresh saliva in her mouth and the rumble of her stomach. *Not far now. Mum will have food in.*

The street narrowed until she could almost touch the whitewashed houses on either side – the old smugglers and fishermen's cottages that were now shops. Lena turned left and through more narrow, winding streets towards the east cliff.

Away from the shops, Lena's thoughts were dominated by her parents. She hadn't hugged her dad for three years. *Will he smell the same? That deodorant and aftershave mix. I doubt it – I haven't given it to him for Christmas. Mum's cooking: roast beef with Yorkshire pudding or even some salmon and a glass of wine. French wine. I can't believe I thought they were traitors just a few weeks ago.*

'Puffins' was the third in a row of mews cottages with brick plant boxes outside. Lena rang the doorbell and hopped from foot to foot as she peered through the round thick glass in the door. *C'mon, c'mon.* The door opened and her father appeared, grey hair tousled, wearing his blue pyjamas.

'Dad,' Lena's voice croaked.

Filip rubbed the sleep from his eyes. 'Lena?' He took a step closer, repeating, 'Lena!' He picked her up and hugged her. 'Welcome home, pumpkin.'

Lena grinned and cried at the same time, the knot in her stomach gone, squeezed out in the safety of her dad's arms.

'Emma, Emma! Look who's home,' Filip shouted into the house.

Lena heard the thud of footsteps down the wooden stairs.

'What's all the fuss about?' Emma stopped with her mouth wide open, thinner than Lena remembered. Her hair was tidy but greyer. 'Pumpkin!' She ran forward in her huge slippers and hugged Lena from the side.

Lena felt the air go out of her lungs but didn't complain. She could stay like this forever.

Tears streamed down her face and her body shook, the emotions of the last twenty-four hours and the misery of the last three years released.

When her sobs had finally subsided, she wriggled out of the embraces. Her parents were both red-faced and wiping tears away.

'Is Alek with you?' Filip said, looking over Lena's shoulder.

'Oh, Dad. I've got so much to tell you.' And she meant it. No more lies, no more looking over her shoulder. She was home.

Epilogue

The kayak hit Alek in the knees and he staggered backwards, slipping in the mud and falling onto the bank. He scrambled to his feet, keeping the pistol aloft, peering across the blackness of the river but there was no sign of Lena. Not that he would have shot her, anyway. 'Why did you threaten her?' he said to himself. 'You idiot!' He was as angry at himself as he was at Lena for leaving. He looked across the river, straining to see anything moving. There was a shape in the water – maybe her head? But it didn't move. *A rock, probably.*

Alek felt for the radio in his pocket, but it was wet and probably put of range. The pursuers should have been told to keep their distance; they wouldn't know where he was now. He pulled the kayak up onto the bank and, putting the rucksack on the grass, he sat on the flat bow. 'You've left this behind, you silly girl.'

He wiped the mud off his hands onto his trousers and returned the pistol to his pocket. *What now?* His mission had been partially successful. He had stopped the Resistance and found one of their escape pipelines. But Lena had escaped. He could always tell Captain Maguire that he had shot her too…but no, she wouldn't believe that.

He picked up Lena's rucksack and walked up the slope to the stile. He could see Jupiter hanging above Venus and thought how close they looked, despite being light years apart. Two planets in orbit around the sun that would never meet.

The quay was only three kilometres away and the nearest checkpoint only one kilometre. Alek set off down the road, tired, wet, cold and alone. The sound of vehicles grumbled towards him and, when he saw dipped headlights, he stuck out a thumb.

In the back of the truck he checked the contents of Lena's rucksack for contraband, finding her sketchpad, water-stained on the outside. As he put it to the side, a photo of Alek and his mum and dad fell out. Alek held it up to the moonlight. He leant back against the truck canopy and closed his eyes. A single tear ran down his cheek.

JAMES MARSHALL

ABOUT THE AUTHOR

James Marshall is a sports coach who lives in Devon, UK.
He specialises in the athletic development of young people.

He is a barbecue aficionado, a raving fan of the Green Bay Packers and a Masters weightlifter.

You can read more about his writing journey here:
https://jamesrmarshall.substack.com/

Printed in Great Britain
by Amazon